Cover and illustrations created by Bill Knapp

Bill Knapp

A Tick in Time
©2021 Bill Knapp

All rights reserved. This book or any portion thereof may not be reproduced or used in any manner whatsoever without the express written permission of the publisher except for the use of brief quotations in a book review.

ISBN: 978-1-66780-518-4

Author's Note

This book had to be written to complete the story started in the novel, "Remember Who You Are". It is a natural progression given the characters developed in the first book. I felt compelled to leave very few questions and provide a suitable and yet gratifying conclusion for the reader.

It is inspired by people that I have met along the way which include my family, my friends and my students. Most of what is written here is true, perhaps not the exact story but the events and situations are real. You don't have to look too far to find similar situations, conflicts and relationships. It has been my hope during the course of writing these books, to not only disclose episodes experienced by me or my relationships but to help you find commonalities.

Originally began in the 1970's the original story was a way to reach my seventh and eighth grade students, to arouse interest and participation in reading and writing as well as listening. More importantly for me was how they related the events of the story to their own lives. Since the original characters were only 14, they could see similarities with their lives and were able to imagine how they would have responded to circumstances described in the story.

Joey, the main character is very much a person I would have aspired to be in my younger days but sadly I've fallen far short of his mettle even as an adult. Perhaps in writing this story it's a way for me to convince myself to view things more like he would.

I would venture to say that you have made a mistake or two in your life. I know I have, in spades! If we lean on those we love to help us through our despair, our grief, and the choices we make, the road becomes a lot smoother. It's tough going it alone. All of us have probably found ourselves alone in the world or at least we thought we were. If we can navigate through the obstacles thrown at us surrounded by genuine people, we not only find our way through, but I believe we become better people.

Your personality and your goals change throughout your life. That is inevitable because you experience new things all the time no matter how old you are, and each experience is part of your metamorphosis. When I look back on my life, I see things I've done that I regret, paths I've chosen that ultimately led to disastrous results and interactions I've had with others that caused pain to both them and me. The older I become the more I realize that regret is merely the past. You don't forget it, but you need to use it as motivation so that you avoid the results your past actions caused. I think it's best to look ahead and approach all you do as positively as you can. For most of us, true enlightenment will never be attained but if we make our motivation love, most things will turn out for the better.

Our lives are so short! It's ridiculous really. In the grand scheme of things our entire lives are comparable to a grain of sand in all the beaches of the universe. It's bizarre, but when you are young and you feel indestructible, and the future is so far away your sense of being small isn't prevalent and you feel like you will live forever. In youth even your memories are more detailed, and the past is longer. You think of a year as this long period of time, especially when you are looking forward to the milestones in your life; your graduation, your first car, your first love, etc. When you are older, and you are rounding the last corner to the finish line it's much different. What's outlandish is the older you get the shorter your life was! Yes, "was". You look back at all the years that you have existed and now all that time seems only a **tick in time**… ironically then, your memory begins to fail you!

So, the moral is, as much as it is difficult at times, we should attack what time is left of our life making love our motivation. If your eyes well up or you flat out cry or the lump in your throat makes you tremble slightly, if you relate experiences you've had that are eerily similar to those found on these pages, or if you laugh at some silliness or humorous action by one of my characters, my job is done.

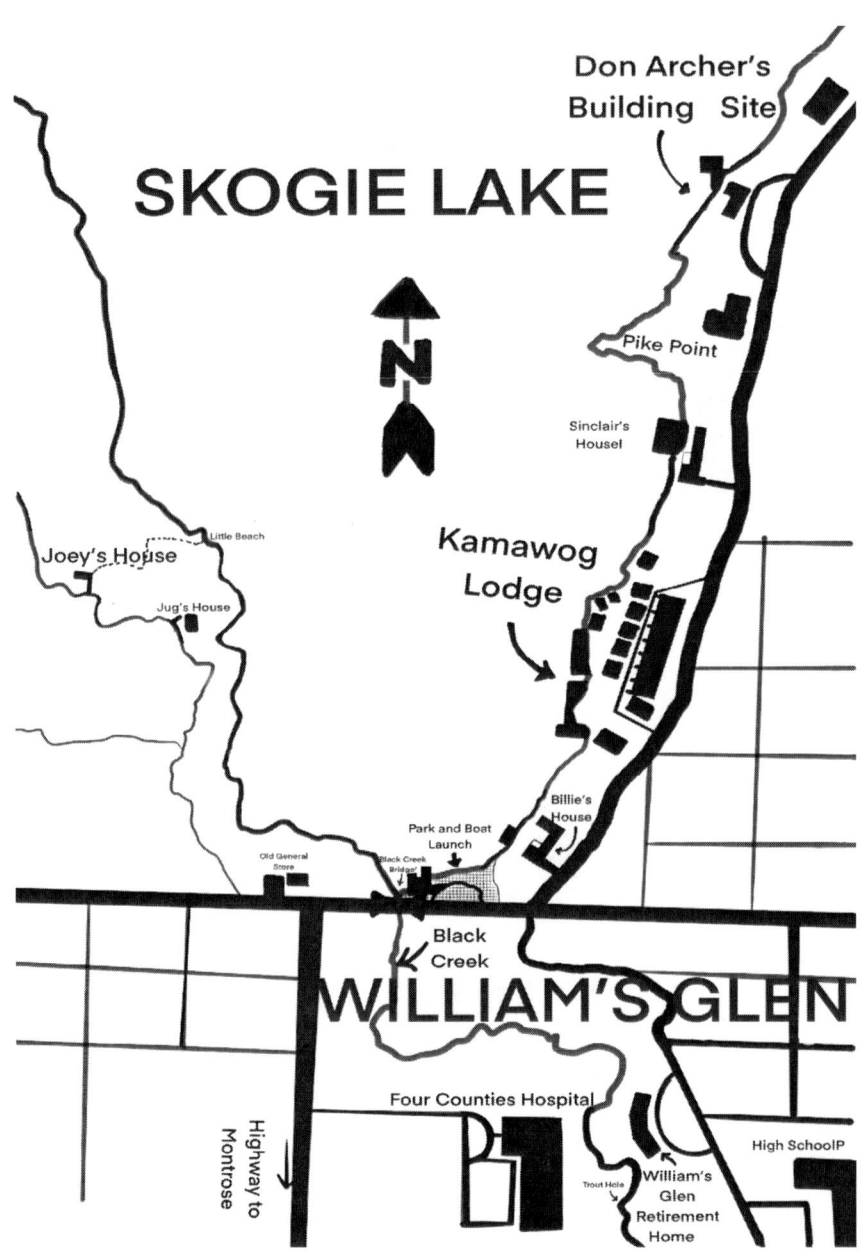
Not to scale

PART ONE

CHAPTER ONE

Joey sat on a warm, flat stone with his feet dangling in the clear flowing water of Black Creek. He didn't bring his fishing pole to try for some speckled trout, like he usually did. He just wanted to be alone at his most special place in the world, to just take in the beauty of the area and contemplate life and its future. Harriet, Joey's Bernese Mountain Dog, was curled up in the shade of a winterberry bush just behind him sleeping, only momentarily waking to snap at an insect which occasionally invaded her personal space. It was here, only just behind him and a little further up the hill, under the giant beech tree, where he had held his first love, Billie. Up there, on an old quilt spread over the soft wild grass, the two of them had shared their secrets and pledged their love for each other.

Joey had admired Billie from a distance for some time during their first year in high school. When he finally summoned the strength to ask her if she would spend some time with him, she agreed and the two immediately found comfort in each other's company.

It was an unlikely relationship, as Joey was from a rather poor and dysfunctional family, and Billie was the daughter of the owner of a large construction company. Her family was affluent, and they lived in a large house on the shore of Skogie Lake, complete with a boathouse and several types of boats. Joey lived just across the lake from Billie, but in a small wooden bungalow in disrepair, set back from the shore on a gravel road and part of the Seneca Reservation. While Billie's neighborhood housed the wealthy, upper-class families of the town of William's Glen, Joey's neighborhood was an older cottage in a rental area just outside of town. His family's house was owned but the property was rented from the "Res". The people that lived in these houses were there because it was affordable. It used to be considered a rather undesirable area due to tension between the white population and the Cayuga Nation in the area. The Cayuga people lost their lands to the white man in the 1700's and have always felt cheated of their birthright. Today they live with their allies on the Seneca reservation. As long as families like Joey's paid their monthly rent on time, there was usually not much friction between the two races these days.

Billie's family was stable and well entrenched in the town's society. Billie's real name was Catherine Magee, but she preferred her nickname, "Billie" and many didn't even know her real given name. The Magee Construction Company bearing their family name, was responsible for many of the larger buildings in the nearby city of Montrose, about 15 minutes to the south. Billie's mom, Sarah, was a popular socialite and benefactor, frequently organizing town functions and fund raisers while William, or Willie, as he was known to the locals, was a member of the town council and a very well-respected businessman. They were also friends with the Sinclair's, another wealthy family that lived further north along the shoreline of the lake.

The Sinclair's also happened to be the parents of Joey's arch enemy, Paul Sinclair, a known bully who often picked on Joey. Paul was continually seeking the affection of Billie – a relationship that Paul's parents would love to see consummated. That union could prove beneficial both from a social and financial aspect, and like Paul, his parents were known to play by their own rules when it came to getting what they wanted. The Sinclair's: Mark and Sally, were co-owners of Sinclair Pulp and Paper and their connection to the Magee Construction had obvious payoffs. If their son were to hook up with the Magee's daughter, that would make the family accord just that much more agreeable to them. Paul was certainly a willing participant in this courtship, and although not really aware of his parents hidden agenda, he had always considered Billie to be his girl. Even though Billie's feelings were not mutual, Paul just figured he would win her in the end. He was a good looking blue-eyed, blond, athletic guy with money. Afterall, what was not to like?

These two families were, on the surface, successful, with solid family values and healthy conjugal relationships.

As Joey sat beside the stream this morning, flicking the odd stick into the water and watching it sail downstream, he found himself constantly wondering how Billie could have chosen him over Paul. He had come to feel that Billie respected him because of the person he was, but his family was far from the typical nuclear arrangement, and money was a constant worry, especially for his mom, Lilley. She held down two jobs: one at the Old General store and the other cleaning houses for the likes of the Sinclair's and the Magee's. Joey's dad was now completely out of the picture. Lilley had finally filed for divorce after months of legal separation from Hank, an abusive, alcoholic husband and father. There was a time when all was good in Joey's family; when his sisters Pamela and Jessica and he would jump in the back seat of the family car with Hank and Lilley in the front seat, and they would head out for ice cream or fries. Some nights, when there was a good movie playing at the Starlight Drive-in, they would all go as a family, bring lawn chairs and the two older kids would sit out in front of the car on the lawn chairs, downing large buckets of buttered popcorn and pop. With Jess passed out in the back seat, Hank and

Lilley would watch from the front seat stealing kisses, arms around each other. Those were the better times, before the drinking began.

Slowly but surely, Hank had found that he needed alcohol above family. In the last 2 years he had become verbally and physically abusive to anyone who crossed him when he arrived home from the bar late at night. What started as a Friday night out with the boys, became every night with whoever was at the Highway Saloon on the way home from Montrose, after his work at the steel mill. Soon his reproachful behavior became unprovoked. He would lash out just because someone might be in his way. After he had attacked and beaten both Lilley and Joey one night a few months back, Lilley had gone to the police and had Hank arrested. After his release he was slapped with a restraining order and could not be within 10 miles of his former loved ones. When Lilley found out that Hank was still being abusive to other women and had become involved in various brawls and altercations in Montrose, she came to the conclusion that he really was never going to change. It was a difficult decision to file for divorce. It was, obviously, not something she had foreseen when she first walked down the aisle with the man that she loved in her arms. Nevertheless, she was forced to protect her children and take the appropriate action.

Joey's older sister, Pam, now seventeen, was staying at a halfway-house and being treated for drug abuse and addiction. She had distanced herself from the family since her dad had abused her several times. She felt safer with her friends and had gradually accumulated a suitcase full of her possessions including clothing, that she took with her, to be as independent as she could. She was an attractive girl underneath the gothic façade of black lipstick and eyeshadow, but she hid her fine facial features and hazel eyes behind her black and purple hair like it was a mask. With no source of income, she would collect bottles and cans and occasionally offer her body to a stranger for cash. Then her life took a turn and Lilley hoped with all her heart that it was for the better. A drug raid at Pam's friend's house a few weeks ago had landed her in jail. Once the police had questioned the users and found the source of the contraband, the court appointed lawyer had arranged for some rehab. Lilley was relieved to know that she was, at least, getting some kind of intervention now. However, it still saddened her to know that one of her babies was in trouble and was not at home.

Jessica, Joey's baby sister, was five and just starting school. She was still able to take most things in stride, although, she would occasionally start to cry for no apparent reason. Joey knew the reason probably better than Jess did, but simple, logical answers to her brooding questions seemed to pacify her for periods of time. Joey and Lilley worried that when she got a little older and realized the extent of the family's dysfunction, she might travel down the same road Pam appeared to be on. She was a wonderfully inquisitive little kid, Joey thought – so innocent and at times hilariously funny. Joey was often amused by her antics and seemingly rhetorical questions.

One day, on a walk along the lakeshore with Joey and Harriet, on seeing a school of minnows flitting away from their shadows, she asked, "Hey, Joey. Do fish ever get thirsty?" It seemed like a perfectly logical question to her.

"I don't think so, Jess. I think they can just open their mouths when they need water." Joey offered, hoping that would satisfy her.

"Well, if they open your mouth under water, wouldn't that choke them?"

Joey laughed and knew if he were to escape these types of conversations, he would have to change the subject. To explain to Jess that fish don't have lungs would inevitably lead to an entire explanation on how fish breathe and what lungs do, and heaven knows what other questions would spring into that little mind.

Instead, he just pointed to the far shore and said, "I bet you don't know how far it is across to the other side." That led to a more innocuous interchange, far less painful than the complete explanation of the human and fish anatomies.

Today, as Joey sat on his flat rock at the trout hole, he reflected on all these things. He recalled Gramps' death just two months ago, and how that had completely devastated him and still caused pain and an acute feeling of emptiness. Ironically, coming to this place where the two of them had spent so much time together, would start the torment, but he did not want to let Gramps go, altogether. Gramps had been the biggest part of his life the last few years. He had gone to him for any number of reasons, from escaping his home life to just enjoying his company either at the picnic bench behind Gramps' residence or fishing down here at the trout hole. This place where he sat today, just about 100 meters behind Gramps' old residence, the William's Glen Retirement Home", was the place where special things happened and where the grim parts of reality were left behind.

Joey was remarkably well adjusted considering the dismal occurrences he had endured in his 14-year life. He had the friendship of a boy down the road from him named Jug. This friend had proven his loyalty time and time again, demonstrating that he had Joey's back. They were long-time companions, and their bond was solid. As Joey looked around and caught a glimpse of Harriet asleep with what looked like a smile etched into her long snout, he realized that he also had her unconditional love, something that Joey valued greatly.

Other than his mother's concern for him, there was really only one clear reason Joey had not lost it totally during his broken and troubled home environment. The thing Joey could count on, the person he could bare his soul to, the only one he absolutely trusted with his heart, was Billie.

CHAPTER 2

Soon Joey would be reunited with his dear friend, Billie. She had gone to visit her cousins in England for the summer. Her cousin, Olivia, was the daughter of Mary and James Wilmot. Mary and Billie's mom Sarah were sisters and before the Wilmot's had moved to England because of a new job opportunity for James, Billie and Olivia spent countless time together here in William's Glen. They were only a month apart in age and were very close friends. The two families had made a deal to give their daughters the opportunity to spend more time together. This summer the Wilmot's would host Billie, and next summer the Magee's would host Olivia. The only expense for the visitor was the cost of the flight, and both families would have no difficulty managing that.

It was a long two months for Joey. He couldn't believe himself, how much he missed Billie. At times he had difficulty believing she had ever said, "I love you, Joey!" and kissed him so passionately on the lips. With two weeks until she returned, he was growing increasingly nervous in anticipation.

He was able to pick up quite a few lawn mowing jobs around town which helped pass the time. From his earnings he was able to buy a used push mower and many mornings you could hear the rattle of the wheels as Joey pushed the machine over the gravel road leading to town. He liked to do the work as soon as the dew had burned off the grass. He could get two or three lawns done by about 1:00 pm, and then he would go home, grab a sandwich and head over to Jug's place, which was on the same road, between Joey's and the town. From there, they would invent some activity for the rest of the day. Often it was hiking along Black Creek or rowing out along the shore in Joey's old rowboat. The two things they always had with them were fishing poles and, of course, Harriet. Harriet loved being with Joey and would sulk at home with her head between her front paws any time Joey could not take her with him. She was almost 8 years-old now and slowing down a bit, but she loved the adventure, and it was not easy for Joey to leave her at home when she pulled the sad face sham.

If Jug was busy, it was just Joey and Harriet. When they didn't go fishing, Joey found time to strum his guitar or sketch with the kit Billie had bought him before she left. Joey's left arm was fresh out of a cast from a compound fracture of his forearm, the result of an altercation with Paul Sinclair. Paul had caught Joey and Billie together on the first day of the summer holidays and attacked Joey while he was on the way home. After a brief fight at the mouth of Black creek, Joey attempted to escape across the shallow, but turbulent, creek. Paul tackled him and Joey's arm had slammed into a boulder, causing a grisly fracture and a protruding bone. The sight of Joey's injury scared off Sinclair and Jug had come by just in time to help Joey as far as his house. From there Jug's mom had taken Joey to emergency at Four Counties Hospital, south of William's Glen.

Although his injury made it difficult to play the guitar, he continued to force himself to practice even with the pain. He used to try out new songs on Gramps from time to time and Gramps was a very good listener. He once played the fiddle himself and still had a good ear for music. He told Joey on numerous occasions that he thought

Joey sounded like Bobby Vinton. Of course, Joey had no idea who Bobby Vinton was but after doing some research and listening to some old recordings, he decided that Gramps was really giving him a huge compliment.

Neither Joey nor Lilley had any up-to-date technology, like a smart phone or a tablet. One day as Joey and Jug were heading home from a hike with Harriet, Jug's mom, Ellen, poked her head out the front door and said, "Hey, guys…Come in here for a sec. Yeah, you too Joey."

They both headed for the door and Ellen said, "I have something for you, Joey. You are likely gonna need Jug's help running it, but the office gave me an ipad to do some of my work. It comes with unlimited internet access…So…"

"Yes, yes, yes!" Joey exclaimed. "Can I use it for a minute?"

"Well, there wouldn't have been much point in me haulin' you guys in here if I wasn't going to let you use it." she laughed. "I thought there might be a certain young lady that hasn't heard much from a certain young man."

"She wrote me, and I wrote her, but it would be great to write her live!"

"I can do better than that. How about a video call?"

"You mean where I actually get to see her?"

"No, it's called a video call so you can hear her," Jug inserted sarcastically, both laughing.

Joey had not even known that you could video call someone all the way from England.

"Can you show me how?" Joey asked enthusiastically.

Ellen looked at her watch, "Sure. We can use the FaceTime app. Can you be here at seven tomorrow morning?"

"Seven? Oh yeah, they are way ahead of us in time, aren't they," Joey answered as more of a statement than a question.

"Yes, so if you get here at seven, it will be noon over there. The chances of you catching her will be better, and hopefully just having lunch. I don't think she would mind the interruption, would she?" Ellen asked facetiously.

"I hope not! Said Joey, half joking. "I'll be here!" Joey made for the door, "See you, Jug. See you, Mrs. Parker."

Later that evening, Joey was in his room imagining what he would say and just excited about the whole prospect of actually seeing Billie again. Since Billie had left about 6 weeks ago, Joey had undergone some personal changes, more like a metamorphosis or evolution. He had taken much more care of his appearance. Zits were less an issue because he was on top of them immediately, using cream and keeping his face cleaner than he ever had before. He bought decent clothes with the money he'd earned cutting grass…not expensive clothes, just clothes with a little more style than functionality. He had actually grown an inch taller in the last couple months and his mom said he was starting to look like Li'l Abner from the old comic strips. That meant nothing to Joey, of course, but when Lilley showed him a picture of Li'l Abner from her scrapbook, he took that to heart. His body was long and lean and seemed as though it was sprouting out beyond the confines of his clothes. In general, he could have passed for any normal high school kid going into grade 10. Before Billie, he only passed for size but stood out because of his country bumpkin appearance. He laughed about his transformation, calling it AB (after Billie) as opposed to BB (before Billie). It was not just a transformation in appearance, it was a genuine growth toward a more positive self-concept. He was more confident because, in his mind, Billie was totally out of his league, but she said she loved him. Those words echoed constantly in his head, and he wanted to be the kind of person that would make her proud. He was still a gawky teen, but he was clean, looked good, and his work in lawn maintenance this summer was starting to make him stronger and more muscular.

It was getting late, and he went out to the living room to tell Lilley about tomorrow. Lilley was sitting on the couch watching an old TV series and was drifting off between sleep and being cognizant of what was actually transpiring on the tube.

"Hey, Mom," Joey said softly, jarring her to attention.

"Hey, Joey. What's up?" Lilley asked as if she was totally switched on an awake.

"I'm getting up at 6 tomorrow, so don't be surprised when you get up and don't know where I am."

"Oh, so where will you be? Something tells me this has something to do with either Jug or Billie."

"I'll take door number two," answered Joey, playing along.

"Really? Is she coming back early?"

"No, but I gotta be over to Parker's before Jug's mom goes to the office. She has a tablet from her work and she's going to let me use her FaceTime to talk to Billie."

"So, you can actually see her and talk? Wow, that's kind of exciting!" then Lilley paused. "I wish I could give you that kind of thing. When your Grampa's estate is settled, I'm going to make sure you have something like that…at least a good phone."

"That would be nice, but I just thought I'd warn you when I was not here in the morning."

"Thanks, Joey. I'm so happy for you!" Joey could see Lilley's eyes moisten. "I don't mean just about tomorrow. I mean, about Billie…she's such a nice girl, and you so much deserve to have her in your life!"

"Thanks, Mom. She really likes you…and she loves Harriet too!"

"Yeah, well, who doesn't love Harriet."

"Okay, well good night, Mom."

"Good night Joey…I love you!"

"Love you too, Mom."

Joey went back to bed recognizing that he had just broken the "I love you" barrier. He couldn't ever remember saying it before to his mom. The awkward teen seemed to be continuing his metamorphosis. Instead of feeling ashamed or embarrassed that he had said it, he just smiled to himself.

Out in the living room, Lilley's watery eyes turned into tears tracing down her cheeks and she let out a slight tremor of joy holding her breath so as not to cry out loud. She had not missed those words from Joey. She knew he loved her but to hear it from him for the first time since he was a toddler, was one of the most validating, pleasing things she could remember. Her moody, hormonal, teenaged son was becoming a man.

The next morning, Joey's alarm clock woke him at 6. He quickly showered and shaved; a practice he started doing about twice a week. He dried himself off and made sure his double crown was sufficiently flattened, slipped on his clean "Beatles" t-shirt with the quote, "And in the end, the love you take is equal to the love you make". It was going to be a warm August day, so he decided a pair of cut-off jeans and sandals would complete the ensemble.

Joey tip-toed out into the kitchen and let Harriet out for her morning pee, making sure that the screen door didn't slap shut and wake Lilley and Jess. He noticed that Harriet was having a little difficulty getting to her feet these days. Joey just chalked it up to sleeping on a hard floor all night and reasoned that he would be stiff too if he had to sleep on the floor. He wolfed down a couple pieces of toast and cherry jam, while saving a small piece for Harriet, and she reappeared at the door. Joey let her in, tossed the piece of toast toward the living room and while Harriet went for the diversion, he was out the door, stealthily, and heading down the laneway. He knew her sad face would be watching him out the living room window, but he wouldn't be tempted to fall for it, so he resisted the urge to look back.

Joey arrived at Jug's about 6:45 and thought he would just sit on the porch steps to give Ellen and Jug time to get ready. The door creaked open behind him, and Jug's head peeked out.

"Hey, Joe. You realize I'm making a big sacrifice getting up this early, eh?"

Joey chuckled, "I know bud. I will definitely owe you one for this."

They sat at the kitchen table and Jug showed Joey how to use Billie's email address to contact her through FaceTime on his mom's ipad. Ellen was busy making her lunch and brewing a cup of coffee but took time to set out a big glass of orange juice for each of the boys.

"Thanks, Mrs. Parker," said Joey politely.

"Yeah, thanks Mom," Jug mimicked.

"Your welcome guys. Just don't be too long. I gotta be outta here by 7:20."

"Yeah, we will be quick," Jug answered. "Okay, Joe, all you do is hit that button and it should connect you. It might take a few seconds for her to answer."

Joey clicked the little green video icon and waited nervously, for her to respond. After about 10 seconds a blurry screen gradually came into focus. Billie's face appeared and trees were going by with a beautiful blue-sky background. She was obviously walking somewhere and holding the phone, steadying it as best she could.

"Joey…Hi! How did you manage to do this?"

Joey was stunned at just being able to see her face. She was even prettier than she was a couple months ago. He hesitated, made sure his image was in the camera and explained to her how he had got up early and was over at jug's place using Ellen's ipad.

"Wow, that's nice of her! I don't have too long though. Olivia and I are walking over to a chicken place for lunch in Brent Cross. We are almost there."

She showed Joey the streets and caught Olivia as she waved to him as if she knew Joey quite well. Joey could see houses all joined together like they were in Montrose in the area of Mrs. Greer, the piano teacher's house, and black wrought iron fencing. The view bounced along with her gait and Joey could hear muffled giggles and conversation. Then Billie pointed her camera to a guy walking along with them on the other side of Olivia.

"This is Harry. He is Olivia's boyfriend. He has promised to show us this great place to eat." Harry waved to the camera. Then Billie could be heard in the background saying, "This is my boyfriend, Joey."

Harry smiled, waved again, and said, "Hi, Joey."

Joey responded with a "Hey."

There was a lot of background noise, giggling out of the two girls, interspersed with barely understandable conversation. It was clear that they were having a lot of fun and that Billie was having a great time. He felt pangs of jealousy and wished ardently that he was there with Billie as her escort.

"It sounds like you guys are having a great time." Joey offered.

"Sorry, Joey. What did you say?" Billie pointed the camera at her face, still laughing from something that had been said.

Joey repeated, "Sounds like you're having a great time."

"Yeah I am. Olivia is fun to be with and Harry's great too. Uncle James took us over to look at Wembley Stadium the other day. It's only about 10 minutes from Olivia's. It's absolutely huge! Your t-shirt reminded me because the Beatles played there, and it was so cool to see where that happened! Is Jug there too?"

Joey turned the ipad to reveal Jug to Billie and they exchanged waves and "Heys".

"Well guys, I'm going to slip outside for a minute so you can have privacy. Don't be too long now. By my watch, you only have about 5 minutes."

"Bye Jug," said Billie, waving again. "I miss you, Joey!"

Joey was relieved to hear that. "I miss you too," he replied. "But you look like you're having too much fun to miss me all that much," Joey half-heartedly chuckled.

Billie held the phone closer as the other two went into a building. "Harry and Olivia are going into the restaurant, but I can talk a little more." She turned her phone to reveal the sign "Chicken Valley" in white letters on the window as the sound seemed to break up a bit on her end.

"Cool," said Joey, at a loss for what to really say next. "Your phone is staticky. It's kinda hard to hear you."

"Yeah, Olivia said the reception is bad down in the middle…town…wifi…cell."

Fearing he would lose her to poor reception, Joey looked into the phone and said, "I love you, Billie!" But Billie was gone and that was it.

Joey returned the ipad to Ellen and thanked her. He told Jug he would see him later today and he headed home to plan his grass cutting for later that morning.

Joey could see Billie's beautiful blue eyes and that twinkle she gave him as he walked along. So clear was her image that he tripped on a branch on the edge of the road. He recalled that the way the sun was hitting Billie's hair gave it a reddish tinge. Perhaps the auburn hues were her Irish background. Joey was happy to have actually seen her but completely saddened by her lack of verbal intimacy. And to make matters worse, just when she had a chance to answer his pledge, her phone lost its signal. He recalled how she once said that she sounded business like on the phone and she had apologized to Joey for that.

Joey was now thinking out loud. "Get a grip on yourself. She's just a girlfriend. Stop being so obsessed." But he couldn't stop thinking about her.

Then he smiled, "Hey you idiot! She introduced you as her boyfriend. And she had said 'I love you' in her snail mail letter." He carried these thoughts with him for the next few days.

He wanted to tell her more but there wasn't time. They had a lot of catching up to do. He wanted to explain how piano lessons were no longer an issue. He had promised his mom that he would find someone to teach him guitar so that he could avoid weekly visits to Mrs. Greer's in Montrose. He hadn't found anybody yet but would ask around if the opportunity arose. He wasn't exactly in a hurry to have his Saturdays interrupted.

That afternoon, Jug called Joey just before Joey was going to head out the door.

"Hey, Joe. Mom's comin' home early and I gotta go with her into Montrose. She bribed me into getting a hair cut by promising some new clothes." Jug announced, laughing.

"Okay, I'll see you tomorrow then. Harriet probably wants to go for a walk anyway. See you later."

"Yeah, see you."

Harriet scratched the floor straining to stand, and walked over to the screen door, looking out, tail wagging.

"Wow, you sure are a smart little girl, aren't you? I might have said your name and walk in the same sentence." The two headed out back of the house in search of nothing in particular.

As Joey and Harriet walked along the pine needle strewn path beside the shore of Skogie Lake, Joey noticed that Harriet was lingering farther and farther behind. After about half an hour, Joey turned around and couldn't see her. He retraced his steps and found her just sitting there on the path waiting for him.

"What's the matter, girl?" he asked, scratching the back of her head. She took the weight off her front legs and lay down resting her head on them.

Joey was getting a little worried about her lack of energy lately. He sat down beside her and rested his back up against a sapling with his hand gently scratching her back.

"That's a good girl. We can have a little rest and then head back." Harriet responded by moving her head over onto Joey's thigh.

He was aware that Bernese Mountain Dogs lifespan averaged around 8 years, but Harriet had always been healthy and even though she was 7 and a half, Joey just assumed that she would buck the odds and live to 10 or 12. Maybe she's just been a little sick the last few days…probably ate something she shouldn't have.

Joey explained Harriet's behavior to Lilley that evening. She agreed and thought she had noticed Harriet slowing down a bit too. She told Joey she would call Dr. Norman, the William's Glen vet, in the morning.

"Isn't that going to be expensive?" Joey asked, worried.

"Well, I used to work after school with him when I was just a little older than you. I cleaned his examining rooms and helped him handle some of the less cooperative animals in his charge. On one of my days off, I was walking by his office when a beautiful little golden retriever escaped his grasp and ran out into the woods behind the clinic. We both ran over and searched the bushes and after almost an hour I found the little guy, coaxed him over with a piece of licorice I had in my pocket, and carried him back to Dr. Norman's office. He had given up the search and was about to call her owners, or parents as we called them, when I showed up with her in my arms. He said that I had saved the day and that he owed me one… Maybe it's time to collect on that promise by having him check out Harriet for us."

"That sounds great. Hopefully, he can get her in soon. She is not eating as much either. Sometimes her night meal is still in her bowl in the morning," Joey added.

"Well, leave it with me. I'll call in the morning and set something up.

Joey turned to head into his bedroom when the phone rang. Joey was just a couple steps away, so he picked up the receiver, expecting it to be for his mom. Lilley didn't even look over.

"Joey?" It was an adult voice calling him 'Joey' and that puzzled him momentarily. "It's Sarah Magee…Billie's mom.

"Oh, hi, Mrs. Magee!" He was pleased to know that Billie had referred to him as Joey and not Joseph and that explained it.

"Hi, listen… Billie's dad and I were thinking about a surprise for Billie. We have really been missing her and Willie said that he thought you would be missing her too."

"Well, he's right. I do miss her. I was able to FaceTime her from Jug's the other day, but we got cut off…poor reception."

"Aw, that's too bad! Well, here's our idea. She arrives at the Montrose airport at 4:30 on Sunday afternoon. We thought it would be a nice surprise if you were there to help us welcome her back home. Is that something you would like to do?"

"Are you serious? I literally won't sleep until then!" Joey's throat was closing and was near tears. He was overjoyed that they had thought of him that way.

"We thought so. We were talking about that when we stopped the car on the way to the airport at the end of June. Willie spotted you and stopped the car so Billie could jump out and say goodbye. That really touched us and made us realize how important you were to her. We will be leaving our place at 2:30. We can pick you up or you can come over here."

"I will be at your place by 2:15!" Joey answered enthusiastically.

"Okay, see you then…bye."

"Bye…thanks!" Joey hung up the phone and looked over at his mom who was grinning from ear to ear.

"You knew!" Joey said, still excited.

"Well, Sarah and I did talk about that possibility. Besides some days this summer you have been rather mopey. I figured that might cheer you up."

"I knew too!" A little voice came out of the hallway behind Joey. Joey turned and picked up Jess and hugged her and set her back down. "Now can I have that ice cream bar, Mommy?"

"You guys!" Joey blurted.

"Yes, you can have the ice cream bar. It's in the bottom freezer in the fridge." Lilley looked up at Joey and shrugged. "Well, she overheard Sarah and me on the phone yesterday and I had to bribe her to keep it a secret from you."

Joey just shook his head smiling, "Thanks, you guys." Then he turned and headed to his room to get ready for bed.

CHAPTER 3

It was a Thursday night and Joey was counting down the hours until Billie would be landing at the airport in Montrose on Sunday. She was such a happy part of his life and he had missed her constantly while she was in England during the summer holidays.

There were, however, holes in his family life that needed mending. His dad was not there, and that was a healthy thing, literally, for his mom, Jess, and him, but he still missed him. Hank, the good father, was fun to be with. He and Joey did things that fathers and sons do, like fishing and going into Montrose to watch a semi-pro baseball game or a stock car race at the Glen, a few miles north of town. Joey found it odd not to have a father. He figured that's why he and Jug got along so well, in part, because Jug's dad had passed away a few years ago and his mom, Ellen was pretty much best friends with Lilley. Living in a single parent home was not all that uncommon, but there still was a void that was once full and happy. He recalled too, how Pam and he would even do some things together before she alienated herself from the family and turned to drugs.

Negative thoughts began to overpower him, and he lay there staring at the tile ceiling of his bedroom feeling confused about how things had come down to this. Would things ever be back to the good days where he would be the son in a normal nuclear family? He guessed not. He couldn't sleep because his brain just wouldn't wind down for the night. He got up and sat in the armchair beside Lilley who was curled up in the corner of the couch reading a novel. It occurred to Joey that she must be even more distressed. She read about steamy romances and loving relationships that were, at least for now, stolen from her.

"Well, what brings you back out here with your mother? What's on your mind, honey?" asked Lilley in a warm tone.

"Nothin', I guess…Well, to be honest, I was missing being a normal family," Joey admitted.

"You mean you miss Pam and maybe even your dad?" Lilley answered quickly, as if she anticipated Joey's thoughts.

"Well…yeah, I guess. I know Pam's in a drug rehab program, but when is she comin' home? I know it's weird for me to miss an aggravating older sister, but I think I do," Joey admitted with a chuckle.

"No, it's not weird," Lilley set her book down on the end table and swiveling around to better face Joey. "I guess you probably know, I have only seen her twice in the last couple of months, and I miss her desperately! She was a really nice kid, and funny too, even just a year ago." She stared ahead as if searching her thoughts. "That's why I want her to get the help she needs. Inside the tough shell she has developed lately, is a warm, loving person, and I want that back…not just for me but for her and everybody."

"How are you even managing to pay for her rehab? Isn't that really expensive?" Joey seemed concerned.

"Yes, it is expensive, but ironically, since we cannot afford it, the government pays for most of it. Right now, your grandpa is also helping."

Joey looked confused. "How is that possible?"

"You are, no doubt, aware of my constant meetings in Montrose, right?"

"Yeah, I figured you were either seeing people about Pam or Dad."

"Just after Pam was taken away, your grandpa gave me some money to help with her if I needed it. She actually progressed very well during the 30 or 40 days in the rehabilitation center. She even reached the point where they would have normally sent her home. Because your dad was…having problems, we felt it would be safer for her to live in Montrose a little longer. She is in a halfway house, or some people call them sober living houses. That requires rent, though, and I'm using your grandpa's money for that at the moment. Now that things have quieted down here, I am working to get her home. If we can work it out, I want her back in the next two weeks."

"That would be really good," Joey said sincerely. "You said things have quieted down. Does that mean Dad will never be coming back?"

"I have applied for a separation which will mean divorce, eventually." Lilley studied Joey's face. "He has been getting himself in trouble in Montrose too. The drinking changed him, Joey!" She began to tear up.

Even though Joey knew she had started the divorce proceedings there was something about hearing her say it that angered him. He wasn't sure why. "Why can't you guys work it out!" Joey said, emotion creeping into his voice.

"Don't you think I tried, Joey?" Lilley was now sobbing.

Joey looked down as if ashamed of his feelings. "Sorry, Mom… I know you did try. You probably tried too hard. I mean you probably gave him too many chances to change. I remember all those late nights and the yelling and the hitting. I remember the night he hurt both of us really bad!" Joey got up and leaned over Lilley hugging her, resting his head on top of hers. Lilley took hold of his arm and squeezed. "Ow!" Joey yelled. Lilley had forgotten about his bad arm and that brought them from sobs to snorts and stifled laughter, both of them wiping their eyes.

"We are quite the mess, eh, Joey?" Lilley was still wiping her eyes half crying, half laughing.

"Yeah, I guess we are…How's Jess these days? I'm always out with Jug or Harriet and we don't talk much anymore." Joey looked a little saddened.

"It's funny you should ask that. She has been constantly asking me when Pammy was coming home for almost two weeks now. All I can offer is to say 'soon.'"

"Well, I hope it is soon. I do kinda miss her annoying self!" Joey smiled attempting to lighten things.

"Joey, I'm sure glad you have Billie. I'll be glad when she gets back too. I don't know if it's her influence or what, but it seems like…like…you're not a little boy anymore. I feel like you are becoming a real genuine, caring young man, and I'm proud of you!"

Blushing, Joey answered, "Thanks, Mom. You know I love you right?"

Lilley looked wary of what was coming next. "…yes."

"Okay, good. So don't expect me to say that every night before I go to bed, okay?" They both laughed and Joey turned to go back to his room.

Joey must have been tired, or the conversation with his mom had somehow relaxed his brain because he slept soundly and did not wake up until 8 the next morning. The house was still quiet except for the faint sound of the TV in living room. He poked his head out from the hallway and saw Jess sitting on the floor cross-legged in front of the coffee table, coloring and watching cartoons. His mom must still be in bed, he thought. He cleaned up got dressed and got Harriet to her feet where she was lying by the door, and they snuck out of the house for a little walk.

Rounding the corner at the back of the house he came upon his mom pinning clothes on the clothesline.

"Whoa, I thought you were still in bed." Joey said surprised to see her.

"Jessie came into my room and asked if she could watch TV, so I got up and found her some cartoons. I thought I might as well put the laundry out since I'm awake now anyway." She answered smiling. "You two going for a little walk?... I'll phone Dr Norman when his office opens at 9 and we will see if we can get him to look at her."

"Okay, sounds good." Joey answered. "We won't be too long. She seems really tired this morning. I hope he can help her."

They took to the path that led to the nearest water's edge. Joey kept turning around to make sure Harriet was still there as she lumbered along behind him. He had all his lawns cut for the week and was free to just enjoy the day…and it was a spectacular one. Boats were already crisscrossing the lake and the warm wind was stirring up patches of darker blue ripples. There were even a couple of sailboats farther north up the lake, their bright, white triangular sails gleaming and reflecting in the water. Joey found his favorite smooth rock and sat examining what his surroundings offered him. At his feet, the shallow water revealed a reddish-brown sandy area with tiny maroon roots tangled in hairy masses and little brown and beige stones. From where he sat, he could reach over and lift up little rocks and watch the crayfish scurry from underneath, frantically searching for another rock to hide under. Harriet was standing with her front paws in the water, her head bent down slurping up some of the cool liquid, then she turned and curled up behind Joey on the rock. Some days he didn't need a fishing pole or a guitar or a pad of paper and some pencils. Some days it was good enough to just "be", especially in the beauty of this area that he loved so much.

Joey thought of the sketch he had done for Billie depicting the trout hole where she had had so much fun squealing in delight as she hooked those little fish a couple months ago. He wondered briefly if the same Billie would come back from her summer in England. Lilley had picked out a cheap frame from the Old General Store. Because she worked there, she got a 20% discount and was happy to be able to provide something for Joey. His sketch was a charcoal drawing and the white matting and black frame made it look very professional. He signed it simply, "Joey", but on the back he risked the words, "For Billie on her return from England. With love from Joey." He was pretty sure he could get away with the "with love" part with Billie's parents. As long as she still felt the same, he would be happy. There was no reason to think she wouldn't, but maybe her time away from William's Glen had broadened her view and made her realize there is more to life… more fish in the sea.

Joey snapped out of his daydream and thought they should head back. Harriet was completely relaxed and sleeping behind Joey, but as soon as he got to his feet, she raised her head and began struggling to her feet. Joey assisted her by reaching under her stomach and lifting her back end up. He felt a little surge of emotion in his throat. He hoped that she wasn't somehow in pain. She had the sweetest disposition imaginable. He recalled how once when they were on a walk to the trout hole, just past the bridge, a dog jumped right out of the window of a parked pickup truck and attacked Harriet. It began to bite

Harriet on the rear and Harriet just turned and looked at her attacker indignant, as if to say, "What the hell are you doing!?" Harriet was twice the size of the other beagle-like dog and when the owner ran over to scold his dog and take it back, he remarked how surprised he was that Harriet hadn't even tried to bite back. Joey knew she was a special soul, and their bond was unbreakable. As he stood there, after getting her to her feet, he looked back out over the lake and right on cue Harriet did what she always did. She stepped on his toe and leaned against his leg like a true Bernese often does to show her love.

When they got back to the house, Lilley was at the sink rinsing out her coffee cup. She didn't have to be at work at the Old General Store until 10 so she sat down to talk to Joey.

"Hi, honey. I phoned Dr. Norman and he said he could see Harriet on Monday around 4 after his last appointment. Do you think she could make it there walking? I won't be done work until 5."

"Oh, I don't know," answered Joey. "Actually, I don't think she can. She was having trouble just now and we only went to the little beach and back."

"Okay, well leave it with me. We will figure something out. I don't want to change the time since he is seeing her for free."

Joey chowed down on some cereal and a couple pieces of toast and headed out, leaving Harriet on the kitchen floor in her familiar spot. She was content to stay there and not follow him like she used to do. Joey would normally have to trick her with a treat to escape, but lately she did not seem interested in accompanying him on his adventures. Even though Joey had to invent ways of getting rid of her, he wished she was up wagging her tail and begging to come with him today.

Joey and Jug had planned an afternoon out on the lake in the rowboat doing a little perch fishing. Once out on the lake they drifted away from shore, lowered their hooked worms into the water and sat back drinking dr. peppers and munching on chips. This was heaven to these two. They would talk and solve all the problems of the world and joke around like two teenagers are prone to do. Sometimes they would shed their shirts and jump in the water and relieve themselves swimming under water. It was a wonderful life for boys their age and they knew they were lucky to live here.

After about 30 minutes, they had realized that they had drifted about half a mile out into the lake and figured they better start rowing back. Joey began rowing and Jug figured it would be a good opportunity to do a little trolling.

"Oh, yeah, sure…use me as your trolling motor," Joey quipped.

"Hey, why not?" Jug laughed. "You row halfway, then I'll row so you can troll after that."

"Sounds good," Joey said looking inquisitively at an approaching boat. "Oh, crap!"

What's wrong?" Jug asked.

"Remember, I told you about when Billie and I were out in her rowboat, and Paul Sinclair came by on skis and soaked us?"

"Yeah." Jug answered, turning to see what Joey was looking at.

"Well…déjà vu! No skier, but I recognize the yellow stripe on the side of that boat and I'm sure he still wants to hassle me. I haven't seen him since I broke my arm and I'm sure he's still pissed off about me and Billie."

"What should we do?" Jug asked slightly panicked.

"Not much we can do out here. I'll just keep rowing for the shore and hope he doesn't do anything too drastic."

Instead of slowing down the approaching speed boat began accelerating, probably because Paul had recognized Joey's rowboat. It came closer and closer and extremely fast.

"Jesus!" Joey shouted. "That stupid bastard is going to hit us! Hold on Jug!"

Paul's boat was near the point where he couldn't avoid hitting the small boat and then it veered sharply away, but too late. The stern of the speed boat slid sideways and slammed into the bow of the rowboat splintering the wood and overturning it sending first Jug and then Joey flying into the water. When Jug landed in the water the bow of the rowboat came crashing down on his head, stunning him. Joey was clear of the boat and saw that Jug was in distress and panicking. He swam quickly over to Jug who was losing consciousness and halfheartedly clawing at the water to keep his head above. Then he seemed to give up and began to sink just as Joey reached him. Joey was able to lift Jug's head enough to rest it on the overturned hull of the partially submerged and upside-down rowboat. Jug's eyes were closed, and he was not responding, as Joey tried to gently slap his cheeks to bring him around. He was breathing but he was not responding.

"Jug! Wake up! Jug! Come on man, you gotta wake up!"

Joey found the bow line, tied it into a large loop using his right hand and his teeth while holding onto Jug with his left. Then he ran the rope under Jug's arms and around his back so that he was securely bound to the upturned hull and in no danger of sinking back under. Oars, life jacket pillows, half empty pop cans and chip bags floated nearby. He checked Jug again – still no response but he could feel a heartbeat in his neck, and he was clearly breathing. It was like he was asleep, but he couldn't wake him up. Joey noticed an abrasion on Jug's forehead and figured the boat must have knocked him out…but he was not waking up, and Joey was becoming more and more frantic. He grabbed an oar and fastened a lifejacket to the end of it by the straps normally used to fasten it too your body. He raised the bright orange life jacket up as high as he could, but he slipped back down into the water. He desperately clamored up onto the hull watching to make sure Jug was still securely fastened. Once on top, he began waving the life jacket again, hoping to catch the attention of a boater or someone on shore. There was only the distant white spray from the back of Paul Sinclair's boat about a mile away heading for the cover of his boathouse and the distant sailboats, too far away to notice their predicament.

Joey, exhausted, laid back down on the underside of the boat to catch his breath almost feeling as though he could pass out too. He checked Jug again and he seemed okay, but he was worried about the cold water and his friend's motionless, partially submerged body. Hypothermia was always a danger especially out deep where they were. Finally, the sound of a small motor could be heard heading their way. Joey looked up and saw a small red and white aluminum fishing boat approaching. The man at the tiller waved and slowed, shut the motor off and coasted in closer to the two stranded boys.

"I saw you guys were in trouble. I actually saw the other boat hit you and then drive off. Is your friend okay?"

"I don't know," Joey answered, shivering and close to tears. "We gotta get him out of the water. He's breathing and he has a pulse, but he is unconscious."

Joey was able to untie Jug and pull him higher onto the overturned rowboat. The man in the aluminum boat grabbed Jug's arms and tried to pull him into his boat but was having trouble. Joey jumped into his boat and grabbed one arm and the man the other. Together they were able to get Jug prone between the seats of the small fishing boat. The man checked Jug over and confirmed Joey's diagnosis.

"Yep, he's alive and seems to have normal vital signs. Did something hit him there on the head?" he pointed to the wound on Jug's forehead.

"Yes, the boat flipped over on top of him. I was barely able to keep him from going under when he passed out. I just tied him here to wave for help." Joey answered extremely agitated.

"Don't worry, son. We'll get him help. You probably saved his life. My name is Don Archer. I was launching my boat over there at the town ramp when I saw this happening. I couldn't get my motor started at first or I would have been here sooner."

The man called Don reached into his pocket and pulled out a cell phone. He dialed and then began to talk on it.

"Hello? Yes, this is Don Archer. I have an unconscious teenager about 14 or 15," he looked at Joey for verification and Joey nodded. "He has been hit in the head and needs an ambulance. We can bring him to the William's Glen boat ramp…Okay, we will look for you."

Quickly and efficiently, Don secured Jug's head with some boat cushions and made sure his neck was straight. There was still no movement from Jug and Joey was beginning to feel nauseated.

"I will send my son out for your rowboat so he can tow it in for you. I'm afraid it looks like a write-off though," he said pursing his lips. "You hold his head still so the bumps don't jostle him around too much.

"Yeah okay, but I don't care about the boat. I just want Jug to be okay."

"We'll get him to Four Counties as soon as we can," reassured Don.

"Thank you," Joey said losing his composure and sobbing openly.

"It's okay, bud. He's going to be okay," he said, completely unsure of that.

By the time they got to the boat ramp, the ambulance had already backed up to the dock area with its lights flashing. There was a small gathering of onlookers starting to gather. They got Jug onto a gurney and into the back of ambulance.

"Can I ride in the back with him?" Joey asked one of the attendants.

"No, I'm sorry son. We are going to Four Counties if you want to find your way there."

Don caught Joey by the elbow, "What's your name bud?"

"Joe Burgess. I just live up the road over there." Joey was still frenzied with worry.

"Okay, Joe, as soon as I get my boat tied up, I'll take you over to the hospital so you can be with your friend. Give me your phone number so I can tell your mom or dad where you are."

"Mom…but she's at the Old General Store. She works there."

"Okay, I'll call her there then."

Don Tied up his boat securely, grabbed a few things out of his boat and motioned Joey over to a black pickup truck with a white trailer on it. Joey jumped in and off they went in the direction of the hospital. When they arrived, Don got his phone back out.

"Do you know the phone number of the store?" he asked.

"Uh, yeah…uh…shit…I can't remember!"

"That's okay, kid. Look, I'll find the number or I'll go back there myself, but I will get in touch with your mother. You go in and find your friend and stay here until I can get hold of your mom and his parents."

"He only has a mom too," Joey responded quickly.

"Alright, whatever. I'll make sure they know what's up…now go!"

Joey ran from the truck into emergency where he was stopped by an elderly volunteer.

"Whoa, son. What's happening?"

Joey told him the story and the man led him into a waiting area and told him that someone would come out to see him soon. Joey told him that both their moms were on their way there. The volunteer went over to the triage nurse's office, whispered something, and came back.

"Try to relax. He is in good hands, and someone will come and tell you what's going on as soon as they can…okay?"

Joey didn't answer. He just drew his knees up toward his face and wrapped his arms around them, still shivering more from worry than being wet and cold.

Don Archer couldn't find the Old General Store using the 411 directory, but he knew where it was. It was likely still under the former owner's name and wasn't registered in the directory yet. He pulled up alongside the store, to leave room for the trailer, and quickly ascended the steps flinging the door open with the bell ringing loudly overhead.

Looking around and spotting Lilley behind the counter he asked, "Are you Mrs. Burgess?"

"Yes, that's me," sensing the urgent look on the man's face. "Why, what's wrong?"

Don introduced himself and explained the situation to Lilley as calmly as he could muster.

"Oh no! I need to get hold of Ellen…That's Josh's mom."

Lilley reached for the store phone, got her purse out, took out a small address book for the number, and dialed Ellen's office in Montrose.

"Hello, Ellen…look, I don't have much time, but…"

"What's the matter Lilley?" Ellen's voice became distraught.

"I can't get into all the details right now. The boys were involved in an accident and Josh has been hurt. Just please meet me at the hospital as soon as you can!" Then, in an effort to keep Ellen from coming apart, she added, "He is in good care so just try to get over when you can."

"I'm on my way," Ellen answered and hung up the phone.

Lilley had walked to work today so she didn't have her car and her shift wasn't over for 3 more hours. She looked around frantically.

"Do you need a ride to the hospital?" Don asked, sensing her plight.

"Well, uh…I…"

"Lilley, go!" the owner shouted from the back room.

"Thanks Mike. I'll make it up to you," Lilley shouted back.

"Don't worry about that. Just go to the boys…and let me know how you make out." Mike said as he walked out toward Lilley. He motioned with both of his arms for them to get going. "Go…hurry. Get outta here."

Lilley grabbed her purse, and they were quickly out the door and on route to the hospital.

"Thank you so much! … "Lilley struggled to remember his name.

"Don, Don Archer. I live in Montrose. I was just up here doing a little fishing when I saw what was going on."

He explained what he had seen and how he managed to get the boys in to shore.

"Thank you so much! Lilley repeated. "You are a real Samaritan!"

"No worries, it's not like I was busy or anything," he tried to force a chuckle but could see that Lilley was far too distressed to be amused.

"Look, since you don't have a car, I'll go back and get my boat back onto the trailer and come back until your friend gets here." Don added, sincerely, as they entered the hospital laneway.

"Thank you again. You are so kind!"

Don dropped Lilley off at the emergency entrance and she ran in quickly, talked briefly with the volunteer who pointed toward the waiting room where Joey was now prone across three of the seats. She walked quickly to him.

"Joey! Are you okay?" As she reached him, Joey got up and hugged her, trembling. "You are soaked and shivering. You need some dry clothes!'

"I'm fine, Mom. It's Jug. He's out cold. It's like he is sleeping and won't wake up. God, mom…it's bad!"

"I'm sure he will be okay," she lied. "Mr. Archer told me what happened. Who hit you guys?"

Joey looked up studying her eyes, pausing as if she could figure it out.

"Really… Paul Sinclair would stoop to this!? I thought it may have just been an accident…not deliberate!"

"Mom, please don't say anything! I can't prove it. I know it was Sinclair's boat, or at least one exactly like it. We were too busy being flung into the lake to get a good look. But I know it was him."

About 10 minutes later, the rapid pace of clicking dress shoes became louder, as Ellen rushed into the room. Lilley gave her a quick hug, and then set her down on a chair close to them and tried to explain things as calmly as possible."

Ellen was crying and took a hanky out to wipe her face, "Joey, you're okay?"

"Yeah, I'm okay, Mrs. Parker. Thanks…just a little soggy," he forced out a phony chuckle.

"Who did this?" she looked back and forth from Lilley to Joey.

"We don't really know. It happened so fast," Joey chimed in.

A kindly looking, young Asian doctor walked into the waiting room. "Is one of you the mother of the boy that was in the boating accident?"

"Yes, me!" Ellen quickly stepped forward. "How is he?"

"Could you come with me please? We need some background information to be able to properly treat him," the doctor answered.

"How is he!?" Ellen asked again in a louder, more flustered voice.

"Come with me," the doctor repeated.

Ellen grabbed her purse and they walked through two swinging doors and back into the inner sanctum of the emergency ward.

"Geez, Joey, let me see if I can get you some scrubs or something!" Lilley offered.

"No, Mom, it's okay, really. I'm drying out anyway and it's warm in here.

They both changed their gaze to the parking lot outside the waiting room windows. A black pickup drove in with a red and white aluminum boat in tow.

"Don! Jeez, I almost forgot about him," announced Lilley

"Yeah, he was amazing, Mom. If it wasn't for him, we might still be out there!"

"Yeah, we owe him for sure. And now he is back to see if Ellen made it here, in case I didn't have a way of getting home. They don't come any nicer than that. Such a good man."

Joey noticed something odd about the way Lilley said that. Perhaps she saw a glimpse of what her husband used to be like. But he shook it off and went over to the emergency doors to greet him.

"Hey Joe, how's things going with your friend," Don said as he walked in through the automatic doors.

"We don't know yet. His mom is in the back there now." Joey pointed to the double doors leading to the back.

They walked in and sat down in the waiting room together.

"Mr. Archer, we owe you a huge debt of gratitude. You don't need to hang around here anymore. Josh's mom is here, and we can get a ride home in her car. It's getting late and I'm sure people are wondering where you are," she continued.

"That's okay. I'll stay in case you need me. She might need to stay a bit longer than you guys." He lowered his voice to speak calmly, attempting to lower the tension. "As a matter of fact, I'm going to head over to the McDonalds on the highway and bring you guys back something to eat. I could use something myself."

"Mr. Archer, you have done more than enough. I'm sure your wife will wonder where you are during the supper hour." Lilley said glancing at her watch.

"Well, there is no Mrs. Archer, and I'm hungry. I'll see you in a few minutes…any favorites?"

"No…but…"

"Okay, back in a flash…" and out he went in quest of food.

"Boy, we were lucky to run into him," Joey said. "You know, Mom, I think he likes you," he winked, trying to bring some levity to the situation.

"Oh, Joey…give it a rest! I just wish your dad could have been the one to look after us." Then, sensing how that comment might affect Joey, she added, "But, yeah, you guys were very lucky he saw you!"

Fifteen minutes later, Don returned, and they realized they were hungrier than they thought. They wolfed down their quarter pounders and fries with milkshakes quite quickly. Lilley phoned the babysitter's house and she assured Lilley that Jess was welcome to stay the night. Still Don refused to leave, insisting that he really had nothing pressing on his agenda and no one who would be missing him.

Then the same doctor that talked to them the first time returned, clipboard in hand, and sat down with them to give them an update in a concerned but controlled manner.

"I'm Dr. Wong. I should have introduced myself earlier. It smells like McDonalds out here." He laughed. "I'm glad you were able to eat something…Unfortunately, not much has changed. He has taken quite a blow to the head. There is no fracture, but he remains unconscious."

Joey stood up and looked out the window. "You mean he is in a coma, don't you?"

"Yes, I'm afraid so. What's your name son?" he asked softly.

"Joe Burgess."

"Well, Joe, your friend has good strong vital signs and that means he has every chance of pulling out of this and recovering."

"How long will he be like that?" Joey interrupted.

"It's impossible to tell. A coma is the brain shutting down to deal with a trauma. So, it depends on the seriousness of the hit he took. Because of his age, I have every reason to believe he will recover, especially if he wakes up in the next few hours. My suggestion to all of you is to go home and get some rest. Mrs. Parker is prepared to stay here for the night. Go get some sleep and check back in the morning and hopefully we will have some good news for you by then. Mrs. Parker told me to tell you that too. She knows you are concerned but she wants you to go get some sleep. If anything happens, Mrs. Burgess, I have your number and I'm pulling an all-nighter, so I'll let you know as soon as he wakes up…Okay, guys?"

"Okay, thanks, Dr.," Lilley offered. "Tell Ellen to call me if she wants me to bring her anything."

"Will do." Dr. Wong turned and disappeared behind the swinging doors.

"Hey guys, I will be happy to give you a lift home," Don spoke up.

"You've already done more than enough Mr. Archer," answered Lilley.

"What…you gonna walk? And my name's Don. It must be a couple miles back to the store and you probably live close to there, right? It's almost 8 o'clock and the doctor's right. You can't really do anything here… I insist."

They made their way to the truck, piled in and Don drove them home following Lilley's directions.

"Hey, Mr. Archer, I kind of got your seat a little wet on the way to the hospital," Joey confessed.

"No worries, that's why I paid the big bucks for the leather seats. Okay, guys, here's my business card." He reached across and handed it to Lilly. "I got a message from my son while I was out getting burgers. He has towed your rowboat in and tied it to the government dock at the boat ramp. It's still upside-down Joe, and he says that it's probably not fixable. The bow is pretty smashed up. If you guys need anything, I'm staying over at the Kamawog Lodge for a few days. My cell number is on that card and I would be happy to help. I would also appreciate knowing how your buddy makes out, Joe."

"Yeah, sure…we sure appreciate all you have done." Joey said. "You have a son in William's Glen?"

"No, not really. He lives in Tilson, about 10 minutes east of William's Glen." Sensing that Joey was probing a little deeper, he added, "I used to live there with his mom."

"Will you come in for a drink or something?" Lilley offered.

"No, thanks. I think I will turn in for the night."

After several more thank yous, Lilley and Joey made their way into the house, greeted Harriet, and sat facing each other at the kitchen table.

"Well, that was a terrible day, Joey. I sure hope everything is okay by morning." Lilley sighed.

Harriet scratched and clawed herself to her feet and was pointing at the door.

"I think your little girl is trying to tell you something," Lilley said, nodding at Harriet.

"Oh, yeah, she must really have to go!"

"I'm going to bed." She kissed Joey on the top of the head.

Joey got up let Harriet out, then waited for her to return and made sure she had water and noticed that there was still food in her bowl. He locked the door, turned out the lights and went to bed. He threw his wet clothes on the floor, grabbed a quick shower and climbed into bed. Exhausted, and despite the worry and concern for Jug, he fell asleep almost instantly.

CHAPTER 4

Joey woke early Saturday morning and was immediately aware that there had been no phone call from the hospital. It was 6:30 so he thought they might not call this early out of courtesy. Then he remembered that the Dr. said he would call whenever Jug woke up and he was on duty all night.

Joey got dressed and took Harriet out for a pee and a short walk. It was already hot outside, and they were calling for a real scorcher. Harriet's tongue was hanging out before they even reached the trees behind the house.

Five miles north, up the other side of the lake, Paul Sinclair was washing his Donzi speed boat and checking the right rear for any telltale signs such as a crack in the fiberglass or green paint that may have come off Joey's old rowboat. He saw only a few scratches in that area and could pawn that off as dock rash. Still, he thought it would be best to have an alibi in case anyone had seen him. Because he had come at Joey and Jug straight on, there was no way they could have seen him and when he turned and hit the rowboat, they were too busy clamoring to stay afloat. By the time he had turned his boat around and headed back north he slumped down in the seat which kept him from view from behind and gunned the throttle. The boat was capable of 75 mph, and he was quickly out of sight by the time Joey had been able to secure Jug and cling to the capsized rowboat. What he was not confident of was whether anyone from another boat or perhaps on shore at the south end of the lake, had seen him. He decided to fess up to his parents so they could hatch a plan…because that is what they would do. Admitting guilt, or that they were wrong in any way was not in the Sinclair genes.

He came into the kitchen through the back door. Sally was frying up some eggs and bacon and the smell was irresistible. Paul had planned to ride his four-wheeler along the train tracks into town and grab something at the diner, but he decided a free breakfast would be cool too. Besides, this might be a good time to approach his mom about his quandary.

"Hey Paul, you want any eggs, or you got something else planned?" Sally asked

"Yeah, sure, Mom. I'll put in a couple pieces of toast and join you."

Sally Sinclair was an attractive, statuesque, almost Amazon-like, blonde woman at least as tall as her husband, Mark. She had sea-green eyes and kept her hair usually up in a bun. She wore frayed cut-off jeans; no doubt made that way and expensive. Her top was a white loosely fitting white button-up floral blouse and short sleeves made to look like long sleeves rolled up and fastened by a ribbon of the same material at the shoulder. She was always fashion conscious, even if she was just in the kitchen of their lake-side mansion making breakfast. Several fine gold chains hung from her neck and disappeared into the deep vee of her blouse. Sally was a fitness freak, and her body was always tanned, even in winter. She jogged, walked or road her mountain bike every day, which kept her thighs and calves shapely and muscular. Her almost 50-year-old body looked years younger. She had the time to pamper herself, because she didn't have to go to work and had all the money she needed to buy herself expensive clothes or whatever else she wanted.

"Where's Dad?" Paul wondered.

"He told me he has an important meeting this afternoon and to leave him in bed to get some extra sleep. Why?" she wondered. Paul would never have cared normally.

"Uh…nothin'" I just wanted to talk to you guys. "No big deal." Paul said nonchalantly.

"Ah, you need something, right? Maybe something for your speedboat or your 4-wheeler or maybe for your trail bike…or perhaps your jet ski?"

Paul caught the sarcasm in her voice and thought it best to use a softer more congenial tone. He too had mastered the art of manipulation…and why not? His parents had taught him well. "Yeah, I know, Mom. You guys have given me a lot of toys…and you're right, I do need something but not a physical thing."

Sally passed him a plate of eggs and bacon, then brought over his toast and shoved the butter dish closer to him.

"Well, that does sound interesting," she said sitting down at the kitchen island across from him. "Let me guess…You want to borrow the jeep…and I've told you that until you get your license, that's not happening."

"No, Mom, nothing like that."

"Well, don't keep me in suspense. Spit it out."

"You remember on Friday when I took the boat out for a spin?"

"Oh…Yeah, I was out tanning on the deck when you left. You didn't stay out too long. What about it?"

"Well, I accidently swamped a little rowboat over by the east shore. It was that stupid Joe Burgess and his buddy Josh Parker. I don't think it's anything to worry about, but I think the back of my boat hit theirs. That boat was probably only worth a hundred bucks anyway, but I was hopin' you could have my back and just say I was home or something if anyone asks. That's about it, I guess," Paul ended the story and looked up to see his mom's eyes widening into green saucers.

"What? What's the big deal?" Paul said, confused, as his mom stood up and started pacing.

"Jesus Christ, Paul! Do you know what you've done?"

"Yeah, I just told you," Paul answered, wondering what the fuss was about.

"Jug Parker's real name is Josh, right? Sally asked.

"Yeah, but…" Sally held her hand up, stopping him, and started pacing again with her hand over her mouth, a horrified look on your face. "Do you know what you've done?... Don't answer that. Josh Parker is in Four Counties in a coma! It's all over town now. There will be an investigation. Some stranger from out of town saw it happen from the boat launch."

"Jesus!" Paul exclaimed. He began to offer an explanation, but Sally stopped him again.

"Go and hide yourself for a while and don't talk about this to anyone… Go!" Sally screamed.

"But I …"

"Go! Go now. Give me time to figure out what to do and how to tell your father…Paul, I don't want to see you right now. Get out of here!"

Paul got up and went down to the boathouse to recheck the boat for evidence. Sally braced herself against the counter over the sink and stared out over the lake pensively, shaking her head and frowning. "Shit, shit, shit, shit! She spat through clenched teeth.

"What the hell is all the fuss out here?" Mark asked scratching his unkempt bedhead.

"Mark, come in here and sit down. We have a problem." Sally took charge, like she usually did.

Mark was a remarkably successful building materials distributor and had a masterful command of the boardroom but when facing Sally in matters of the heart or family, he was warm putty. He sat down as directed and reached for the paper as was his custom in the morning. Sally quickly snagged the paper and shoved it out of his reach.

"I need your attention!" she snapped.

"Whoa, okay, you have it. What could be so important?"

Sally sat down facing him as she had done with Paul a few minutes earlier. She laid out the events that occurred and that she was sure it wasn't Paul's fault, and that he did come and tell her rather than trying to hide it.

Sally was attempting to take the lead, but this was potentially a business problem. Mark's face began turning red and his heart began beating faster, his anger building. His reputation could not be tarnished. He relied on the surrounding communities for his livelihood and Paul was working parttime at the business and was also heir to family empire. Sally eased gradually up to the part about one boy ending up in the hospital and was knocked out.

Mark at 47, was not an intimidating man but he knew how to control a situation. He stood about 5' 11" and had a stocky build and the requisite burgeoning belly of a well-fed businessman. Money was his main love and almost everything else came in second. Although his current lumber and building material business was above-board and his clientele was largely happy, he had built this business by selling inferior products to gullible retailers and unethical dealings that ruined more scrupulous competitors. His slicked-back black hair was beginning to reveal receding grey patches on each side of his head. His modus operandi was also very slick, borderline psychopathic. If he thought he would gain from it, he would present a very glossy, sunny personality. If things didn't go his way, he would gut you and throw you to the rats with no remorse. He could dominate a meeting, and this present situation was evolving into something that could hurt him where he felt it most – his wallet.

Mark stood up partially and stretched to retrieve the morning paper. He leafed through to the local news in the second section.

"Local William's Glen teen in coma after boating accident." He read down further as Sally came around behind him to see what he had found. "Unnamed witnesses, claim that the small punt he was in was hit by a larger speed boat. An investigation into the incident is ongoing."

"For Christ's sake! Where is that boy? And how in the hell did this get in the papers that fast? That kid is in a goddamn coma for Christ's sake!" Mark was livid, puffing up his cheeks and blowing air out angrily.

"Paul's down at the boathouse. But…we need to think about how to handle this." Sally postured.

"Yeah, well, that's stating the obvious!" he snorted in disgust.

Mark walked over to the back entrance, opened the door and yelled toward the boathouse, "Paul!"

A sheepish and distant, "Yeah?" came from within.

"Get your ass up here, now!" Mark slammed the door and sat back down at the island with his hand on his forehead stewing and shaking his head, as if searching for answers.

Joey sat in the shade, his back propped up against a tall white pine, his hand gently scratching Harriet behind the ears. He stayed close to the house, hoping to hear the phone ring and some news from the hospital. He was overcome with thoughts of bad endings to the situation. The thought of the prospect of Jug dying filled him with fear and ultimately anger. Regardless of what happened, he wanted to somehow get revenge on Paul Sinclair.

Finally, just after 9:30 the phone rang, and Lilley answered it. It was Ellen. Joey could hear a muffled conversation from his position about 20 feet outside the screen door of the house. After a couple minutes, Lilley appeared at the door sat down on the steps and faced Joey who was still sitting under the pine tree just across the driveway.

"He isn't awake yet, honey, so nothing has really changed. Ellen is really having trouble dealing with this and she needs some clothes and things, so I'm going back up to the hospital. The Wilson's are keeping Jessie for now. They are aware of what's going on and Jessie thinks she's on some kind of fun holiday so…if you'd like to come with me, you can, but there won't be much for you to do."

"Okay, I think Harriet will be okay here. I'll put her bowls out here where it's cool in the shade. I want to be there, so I know what's going on. This is going to upset Billie too. She is a good friend of Jug too."

"It's upsetting for everyone involved, honey. We won't stay too long."

About a mile south of the Sinclair's in a beautiful little chalet at Kamawog Lodge, Don Archer was getting ready to head out on the lake for some fishing. Don was a bachelor, the result of a fatal car accident that claimed the life of his wife, Wendy. She had been on her way to William's Glen 3 summers ago when a semi t-boned her small Honda about a mile north of Montrose. She was instantly knocked unconscious, and died a couple hours later at Montrose General, with Don at her bedside, never regaining consciousness. She had been on her way to join Don for a second honeymoon at the Lodge on Skogie Lake. It took a good two years before Don could summon the courage to go back to Kamawog and enjoy his favorite pastime of fishing. In the last two years, he had only driven straight through William's Glen, on the way to Tilsen to visit his son. Reminders of that awful day were still ever present and, he reasoned, would always be there. There were some things that you just never forget, you only try to carry on.

Don was a good-looking man, well groomed, with short black hair and matching chevron shaped moustache and an angular jawline. His Romanesque nose, and sparkling blue eyes framed by understated black brows, had been lady killers since his high school days. He stood just over 6 feet and now at 47, his once athletic abdomen was only now starting to show a slight paunch. His shoulders and chest were still very much toned and muscular, accented by a natural light brown skin tone.

Reflecting on the events of yesterday, he remembered something he had heard Joey and Lilley say. They mentioned the name,

Paul Sinclair. He wondered if it was the same Sinclair that had swindled him years ago leaving him temporarily bankrupt. He knew the Sinclairs were in this region. Mark Sinclair had sold him thousands of faulty electronic components that Don had distributed to a large HVAC company developing high end homes in a large subdivision in Montrose. When they failed to work and caused a potentially dangerous fire threat, the HVAC company was sued, and Don was libel because of some fine print Sinclair had written into the contract. After recovering from that, Don had developed a lucrative business, invented some building software, and sold the rights to a large tech corporation for millions. He still had a bitter taste in his mouth for the name Sinclair and his curiosity was tempting him to find out more. He had all the time in the world now.

His son, Greg, was looking after his wiring and technology business as well as his retail outlet up in Tilson, and that was pretty much on autopilot. Every once in a while, Greg would call him on business matters and occasionally Don would drive up there and help him out. Greg was doing very well and was well on his way to a successful career. He had brought his boat down to William's Glen yesterday to help his dad out by towing Joey's heavily damaged rowboat back to the government dock beside the boat ramp as his dad asked. He was aware of the news and the injury to Jug but didn't know the boys at all. He was simply doing his dad a favor and he left it at that. He knew his dad would fill him in on the details and he did later that night.

Don paused his walk toward his truck and boat, turned around and returned to the porch of his chalet, and coffee still in hand, nestled into a large red Adirondack chair, rethinking his plans for the day. He chuckled to himself. He had only been up to the lodge one day and already he had rescued two kids and met two attractive and seemingly unattached women. It must be his magnetic personality, he thought.

He smiled, though no one was there to see. But then he thought more about Jug and wondered how all those involved were doing. He felt some attraction to these people and some responsibility to see the events lead to a positive ending.

The Sinclair family had talked it over extensively. Mark and Paul made a closer inspection to the boat and once more found no incriminating evidence of any sort. They resolved to cover it up and designed an alibi for Paul's whereabouts Friday morning. The story was to be that Paul was at home the whole time staining the deck. They had stain in the boathouse storage locker and the three of them immediately began painting the deck so that it looked like a couple days work had already been done. Paul did not have to pretend to get stain all over him and his shoes, so that would be handy additional proof that he was at least doing the work. If no one offered irrefutable proof, it should work. There were 4 or 5 yellow and white Donzi Sweet Sixteen's in the area, and there were no distinctive markings on their boat. Someone would have had to be on shore training high-powered binoculars or a telescope on Paul to have identified him conclusively. Even if they were certain, it was just their word against the Sinclair's.

There had never been a thought to admitting Paul's wrongdoing, only how to cover it up. Saving face and retaining his innocence was the main priority here. Honesty was not ever their first thought, and it was easy to see why Paul was the bully that he was. They did discuss the fact that Joey was friends with Billie and that made it mandatory to disavow any involvement. Billie's parents were crucial business partners and without their business, the Sinclair's could lose millions.

Joey and Lilley arrived at Four Counties hospital around noon and found Ellen on the third floor in a semi-private room that her work's benefits had fortunately covered. She was standing looking down at Jug, a damp handkerchief in one hand. They both hugged Ellen in turn, and she shuddered with grief each time, holding back an all-out cry. Just looking at her face, Joey could barely stand it. She was usually the most vibrant, cheerful woman and now she was so scared and helpless looking!

They turned to look at Jug, lying there seemingly just asleep. He looked as though he could wake up if you just shook him a little. Joey teared up again and wanted to leave the room. Before he could escape, Dr. Wong, the doctor who had admitted Jug in emergency came in the room with his clipboard.

"Hi, folks," he said, mustering his most cheerful voice. "So, his breathing is strong which is a good sign and that means no breathing tube. We are feeding him and keeping him hydrated by the intravenous lines you see here. We are also giving him some medication to bring down the swelling in his brain. In a coma, the brain shuts much of its functioning down and just completes the basic function like breathing and heart contractions. If the pressure comes down from the medication, then that would be another good sign. The pressure is usually caused by blood between the brain and the skull. There is a chance that we may have to operate to relieve the pressure. That could happen today if we think it's necessary."

No one asked any questions because they were still just stunned by the whole thing. It was difficult to believe that just a little more than 24 hours ago, the boy that lay in front of them was a fun loving, wise cracking teenager, enjoying life.

"Uhm... I'm going for a walk," Joey said, almost in a whisper. He turned and left the room.

Joey exited the elevator and walked past the gift shop and the admitting area and straight outside. He found some shade under a tree on one of the parking lot's grass strips between rows of cars and sat down chewing on some grass.

A couple minutes later a familiar pickup towing a boat parked a few rows over taking up several spots. Joey recognized right away that it was Don Archer, the man who had rescued them. He got up and approached Don as he exited his truck.

"Hey, Joe, any news?" Don asked in a hopeful tone.

"No, not much has changed at all. They might even have to operate to bring down the swelling in the brain," Joey explained.

"Yeah, let me see if I can remember…a subdural hematoma I believe it's called."

"How do you know that?" Joey asked.

Don didn't answer but pointed to a picnic table in the shade, on the grass on the east side of the hospital.

"Let's get out of this heat. It must be a hundred degrees today," said Don.

They found the table and sat facing each other. Joey was reminded of how many times he had sat across from his grandfather on the picnic table behind the William's Glen Retirement home. A sudden wave of sadness fell over him. God, he missed him!

"You look really sad, Joe. Is there anything I can do?"

"No, it's okay. It's just that I lost Gramps a couple months ago and we used to sit like this and talk," Joey looked down digging his fingernails into the soft wood of the picnic table.

"Aw, man, sorry to hear that. You've had a lot of pain recently… When you asked me how I knew what a subdural hematoma is, it reminded me of Wendy."

"Who's Wendy?" Joey asked.

"Wendy was my wife. She died in a car accident three years ago. She had many injuries, and one was a subdural hematoma. She was on life support with so many life-threatening injuries that she just couldn't be kept alive." Don looked away a little watery eyed.

"Jeez, I'm sorry! I can't imagine that!" Joey offered, but he could imagine it.

"We were both married when we were only 20. Next month would have been our 28th wedding anniversary." Then giving his head a little shake, he changed the subject. "So, is there anything I can do or get for you guys?"

"Mr. Archer…how come you came back here today? You don't really know us, and you already did so much." Joey was genuinely curious.

"You know what, I asked myself the same question this morning. Why aren't you out on the lake fishing like you came up here to do? I still don't know the answer, but I just feel like I might be able to help out and I like you guys. I saw you get hit out there on the lake. I think there might be something we can do about that." he said, thoughtfully.

"Well, that's pretty nice of you. I can't imagine what we can do. I'd like to find a gun and walk over to Paul Sinclair's house and blow his head off," Joey said carelessly.

"No, you wouldn't. You are not like him. Thinking about how you can get even is pointless if you just think of it in terms of causing him physical pain. By the way, his dad's name wouldn't be Mark, would it"

"Yeah, how'd you know that?"

"Well, let's just say, we go back a few years and there are some scores I would like to settle with him, too. Maybe we could put our heads together and come up with a plan. What do you think?"

"You mean it?" Joey asked, surprised. "You would help me get even…I mean get back at Paul Sinclair?

"Yep, I think I would.

"Mr. Archer, I have a small favor to ask."

"Sure, Joey, what is it?"

"I left my dog under a shade tree at home, and it's so hot…"

"Let's go. We'll refresh the water and make sure everything's okay."

They hopped into the truck, stopped by the house and Harriet was still where Joey had left her. Her head perked up and she wagged her tail but did not stand.

"Wow, what a beautiful dog!" Don remarked.

"Thanks, her name is Harriet. She has always been my best friend. She follows me everywhere…or at least she did. She hasn't been feeling that well lately."

"Well, she is a really nice Bernese Mountain Dog, that's for sure! How old is she?

"She will be 8 in about 3 weeks," Joey answered. "I guess that's kinda old for her breed."

"Yeah well, you never know," Don tried to be positive, but he knew that Bernese have very short life spans and rarely go past 8 or 9. Joey had enough heartache at the moment, so he changed the subject. "Hey… you sit down and pet her. She seems to miss you. I'll grab her water bowl and fill it up with the hose here."

Don took the bowl over to the hose hung on the side of the house and ran the water over his hand until it ran cold and filled up the bowl.

"There you go, Harriet!" He bent down and scratched her behind the ear. "What a beautiful girl you are…We better get back to the hospital or your mom will wonder where you are."

"Yeah, good point," Joey answered. "Hey, thanks for this."

"No problem bud, dogs are family too."

Joey didn't say much on the way back to the hospital, but he thought how this man seemed almost too good to be true. Did he come into his life to replace Gramps somehow? Then the thought occurred that he didn't even live around here, and he would likely be gone back home tomorrow. This thought vanished when they got back to the parking lot of the hospital.

"Joe, I have a plan. I would like to bring supper over to your house tonight. What time do you eat?

"Ah, well, usually around 5:30 or 6:00, I guess," answered Joey, wondering what Don's angle was.

"Okay, like I said, I have a plan that we need to discuss. Here's my card with my cell number. I'll be at your place with food at 6 pm. Call me if your mom thinks it's a bad idea but I think we might be able to prove that it was Paul Sinclair."

CHAPTER 5

At almost 6:00 pm on the dot, Don Archer pulled up into the laneway. He had left the boat and trailer back at Kamawog Lodge to avoid trying to turn it around on the narrow gravel road. It had not taken Joey much convincing to get Lilley to agree to a catered dinner and the sound of Don Archer's proposal about proving Paul Sinclair's involvement with the boating incident was intriguing.

Don brought enough Chinese food to feed a small army and they all enjoyed talking about the area, the weather, fishing… everything but Jug. Finally, Don broke out the plan he had in mind.

"So, Lilley, I don't know if Joe told you, but I think I have an idea on how we can prove it was the Sinclair kid that caused the accident intentionally."

"Joey told me, and I am definitely interested, and he also told me why you would be particularly interested. There is something you need to know too. I'm quite sure you haven't told Don about your relationship with Billie, have you dear?"

"No, but I don't see the reason to…" He stopped short, realizing what Lilley was getting at. "Oh, I see what you mean…I guess I should tell the story." Joey admitted.

"Okay, well my girlfriend, Billie is coming home from England tomorrow. She's been away all summer and I really can't wait to see her," Joey began.

"Oooookaaaay?" Don responded confused at the relevance. "What has that got to do with our plans?"

"Maybe nothing, but it's a factor we got to consider," answered Joey.

Lilley was growing impatient, "Joey, get to the point please!"

"Okay, okay…Well her real name is Catherine Magee," Joey paused studying Don's reaction.

"Oh…and I suppose that's Willie Magee's little girl?" Don asked. "Well, the plot thickens. Aren't the Magee's and the Sinclair's kind of tight, as in personal friends as well as business associates?" He paused as Joey nodded. "Wait, let me wrap my head around this. You and Catherine, er Billie are a thing. Magees and Sinclairs are a thing. If we bring down the Sinclairs we might damage your relationship with Billie?"

"Well, I don't really think so. I think Billie is above all that and I don't see Billie's Mom and Dad as dishonest businesspeople or anything. It might make it awkward but…I don't know."

"You are a good judge of character, Joe. Willie and Sara are two of the most upstanding and honest people I know. The crazy part of all this is that I know these people at all. I mean you run across this stranger from out of town and he knows the exact problem you are dealing with. Did you ever think I was somehow placed here by some kind of divine intervention?"

"Actually, that thought occurred to me this afternoon when you helped me with Harriet," Joey chuckled.

"This could work out for all of us. Willie Magee was one of my biggest supporters and endorsed my software to the interested tech companies that were vying to buy it. He is probably the reason I have the life I have today and can take off and go fishing anytime I feel like it."

Lilley sat there, not able to add to the exchange but stunned by the unlikelihood of all this.

"Joe, like I was saying…I think you are right about the Magees. Willie is a heck of a builder, smart and honest, a combination that is rare in the construction business. Mark Sinclair has way more to lose if the relationship goes sour. Willie could get his materials from many other companies, but Sinclair would lose his main customer if they severed their relationship…No wonder, the Sinclairs didn't come forward. I would bet they know everything. At first, I was kind of thinking that Paul might be hiding the incident from his parents. If he told them what happened, it will be difficult to prosecute Paul. Either way, I have a plan but there might be some risk involved."

Lilley sat more upright, "What kind of risks are we talking about?"

"We need to find evidence and the best evidence could be on their boat," Don suggested.

"They would have checked for scratches or paint off my rowboat, I would think," Joey said.

"Maybe not…That is the key to my proposal. When I saw him coming at you, I couldn't see many details but when he swerved, the only thing you could see was the bottom of the hull as it hit you."

"Oh…I see what you're saying. They probably wouldn't think to look at the bottom. They likely checked out what they could see or shone a light on the sides from the dock and not think of going under the boat."

"Exactly," Don confirmed.

"So how are we going to see if there is evidence on the bottom of the hull?" added Lilley with a puzzled look.

"I thought you would never ask," Don joked. "I have a little hobby. When I have a good fish on, I take videos of them as they fight. I'm in the tech business and one of my products is the 'Aqua Viewer'. It is camera mounted to a telescopic pole and it has its own built-in light. It is able to take underwater pictures and videos in basically any light."

Joey was beginning to see where this was going so he added, "At night…we could sneak up on the boathouse and take pictures of the bottom of their boat!"

"Bingo!... If there are no marks then we have to go back to the drawing board…but if there is, we are golden. I don't think they could charge us for trespassing or illegally gathering evidence because we can do this without setting foot on their property or even touching their boat for that matter."

"I think I like the idea," Lilley interjected, "but where does the element of risk come in?"

"I know Mark Sinclair. He's the kind that shoots and then yells run. I can't guarantee what he might do if he sees us. We can't bring a large powerboat too close, but we could take my boat up from the lodge, shut the motor off about half a mile away and row in near silence. If they do see us, we would be no match for that Donzi of theirs."

"Well, then we will have to find out when they won't be home," Joey suggested.

"I like the way you think, kid," Don reached over and cuffed Joey's arm and smiled.

"Well, Don," Lilley piped up. "I think your idea could work but right now, Josh's health is my main concern and probably Joey's too. Joey also has a big day tomorrow with Billie's homecoming. I also think that if it was possible, the Magees should be in on this. Like you said, they really don't have much to lose. Billie is a close friend of Josh's too and I'm sure she will know these plans from Joey before too long, because if I know you, Joey, you won't keep anything from her."

"Absolutely not. It's part of our pact, that we don't keep secrets," Joey confided.

Don got to his feet, "Well, I have overstayed my welcome and I need to let you folks get some sleep. I understand you have a couple sisters too Joey?"

"Uh… yeah. Jessie's at the babysitter's and Pam will be home in a few days," Joey said, quickly, careful not to give away too many details.

"Will if I'm going to hang around here and play detective for a few days, I look forward to meeting them. Okay, well I'll leave you then. We will talk again maybe tomorrow night or Monday. You have my card, and you know where I'm staying if you need me." Don started for the door.

"Don," Lilley piped up, "you did not overstay your welcome. You brought us a wonderful dinner…One we never usually can afford to have…and you gave us hope that we might see justice done and you rescued our boys from the lake. We owe you more than you think."

With an understanding nod, Don answered with, "Good night, Lilley…'night Joe," he bent down and gave Harriet a little scratch. "Good night beautiful!"

Joey and Lilley both said, "Good night," in unison as he disappeared out the door.

"Let's sit in the living room," Lilley suggested.

Just as they got up out of their seats, the phone rang and Lilley answered it, "Oh, hi Sarah…yes, still the same I'm afraid. Poor Ellen is beside herself! Yeah, I was wondering about that myself, but I'm quite sure I know his answer," Lilley gave a short chuckle. "Well, he's right here. Why don't you ask him yourself? Okay, just a sec…" she gestured with the receiver to Joey who had been watching propped against the hallway entrance. He tilted his head and gave a confused look and took the receiver from Lilley.

"Hello?"

"Hey, Joe. It's Sarah Magee, Billie's mom."

"Oh, hey, I thought that was who she was talking to. Is something wrong?" Joey was desperately afraid something would spoil Billie's homecoming.

"No, well…Willie and I just want to tell you how sorry we are about you friend Josh. I guess you guys call him Jug. It's a terrible thing and we sure hope he gets better soon."

"Thanks, Mrs. Magee," Joey began to choke up a little. His emotions were so close to the surface.

"Billie and I text just about every day so she's up with all the goings on around here. This afternoon, I talked to her on her cell and told her about the accident. She was very upset and it upset Willie and me too. We had her on speaker phone, and she started crying." Joey was tearing up again for 1000th time today. "She was crying for you, Joey. She knows how close you and Jug are … She really misses you too, but that's not really why I called. Willie and I were thinking that maybe you would sooner stay here with Jug than go into the city with us. It wouldn't hurt our feelings if you decided to stay."

"Thanks, Mrs. Magee. I have trouble seeing him actually. It's like he is pretend sleeping or something. I appreciate that you are giving me a way out though, but if you knew how long this summer was for me, you would know the answer. I really don't want to wait another day if I don't have to."

"Your mom and I thought that would be your answer. You sure don't sound like a 14-year-old…I wanted to tell you too…Every time Willie and I texted, emailed or talked on the phone to Billie, your name seemed to come up every time. I thought you might like to know that."

Joey had trouble talking. His larynx seemed to be in his mouth. "Thanks…for that," he managed. "I want to say something to you to," Joey realized that this thought had been with him since he first met Sarah and Willie Magee. "I appreciate how you and Mr. Magee have…I don't know how to say it…accepted me…treated me so nice and everything." Joey was totally choking up.

"Aw, honey, that's okay! We should be thanking you. You make our daughter happy, and we are both grateful to you for that. I can't wait to see my little girl tomorrow, but I also can't wait to see her face when she sees you! Good night Joe. See you tomorrow."

"Good night Mrs. Magee. I can't wait but I hope I have good news about Jug too."

"Yes, for sure," answered Sarah and she hung up the phone.

Lilley was waiting, sitting on the couch with her feet tucked up under her, leaning on the pillowed arm and turned toward Joey.

"That was a nice conversation. Not that I was listening or anything," she winked at Joey.

"Yeah," Joey plopped down on the armchair beside her. "I can't believe how nice that family is to me. I also can't believe how they could really be friends with the Sinclair's."

"Well, if what Don Archer says is true, maybe the Magees are just being polite or courteous. They will probably get to know the real Sinclairs as time goes on. If we were able to find evidence that would prove their son's deliberate involvement in the boat incident, that would definitely cause the Magee family to question their friendship."

Joey remembered something and spoke up, "If you remember, Mom…Willie Magee saw Paul chasing me down by the bridge, the day he tackled me and broke my arm. I think they already have negative vibes about the Sinclairs."

Lilley studied her son lovingly, "Where did that grass-stained, grimy little boy of mine go?" she laughed. "It seemed like yesterday; you were 5 years old standing at the doorway with a rock bass flopping away on your fishing line. You had no shoes on, your t-shirt was dirty and torn and your cut-offs were soaked from wading in the water down at little beach. You were so proud that you caught that fish all by yourself…'a tick in time' she muttered.

"What was that?" Joey asked

"A tick in time," another one of your grandfather's sayings. "Whenever he reflected on his life, he would remind us of how brief our time here on earth really is. He said that our lives are just a tick in time compared to the grand scheme of things."

"Billie and I have talked about things like that. It kind of helped me get through this long summer, waiting for her to get back. We told each other that in September we would look back and think that it was only really a moment of time in our lives. I'll have to remember that though. His best one was 'remember who you are' but that's good too."

"Yeah, he was a smart man," she said thoughtfully. "Speaking of smart men, what do you think of our friend Don Archer?"

"I think it's almost freaky how he appeared out of nowhere," Jug answered. "I was trying to imagine what would have happened if he hadn't shown up that day when we were in the water hanging on to the rowboat for dear life…and now…he just happens to know everybody. It's almost too good to be true." Joey paused. "Did you know that his wife was killed in a car accident about 3 years ago?"

"No, aw…that's horrible! The poor guy! Well, I guess we will just have to see how things play out. Maybe he is too good to be true but I'm willing to take a chance on him for now."

There was something a little wistful about how Lilley said those last words. Joey thought that if the time was right, Don Archer would be a great companion for his mom. He knew, of course, that it was way too soon for her to think that way. She wasn't even officially divorced yet, but it seemed to Joey that she didn't miss his dad now that he was being kept away from them. In fact, she seemed much happier since he'd left. He then realized that he had been happier too. Maybe it wasn't just Billie being part of his life that was beginning to change him.

Joey lay in bed and knew that sleep would not come easy tonight, excited for the return of Billie. He glanced over at the charcoal drawing he had made for her the day after she had left for England. He knew how much she would love that. Then, there were three light knocks on his door.

"Yeah, mom, come in."

Lilley stood in the threshold, "I don't know how I forgot to tell you this, but Pam is coming home next week.

"Really?" Joey sat up. "That's awesome! How long will she be staying?

"I hope, for good. It depends on her. I sure hope she has changed. Jessie will be so glad to see her. I am picking Jessie up in the morning. The Wilson's have been amazing keeping her this long. The thought of Pam coming home should keep her excited for a while…Good night…again." She chuckled.

"'Night, Mom."

CHAPTER 6

Another warm day in the lake district and Joey was up with the birds and walking slowly toward Little Beach with Harriet plodding laboriously behind him. He hated how she was so slow and lethargic. It was only a few weeks ago she had been playfully pawing the waves at Little Beach and chasing the darting minnows. He wondered what it was that had made her suddenly seem so much older and tired. Still, her will to be with Joey and experience that relationship was strong and there were many days that Joey needed her company every bit as much as she needed his. They sat again on the flat rock beside Little Beach, Harriet laying down behind him with her nose resting on her forepaws and Joey flinging small stones into the lake. The mist was still burning off and the steam rising up into the air created a surreal scene; seemingly enclosed and cut off. It was only possible to see a few hundred feet out into the lake and their world was encapsulated by the thick moisture-laden air.

This was the day Joey had been waiting for all summer. He prayed that it would be like the day after he had last seen Billie as if no time at all had passed, with all the emotion and feelings for each other intact. Today, she was coming back and what had seemed like a long summer now was indeed feeling like a tick in time. Yet, so much had happened, especially recently. Joey felt guilty, suddenly, realizing that he was so caught up with the return of Billie and his own feelings that those thoughts almost overshadowed the gravity of Jug's condition. He felt the need to see him.

After refreshing Harriet's water bowl and leaving a note for his mom, he threw a leg over his old mountain bike and made his way toward town. It took about fifteen minutes of strong pedaling to reach his destination. After securing the bike with his cable-lock to the bike stands he entered the hospital. He had learned that if you want to avoid being questioned by a volunteer or a nurse at the nurse's station, it was best to walk briskly, giving off the illusion that you were on an important mission and you were supposed to be here, whether it was during or outside visitation time. When he reached Jug's room, he realized how early he was. Ellen was curled up in the recliner beside Jug's bed with a couple hospital blankets wrapped around her, sleeping. Jug was lying there in exactly the same position Joey had last seen him. The nurses must have moved him from time to time, Joey thought, but he could only really lie on his back because of the tubes attached to him. Joey moved closer and sat on the side of a table between Jug's bed and an unused bed. Ellen did not move a muscle. She was on the window side facing Jug. The blinds were closed, and it was only just light enough to see the details of the room.

Joey put his hand on Jug's left forearm and was mildly pleased that his arm felt warm; much warmer than when he had last touched him before being loaded onto the gurney at the town dock. The events of that day flooded into Joey's brain as if it was being transmitted to him from Jug's body through his arm. He was transported back two days to the scene of the accident, and he pictured it more clearly than ever before. He saw the boat coming at them and just before it hit them, and he did see the underside of the hull just like Don said he had seen. He suddenly realized something else; Sinclair's boat had a name on the back. It wasn't something he had noticed during the collision, but he had seen the name many times. Why had he not thought to mention that to Don? The boat was called "Dreadknot" a clever wordplay, like dreadnaught but done in wood grain letters and obviously a reference to their lumber business. Joey wasn't sure how significant knowing that was, but he thought he should tell Don the next time he saw him.

Joey couldn't resist the urge to talk to Jug. He had seen TV shows where people had been helped through a coma by being comforted by the words of a loved one or a friend. There was always the controversy as to whether a person in a coma can actually hear people around them while they are in that state. There were even cases where the person in the coma was supposed to come out of it sooner by hearing familiar voices, like it somehow stimulated the brain.

"Hang in there bud," Joe whispered. "We are all pulling for you. I hope you can somehow sense that, and that part of your brain is still working a little." Then Joey, trying to appeal to Jug's sense of humor, added, "God knows there was never much going on up there before the accident!" Joey laughed to himself and then clouded back over quickly as he observed Jug's expressionless face.

Joey noticed that it was almost 8 am and the room was becoming brighter. Ellen stirred, lifted her head up sideways and grabbed her neck.

"Joe?" she moaned, "Whoa, my neck is totally messed up. How long have you been here?"

"Just maybe 10 minutes. Billie's coming home today so I wanted to see Jug this morning. I'm going to greet her at the airport."

"That's nice. "I'm happy for you," she added, agonizingly rotating her body around to look out the window. Then she grabbed the lever on the side of the chair and lowered the footrest.

Joey felt like he was being insensitive, and guilt crept in again for letting his happy thoughts rule over her anguish for her son. He tried to soften the comment by adding, "Mrs. Magee told me that Billie knows about Jug and she was pretty sad to hear the news. She even cried while she was on the phone."

"Aw, she is such a sweet kid! You are lucky…both you and Josh are…to have a friend like her. Maybe he will wake up in time to greet her when she gets into town today."

Joey said, "Yeah, hopefully," but he knew the odds of that happening were slim. He had heard about how people recover from comas and it was usually a gradual process. It's not like you see in some Hollywood movies where they wake up and say, "Hi, Mom. How long was I out for? I'm really hungry."

Joey had cornered Dr Wong the other day shortly after Jug was admitted and asked him if he thought Jug was going to be alright. Dr. Wong had said what Joey thought was likely a standard scripted answer… "We have no way of knowing how he will come out of it. Some people have little or no aftereffects, while others must relearn things…like walking or even speaking. Some have permanent disabilities. But he is young and has a better chance than most to make a full recovery."

That was not exactly reassuring but there was a glimmer of hope and Joey would dwell on the idea that he could make a full recovery.

The cafeteria was not open until 9 am but he managed to rustle up a coffee from the machine just outside the cafeteria's barred entrance doors. He returned to the room and handed it to Ellen.

"He will recover," Joey stated adamantly. "I know he will."

"Thanks, Joe. You are a good friend…to both of us. We both value that. Now, get back home and get something to eat so you can be ready for your little sweetheart!"

She set the coffee on the window ledge, stood up and gave Joey a big hug. Joey took another look at his lifeless friend and left, still trying to hold back the tears.

It was lunchtime and Joey was outside playing with Jess and Harriet in the shade of the huge white pine beside their laneway. They were sitting in the soft pine needles and tossing a ball back and forth. Joey praised Jess every time she happened to catch it and Joey did his best to try and toss it directly into her open hands. Harriet, with her snout on her paws, followed the flight of the ball with just her big, brown eyes. Joey thought about how just a few weeks ago she would have lunged back and forth from the thrower to the receiver to be part of the game. It was a little orange ball hockey ball, and it was covered with teeth marks that represented a friskier time in her life.

Lilley called them in, and they sat around the kitchen table, a rare family sit-down meal. Joey wolfed down 3 hot dogs and disappeared into his room reemerging with unblemished blue jean shorts and a nice freshly washed t-shirt; the one that said, "Beatles – In the end, the love you take is equal to the love you make." Billie had said how much she liked that shirt, so it seemed appropriate to wear today. Joey noticed that the shirt was fitting a little tighter than a couple months ago, especially around the neck and biceps.

"Mommy, Joey's going to see his girlfriend," giggled Jess.

"Yes, I know. Isn't that nice?" Lilley answered.

"Yeah, but not as nice as it used to be," Jess looked down frowning.

"What do you mean, dear?"

"It used to be more funny, now it's just a thing and it doesn't feel funny anymore," Jess said, pouting. Both Lilley and Joey laughed heartily at the blatant honesty of an almost-six-year-old.

"Are you off now, Joey?" asked Lilley.

"Yeah, I guess," answered Joey. "I think I'm almost nervous."

"Of course you are. That's just natural. Think of it as more excited than nervous." She encouraged.

"Yeah, I guess you're right." Joey conceded. "I think I'm gonna go down to the park for a while first. Oh, Mom, I just remembered. I know the name on the back of Paul Sinclair's boat. Do you think that would help prove it was him?"

"It might, if you find any green paint marks on the bottom, but let's leave that for another day. Go and have a great time. From what Sarah Magee has told me, you won't be disappointed."

Joey walked over to hug his mom and Jessie stood up on her chair beside them and shouted, "Me too! Me too! …they had a little group hug and Joey left, letting the screen door double slap behind him. Harriet was still under the shade of the pine, so Joey walked over and tousled the hair on her head as she looked up.

"Wish me luck, little girl. No parties, eh?" he chuckled as he walked out the lane, followed only by Harriet's eyes.

Joey sat on the bench in the boat launch park where just two and a half months ago, he had met Billie for their first little rendezvous. He had about 15 minutes before he had to go the remaining 100 yards or so up to her parent's front door. He remembered how pretty she looked to him; her piercing blue eyes and that cute squint-like wink she gave only him, her slender body and the auburn highlights in her hair as it bounced when she turned her head toward him.

"Wow!" he thought. "I'm really in deep here. What is it about her that makes me like this? Is this what being in love is like? If it is, no wonder they write movies and books about it!"

It was time. He got up and walked into the bushes at the shoreline and found the path that led past Billie's little rowboat. He paused and smiled as the memories of that day flooded through him again. Then he came out in the clearing of the Magee's back yard and walked around to the front door and rang the doorbell. The Magee's black Lincoln mkz was parked in the laneway waiting for the trip to the airport. The door opened and Sara Magee greeted Joey with hug and invited him in. Joey instantly recognized her eyes. They were Billie's, and her dark brown hair had the same reddish tint. She was very neatly dressed in white shorts and blue patterned blouse. She seems about the same height as Billie too. He kicked off his running shoes, left them on a mat inside the door and walked in.

"Have a seat, Joe." She pointed to a beautiful big brown leather recliner and then disappeared down the hallway toward what Joey assumed would be the bedroom/bathroom area.

Joey sat down and took in the grandeur of the house's interior. He imagined that Willie Magee probably entertained prospective clients here, clearly demonstrating his design and building expertise. The ceiling was vaulted and had a great fan near the peak and the blades were leaf-like like the leaves on a thatched roof. The room had a great stone wall at one end with a huge flat screen TV fastened to the stone chimney. The chimney narrowed after that and pierced through the ceiling some 20 feet up at its peak. Joey got back to his feet to take in the rich features of the room. On the other side the room melded into the kitchen like it was part of the TV room. It was like one you would see in Better Homes and Garden magazine, with white cupboards and dark marble countertops that contained an oversized copper sink with an overhanging faucet. The sink itself was probably 4 feet long and there was a large, framed opening or passthrough to a dining room behind the sink. About 6 feet to the right of the sink was the largest fridge Joey had ever seen. He was tempted to look inside but resisted. Between the fireplace room and the kitchen was a large island with 8 stylish stools in a semi-circle around it. The island had the same dark marble as the other countertop, and it stuck out over white louvered cupboards matching the ones over the other counter, leaving ample leg room for dining. The floors were gleaming reddish-brown hardwood and the cracks between the wood slats all seemed to point to the amazing wall of windows that looked out over the lake and the stone patio. There was a total of three patio doors side-by-side and above that more windows reaching up to the peak of the ceiling. He walked over to the bank of windows and looked across the lake. He could see the where Little Beach would be along the far shore, probably half a mile across the water.

As he stared out on the lake Willie Magee came up silently behind him, "Hey Joe," he said extending his hand.

Startled, Joey took his hand as firmly as he could but was no match for the big Irishman. "Hey Mr. Magee. You kinda scared me there. This is a beautiful house. I love the design of the kitchen and family room area, and the view you get from each room."

"Thank you… That is not what I would expect a boy of your age to say. But Billie did tell me you had a great eye for art, and you are really quite the young artist."

Slightly embarrassed, "Well, I don't know about that, but I do enjoy sketching."

"Well, maybe someday you can come and work with us in our design department." Willie winked.

"Wow, would that ever be awesome!" Joey beamed out.

The two of them stood there for a few minutes engaged in small talk. Joey noticed that Willie was probably almost 6 inches taller than him and quite distinguished looking, slightly barrel-chested with a receding hairline that was red on the top graduating to grey along the sides. He wore a bright red polo shirt and tucked neatly into some plaid, but mostly white shorts held up with a braided Nike belt and white anklet socks.

"Well, you gentlemen ready to go?" Sarah had reentered the room behind them.

Turning toward her, Willie said, "Us? We were waiting for you." They all walked toward the door chuckling.

On the way out of town, Willie glanced back to Joey sitting comfortably on the soft white leather upholstery of the Lincoln. "You remember this place, Joe?"

Joey looked out the side window to his left, "Every time I go by here, I think about that. I definitely owe you one for that."

Willie laughed, "You don't owe me anything. The look in my little girl's eyes and the kiss on the back my head when I stopped the car for her last goodbye to you is all the payment I will ever need."

Sarah piped up, "Hey, mister, what about the kiss I gave you for stopping."

"Oh, yeah…that too." They all laughed heartily as they accelerated away from town.

Sarah swiveled around, put her arm on the back of her seat tilted it back to almost face Joey, "Willie and I have kind of a plan for when Billie gets off the plane to surprise her. We thought we would…

CHAPTER 7

They sat in the waiting area watching planes take off and land at the Montrose International airport. Not a huge airport, Montrose wasn't a big city with a population of about 400 000, and most of the planes were smaller private planes and business jets. Only a couple of passenger liners were parked with the long tentacle-arms of the closed-in walkways reaching out to the openings in the fuselages of those bigger birds.

At precisely 4 pm a huge BOAC 747 landed on the longest runway; a plume of smoke puffed out of the tires that hit down first. Joey watched the plane taxi to the end of the runway and pause before turning toward the terminal. He watched as the big jet inched its way toward the docking area. The long arm of the boarding tunnel telescoped out and rested against the fuselage just behind the cockpit area. A small vehicle towing 4 flatbed cars behind it circled close to the belly of the aircraft and the doors on the underbelly slowly opened like little wings. Three men rushed to load the luggage coming down from the ramp of the plane onto the waiting wagons. It seemed like the process lasted for hours, but then there was a ding and an announcement, "Flight 649 from Heathrow and Le Guardia now disembarking."

Sarah said excitedly, half whispering, "Okay, Joey, take your position like we talked about."

Joey walked back toward the tables at the airport restaurant where he could get a good view of the opening to the tunnel that Billie would be coming out.

There must have been a hundred people stream through so far and no Billie yet. He watched as Willie and Sarah waved toward the opening to the ramp and then both closed in on Billie with hugs and kisses. Joey stood up and started walking slowly toward them as planned. Willie and Sara, standing side by side turned to make an opening to reveal Joey to Billie. She looked up, dropped her carry-on bag, and ran to Joey, leaping into his embrace.

"Joey! I'm so sorry about Jug! I missed you so much!"

"I missed you too!" Joey replied, holding her tight. "I love you!"

"Hey, you seem a little taller…I love you to, Joey!" Joey sighed with relief. That was really the only thing he wanted to hear today… that, and some good news about Jug. Then the tears came from both simultaneously.

Sarah and Willie stood there, watching their young daughter run into the arms of a boy they barely knew. They reached for each other's hands and stood there. Sara cupped her hand over her mouth blubbering with tears of joy for her daughter's happiness. Willie's eyes were also watery as he watched Billie throw herself to Joey. The two young people they were watching just stood there holding each other without a sound just quivering with emotion, both crying and not knowing what to say to each other.

Sarah looked up at Willie, "These kids are so young. How could they have found real love at this age?"

"I don't know," replied Willie, "but it looks pretty real to me."

Then they turned and they too embraced each other. Then Willie picked up Billie's carry-on bag and the two walked toward Billie and Joey, hand in hand. The young couple and the older couple walked linked together down the long hallway to the baggage handling area. Billie spotted her bag on the carousel, pointed to it and Joey grabbed it. Then they headed for the escalator that carried them up to the exit, both couples' hands still clasped together.

As they left the airport grounds in the car, Willie glanced at the rear-view mirror and caught a glimpse of Billie and Joey sitting wrapped in each other's arms. "Are you sure you guys are only 14?"

"Fourteen and a half," said Joey. They all laughed.

Willie drove around to Joey's house and stopped in the laneway. In spite of her parents close proximity, Joey risked a kiss on Billie's cheek, reached over to the door handle on the other side of him. Billie still clung to his hand and he gave it a squeeze as she released her grip.

"See you tomorrow?" Joey asked.

"I sure hope so," Billie answered with that coy twinkle in her eyes.

He slid across the seat to the door and exited the car. He stood for a second outside the driver's side door and Willie powered the window down and looked up to Joey.

"Thank you, Mr. Magee," then Joey bent down to see Sara, "and Mrs. Magee…for letting me come with you today and be … you know, part of this." Joey didn't really know where this newfound bravery was coming from, but it just felt right to thank them. "I hope you know how much that meant to me."

"Hey, bud." Willie replied, "Why do you think we brought you along today?"

Joey backed away from the car and saw Billie blowing him a kiss from the back seat. He waved to her then, with difficulty, he turned his back to their car and walked toward his house not turning back.

It was almost 7pm and Jessie and Lilley had already eaten. Lilley was cleaning up the kitchen as Joey came in.

"Hey, Joey, how did it go today?" Lilley asked with a wink.

"Hi, Joey," Jess spoke up as she was playing with some play dough at the table. "Did you kiss her?"

Joey reached down to give Harriet a quick scratch behind her ear and ignored his baby sister

"It went awesome! She was totally surprised. Her parents are great mom. They said Billie and I don't act like 14-year-olds, though, and I'm not quite sure what that means.

"No, you guys sure don't. Lilley paused. "But I have a theory…"

"Oh, really, are you going to tell me?"

"Well, it's pretty common knowledge that a girl your age is more mature both physically and mentally than a boy is at your age. But, in your case it's different, I think." She turned away from the sink where she was drying some dishes to face Joey, put the towel over her shoulder and leaned back on the counter. "You have had to go through a lot of experiences in your life that you have learned from. I don't want to list them all right now," she nodded at Jessie and Joey nodded back with understanding. "Have you heard the saying, 'What ever doesn't kill you makes you stronger' or something like that.

"Yeah, I think so," Joey replied still a little puzzled. There was a pause, and then he began to recognize what his mom was saying. He glanced quickly back at Jessie, "So, all the kind of, negative things that have happened in my life, taught me lessons…even certain injuries and losses and that?"

Jess was totally in on the conversation and quickly added, "Yeah when that bully hurt your arm, you learned that bullying was mean, didn't ya, Joey?"

Joey laughed, "You little monkey! Nothing gets by you, does it?" He reached over and tousled her hair while she giggled.

Lilley shook her head and let out a little chortle too. "Yeah, Joey, that's it, but there is more to it." She paused. "Jess, go and brush your teeth and get your pj's on."

"Aw, Mom!" Jessie moaned.

"Go on, squirt," Joey injected. "I'll read you a story tonight after your in bed."

"Oh…that's different!" Jess jumped up and disappeared down the hallway.

Laughing again the two continued the conversation, Lilley began, "You know some kids that have gone through things you have, react quite differently. I mean things like, you know…with your dad and stuff. A lot of kids go the wrong way. They rebel and get in trouble with the law and…" she stopped.

"Drugs," Joey said, knowing that was a direct reference to his sister, Pam.

"Well, you and Pam are perfect examples of the opposite ways some kids react to dysfunctional families, I guess."

"It's nice that you think of me like that, Mom. But I think it's because I've had you to help me…and I wanted to be there for you too."

"How come you're so smart?" Lilley took a couple steps over to Joey, who was half sitting on the kitchen table, and gave him a big hug. "I sure love you kid!"

"Love you too, Mom!"

"Aha, two I love you's in one month! Lilley pointed an accusing finger at Joey.

"I guess you got me there," Joey laughed.

"I'm gonna go read Jess a story and then turn in. I'm tired."

"Aren't you going to eat anything?"

"Nah, I need some sleep…Oh, did you figure out how to get Harriet to the vet?"

"Yeah, Mike said I could leave work for a while. You and I can both go and it's better that way because you know how she hates riding in the car."

"Yeah, okay good. Well, 'night, Mom."

"'Night, love you!" Lilley answered dramatically.

Joey just chuckled, turned and formed a heart with his fingers and kept walking.

After Joey had read Jessie a story and she was about to sleep he bid her good night and realized that his mom was right… he was hungry. He found a couple hotdog buns and wieners and set about boiling the wieners.

Lilley was settled into her favorite spot on the couch and glanced over. "I told you."

"Yah, yah," Joey scoffed.

The phone rang and Joey picked it up quickly thinking it might be news about Jug.

"Hello?" he answered anxiously.

"Hi," It was Billie. "Were you expecting someone more exciting?"

"Oh, it's just you," Joey joked.

Laughing Billie said, "Watch it mister! I called for two reasons really…maybe three. The first is… how is Jug?"

"Still no change," answered Joey lowering his voice.

"Aw, that's too bad. You can call me any time of the day or night if you hear something, though. I just figured out why you sounded excited when you answered the phone and I totally get it. We are all waiting for some good news. The second thing is…where do you want to meet tomorrow?"

"I didn't want to rush you," Joey said. "I figured you'd have a lot of unpacking and stuff to do and…

"All done with that," she interrupted.

Joey continued, "How about at the big tree? You know, *our* big tree. I have a couple surprises for you. Would 10 am work for you? We are taking Harriet to the Dr. Norman's for 4:30."

"Yeah, that would be great! I'll meet you at the bridge. I sure hope Harriet is okay. She is such a sweetheart!'

"Me too," Joey answered with a pang of sadness.

"Well, see you at 10 then. I'll bring lunch and my quilt…love ya."

"Wait!" Joey said urgently. "You said there were three reasons you wanted to call me."

"Oh, yeah…Were you glad I called?"

"Of course."

"Were you glad to hear my voice?"

"Absolutely!" There was a pause. "Oh, okay…I guess I'm a little slow at this boyfriend, girlfriend thing. Afterall, we are only 14." That brought laughter from Billie and Lilley in the living room. Joey glanced over and Lilley was holding her mouth. "Yeah, Mom heard that. I really need to take my lawn mowing money and buy a cell phone. It was great to hear your voice! It always is…'night, love ya."

"'Night, Joey,"

"Oh…so you can say it to her every day but not to your mother who has loved you for…14 years?" Lilley was nodding and throwing her hands up in a questioning gesture.

Joey just waved her off and went to bed.

CHAPTER 8

It was another very hot day for late August. Joey and Billie met at the bridge as planned. Joey grabbed the cooler in one hand and fishing pole and tackle box in the other and off across the road and along the east side of Black Creek they walked, disappearing into the foliage. They found the big beech tree where Billie spread the quilt out over the level grassy area and they both arranged the assorted paraphernalia around the perimeter. They sat, side by side facing each other propped up with their hands behind them.

"So, how tall are you exactly now?" asked Billie.

"Six foot, 2 inches," Joey answered proudly.

"Jeez…you can stop now," Billie joked. "I guess you would have told me if there were any news about Jug, eh?"

"Yeah, no, nothing yet."

Billie turned her head to look in the direction of the stream, "Oh…my…God! You carved our names into the tree!" She began to cry, sat up and threw her arms around Joey. They both held each other tightly and then kissed deeply.

"And I have something for you too." Joey reached for his tackle box and set it between them."

"What, you bought me a lure?" Billie joked.

"No, it's something we both really like," Joey teased.

Billie was baffled. What could possibly fit in a tackle box that they both really liked. Any number of things, she guessed, "I give up open it. The suspense is killing me!'

He opened the latch and lifted the two little trays of lures to reveal a rolled up piece of sketch paper tied with a thin red ribbon Joey had stolen from his mother's sewing table.

"You did it! You used the art kit I gave you!"

"Yeah, and Mom bought me a frame for it too. I didn't think I could hide it from you in the frame today, but I'll mount it for you later."

He handed it to her, and she carefully pulled the bow open and unrolled the thick drawing paper to reveal a charcoal sketch of the place at the stream Joey referred to as the "trout hole". She studied it carefully and bit her bottom lip trying not to cry again but it was futile. She broke down once again, set the paper down and threw her arms around Joey for the second time. Billie picked up the artwork again and studied it. "Joey" was signed on the bottom right corner. She turned it over and there was writing on the back, "To Billie on her return from England – love, Joey"

"You know Joey, sometimes you kind of piss me off!"

Joey looked bemused at her comment, "What do you mean?" he half chuckled.

"You are so damn…I don't know…"

"Handsome, intelligent?" Joey offered with a laugh.

"You keep making me cry. Guys aren't supposed to make girls cry! They held each other again. "But I guess I'll forgive you." Neither could see the other's smile, but they felt it.

Releasing her hold slightly and backing her head away a few inches she wiped away a tear, as did Joey. "That day up here with you before I went away…it was probably the best day I've ever had in my life! I really mean that! And now, this!"

"It was definitely mine too up until now. It's still a mystery to me that you chose me over so many other guys. You are so pretty and so…well, classier than me. I can't give you what others can. But I'm so thankful that you do."

"Hey, we've talked about this before. I have lots of things and I don't need money and all that, but you can't buy what I feel for you!" They wrapped each other in their arms again and then backed away leaning back on their hands to talk.

Joey began to sing softly while Billie watched slightly blushing, "I'll give you all I have to give, if you say you love me too," Then Billie joined in, "I may not have a lot to give but what

I've got I'll give to you. I don't care too much for money, for money can't buy me love."

They turned onto their sides to face each other while laughing and singing. It was a break in the sadness and the reality facing them…a much-needed break.

"How would you know that song?" Joey asked. "It must be like 50 years old."

"My parents have every vinyl record the Beatles ever made… and I actually really like them."

Joey chuckled, "Well, that's something we sure have in common. I don't have all their recordings, but I have a guitar book with most of their songs. It's classic stuff."

"Sometimes I wish we were a little older and could just run away together…you know? I mean…and it would be okay because we wouldn't be just kids."

"You're preachin' to the choir is the way I think the saying goes. I've always felt out of control as far back as I can remember. But there is one thing we can control … us."

"I agree," said Billie. "No one can tell us we can't be together. I mean school and other people might pull us apart for a while like this summer, but no one can keep us apart here," She made fist and held it over her heart. "I thought this summer was so long and now that we are together it seems like it was just a tick in time."

Joey cocked his head to one side looking surprised, "What did you just say?"

"It doesn't seem so long…"

"No," Joey interrupted. "What were the exact words you just said?"

"It was just a tick in time?"

"Yeah, that…where did you hear that expression?"

"My grandma used to say that about life because it's so short compared to time itself."

"I wonder if your grandma knew Gramps, because that's what he used to say too, and for the same reason."

"I thought your grandpa's famous saying was, 'remember who you are'.

Joey chuckled, "Yeah, he had a lot of them. Come to think of it I bet they did know each other. It might be fun to find out somehow. I think we were meant to be together."

The two of them spent the next three hours just talking and laughing, only interrupted by sandwiches, bananas, cokes and the odd kiss or hug. They were never happier than when they were together and to them, there was no force on earth that could change that. As the time for Harriet's vet appointment drew nearer, they packed up and walked down to the stream. Joey allowed some time for Billie to catch a few little fish, something he really enjoyed watching. Her excitement, the looks of anguish and joy the next second, the squeals, the way she stuck her tongue out as she was winding in the line, was great entertainment and hilariously fun to watch for Joey.

Walking back hand in hand with their other hands loaded with picnic equipment, both in t-shirts and cut-off jeans they looked a little like Tom Sawyer and a rather curvy, little Huckleberry Finn. As they reached the open area close to the bridge, Billie stopped them and pulled Joey around to face her.

"Joey, do you think it would be alright if I came with you and your mom when you go to the vet today?"

"Sure, absolutely. I know you love Harriet too. I was wondering… why don't you guys have a dog? You're so good with Harriet and she obviously loves you."

"I never told you, I guess. I barely remember. I must have been about 3. We had a dog. His name was Rusty, and I do remember his beautiful long rust-colored hair. He was a golden retriever with a personality something like Harriet. At least it sounded that way by my mom's description of him. She really loved that dog. She used to tell me that when she was home alone and Dad was out at some construction site, they would go for walks exploring along the seashore."

"Just like Harriet and me," Joey said. "What happened to him?"

"One day, Rusty followed Mom out to the mailbox on Lakeshore and he saw a squirrel on the other side of the road and…

"Okay, I get it," Joey interrupted. "Your poor mom! I can't imagine that…and to be there and see that…god!"

"Yeah, well, she has never forgiven herself. She still cries when she talks to Dad about it and swears she will never have another dog around because she doesn't want the heartache of losing it."

"I would," Joey said. "They give so much more love to you than they take with them."

"And that right there…you big jerk, is why I love you." She reached up on her tip-toes and gave him a big kiss on the lips with a "mmwwaa."

Joey walked her home with all her stuff and set down his fishing pole and tackle box on the side of driveway.

"We'll pick you up in about a half hour. I can throw my fishing stuff in the trunk then."

He returned the "mmwwaa," and took off running through the bushes near the shoreline, through the park and the launch ramp, which now held ominous memories, over the bridge and turned right down the winding gravel road. Lilley's car was already in the laneway. Out of breath he reached the house and sprayed his face with the hose and intentionally got his hair wet and entered the kitchen.

"What happened?" Lilley asked curiously. "How come you're all wet?

"Just the hose. It's so hot out and I ran from Billie's house."

"I see…maximizing your time with her I presume?"

"Pretty good guess, Mom. How's Harriet?"

They both looked over at her laying on relatively cool kitchen floor. "I don't know. She hasn't really moved much, and she looks funny when she looks at you. She did get up when I got home, and she went slowly outside. I watched her and she had a pee and came back in and plopped herself right back here again."

Joey went over to Harriet and sat down with her. She raised her head and her beautiful big brown eyes looked somehow different; sadder or something.

"I think I'm going to have to carry her to the car," Joey said. "She has trouble walking anyway, and her limp seemed worse this morning. She won't voluntarily get in the car either."

Joey got Harriet to her feet, and he wrapped his arms around her like a shepherd carrying a lost lamb back to the fold. Lilley opened the screen door for Joey and walked ahead to open the back door of the car. Joey placed Harriet on the seat with surprisingly little objection, rolled the window down and closed the door carefully making sure her tail didn't get pinched.

"Look at me Joey," Lilley said comically as she opened the driver's door.

"Wow!" The driver's side door had been seized shut since last fall. When did you get that fixed? Mike, my boss said he had a similar problem after he saw me sliding across to the passenger side to get out. I'm not sure what he did, but it only took him about five minutes. He used a large screwdriver and a spray can of something, and it now magically works."

"It's still a piece of junk but at least the doors all work now," Joey laughed. "Oh, can we swing by Billie's? She wants to go too."

"Yeah, sure," Lilley answered apprehensively. "Are you sure you want her there. I mean it could be…"

"We share everything, Joey interrupted.

"Oh, alright then, if you're sure."

About halfway down their road Lilley looked rather pensive, "When you said you guys share everything, did you mean…"

"No, Mom, jeez! She…we aren't ready for that."

"Well, I…

"Mom, can we drop it, please!"

"Okay, okay…just being a mom."

Joey thought about what she was insinuating and thought maybe they might have progressed farther in the sex department. It was just not something that dominated their thoughts when they were together. He would be lying to himself if he said he hadn't thought about touching her body that way or wasn't tempted to make more passionate physical advances. He was well aware of the stories told by other guys from school and their escapades. One kid; Arnie was always going on how he had to make sure he picked up some "trojans" at the drugstore before they hit the drive-in theatre. Of course, he was old enough to drive and Joey still had a year and a half to go. With stuff going on with Jug and now with Harriet in the back of his mind there just wasn't that kind of drive right now. Besides that, he really did love her. When she said she wasn't ready, he respected that. He would do whatever it took to make her happy. Judging by the way the other kids at school talked, he figured he was different than them when it came to girls. Since he found his love for Billie, no other girl attracted him in the slightest. "I guess I'm a one-woman man," he thought, remembering that line from some song, somewhere.

They arrived at the Magee's and Billie was waiting on the front steps holding Joey's fishing pole and tackle box. Lilley popped the trunk and Joey got out and stowed them in the trunk. He motioned to Billie to get in the front seat and she scooched over to the middle.

The old chevy had ample bench seats and there was plenty of room for the three of them.

"Hi Mrs. Burgess. I hope Harriet will be okay," was all she could think of to say.

"Hi Billie," Lilley returned. "I don't have a good feeling, but we'll see what's wrong shortly, I guess."

Joey looked out the window and felt Billie's hand on his to let him know she understood his feelings.

Then she turned around and reached back to pet Harriet's head… "Hi, there pretty girl." There was a feeble wag of her tail and Harriet lifted her head to look at Billie. "Aw, don't be sad. Everything's going to be okay."

"You see it too, don't you?" Joey said.

"What?… That her eyes look sad? Yeah, I guess so."

"Mom and I see that too. I can't help thinking that she is in pain." Joey started to tremble and Billie squeezed his hand tighter.

"You guys are going to make me cry, and I'm trying to drive here," Lilley said sadly.

They drove into the parking lot and got out of the car. Joey carried Harriet into the waiting room while Billie held the door. The sterile smell of chemicals and antiseptics was unmistakable, the same as any medical office, Joey supposed. It reminded him briefly, of the hospital and his friend lying in a coma. Joey sat down with Harriet on his lap and Billie beside him. Lilley went to the reception desk and announced their arrival. A tall sandy-haired man in his twenties, dressed in blue short-sleeved scrubs and matching pants opened the door to the hallway and looked into the room and down at a paper in his hand, "Harriet?"

Lilley spoke up and pointed to Joey, even though there were no other animals in the place, "Yes, that's her."

"Hi, my name is Dr. Marshall. I work with Dr. Norman. Dr. Norman would like to get some x-rays of Harriet before he does a complete examination."

"Well, she has a little trouble getting around," said Joey but I could carry her.

"Well…sorry, what's your name bud?" Dr. Marshall asked in a kind voice.

"It's Joe Burgess, sir," Joey answered politely.

"Wow, sir, is it? I haven't been called that since that slimy guy in Montrose tried to sell me a used car," he chuckled. He saw only a slight smile on Joey, so he got back to business. "We don't allow the pet owners into the x-ray area, so I'll bring out a cart."

He opened the door to the hallway and reached for something. The cart was obviously close by in case of situations like this. It was a light steel cart with four wheels like an A.V. cart used for projectors or TV's and it had a canvas stretcher on the top with two tie-down straps.

"Okay," Dr Marshall continued, "let's get her up on this."

Joey placed Harriet carefully on top of the stretcher and Dr Marshall wrapped the straps around her. He was careful to attach the straps loosely and not catch her fur. They clipped together something like a seatbelt.

"Okay, we'll be back in a few minutes after we get some pictures."

Harriet had her head up looking back to the room where the people she loved were sitting. Joey had his head down and his hand covered his eyes. Lilley moved over and sat on his left with her right hand on his shoulder and Billie on his right doing the same with her left.

Suddenly Joey jumped to his feet, "Jesus I hate this! He walked out the front doors and down the steps to the car stooped over it leaning with both hands trying not to cry out loud."

Lilley was now crying and dabbing her eyes with a white tissue she took from her purse. "I knew this would be a bad day. I just didn't know how bad!"

Billie scooched over to her and put both arms around her while tears traced down her cheeks as well.

"Thank you, Billie! I think I know what my son sees in you. You are a wonderful caring person!"

"Thanks, Mrs. Magee. Do you think it's as bad as Joey thinks?"

"Yes, I do. No one knows that dog better than he does. He would sooner have one of his legs cut off than lose her. He's watched the steady decline and he knows that Bernese Mountain Dogs have an average life span of 8 years… I don't think we are going home with her!" they both cried holding each other.

The door opened again, and Dr. Norman entered the room without Harriet, holding a sheet of Xray film. He clipped the film to the viewer on the end wall of the waiting room as Joey reentered through the main doors. Dr. Norman was a giant of a man. He was about 60 years old with a pot belly with very little white hair remaining on his balding head. He had a kind face with many wrinkles around his eyes like someone who had smiled much of his life. He was clean shaven and if it wasn't for that he could have passed for Santa Clause. The twinkle in his eyes was that of a man who had cared for thousands of animals during his practice here in William's Glen. He cared greatly for all life. His wife, Angela, ran a shelter for abandoned dogs, particularly older ones. She took them in when their owners either passed away or for various reasons could no longer look after them. He wasn't in the veterinary game for money and his life and family were a glowing testament to that. People knew that their pets or farm animals were in the best possible hands. Now, he faced yet another challenge as he turned around and faced his audience. Looking back at 3 sets of red teary eyes is not something you ever get used to.

Joey was still standing beside Lilley with his right hand on her shoulder. Billie still had her arms around Lillie but reached up and held on to Joey's hand too.

"Well, it almost looks like you know what I'm going to say… She is a wonderful dog with a great temperament. She didn't mind us holding her down or put up any resistance while we took the Xrays."

"Yeah, butter us up, and then let us have the bitter truth," Joey thought to himself.

"Can you guys come over here a little closer?"

The two girls stood up and the three stood facing the screen, arms around each other with Joey in the middle.

"Do you see this here?" He pointed to her hip joint. "This shows some dysplasia which would account for the limping you mentioned on the phone, Lilley. It could be fixed with surgery; however, I wouldn't want to do that on this breed and at this age. It is not that she is not worth it but the most effective thing to do would be total hip replacement. The problem is really this.".… He pointed to a few darker smudges and there were hundreds all throughout her internal organs. "I'm afraid these are cancer tumors and the reason she has deteriorated so quickly is that they are metastasizing or spreading rapidly."

The tension in the room was unbearable. Joey was sure he was hurting his mom and Billie with his grip, and he tried desperately to control his deep breathing.

"How long does she have?" Joey blurted out bravely.

"Not long, son. You have a hard decision to make, and I'm not going to soften it for you. It's one of the hardest decisions anyone has to make."

"Is she in pain?" asked Billie. She knew what everyone was thinking.

"Yes, I'm afraid so. Lilley, does she eat well still?"

"No, hardly at all," Lilley answered, "and she is shaky, panting all the time, and constantly licking herself."

"All signs of pain, I'm afraid. I can give her something for that, in fact I took the liberty to do that already. I will send you home with some pain pills. The reason I am sending you guys home is because you need time to say goodbye."

The old doctor's eyes looked watery, like Gramps' eyes before he passed away, Joey thought. They stood there stunned and, in their hearts, they knew he was right.

"When?" said Joey, with no explanation. Then summoning more courage, he asked, "When do we bring her back?"

"Does she have a favorite place?"

"Yes," Joey took a deep breath. "She loves to lay down under the pine by our laneway in the shade." Billie reached down and squeezed Joey's hand. That was enough to give him fuel needed to finish his answer. "She can see the people and cars coming and going down the road and if I'm going somewhere she used to ask me if she could come too. I mean before she got sick."

"Okay, then…he paused and looked at Billie. "I now just figured out who you are. You're Catherine Magee, aren't you? I've seen you around with your mom and dad. Their golden was…" He stopped not wanting to bring back those memories. "Sorry, sometimes I don't know when to shut up."

"That's okay, Dr. Norman, I don't hardly remember back then."

"So, you two…" He pointed alternately back and forth from Billie to Joey.

"Yeah, I guess we are a thing," Billie offered.

"Well, from what I know about you two, you will make a fine young couple…and that's rare these days…Now, about Harriet. You give me a call in a couple days, and I'll come over to your place."

"Just a couple days?" Joey asked searching Dr. Norman's eyes.

"Yes, son, I wouldn't leave it too long. Dogs can talk. Not like you and I but nevertheless they can talk just as sure as I'm talking to you right now. I'll bet she has already looked at you differently these last few days, hasn't she?"

"Yes…yes she has." All three of them nodded and looked back and forth at each other.

"Do you know what she is telling you?"

"Yes, I think I do," offered Joey. "I think she is saying, help me," Joey could barely speak, "I…I…I'm hurting!"

"See, you are a dog whisperer and I know she has been loved by you because you are sensitive to her. Do what she asks. At the rate the cancer is spreading sooner is better than later. Like I said, just call me and I will come over that evening. I owe your mom one and I plan on helping you out however I can. In fact, I would help you guys out even if I didn't owe you. We will let her fall asleep in her favorite place and I will do the rest."

Dr Marshall wheeled Harriet back out and Joey grabbed her in his arms and held her with his head down in her fur. Both Lilley and Billie gave Dr. Norman a polite hug and they left the office and drove away to Billie's house.

Joey walked Billie to the front door and Billie faced him, up one step to be at his eye level. "You really do have to stop growing," she quipped.

"Thanks for being there today," Joey managed, his lower lip still slightly quivering.

"Isn't that what people who love each other do?" she answered.

"I wouldn't know. I'm only 14." They held each other cry-laughing. Then Joey left her standing on the porch waving to them as they drove off.

CHAPTER 9

That night was probably the longest night that Joey had ever experienced since Gramps died, and it was still only 3 am. He sat on the kitchen floor long after Jessie and his mom had gone to bed, just petting Harriet gently. He worried constantly about what to do. Well, that's not exactly true. He knew what to do, he was just tormented about doing it. To put Harriet to sleep felt like such a traitorous thing, and yet he knew it was for her and he must. The more he thought about it the stronger he got. He thought about how Dr. Norman was so right on, about needing just a little more time. Now Joey realized fully that he was the one that would hurt and by taking this hurt he could stop Harriet's hurting. He also fully realized that it had to be as soon as possible.

He left Harriet and went to his mom's bedroom door which was always about half open. He brought his hand up to knock gently to see if his mom would respond.

"Come in Joey, I can't sleep much either."

"Mom, I want to do it tomorrow, or I guess that would be today."

"I knew you would say that. I have been hearing Dr. Norman's voice in my head too. I will call him in the morning."

"I wish I could talk to Billie right now!"

"So, I'm not good enough?" was Lilley's attempt at humor.

"Of course, you are but..."

"Joey, I think it's time we got you a cell phone. Then you can text all night if you want."

"We can't afford that, can we?" Joey wondered. "I do have almost $300 saved, but phones are way more expensive than that."

"I think if you are going to be Detective Joseph Burgess, you might need one to communicate with the other field agents," Lilley laughed.

"Huh? You mean about Sinclair and stuff...Yeah, I get it. You've been reading too many stories about the FBI and the CIA. I imagine Mr. Archer will be getting in touch with us soon. Hey Mom, he is in the tech business. Maybe we can get phones from him somehow."

"We'll talk about it later...we really do need to sleep. Even an hour or two would be better than nothing. I need to be half ways awake tomorrow because I have to go into Montrose and sign some legal papers.

Earlier that night, shortly after Joey and Lilley dropped her off, Billie was sitting on the back deck looking out over the water deep in thought, when her mom, Sarah, came out and sat next to her.

"So, how did it go with Joe today? Is his dog going to be okay?

"No, Mom, she isn't. They have to put her down and it's killing Joey." She started to cry. "Mom, why do I cry so much. It doesn't seem...I don't know, normal or something."

"Aw, honey, you are just a sensitive person, and it looks like you're hooked up with a pretty sensitive boy." She touched Billie's shoulder and gently squeezed.

"And that's kinda bothering me too...I love him, Mom, but he is just a boy ...and we are only 14! Everything says we won't make it as a couple. Anything I've read about teenage romance says it almost never lasts. Does that mean more heartache for Joey and me? He's like…too good to be true, and you know what you've always told me…if it's too good to be true, it probably is."

Sarah interrupted, "Honey, you need to live each day at a time and not worry about your future so much. If it's meant to be, it just will be. You two are amazing kids. Your dad and I are just floored by how mature you and Joey are. If there are two young people that can buck those odds, you two are definitely it."

"You know, one thing that I really like," Billie added, "is that we swore to be honest and not keep anything from the other person… no lies. The weird thing is, I don't feel trapped by it or, you know like, tied down or something. I feel like we're both the same that way."

"I understand what you mean because your dad and I have a no secrets, kind of a deal in our marriage. So, I rest my case. You guys are not even close to most 14-year-olds when it comes to your relationship. You just made me proud of you and like Joey even more. My only advice to you would be to just roll with the flow. I mean, you can't possibly tell what's going to happen in the future. It is possible that you two could develop other interests that make you drift apart. You are very young to say, 'that's it, I've made up my mind. I want to be with him forever'. But on the other hand, if you've pledged to be honest with each other, then you should be able to handle anything that comes along. I would say that when you are finished high school and you two still feel the way you do now, that would be the time to think seriously about your future together. For now, just enjoy each other's company and develop your friendship because, in the end, that is the most important thing. Just ask your dad who his best friend is."

"Joey's right...my parents are amazing! Thanks Mom." Billie moved over to Sarah's chez lounge so that she could lean in closer and hug her.

"Don't ever change," Sarah said, as she gently ran her fingers through the hair on the back of Billie's head.

Billie sat up. "I'm worried about Joey, though. I don't know how he's going to handle losing Harriet and with Jug still in a coma, it's just too much for one guy to deal with...and then there is his older sister, Pam. You probably heard about her drug problems. She might be released any day now, Joey says."

"I guess that's where you come in. Just go with your instincts and be there for him. Your dad got me through a pretty rough time with Rusty...God it still hurts to say his name after all these years!" she wiped away a tear.

"I guess I'm not the only emotional one in this family, eh, Mom."

"No, I guess you come by it honestly."

"Lilley got up and prepared herself for a meeting in the city. It was time for cross-examinations and other things she really didn't understand fully, but it was all to do with the divorce proceedings. She had heard via the gossipy townsfolk that frequented the Old General Store, that Hank was living with another woman now. Lilley didn't even have a pang of jealousy or regret and in fact, that news just made it easier to follow through and make it an official divorce, a break from a couple years of painful abuse at the hands of someone she once loved.

She got Jessie up and tried to explain to her about Harriet, in the limited time she had this particular morning. By relating Harriet to the passing of her grandpa, she was reasonably confident that Jessie would understand to some limited degree.

Joey was out under the pine tree with Harriet. When they brought Harriet home from the vet yesterday, she started perking up a little and that strain in her eyes seemed gone. This morning when she looked over at Joey the pleading look was back. "I hear you little girl. Soon you will have no pain." He bowed his head and held his eyes with his hand, tears streaming again. He wondered once more if life was just like this – a series of painful events. He remembered his times with Billie and weighed it in his mind. He tried to figure out if the good times balanced the bad times or kind of cancelled them out. When he was going through the hard times the good times seemed insignificant and when he was with Billie and having a good time, the bad times seemed lost. He could hear the health teacher and even his mom talking about hormones and mood swings and all that but knowing that doesn't really help. If you are hurtling towards the earth and you know the airplane you're on doesn't have wings, it doesn't lessen the impact when you hit the ground. It's easy to label problems but quite another to experience them.

Mom and Jessie came out of the house and got into the car and Joey walked around to the driver's side.

"Hey, Mom, did you call Dr. Norman?"

"No, I'm going to drop in there on the way through town and see if he can come out tonight. How's she doing? I gave her her pain pill this morning, but she didn't even want it rolled up in cheese. I opened a can of tuna and that seemed to work."

"Well, she has that look again. I know she is hurting, and she can barely move. I will give her another pill before I go. I want to go see Mrs. Parker for a while, later." Joey realized that he hadn't said that he was going to see Jug and that bothered him. It was like Jug really wasn't there anymore.

"That would be nice," replied Lilley. "I am stopping by there too. I bring her a breakfast sandwich every morning. I have a key for her house too so I can grab things like clean clothes for her. I even wash her clothes in their washer some days on the way home. She insists on staying there at the hospital. She won't leave his side. She even talks to him regularly thinking that somehow, he hears her. I am starting to worry as much about her as about Jug. Her eyes are so tired and sunken, and her general appearance is quite sickly."

About 10 minutes after Lilley left, a familiar black F-150 drove up with a flatbed trailer loaded with a bunch of lumber. It was Don Archer. He pulled over to the side of the road in front of Joey's house, got out and walked up the laneway and shook hands with Joey.

"How's the pooch doin' Joe?" Don asked, as he crouched down and petted Harriet. Only a very slight wag of her tail was noticed. "Hmm, she isn't well, is she?"

"No, sir. She has cancer and she is going to...go to sleep tonight."

"Aw, man, I'm so sorry, bud." Don said as he struggled to keep his composure.

"Yeah, it's pretty tough, Mr. Archer, but I know now it's the best thing for her."

"That's an extremely grown-up way to think, Joe. I bet your mom is proud of you for that. Hey Joe, please just call me Don, okay...no more sirs or Mr. Archers."

"Okay, and thanks, but I don't feel very grown-up right now. I feel like if one more bad thing happens, my brain is going to blow!"

"I remember having days like that when my business was tanking because of the a-hole Sinclair. Speaking of Sinclair...what's it been, about 5 days since the accident? And he's living up there in his nice house hunkered down, hoping this thing will blow over. I think we should start with our plan right away before the coals cool, as they say…Are you busy?"

"Well, I was going to go see Jug but what are you thinking of doing?"

"Have you told your little lady friend about our plans?"

"No, not yet but I thought I would today."

"Still no news about your Josh, er Jug, eh?"

"No, still hasn't woke up and his mom isn't in that great a shape either."

"Well, I got a proposal for you." He stood there scratching the stubble on his chin and pointed to the trailer full of lumber. "You see that lumber over there?"

"Yeah, what are you making?"

"Have you ever built a dock, Joey?"

"Ah, nope." Joey answered with a confused look on his face.

"The other day you mentioned that there was a little sheltered clearing near you house, right?"

"Yeah, we call it little beach,"

"Do you think that would be a good spot for a dock, say about 20 feet long sticking out into the lake?"

"Yeah but…how are you…why are you…I'm a little confused here."

"Okay, if the water there is over 3 feet deep about 20 feet offshore and there are plenty of large rocks around, we are going to build a dock there."

Joey was starting to understand what Don was saying. "Yeah, it's probably real close to 3 feet deep that far out and there are tons of rocks around…You mean it would be like a base or something, right, where we could have your boat tied up and do what we talked about doing right from here?"

"Exactly, there's no point in a bunch of lights and carrying on at the boat launch. We might have to do a couple of surveillance trips to work out our timing and stuff so it would be way easier if the boat was in the water already."

"Why can't you just pull your boat up on the shore? Why do we need a dock? I also think you need some kind of permission because this is really native land, and we don't actually own it."

"I knew you were a smart kid. Now, I'm sure. We need a dock because you need a dock. When we take Sinclair to court and he has to replace your boat, wouldn't it nice to have a dock to tie up to, or fish from, or even just jump off."

"Well, yeah, that would be awesome, but wood and stuff is expensive…"

"You let me worry about that. The answer to your other question was solved earlier this morning. I drove up to the band council office and we have written permission to build a small dock. My company did all the wiring and tech installs at the band office, the community center and the school for the Res, and I know Chief Charlie Hunter from a way back. I gave him a great deal and now he gave me a favor. That's kind of how the native people have been doing things for thousands of years. They have been trading things and favors since before money was invented."

"Bartering," Joey said quietly.

"You got it. Now, you want to visit Jug, right?" Joey nodded. "And since your girlfriend would probably like to be in on this little mission of ours here's what we do…"

Joey went in the house and phoned Billie and asked her to meet him at the park to go and visit Jug. She agreed but had no idea that a man in a pickup would be picking her up. When they got there, Joey hopped out of the truck and walked over to Billie. She heard them arrive and was also walking his way.

"Okay, what's going on?" Billie asked, baffled by the stranger in a big black pickup pulling a large trailer full of lumber!

Joey gave a perplexed Billie a kiss on the cheek, took her hand and began leading her toward the truck, "It would have taken too long to explain over the phone. Just trust me, Okay?"

Joey introduced her to Don as the man who rescued Joey and Jug and that eased Billie's mind somewhat. During the next 15 minutes, Billie was brought up to date on the plans for nailing Sinclair.

Then Don asked, "Billie, does the fact that your families are friends put you in an awkward position at all?"

Billie thought for a moment. "Actually, not really. My parents and Paul's parents have what my dad calls a working relationship. They kind of have things the other wants for building but it's more like Dad just buys materials from Mark Sinclair. I guess we are kind of friends with them because we do barbeques and stuff but that's just so my dad and Paul's dad can talk business, and Sally Sinclair can show off her latest clothes, or jewelry, or whatever to my mom. I've heard Mom and Dad talk about the Sinclair's and I really don't think they totally trust them."

"That's music to my ears. I have done lots of business with your family and the Sinclair's and believe me your parents are polar opposites to the Sinclair's, and I mean that in the best way possible."

"Wait a minute," Billie said. "Don Archer…I've heard my dad say your name lots of times. Duh…it took me a minute but now I see the connection."

"Well, I hope it was all positive," he smiled.

"It was. I remember them saying you did pretty well selling some software or something to some big company."

"I guess I did all right…so, let's get you kids to the hospital."

Don pulled into the parking lot at Four Counties and stopped spanning about 8 parking spots. Then he reached into his pocket and brought out his cell phone. "I got some calls to make so you guys take your time. If they come to give me flack about taking up all this room, I'll just move the truck out onto the road somewhere. When you want to start on the dock I'll be here."

"Okay, thanks Mr. Arch… I mean, Don," Joey smiled.

Billie and Joey walked into the hospital hand in hand but apprehensive, knowing there was likely no change. They knocked on Jug's room and Ellen came to the door, looking every bit as haggard as Lilley had described. They both greeted her with hugs and walked over to Jug's bed and stared down at him with their emotions starting to well up inside them. It was so bazaar to see their friend just lying there, for all intents and purposes, sleeping. Fearing that they might break down entirely, Joey turned to Ellen.

"Has there been any change or anything?"

Ellen turned from looking out the window, "Not really. Is that Don Archer's truck and trailer over at the far end of the parking lot?"

"Yes, it is. He gave us a ride here. After this we are going to start working to find evidence to pin Paul Sinclair to this so-called accident.

Don saw it happen and he said there was nothing accidental about it, but that could be hard to prove."

"I wish I never knew the Sinclair's at all," Billie chimed in.

"Mrs. Parker, you said not really, when I asked you if there was a change in Jug. Does that mean there might have been something? Joey probed.

"There is a new Dr. looking in on him. His name is Dr. Jordan. He's been assigned to Josh specifically. Late yesterday afternoon, he thought there was some slight straightening of his fingers and a very faint arm twitch. I have not seen anything but maybe it's a sign. All we can do is wait."

"That's something, I guess," Joey said. "Is there anything we can bring to you?"

"No, dear. Your mother seems to be taking pretty good care of me. Thanks for offering though."

"Okay, well, keep us posted and we will let you know if we make any progress too."

"I will and thank you. It's nice of you to come too Billie. Josh is fond of both of you. I'm hoping that he can somehow hear you."

Joey sighed and hugged Ellen goodbye and Billie followed suit. They found Don pacing in the median of the parking lot talking and gesturing with his hands as if the person he was talking to could see him.

"Hey, Joey," Don yelled over. "What's your house number?"

Joey yelled back, "seventy-seven."

Don gave Joey a thumbs up and continued talking. Then he poked his phone and returned to the truck.

"Why did you need my house number?" Joey asked Don, as they began pulling out of the parking lot.

"Well, first I was talking to your mother so she would know what we are up to and then my warehouse and then my retail outlet in Tilson. Well, that would be my son Greg, in Tilson. I am having some technology sent over to your place this afternoon. I should probably leave your place around 4. Greg wants me to sign something."

"What kind of technology?" Joey and Billie looked at each other shrugging.

"Well let's call it a little mystery,"

Don backed the trailer into Joey's laneway. Harriet lifted her head set it back down as if she didn't care who was there. Normally, Joey thought, she would have been dancing all over the place. Joey and Billie spent a few minutes with Harriet, changed her water and then turned to the trailer where Don was loosening all the tie downs.

"How close is this Little Beach of yours?"

"Just through there." Joey pointed to his right. "It's probably less than a hundred feet away."

"Perfect, oh yeah I can see the water through the trees. Well let's get at it. This lumber needs to be over there, and I don't see a forklift handy."

The three of them worked for almost an hour carrying planks and beams to the shore. The heavier 8 by 8 posts were about six feet long and handled by Don and Joey, one on each end. Billie was able to bring deck boards, 6 at a time. By about 11:30 all the wood was off the trailer and piled along the pathway down at Little Beach. They walked back up to the house and Joey grabbed everyone a coke and they took turns spraying their faces with the hose. They decided to rest for a while and sat with their backs against the trees near Harriet.

"Billie, I've decided that Harriet is going to be pain free tonight, if Dr. Norman can make it."

"Sorry, Joey, I will stay if you want me to."

"I appreciate that." Joey nodded and flicked away a tear like it was a filthy bug.

Don looked on sipping on his coke and shaking his head, marveling at the relationship these two kids had.

"There it is." Don got up as a white courier van drove up and stopped behind Don's truck.

Billie and Joey looked up, "That must be the technology Don was talking about. Maybe it's our superpower suits or our bat rings or something to help us on our top-secret mission," Joey dramatically announced.

"Yeah right," Billie laughed. "More likely hi-tech tools to put all that lumber together."

The van doors slammed, and the white van drove off. Don returned carrying two boxes and handed them to Joey.

"Cell phones!" Joey said excitedly. He sat down with Billie and started opening one of the boxes. Billie looked on with one elbow on Joey's shoulder.

"Here's the deal," Don began, "These things don't cost me hardly anything and I have amazing plans with almost all the carriers because they need my tech and services.

"How much do you make cutting grass, Joe?"

"In a whole month in the summer, I can make over $1000," Joey said proudly.

"Perfect. I can give you and your mom these phones for 50 bucks a month. What do you think of that?"

"Sounds, great but how do we pay for the actual phone?" Joey wondered.

"50 bucks a month is your total. That's two phones with unlimited texting and data for $50 bucks a month. But if that doesn't work for you and you don't need to text anyone…" Don and Billie exchanged winks and smiles.

"No, no…I mean, that's amazing! Why would you do all this for us?"

"Your mom asked the same question, and like I told her, I've been waiting for a long time to get even with the Sinclair's. If you knew the headaches that Mark Sinclair caused me with his shady business practices, you would understand. This is a great opportunity for me and to help you guys out at the same time… well, it's a no-brainer."

Then Don took orders for lunch, unhooked his trailer and took off in quest of food in the truck leaving Billie and Joey sitting with Harriet.

"Wow, do you know what this means? We can talk to each other whenever we want!" Billie said excitedly.

"Be careful what you wish for when I wake up in the middle of the night thinking about you." Joey shook her gently by the shoulder.

Billie laughed and leaned over and kissed Joey, intensely. "You would be my first, you know. I mean when the time comes."

Joey looked into her eyes and smiled, "Me, too. You know, I must be different from most guys because I don't even notice other girls at all anymore. It's like if anything happened to us it would be devastating. I honestly don't think I could handle it."

"Yes, you could. Look what you've been through already. Anyway, that's not going to happen, is it."

Just then Lilley returned and pulled the car up beside Don's trailer, got out and walked over to Joey and Billie. She looked in some way, better, perhaps happier.

"Hey, Mom."

"Hi, Mrs. Burgess."

"Hey, guys, I see you got the lumber all unloaded already," Lilley said looking back at the trailer. That Don Archer has turned out to be quite a find, hasn't he?"

"Yeah, no kidding. He's gone to pick up lunch and then we will start building the dock." Joey answered.

"What do you think, Billie?" Lilley studied Billie's face.

"I think it's great. If we can pull this off, I think I will be rid of Paul Sinclair and his idea that he thinks he owns me and that we will be together someday."

"Don't even say that," Joey cringed.

Lilley cocked her head to the side looking for more explanation. "What do you mean dear?"

Billie stood up and brushed the dirt and pine needles off her bare legs. "If we can successfully prove that Paul did this and it is made public, he will be punished, and my parents will not associate with the Sinclair's. I can guarantee that. The best part is I won't have to go to any social functions where that moron will be. It's kind of a win-win."

"Well, I hope you're right," said Lilley. "I have two bits of news for you Joey, and I will share it with you too, Billie, since you two seem to be joined at the hip." Billie blushed and looked down coyly. The divorce will likely be final by October and your father will have to pay child support until Jessie is 18. That means I can stop cleaning houses and just work at the store three days a week…and start being a decent mother."

"Whoa, that's great!" Joey said and gave Lilley a hug. "But you've always been a good mother and you've always tried your best in spite of being so badly treated by Dad."

"Aw, that's so sweet!" Billie said wiping her eyes. She took a step over and joined in a group hug. You see, Mrs. Burgess, why I fell for this guy?"

"Yes, I do, and I sure see why he fell for you too dear." They all stepped back, Joey and Billie holding hands. "The other little bit of news is…Pam is coming home at three this afternoon."

"That's really great!" Joey said, with moderate enthusiasm. "I only just wonder which Pam will show up. But I'm happy she is coming home. She deserves another chance to have a family and without Dad here maybe things will be different."

"That is exactly my wish too, Joey," said Lilley.

"I remember her to see her, but I haven't really met her. I can't wait to meet her, you know, properly," added Billie.

Don returned and they sat on the side of the trailer and ate their lunches. They told Don about Pam and Lilley came back out of the house and sat beside him with a tray of iced tea. Joey tried feeding Harriet some fries, but she wasn't interested. He decided to sit beside her realizing his time with her was limited. Billie sat on the other side of Harriet and she looked up at them with eyes that looked anxious and strained but still managed a slight tail wag.

"I know you are hurting, girl. I hope you know how much we will miss you!" Billie started crying and Joey reached over and took her hand.

"You know what, guys," Don spoke up. "You have a lot of family things to take care of today. How about I come back tomorrow around 10 or so and we can start on the dock."

Joey helped Don hook up his trailer and Lilley came over to see him off, while Billie stayed sitting with Harriet.

"Thanks, so much Mr. Arch…oops…Don, for everything! We really appreciate you helping us so much!

"You are very welcome, and I look forward to our mission." He smiled back and forth to Lilley and Joey.

Lilley stepped up with open arms and gave Don a big hug. "Thanks so much!"

"Okay, gotta go now…" He looked at Joey. "Be strong, kid. You got this!"

CHAPTER 10

Billie and Joey took a walk just to be alone together, back down to Little Beach. They sat on the lumber they had stacked down there, cross-legged facing each other.

"I seriously don't know what I'd do without you, Billie! And I must admit, I don't know how I'm gonna handle this thing tonight. I really love that damn dog! It makes me so, I don't know…mad is the only word I can think of. Why do things you love get taken away from you?"

"You can tell so much about a person by how they treat and feel about their pets," Billie replied. "It's one of those things that shows a person's kindness and their ability to love, I think…And I sure love you!" she leaned forward for very passionate kiss.

"Ahem…." Joey and Billie quickly broke their lip lock and glanced back at the path.

Lilley and Pam were walking, arms around each other toward them and then stopped.

"Well, aren't you gonna say something?" Pam asked.

"Yeah," said Joey. "Who are you and what did you do with my big sister?" Joey laughed and jumped down off the pile of lumber and into Pam's outstretched arms."

"I missed you little bro!" said Pam, hanging onto Joey tightly.

"I missed you too, sis! There hasn't been anyone around here to argue with lately." Said Joey, teasing.

Joey backed up still holding both of Pam's hands. He couldn't believe what he saw. It was as if Pam had all the features she had when she was about 10 years old, but just older looking. There was no harsh black makeup, no knotted, weirdly colored hair, no gothic clothing. She wore a t-shirt that had "pink" across the front, normal jeans and tennis shoes. Joey was actually quite shocked. She was a very pretty girl with wavey, shoulder length brown hair parted in the middle to show off her high cheek bones and dazzling hazel eyes. She looked healthy and her facial skin color was not painted on but natural, with a wholesome farm girl look.

"You look like you've seen a ghost!" Pam remarked.

"Well...you look amazing!"

"Thank you, little bro, and you look damn good yourself and, like a foot taller. How did that happen so fast?"

"You, know, if she wasn't your sister, I might be jealous," Billie cut in with a big smile.

Pam motioned her over for a hug, "You must be the famous Billie. Get over here and hug your beau's big sister. Wow, you are beautiful! I only remember you as the little Magee girl."

"I'm going to leave you guys for a while. I'm going to get Jessie and then start supper. I assume you are staying for a bite, Billie? Lilley asked.

"Yes, if that's no trouble," Billie answered.

"And manners, too!" Pam interjected with a look of approval and a thumbs up.

"Trouble? Yeah, you're such a pain," Lilley joked sarcastically, bringing laughs all around,

Lilley left and the three of them sat back down on the make-shift lumber pile bench.

"I know we got a lot of catching up to do Joe and we can do that later. I understand that you've had a hard time with Dad leavin' and Gramps and…Mom told me about Harriet, and I know what she means to you."

"Really…where's my sister? The last time I saw her she was more worried about…" Joey stopped himself and knew it would not be kind to finish that thought.

"Drugs, dope, drinking, asshole friends…that's okay Joe, because you're right. Sometimes it takes being brought down to your knees before you realize how you got there. I just needed time and a clean mind to remember what and who really matters. I'm so glad you have Billie here, because I'm not the only one who looks different. You seem happier, less angry and way more mature."

They spent almost an hour there talking about everything that had happened since Pam had been taken away. Joey and Billie filled her in on what happened to Jug. Pam had heard about the accident but now she knew the background behind it and seemed eager to take part in the mission. Joey told her all about how much help Don Archer had been and showed off his new cell phone. Then he explained the nitty gritty about how they planned to prove Paul Sinclair's guilt.

"The only thing I can't figure out," Joey mused, "So we get a picture of the bottom of Sinclair's boat. How does that prove that the photo is of his particular boat? Even if we get a photo of the name "Dreadknot" on the stern, that doesn't prove it's the same boat."

Pam looked like she was in deep thought. Then she stood up and started pacing pointing her finger as she talked. "I would bet that this Don guy has a video function on his camera. If he's into taking photos of fish underwater while he's fishing, wouldn't he want to see how they fight as there are being reeled in?"

"Yeah, duh…I forgot about that. He even told me he could take videos."

Pam continued, "So if he starts the video above the water with the name of the boat clearly shown and slowly pans the video down and into the water to reveal the evidence on the bottom…busted!"

"Wow, did you ever come home at the right time, Sherlock!"

"What if Paul decides that the name might be a problem and he takes the letters off?" suggested Billie.

Pam was still pacing, "I've seen boats around here that had their names removed but after years of being out in the sun, you could still make out the words on the faded surface. Just to make sure, either way we need a picture of Paul in the boat, preferably driving it."

"I think I can get that from him with a little persuasion," offered Billie.

"I don't want to know what you're going to do to pry that out of him," said Joey, half joking.

"Hey mister, you should know by now how I feel about him. You better trust me on this…Actually, I know exactly where a picture like this is."

"Where?" both Pam and Joey spoke at once.

"On the bookshelf, in their living room…All I need is to get close to it long enough to get a photo of it on my phone. I might have to get my parents in on this to get access, but I'll think about it."

"Pammie!" Jessie came running down the pathway with her arms straight out in front of her and Pam turned and swooped her up into her arms. Jessie buried her head into Pam's neck and Pam looked toward Joey and Billie, tears forming in her eyes.

"Oh, I missed you Jessie! You got taller too!" said Pam, emotionally.

"I missed you too! Did you see Billie…she's Joey's girlfriend!" Everyone laughed. Jess had an obsession with the idea. "Isn't she pretty? You're pretty too now, Pammie!"

Joey was amazed how a young child like Jess could paint the entire picture, simply and succinctly in just a few honest observations. Words that older siblings or adults would consider too forward or awkward to just blurt out in this way.

After a supper of juicy hamburgers made on the barbeque, Joey got up from the table and went outside without saying anything and slipped out the doorway. He walked over to Harriet who looked up at Joey with only her eyes now.

Billie stood up from the table and looked at Lilley, "May I be excused?"

"Of course, dear. You don't have to be formal around here. I'm sure Joey needs you now." Lilley smiled.

"Why does Joey need Billie now?" Jess innocently asked.

"Hey, Mom," Pam winked. "Can me and Jess play snakes and ladders in the bedroom?"

Lilley sensing what Pam was up to answered, "Sure, as soon as you put all the dishes in the sink and the rest of the stuff away."

It was almost 7 pm and time for Dr Norman's visit. The two girls helped Lilley in the kitchen and Pam ushered Jess into the bedroom. Lilley left the dishes in the sink and went to join Joey and Billie who were outside sitting on the ground, one on each side of Harriet. As if on cue, the white VW Jetta of Dr. Norman's pulled in and stopped at the end of the laneway. After a few seconds the big Santa look-a-like emerged from the car with a small black bag, almost like a small woman's purse. He had on overalls with narrow, vertical blue and white stripes, like a stereotypical train engineer's outfit with straps over a white t-shirt.

They exchanged greetings and Joey went over and grabbed a couple of lawn chairs from the front porch and dusted them off with his hands as he walked back. He set one in front of Lilley and one beside Harriet and motioned Dr. Norman to take a seat.

Billie was already wiping tears from her face. Even though Harriet was not her dog, she had come to love her but most of the pain she was feeling was for her best friend. Joey reached across and grabbed her hand buoyed by some inner strength from a source that puzzled him.

"Well folks, I want you to think of this as a happy time for Harriet, here. I thought of something that might ease your pain. Perhaps you have heard or read things about ADE's, or afterlife death experiences?"

Everyone nodded reluctantly but understood his premise.

Dr. Norman continued as he bent over and unzipped the small black bag, took out a vial and a syringe and drew some clear fluid into the syringe. "In almost every documented case I've read about, it's the same story. I believe animals have souls and they have a spirit life like we do. These people who had ADE's said they felt like they left their bodies, and they went to a place full of love. Once they were out of their body and surrounded by what most of them described as a bright light, they did not want to come back.

Joey held Harriet's head in his hands, Billie was near Harriet's back legs beside Dr. Norman. The Dr. felt around on Harriet's hip for a fleshy part, stuck the syringe in and started talking while he was draining the fluid into Harriet's hip.

"Joey, Billie, Lilley, you all know that Harriet was Harriet because of the love she gave you, not because of her body, but because of her spirit."

As he said those words, Joey felt Harriet's head relax and go perfectly limp. He rested her head back on the ground and said, "Thank you, Dr. Norman. Goodbye my sweet Girl!" as Billie and Lilley both sat there crying.

Dr. Norman put away his equipment and rested the small bag on this lap and bowed his head as Joey stood up and walked away, disappearing down the pathway to Little Beach. Lilley looked at Billie, wiped the tears from her face and nodded with her head for Billie to go to Joey. Billie stood up, using the back off her wrist and arm to wipe away her tears and walked after Joey.

Dr. Norman looked up, "That boy of yours is a strong kid. Every time I do this … I'll call it 'act of mercy', it never gets any easier. In fact, the older I get, the softer I get."

"Thank you so much Dr. Norman," Lilley managed, then turned and looked toward the path the kids had just walked down.

"Grant, please Lilley."

"Okay, Grant…you don't realize how much you've done for us. We should probably bury her here under her favorite tree."

Grant screwed up his face with doubt. "Lilley unless you have dynamite or a huge jack-hammer you're not going to be burying anything around her. We're standing on solid granite and pine roots."

Lilley nodded, "I guess you're right. What should we do then?"

"Well, I'm not going to leave one of my favorite employees, ever with a body and just drive off. Wait here a minute."

Grant got up and went back to his car, opened the trunk and got out a canvas duffel bag with straps like a sports equipment bag would have. He knelt down beside Harriet's flaccid body, unzipped the bag and spread it open. He put one of his large, soft hands under Harriet's head and pulled her legs and torso around with the other hand, rolling her into the bag. He zipped up the opening and carefully lifted her up as though she was still alive and didn't want to hurt her. With surprising ease, he carried her too his car. With Lilley looking, on he placed the duffel in his back seat rather than the trunk, in a gesture of respect. Then he came back and adjusted his lawn chair to face Lilley and sat down, elbows on knees and fingers clasped in front of his chin.

"So, what do we do?" Lilley asked again.

"You don't do anything. I will look after everything from here. You obviously can't bury her here. You could have her cremated and memorialized in a nice wooden box with her name on it. Is that something you would like? That way Joey and you could decide if you wanted to spread the ashes somewhere or just keep the box in special place somewhere or whatever. The process should take about a week, and I can phone you when it's done."

"That sounds wonderful but…"

"Lilley, let me worry about the 'but'. You owe me nothing. It's the least I can do. What do you think you and Joey would want printed on the box?"

"Joey said the other night when we knew she was fading, that the best words to describe her were 'loved and loving'.

"Okay, done." Grant nodded.

He stood up and grabbed the little syringe bag from the ground where he had placed it beside the lawn chair. Lilley got up too and walked over and embraced the plump old vet and kissed him on the cheek.

"Thank you. We will never forget your kindness!" Lilley said, sincerely.

"There, you see. That's what I call payment for services rendered," Grant smiled and nodded goodbye and turned and walked to the car. Lilley stood in the laneway waving as he drove off.

Down at Little Beach, Billie found Joey up to his knees in the lake skipping stones out on the still water of the lake. Billie slipped off her shoes and placed them beside Joey's on the lumber pile and waded in. The water reached mid-thigh on her. She reached for his hand without a word, and he took it without even looking at her. They stood hand in hand staring out over the water.

Finally, Joey broke the silence, "You know, since I left you guys back there, I have barely cried a tear. Well, maybe a couple little ones, remembering her playing back there on the beach chasing minnows." Joey swallowed and gave out a disingenuous chuckle. "I thought I would absolutely lose it tonight. Why aren't I bawling my eyes out?"

"I think I might know," Billie paused. "I think you have been crying both inside and out when you finally knew you were going to lose her." Billie started to sob slightly but held her breath to continue. "I think in your heart, you knew there was only one out that was best for her and you took it… plus Dr. Norman was amazing!"

Joey, turned to face Billie and took her other hand. "You are pretty damn amazing too! I love you so much!"

As the sky faded from light yellow cotton balls to wispy orange feathers, they embraced still standing in the water. They held each other tightly, now both crying unashamedly, forming a single dark silhouette against the sky's reflection in the gently undulating surface of the lake.

Joey knew that his mom had somehow looked after Harriet's body and didn't really ask but to say, "Dr. Norman is taking things from here?"

"Yes, he is," was all she said back.

Since it was now dusk, Lilley, Billie and Joey jumped into the front seat of the old impala and took Billie home. On the way back they remarked about how this day had been such an extremely good day and such a horribly bad day all in one.

About an hour later, Joey had just reclined in his bed when a light rap sounded on his door.

"Come in, it's open," Joey said, half whispering.

Pam came in dressed in flannel two-piece pajamas and sat at the foot of Joey's bed.

"How's Jess? Does she know what happened tonight with Harriet?" Joey wondered.

"Yeah, she knows, and she's cool with it," answered Pam. "She felt bad for you though because she thought Harriet was really your dog. She's such a cute kid…but I came in to see how you were holding up."

"I'm surprisingly…okay, which still kind of seems weird to me. Billie thinks it's because I already did all my mourning or whatever, you know, like…before she actually died."

Pam swatted Joey's foot, "Well, I've only been gone, what, three months? Things are so different here. You seem so grown up and not the introverted little nerd you were before I left."

"Hey!" Joey said, as if insulted.

"Well, you were! I know I was a sullen little wannabe gothic bitch back then too. It's amazing how your outlook can change. There are a lot of things that happened these past few months for both of us. For me it was drying out, rehab, counseling and a real self-awakening, a realization of who was really important in my life. I think that was really brought home when Gramps died. For you it was your run in with that creepy Sinclair kid, Gramps' death, Jug's injuries and now Harriet's passing."

"I know," Joe responded. "It's like bad things can sometimes change you for the better. They are like wake-up calls, so you forget the things that don't matter, and you get focused on what really matters."

"Okay, I'm going to use your line. Who are you and what have you done to my little brother?" They both laughed. Pam added, "The biggest change in your life that I could plainly see today is that little honey of yours. You love her don't you, Joey?"

"Yes, I do, very much."

"Hmm…you sure wouldn't have admitted that to me a few months ago. But I guess I would have just made fun of you, so I know why."

"Well, you wouldn't have called me 'Joey' a few months ago either, unless you wanted something."

CHAPTER 11

Billie and Joey arranged to meet by texting. They had each said goodnight three times and kept texting each other for what seemed like half the night. Joey was in love with his new toy almost as much as with Billie. It helped Joey get through the night without over thinking his loss of Harriet and Billie didn't mind. They planned a morning out on Billie's rowboat and doing some fishing with worms while drifting close to the shore.

After breakfast, Joey dug up some worms from a boggy area about 100 yards back in the woods behind their house. They met at Billie's rowboat at 9:30 and Billie brought an old fishing pole of her dad's, some chips and a couple cans of pop. Joey brought his pole and tackle box along with 2 buckets: one with worms, the other a stainless-steel ice bucket of Lilley's.

As he appeared in the clearing, Billie was already loading her things into the rowboat.

"Wow, you got a lot of stuff today!" she said. "What's with the ice bucket?"

"That's kind of a surprise," Joey answered. "You'll see…I hope."

"Hmm, well that's an interesting answer."

Billie scampered over to Joey's side of the boat and caught him with both hands full unloading the gear into the boat. She leaned in and kissed him on the cheek and ran back to the other side before he could react.

"What was that for?" Joey asked with a shy smile.

"Can't a girl give her man a good morning kiss?" she teased.

"But I was defenseless." Joey played along. "That's okay. I'll get you back, don't worry."

They jumped in and silently floated out into the calm morning waters, steam still rising from the shallow water near the shore. Joey rowed to a spot just west of the town dock, where he knew there was usually a good chance at catching some perch. He often would bring perch home to eat and it was a favorite in his family.

"So today, we are after some perch., one of the best eating fish in the lake," Joey announced like a tour guide.

"Okay, as long as you do the worms and the unhooking and all that," Billie screwed up her face in disgust.

Joey laughed, "Deal."

They sat drifting along the shoreline. Joey had more in his plans than he revealed to Billie and hoped it would all come together smoothly.

As they sat at one point almost stalled in the still water, Joey was starting to crumble slightly from the weight of the night before. The quiet made for too much thinking and reflection. Billie sensed a noticeable silence and turned to see Joey's head was down and he was wiping away a tear. Billie wound up her line and sat at the back beside him with her arm around his back and her head on his shoulder.

"I love you, Joey! We will get through this."

There was a long pause then, "Yeah, you're right, of course, but it's so hard. I don't know how I can even be here…you know out here fishing, like nothing happened. I feel like I'm in a pressure tank or something. It's a weird feeling. I don't feel bad at some points because I know what I did was right, but I feel some sort of pressure building inside me like I might explode…I could not do this without you! I love you too!"

It wasn't long before they were both hauling up crappies, small perch and even a small catfish. Each time Joey would bait her hook, Billie would stick her tongue out and looked disgusted and sometimes just looked away. Each time Billie caught one she squealed in delight and quickly wound her line in and swung her catch over for Joey to unhook. Then Joey hooked a good fish.

"Finally," Joey said, struggling slightly with the line.

"What? Is it a big one?" Billie asked excitedly.

"Bigger but not all that big. You don't want them too big. Just big enough for the frying pan."

Joey landed a good-sized perch. He unhooked it and weighed it with his spring scale. He got out a chain and hooked it through the fish's gills and tied the other end to the oar lock and plopping the fish back in the water to keep it fresh.

"1 pound 6 ounces…perfect for eating," Joey reported.

"I like the orange stripes," said Billie. "They're kind of cute."

"This is going to be harder than I thought," Joey thought. He'd never thought a fish was particularly cute. Then he sighed and said, "Billie, just look away until I say it's okay."

"Why?" she looked puzzled.

"There are some things I must do that you may not like, if we are going to eat this fish."

"Oh…oh!" She looked away. There was a clunk sound and some jiggling behind her, but she didn't look.

In less than two minutes, Joey had killed the fish humanely and filleted it into two boneless slabs of meat and put them on ice in the ice bucket.

"Okay," Joey announced. "You can look now."

Billie turned around and looked expecting to see some gross murder scene. "What? I don't see anything. Where's the fish?

As the fish entrails floated away out of sight behind him, Joey lifted the lid on the ice bucket and pushed some ice aside and revealed two perfect little fillets.

"Holy cow, that just looks like how you buy them at the food market. How did you do that so fast?" she wondered in amazement.

"Next time you can watch me," Joey suggested, looking for a reaction.

"That's okay," Billie answered quickly. "I'll just stay in suspense. How come you can do that to a fish, but you are so kind to other animals?"

"That, I have always wondered about myself," Joe answered. "Even hooking the worm seems hypocritical really. I guess I grew up doing it and have become hardened to it…not sure, really."

They caught 6 perch altogether, two of which were landed by Billie. Each time she turned away to avoid the reality of the fish slaughter. Joey's plan was beginning to work out perfectly, because they had drifted conveniently close to Little Beach. Joey heard a car door slam, and although he couldn't see through all the foliage, he knew that was Don returning to start work on the dock.

"Can you stay today and maybe have a fish fry tonight? Joey asked. Don is here and we are going to start work on the dock."

"Hey, isn't that the little beach?" Billie pointed.

"Yep, now Don's here and we are going to get to work."

"I'd like to, but Mom and I are going into Montrose this afternoon to buy stuff for school. I want to ease my parents into our little plan, so I thought that might be a good time to talk to her. I can drop you off here and row back to my place. I'll come back tonight for the fish fry around 5 if that's okay?"

"Yeah, okay. It's a good idea to let your parents in on things too. I just wanted to spend as much time with you as possible since we are both starting school next week."

"Me, too Joey, but if Mom's willing to equip me with cool stuff for school, I should go. I promise, to spend the rest of the week with you. It's only Thursday, and I don't check-in to the dorm at school until Tuesday, so we still have Friday, Saturday, Sunday, Monday, and part of Tuesday. Okay, that's not quite a week…I'll get Mom to drop me off here when we get back."

Joey positioned the rowboat at Little Beach careful to keep it from running aground then jumped into the water which was barely a foot deep. He reached in and grabbed his fishing pole and tackle box.

"Hey, Billie could you hand me the pale of worms and the ice bucket?"

"Sure." She leaned over to hand them to Joey, and Joey leaned in and kissed her on the lips while she had both her hands full. She did not resist, and their mouths opened passionately during a good 30 second smooch. There was something really very exciting about kissing this way, where only their faces touched and nothing else. They both sighed and Joey stepped back.

"I told you I would get you back," Joey winked.

"Anytime, Joey!" Billie laughed. Then she handed him the pails and took Joey's position and started rowing away. "See you later."

Joey carried all his paraphernalia up to the house where Don was standing beside his truck. He waved at Joey and started pacing toward the road with his cell phone up to his ear. When Joey got to the kitchen, Lilley was scurrying around, a bobby pin in her teeth, her hands attempting to put her hair up in a bun and her feet were trying to slip themselves into her canvas running shoes. She started bouncing on foot, losing her balance and then finally sat down at the kitchen table to complete her preparations.

"Where's Pam and Jess?" Joey asked.

"Pam took Jess into town to the dollar store." There was a noticeable silence and Joey looked a bit confused.

"She took the car?"

"Yes, she did…I know what you're thinking, and I wondered about it too, but we have to start trusting her some time.

"Yeah, I guess you're right," Joey admitted. But he was having a little difficulty believing the apparent transformation of Pam from the rebellious drug addict into a responsible sister in such a short time. Still, people change, and he would roll with it for now.

"You look like you're in a hurry. Are you going somewhere?" Joey asked.

"No, but Don just drove in and I don't want him to see me like I just got out of bed."

"You don't seem to care when the plumber guy comes," Joey saw an opportunity to tease Lilley. "Must be something special about Don, eh?"

"Don't be crazy, Joey. It's just that…he's our friend…and…well…a girl doesn't like to appear unkempt around her friends, that's all."

"Okay, Mom, if you say so, but I think he likes you," continued Joey.

"Oh, just give it up, will you!" Lilley got the tea towel hanging from the drawer handle in front of the sink and rolled it up like she was going to snap it at Joey. She tried one fling and she missed as he dodged the attempt. Then Joey bolted for the door laughing, with Lilley chasing him out to the laneway.

"Hey, that's abuse," Joey laughed

"Well, so that's how you parent your children, Mrs. Burgess?" Don said with a laugh, walking their way.

"Ha…trouble is, I can't catch him anymore," Lilley joked. "So, you two are going to start building a dock today, I take it?"

"Yeah, let's call it, mission preparation. Hopefully, we can get it done in a couple days."

"Okay, well you two have fun…don't hurt yourselves," she winked at Don.

Joey and Don headed toward the path for Little Beach, Don strapping on a tool belt as he walked. Then Joey stopped and ran back.

"I'll be back in a minute. I forgot to tell Mom something."

He got back to the house and stuck his head inside the door. "Hey, Mom, Billie and I caught 6 perch this morning. They are in the ice bucket. Could you do your awesome batter thing and fry them up for supper? Billie's coming and I'm gonna try to talk Don into stayin' too."

"Okay," Lilley yelled from somewhere back near bedroom area.

Don and Joey spent about 5 hours straight working at the making of the cribs for the dock. Joey enjoyed being partially submerged and working at the same time. Anytime he was at or in the lake was a good scenario for him. Keeping busy like they were today, was also the perfect tonic for his general sadness. Don showed him how to make boxes from the beams. They were more like big square baskets with a layer of beams on the bottom of the box. They positioned them by using some nearby rocks to sink them and after making sure they were level they began filling them up with more rocks. They lined it up with the smaller box they made earlier only about 2 feet from the shoreline, then joined the two with 20-foot pressure treated 2 by 10's so that the alignment would hold during the rest of the construction. When both boxes were filled to the top, they would start with the deck part of the dock.

"It's cool, eh, how you can carry rocks while they are under water but once you get them out of water you can barely lift them to get them into the crib." Joey mused.

"Yep, two thirds. They weigh two thirds their actual weight. So, a hundred-pound rock would be sixty-six pounds in the water."

They each walked out from the cribs, Joey walked north, and Don walked south, finding suitable rocks. After a while they became better judges of the size they needed, both for moving them and then lifting them out into the air and over the edge of the crib. The small crib near the shore was only a couple feet high but the one out in deeper water was 5 feet high so that it was 2 feet above the water level.

"What's Billie taking at school in Montrose?" Don asked? He was cleverly leading Joey away from what was still gnawing at him. He knew Joey couldn't shake the guilt of Harriet and figured the best idea was to keep Joey's mind occupied with other thoughts.

"She wants to take advanced biology courses. She's pretty smart but it's kind of funny though. She won't look at a worm or the insides of a fish, but she wants to study biology. I'm a little worried about her when the teacher announces that they're going to dissect frogs today!" They both laughed.

"Why biology? Does she know what she wants to be?"

"Not exactly, but she's kicking around the idea of being a nurse, which I think she would be awesome at. The Elmvale private school in Montrose has the best medically related biology courses."

"A nurse, uh, yeah, I can see that," Don agreed. "What about you? What do you think you will end up doing with your life?"

"Not sure, really. I might get into design or something involving art. Billie's dad suggested I might be able to come and work for him someday, but I know he was just being nice to me."

"Hey, you never know, Joe… That would be a rather cozy arrangement though, wouldn't it?" Don chuckled.

"Yeah, that would definitely work for me," Joey smiled back catching Don's eye.

During that day working side-by-side in the late summer sun and getting to know one another was the perfect medicine for Joey. At one point, Joey lost his grip on his rock just as he was about to lift it into the crib. As he stepped back and let it fall, two small minnows darted away. Joey bent over to pick up the rock and in the reflection of the water he saw Harriet playfully pawing at minnows and her silly face as she bared her teeth into a goofy smile. He stayed bent over as emotion paralyzed his body. Don had just loaded a large rock into the crib with a splash and noticed Joey bent over with his head turned toward the open lake to hide his face. Don walked over to Joey, and just gently put his hand on Joey's shoulder as he trembled. Joey nodded his head in appreciation, wiped away the tears and fished out the rock and flung it into the crib as if it were light as a feather. Neither needed to say a word, but so much was spoken, and an undeniable bond was starting to form.

After filling the cribs to Don's satisfaction, they used corner irons to bolt the 2 by 10's into a large box around both cribs which would be the initial frame on which the deck boards would be fastened forming the floor of the dock. One more 2 by 10 was cut to run up the middle of the frame for added stability ensuring that the deck boards would not sag in the middle.

"Looks like we are ready for the deck boards," Don announced. But it's getting hungry time for me. I think we can finish 'er off tomorrow. I'll pick up some dock cleats tomorrow and that will be a nice finishing touch to it, oh, and some edging to protect the boat from being scratched when it's choppy."

"Hi, guys." It was Billie returned from her afternoon of shopping in Montrose.

"Hey," Joey and Don answered almost simultaneously.

"Wow, you got a lot done today!" She slipped off her shoes and waded about knee high, leaning on the 2 by 10 span between the cribs. "I wondered if you were going to build a floating dock or this…"

"They're called cribs," Joey spoke up, proud of his newly acquired knowledge.

"Hmm, well, I see where they got their name," Billie nodded.

"With what has been happening around here lately, this type of dock cannot be ruined or stolen as easily," Don explained.

Joey walked over to Billie and gave her a kiss and stood with his arm around her.

"Your mom told me to come and get you guys for supper. I brought some corn on the cob and she has the fish all fried up and I think Pam and Jessie are making fries"

"I like the sound of that!" said Joey, licking his lips. "Don, Billie and I caught some perch this morning and we are having a fish fry and we want you to join us."

"I would be happy to. Thanks, guys. I don't want to impose thought."

Joey and Billie looked at each other and then laughed. "Yeah, you're just a pain in the ass, Don," Then Don laughed with them. "Besides, Mom could use some adult company. I'm sure you wouldn't mind that, eh, Don?" Joey teased. Billie bit her finger to stifle a giggle.

"Hehe, I'd be lying if I said I didn't think your mom was attractive. She's a good person too, which is even more important." Then he added slyly, "And, perch is my favorite!"

They had a great time sitting around kitchen table. With all the conversations and laughter no one, not even Jessie brought up the subject of Harriet. Pam had taken some time to explain things to her to insure that didn't happen. During the meal, Joey looked up and caught Pam smiling at Joey and Billie sitting together. Pam pursed her lips, nodded and winked at the same time showing her approval and love for her little brother. Joey nodded back with a smile and thought, "She's back. She's really back!"

After the table was cleared, everyone stood up and formed an assembly line making short work of the dishes.

"Hey, Lilley, I was thinking," said Don. "Maybe we could go over to the Lodge and get my boat and do a dry run tonight?"

"Dry run? Oh…right. Sounds good. Yeah, you guys go ahead and scout out your mission."

"Well, I was hoping you might come along too."

Joey and Billie turned and smiled at each other with raised eyebrows.

"Oh…Well, I haven't been in a boat for a while, but. Okay… might be fun, I guess. Pam, do you mind staying here with Jessie for an hour or so."

"Sure, I got to get even with her for beating me at snakes and ladders." She poked Jessie and they both giggled.

"We should go at dusk like we would for real. It's starting to get dark around 8:45, so I'll meet you guys at the town ramp then?"

Everyone agreed, Don thanked the girls for the great meal and left to prepare his boat.

At 8:15, Billie, Joey and his mom piled in the car and headed for town. When they got there, Don's boat was already in the water, and he was fastening on the portable lights; a small clamp-on green light on the right or starboard side of the bow and red one on the left or port side. Then he clamped a telescoping chrome light post to the stern with a white light that stuck up about 3 feet.

"There, now, we're legal. Untie us, Joe. You guys can hop in. Just try to balance yourselves so that the boat isn't tipped too much."

It was a small 16-foot aluminum boat with a 30 horse Evinrude rear tiller motor. Don had an electric start system added. He pressed the button, as Joey jumped in, and the motor sprang to life immediately. It was surprisingly quiet, as most of the modern outboards have become. Don was in the stern on the right side and Lilley was one seat forward on the left. Billie and Joey were in the next seat forward. Balancing the boat wasn't a problem for Billie and Joey as sitting together in the middle suited them just fine.

As planned, they headed for the eastern coastline of the lake. Don powered it up and the small boat was able to plane out and run quite smoothly. They passed in front of Kamawog Lodge and north up the shoreline for about 5 minutes. The cooling air of late summer was refreshing and there was a hint of fall in the air. Don had scouted out the approximate place to slow down and begin rowing. It was now after nine and quite dark. Don cut the engine and held his finger to his mouth for everyone to be silent. They drifted about a minute silently. Not hearing or seeing anybody on shore or any boat traffic, Don tapped out the lights, using an app on his phone (always the techie).

Don whispered loudly, "Joe, you and your mom change seats. You can do the rowing and I will be doing the camera work from the stern here on the actual night."

Lilley and Joey changed seats while Don pulled one oar out of its place along the right side just under the gunwale and Joey pulled out the other from the left side, both trying to be a careful as possible to be quiet and not hit anything with the oars.

There was just enough light from the various homes and cottages as well as moonlight from a partly cloudy sky for Joey to get his bearings. He rowed slowly toward the shore and then about 20 yards offshore just as he turned to head north along the coast, one of the oarlocks started squeaking. Don tapped Joey's knee and held an index finger up telling Joey to stop for a minute. Don reached around for his tackle box in the stern beside the gas tank and brought out a spray can of sunblock. He reasoned that since it was supposed to stay on even when the skin got wet it must have some sort of oil base. He sprayed the oarlocks thoroughly and Joey moved the oars back and forth. There was a little squeak and then nothing. Perfect!

They continued up the coast for another five minutes as stealthily as they could. There was just the swish of water as the oars slid in and out of the water's surface. When Joey pulled on the oars, the odd time one of them would hit the side of the boat lightly making a muffled clunk. He worked hard to eliminate those times and perfected a near silent rowing technique. When they were a couple hundred feet away from the Sinclair's, Don stood up to survey their location and Joey held the oars out of the water. Don signaled to be extra quiet now because the target boathouse was in sight. Don nodded his head and moved his hand in a circular motion to Joey, meaning it was okay to resume rowing. He also used two hands gesturing in a push down motion to go slow and easy. Just then one of the oars touched the hull ever so slightly resulting in a faint clunk.

"Shit!" whispered Joey.

"Joey!" Lilley whispered back and Billie covered her mouth trying not to laugh.

Then there was a growling sound, and a dog ran to the edge of the water barking and running back and forth agitated as if guarding some king's treasure. It was impossible to tell what kind of dog it was. There was the odd glint from his eyes, reflecting the moonlight but the dog was incensed and now in the water up to his belly and creating a clamor that was clearly heard for quite a distance. The back door of a house opened, and the light from the open door revealed the silhouette of a person on the edge of a deck. The figure then quickly descended some steps on the side of the deck and in short order was at the edge of the lake tying to find where the dog was.

"Jake, be quiet!" But jake continued to bark stomach-deep in the water, wagging his tail and looking out to the lake. Then the man spotted the dog and the silhouette of the boat just a few yards offshore.

"Hey! Who's there?" the man yelled as if he meant business.

Thinking quickly, Don replied. "Sorry sir! We are just drift fishing out here for catfish. We will move on down the shoreline. Sorry for the commotion."

"Well, okay then. Sorry if my dog scared you but you should be careful fishing at night with no lights."

Relieved, Don replied again, "Yeah, you're right. We are going to head in now. Have a good night."

Don started the motor and turned the boat back toward town at a very slow speed until they were out of the man's line of vision. Then he switched on the lights and high-tailed it back to the boat launch. They tied up and sat there for a few minutes.

"Well, we know that's not going to work." Joey offered.

"Actually, that was kind of exciting," Lilley giggled and nudged Billie with her shoulder.

"Yeah, and almost funny, if you don't think about why we are doing this," said Billie.

"I got another idea," Don was scratching his chin, obviously scheming something. "When the dock is built, we will go up the coast from your place and then cross the lake and come at the Sinclair's from the north. I drove up past the Sinclair's today to see what was on the highway both north and south of them. There's a bait shop which is closed at night, and a vacant lot just north of the Sinclair's and then Pike Point. If we go north of Pike Point and then row around the point and south, there shouldn't be anyone or dogs around. Let's try it again tomorrow night."

"Sounds good," said Lilley. "Let's get Billie home before her parents issue a missing persons bulletin."

Billie laughed. "I actually told Mom what we were going to do tonight and as a matter of fact I told her the whole idea about our mission. She said that she had already sort of thought that Paul Sinclair could be behind the boat incident. She and Dad knew about Joey's broken arm and how Paul had caused that to happen…" She paused and looked at Joey. "And they know why Paul was after Joey. I feel responsible in a way." Billie looked down trying to find the right words.

"Aw, don't say that dear," Lilley interrupted. "We all know how you feel about Joey, and we know you wouldn't want anything bad to happen to him." Lilley put her arm around Billie and patted her back gently.

"That's just it," Billie responded. "We know it and my parents know it, but I need to make sure Paul knows it, and loud and clear. If he knows he doesn't have a chance with me, maybe he will back off. I am going to make sure that happens, the first opportunity I get!"

"Okay, we should plan out the next few days," suggested Don. "There might be a little fly in the ointment. The weather is supposed to turn crappy for the whole weekend. They are talking about rain, colder temperatures and some wind. It doesn't look like it's going to work out for what we have planned until later next week... Billie, when do you have to be at school??

"I check in on Tuesday and I'm there until Friday night." Billie answered.

"I want at least you, Joe and myself to be there when or if we find the evidence. When we present it, the more people we have testifying, the stronger our case. Your friend, Jug deserves justice and you guys do too, and I want to make sure that's exactly what happens. So, I'm thinking that we should plan to do the actual mission next Saturday and keep a close eye on the weather. If it looks bad for Saturday, we could do it Sunday or even move it ahead to Friday if Billie's back in time.

"I'll easily be back by 4 on Friday depending on who picks me up. I'm out of class by 2:30," said Billie.

Later that night, Joey was lying in bed and almost asleep as the train whistle sound he picked for his text ring blared and he quickly widened his eyes. He kept his phone plugged in, not more than a foot from his head on the nightstand and it was his lifeline to Billie.

"Hey," Joey texted.

"I just wanted to say good night. Is it okay to talk out loud? Can I phone you?"

"Sure," answered Joey. They hung up and Billie called right away. Joey had a much softer ringtone for an actual phone call so that it wouldn't wake people in the house. That way he could talk without any eavesdroppers.

"Hi," he answered.

"Hi," Billie replied. It is kind of sexy, isn't it?"

"You mean talking to each other while we are in bed? Yes, my thoughts exactly. A little taste of what's in our future, I hope."

"I want that more than I want anything else in the world, Joey. I want you in every way, if you know what I mean? But I don't want anything to ruin it for us, so we have to wait. I'm sorry Joey!"

"Don't be sorry. Why would I mind that you want us to be together forever? I have wanted that since the day I awkwardly asked to meet with you in art class last year."

"I will always remember that moment. You couldn't quite get the words out and I finished the sentence for you," Billie chuckled. "Obviously, I wanted that then too."

"I just don't want you to think I own you or anything but… I've come to realize that I'm not like most other guys. I can't seem to just play the field and basically try out other girls to see if they're the one for me. You are the one for me and I will do anything to make it forever!"

"I know that Joey. I am the same as you that way. I don't feel owned. I feel loved. We both know that, if for some grotesque reason I had to let you go, it would be because you wanted it and it would be for your happiness. But that's not going to happen because I know you love me too. I'll call you tomorrow. I love you so much! Good night Joey."

"I love you, more than I can really put into words! Good night Billie."

They both shut off their phones and rolled over in bed, as happy tears fell onto their pillow covers.

CHAPTER 12

Joey walked down to Little Beach around 8:30 in the morning. The breeze was noticeably cooler than yesterday, but the lake was still calm. He sat on the small dock crib with his sandaled feet in about 6 inches of water. They had taken so many rocks from the area that it was turning into an actual beach with sand. Maybe a nice little beach for Jessie to play in, Joey thought. The flat rock where he and Harriet used to sit was not surrounded with bigger boulders anymore, since most had been used to fill the cribs. Joey went over and sat on the rock. The morning sun, although weaker now, was beginning to warm it and it felt good on his butt, but his heart became flooded with memories of Harriet.

"Harriet, why did you have to go! I hope you forgive me! I hope you are happy and don't have any more pain…God, I miss you!" He drew up his knees and buried his face between them.

Joey wiped the tears and stood up thinking to himself. "People say I'm mature, and Billie and I have a mature relationship. Ha! Does a mature guy cry his eyes out over a stupid dog?"

He picked up a piece of rock and instead of skipping it out on the lake, he angrily threw it as hard as he could against the flat rock, and it broke in several pieces making little plops on the water's surface beside the partly finished dock.

Later that morning, Don and Joey finished the decking and installed the mooring cleats and the padded edging along the sides where it would make contact with a boat's hull. They stood back to admire their work.

"That looks awesome!" said Joey.

"Yeah, it does. We make a good team, I'd say," said Don, as he gave Joey a phony punch to the shoulder. "I'm going to bring my boat over later and tie it up on the south side where it's probably going to get fewer waves. Your mom and me are going to do a little fishing this afternoon."

"Oh, that's cool," Joey remarked. He paused but had been waiting to get something off his chest, "Do you think Mom and you might… you know… get together sometime?" Joey was surprised at himself for being so forward, but he didn't retract the question.

"You don't pull any punches, do you?" Don grinned. "There is no way of knowing what will happen in the future. I have just felt that I am ready for some company again, and your mom and I seem to get along so…who knows?"

"Just between you and me," Joey pulled closer to Don. "I think she likes you."

Joey realized there was a vacancy in the proverbial Burgess Motel, of course, but he really liked him. Any doubts about Don's ulterior intentions were slowly beginning to fade, the more they spent time together.

"I know you probably would have told me, but…any news about Jug?" asked Don.

"No, nothing yet," Joey replied. "It's been a week and he still hasn't woken up. That can't be good, I don't think."

Don looked out over the lake. "After Wendy's accident, I researched a little about comas. I guess part of me wanted to believe that she could hear me during her last few hours in hospital. It turns out that many people do report remembering things that people said while they were asleep. As to how long you can be in a coma and still recover, the reading I've done says after 2 to 4 weeks there is real risk of permanent disability of some kind. Some have been in coma for months and recovered almost completely though. In Jug's case it was likely a brain injury, so it depends on what part of the brain was injured. In my wife's case her cerebellum," Don reached and tapped the lower back of his skull, "and her brain stem were severely damaged and almost severed, so she would have been on life support… if she survived at all. The area around the brain stem is responsible for keeping your heart beating and your lungs breathing on their own. The cerebellum is more for balance and motor function so if it was just that, she might have had a chance and at worst been crippled, but she had other internal injuries too. I saw the mark on Jug's head…"

Joey interrupted, "Yeah, it looked like he got hit high on the left side of his forehead. He was probably looking up and then just turned his head when he saw the boat coming down on him. What can that affect?"

"I'm not a doctor, so I shouldn't give you any false hope, but I don't think that would be as serious. If he… *when* he recovers, he might just have some minor problems with personality or behavior. But, like I said, I'm not a doctor and it's been 3 years, so I've forgotten about a lot of this stuff. I didn't go into it in too much depth either because she didn't…" Don took a deep breath and raised his eyebrows as if he didn't want to finish that thought. "Well, let's get your mom and show her our handiwork."

"Okay, I'll go get her," Joey said eagerly.

That was the first real bit of emotion he'd seen from Don. He was obviously capable of really caring for someone. The problem would be getting over his first wife, Wendy. It seemed like he hadn't really let her go. Maybe you never do. He thought about Billie. What would he do if she was suddenly killed in a car accident?

"God why am I even thinking such terrible things! I'm not even old enough to drive and I'm thinking about spending my life with one person. That's got to be weird!"

Joey ran up to the house and brought Lilley back to see the dock. Pam and Jessie wanted to see too so they trailed after them once Jessie had her shoes on the right feet.

"Holy cow!" Lilley exclaimed. "You guys should go into the business. That's amazing!"

"Teamwork," Don said. "Joe's a good worker and learns fast."

"Yes, he does, and it looks like he had a good teacher," Lilley winked.

The two girls, running down the path, burst onto the scene and of course the first thing Jessie wanted to do was run to the end of the dock and back.

"Hey, be careful!" Lilley yelled.

"We could run and jump right out into the water and go swimming!" Jessie yelled back

"It's only a little over 3 feet deep at the end of the dock, Mom," said Joey.

"Well, she's barely over 4 feet and isn't the greatest swimmer yet. I guess this would be a good place for her to learn though."

"Yeah, and there's more beach now after they took the big rocks away," Pam added. The dock looks great, Don, Joey."

"Thank you. So, I was wondering, Pam, since you are the highest-ranking Burgess here, other than your mom," Don gestured in a thinking pose, fingering his chin. "If your mom is agreeable, would you consider allowing me to take her fishing this afternoon?"

Jessie, excitedly said, "Can I come? Can I…" Pam stopped her with a wave and a finger to her mouth shushing her.

"Well, what do you think, Joey, should we allow Mom to go out into the deep water with this handsome man here?" Pam had a flare for the dramatic and was eating this up.

Laughing, Lilley said, "Hey, don't I get say in this?"

Joey ignored her and looked at Pam, "I think as long as she lets you have the car to take Billie and me to the hospital to visit Jug, we could let her go for a while."

It was a light-hearted exchange in which Lilley finally conceded and admitted that it might be fun. Don said that he would love to have Jessie come along too if it was alright with Lilley and provided she wore a life jacket. In the end everyone was happy.

They all headed back up to the house for lunch, which consisted of hotdogs or tube steaks as Joey liked to call them. About 12:30 a text came in from Billie, and of course everyone laughed at the train whistle text notification that blared from Joey's phone.

"Hey Joey, Mom and Dad and I are going to the Sinclair's on Sunday for a barbeque. This fits with our plans. While I'm there I can get a photo of the pic with Paul in his boat."

"Perfect…" As he was one-finger texting, Joey thought about what she just said. Not long ago, if she had said she was going to Paul Sinclair's for supper he would have been jealous and angry. Now, he trusted the relationship and her completely. "Pam's gonna take us to the hospital to see Jug. Can you go? We could pick you up around 1:15."

"Yes, sounds good. See you then."

An hour later, Don had brought his boat over and tied it to the new dock at Little Beach. Lilley and Jessie were standing on the dock waiting, both carrying sweatshirts and Lilley had a small cooler with her. They climbed aboard and Don helped lift Jessie in and set her up in the bow seat.

"Your job is to look out for rocks, okay?" Don asked Jessie. "It's an important job," he added as he winked.

"Yessir, captain," Jessie replied. A surprisingly appropriate and funny response from a 6-year-old, which got a hearty laugh from Don and a teeter out of Lilley.

They headed north up the coastline trolling at not much more than an idle. Lilley was quite used to fishing in her younger days. She was Gramps' daughter, after all. Lilley had a couple strikes and was able to bring in a nice 2-pound smallmouth bass. It breached the surface several times, jumping about 2 feet above the surface. Smallmouth are known for putting up a tenacious fight. Don helped her by netting it and they decided to just do catch and release today, so he used his pliers to unhook the fish and gently saw it off to live another day.

"Okay, the score is one-nothing for you," Don said as he motioned with his eyes for Lilley to look at Jessie. She was sound asleep, with her mouth hanging open, laying on a boat pillow and extra life jacket. She was also wearing a life vest, which added to the cushioning.

The wind was starting to pick up out of the west. They were heading north so the offshore wind didn't bother their little boat, but there was starting to be a nip in the air. Don got a blanket out of a storage drawer under his seat and motioned again to Jessie. Lilley wound her line in and wrapped the blanket around Jessie tucking the corners under her body and her makeshift bed. Lilley and Don both put hoodies on, changed their lures to spoons and continued trolling up the coast. It was cool but not cold and Lilley was thoroughly enjoying being out on the lake with Don. This was the life she had envisioned with Hank, and for a brief period, it was like this.

"Don, this is great, thanks! I had forgotten how much I loved being out on the lake. The last few years have been just working, looking after kids and…" she literally couldn't find an appropriate word. She opened the cooler and handed Don a coke.

"It's okay Lilley, Joey told me about how life was for you guys before. It was sure not your fault that things were like the way they were. I'd say from my point of view, you did an amazing job with those kids. Joe just keeps surprising me by the things he says. He's just a teenager but he has remarkable wisdom for his age."

"Unfortunately, he has had to grow up too fast. He is remarkable but there is pain deep down. He feels it all the time. I can sense it. I know he tries to make sure it doesn't flare up, which, in itself, is quite a mature thing to do. I hope it goes smooth for him so that it never boils over. That's why Billie has been such a great influence on him. As soon as he discovered her, he started becoming a much happier, well-adjusted guy."

"Whoa!" Don yelled, put the engine in neutral and stood up. "Reel in quick, Lilley, I'm gonna need your help with this one.

Don fought to keep the line as taught as possible but then was forced to let the line out. The drag on his reel was clicking and he turned it tighter, but the line still continued to run out.

"Do you know what?" Don was almost yelling now. "I've been coming up here for years and I've never caught a salmon or a lake trout, but I think I've got one on the line!" Don was trying to keep the line from pulling out, but the bale wouldn't hold it and he was afraid that his 20-pound test line was going to snap.

"Do you know how to drive, Lilley"

"Yeah sure," she responded quickly.

"Okay, let's switch places …right…now!" They switched seats and Don continued fighting the fish and looking back at Lilley. "Okay, this is an old trick I learned from my dad…"

"I'm already doing it," Lilley said as she began a slow turn in the direction of the fish."

"Ha, oh yeah, I guess you had a fisherman Dad too. Great job! Okay, you know what to do then."

Lilley headed toward the fish and each time Don's line became dangerously taught, she hit the throttle a little to give his line some slack. By doing this Don was able to make some ground and wind the line in bit by bit.

With the commotion and Don's gyrations, the boat pitched side to side and Jess woke and sat up.

"What's going on! Wow, you got a big fish on?" Jessie asked wide-eyed.

"Jess, you sit still, okay and if Don's line comes your way you just duck," Lilley instructed.

"Jessie clapped her hands, "OOO, this is exciting!" She followed Don's line and watched on eagerly. "How big is it, Don?"

"Not sure, sweetie but if it's a lake trout, we may not be able to get it in the boat," answered Don, fighting with his reel vigorously. "Lake trout can go over 70 pounds even up to 100, but I've never caught one…especially on fishing line meant for no more than a good-sized pickerel. And if you add the water that it will bring along it could weigh more than that."

The spool on Don's spinning reel was gradually filling up with more mono filament, meaning the fish was getting closer and closer. Then the line went limp.

"Lille, hit reverse, quick!" She quickly found the shifter on the handle and set it back to the rear position and boat slowed and began backing up.

"This thing is smart!" Don managed to say as he wound the reel in as fast as he could. "It's swimming at us to get slack and then it's going to…"

With the words not even out of his mouth the silvery body of a huge lake trout breached four feet in the air and shook its head furiously, about two boat lengths away, just as Don was able to catch up and pull the line tight. It was still on, and now the original problem was back. The bale started whining and the fish was once again pulling.

"Woohoo! Did you see that!" Jessie shouted. "That was like a shark or something!"

Lilley instinctively knew to throw the motor back into forward and follow the fish and Don responded by taking in the slack again.

"It wasn't a shark, but it had to be almost 4 feet long!" Don said excitedly. "I'm taking you guys fishing more often. This is the most fun I've had in years!"

Gradually the pull of the fish began to weaken as the great trout tired. After another 10 more minutes of regaining the line, the fish was getting within just a few feet of the boat. Lilley put the motor in neutral and grabbed the net. Then they saw it, and it was gigantic!

"Geez, we're gonna need a bigger net!" Lilley exclaimed.

"It should fit in there curled up, but there's no way to lift that fish up into the boat. He's pretty tired now. Take the pole, Lilley, and keep it tight while I grab my pliers.

The trout was alongside the boat now, and it was every bit of 4 feet in length. Don kneeled down in the boat and scooped the net under the fish from its tail toward the head and its body curled just enough to fit into the mesh. He lifted the head out of the water using the net as a lever against the gunwale. The fish was spent of all energy and did not resist. Don reached into the mouth following the line and found the treble hook totally bent with only one barbed point left anchored into the corner of its mouth. Don quickly removed the hook with his pliers and Lilley wound up the remaining line and set the pole down.

"What do you want me to do, Don?" Lilley asked.

"Get your phone out and ready to take a picture and go to the seat in front of Jessie."

Lilley moved as smoothly as she could toward the bow trying not to cause the boat to rock.

"I gotta do this fast. If this big fella revives too soon, we're in trouble."

With all his strength he pulled up, hanging on to the hoop of the net and brought the giant trout over the gunwale and onto the floor of the boat.

"Okay, Lilley, get ready!"

Lilley readied her phone.

As if lifting a weight in the clean and jerk competition he hoisted the fish on to his lap. He tried to stand up with it but it was just too heavy, so he held the fish on his lap, the head at the right gunwale and the tale touching the left gunwale. Then he looked, up cradling the fish and smiled.

"Okay, now!"

As soon as he said that, the fish began to contract its body. The fish was turning into more of a green color making the spots show up vividly and its yellowish belly was now exposed. Don knew he had little time, so he quickly turned his body toward the gunwale while the girls moved to the opposite side of the boat as counterweights. He heaved the trout over the edge and back into the water. The fish was back in its domain, and it sat partially submerged and level with its long snout pointed out from the boat. Don held the tail as the gill covers flapped pumping water through the gill filaments.

"Hey! Why are you putting it back in the water?" Jessie yelled. "Aren't we going to take it home to show Joey and Pam…or eat it?"

On his knees, still hanging on to its tail, waiting for the trout to fully revive, Don turned to Jessie. "I can't do it sweetie. Do you think it would be okay to kill such a beautiful animal when we really don't need it to live?"

"I guess not," she answered slowly.

"There are a lot of poorer people up the coast from here on the reserve that would use every bit of a fish like this and live on it for days. Besides this is a female and it can have lots of babies."

"How do you know?" asked Jessie curiously.

"Yeah, how **do** you know?" repeated Lilley, raising her eyebrows comically.

"Ha…well it's not what you guys are thinking. A female has a smaller more rounded mouth. A male has a longer mouth, and some are slightly hooked like pictures you may have seen of salmon out west or the arctic char. Salmon and trout are sort of related."

They watched as Don released the tail and it slowly slithered back into the deep black abyss.

"Wow, that was just amazing!" said Lilley. Then she and Don stood up and high fived each other with a little hug.

"Then Jessie, never wanting to be left out, piped up, "Me too, me too!" So, they all stood up again and had a big group hug.

"Let's see that photo!" said Don in anticipation.

Lilley pointed her phone to each of them in turn.

"Holy smokes, that was a great fish. You got to email that to me so I can print a trophy photo."

"You know, Don, most guys would have taken that fish home to brag about it or had it stuffed and mounted over their fireplace.

"Well, I guess I'm not like that, I don't know,"

"No, you're not," Lilley answered as she nodded with a knowing smile.

During the time it took to land the lake trout, they had drifted almost out to the middle of the lake, and it was a choppy ride back to the dock, but they were all smiles and thrilled with their little adventure.

Pam and Joey arrived at Billie's house and Billie was waiting on the front steps as the old blue chevy rolled up the laneway with its characteristic tick. The valves were likely going, and the lifter tick was louder every month. Major engine repair just wasn't an option for Lilley at this point in time.

Billie jumped up and ran over to the car and Joey got out to let her slide into the middle. This was the best arrangement for Joey's longer legs.

"Hey, Billie," Pam said.

"Hey, Pam, thanks for taking me," Billie answered.

"It's not like I could take Joey somewhere without you, is it?" Pam joked. "You guys seem pretty tight, and I'm glad for both of you. Joey tells me that you might be interested in nursing some day?"

Billie turned and smiled at Joey and gave him a quick kiss on his cheek.

"Yeah, maybe, I'm not a hundred percent sure of anything yet but I am interested in that area for sure."

Joey sat back and let the two of them get to know each other. He was satisfied just sitting beside Billie with his arm around her on the back of the seat.

Pam continued, "I'm sure everybody knows by now that I was in a bit of trouble. It wasn't just trouble with the law. I had serious physical and mental problems and if it weren't for caring nurses and other people like that, I'm not sure where I'd be right now, so it's great that you are thinking about that line of work."

"Thanks, it's only the blood and guts part of biology that kind of bothers me but I'm more interested in how organs and other things work. I guess I should be a brain surgeon because there's not as much blood."

"You could always teach biology," Pam suggested.

"Yeah, that could work too…still young enough to change directions."

"For sure…

The two of them talked all the way to the hospital and Joey didn't get a word in edgewise. He made a mental note, "Do not bring Pam when I want to talk to Billie." But he was happy that they hit it off so well.

The visit with Jug was the same as always. He confirmed that the mark on Jug's head was on the upper left forehead but didn't want to talk about possible long-term injuries with Ellen. She was still looking rough, and it was easy to tell that she wasn't eating. When she saw Pam, she lit up and came over to hug her and exchange pleasantries. In that instance Joey could see flashes of Ellen's old bubbly nature, but the distress quickly returned to her face. Right now, her life revolved around her seemingly lifeless son lying beside her.

Joey and Billie shared in more detail, the plans they had for making a case against Paul Sinclair. While Ellen was in favor of punishing whoever had done this to her son, because of her experience as a legal assistant, she also knew that to really proceed with anything formally there would be stalling and mountains of legalize jargon and paperwork that would be produced.

"You guys should know that with Mark Sinclair's money and influence, actually getting him punished will be a long process. I've been thinking about it a little since you first mentioned that you thought it might be him. He's a minor, 15, think. They will jail him in juvenile court if he is found guilty if you can get the charges trumped up and prove intent but…I have a better idea. It might hit the Sinclair's where it hurts the most…not that it will help Josh, but…"

Joey pulled up the only other chair and Billie sat on his knee and Pam sat on the edge of the other vacant bed. "We are listening…" said Joey.

"Well, the most common punishment dished out around here for minors, seems to be restitution."

Joey looked a little lost, "What's that? Is that like where you work your sentence off?"

"Yes, answered Ellen, "but it doesn't have to be labor. It could be payment of money or other things. I think you need to present your case to someone who would know exactly what the charges against him are likely to be. Someone like…Constable Roberts, down at the police station."

"I know that name," Joey spoke up.

"You should," said Pam. "He is the one that came to arrest me. He's actually a really nice guy. If I was a little order, I… Anyway, he would listen, I'm sure. He would legally want to know the name and everything, but you might be able to put it to him in a hypothetical way."

"So, anyway," Ellen continued. "Once Paul Sinclair and his dad know what kind of trouble Paul is in and he knows you can prove it, then you got him. Why take it to court and let them chat about it for a couple years to figure out what to charge him with? Then he gets sentenced and when he gets out, he still wants to get even, or more hate has grown inside him to the point that he might be capable of more serious things against you. If Mark Sinclair is presented with proof that his son is guilty, he will want to buy you with hush money.

Evil minds just think that way. They think they can pay their way out of trouble. This way, Paul gets reprimanded by his family and likely cut off from some of the perks of being a Sinclair. Mark would likely keep close tabs on Paul, too, to make sure he doesn't go after you and stain the Sinclair name anymore. Best of all, you and Josh would receive some kind of compensation immediately, just to keep your mouth shut about what happened. Do you think you could do that…I mean bring your evidence to the cops and find out the charges?"

"Yes, I do…and I know just the man that would go with me." Joey turned and looked at Billie and she turned and searched Joey's eyes. Simultaneously they both said, "Don."

On the way out of the hospital, they noticed that the gift shop was open. Joey, rather reluctantly followed Billie in.

Pam continued toward the parking lot, "Take your time guys, I'm going for a walk for a few minutes."

"You should get Jug something for when he wakes up," Billie suggested.

"That's a good idea," Joey admitted.

They looked around for a while, each holding different things up and the other nodding approval or shaking their heads. Joey noticed that Billie was looking at a silver colored…he couldn't quite make out what it was. Then a couple minutes later, as he was about to show Billie a talking plastic perch mounted on a wooden plaque he turned and noticed she'd gone back to the same display and pulled, what looked like the same little box out. She was trying on a ring. It was a beautiful silver ring. The mount was a rendering of two fish jumping out of the water and crisscrossing in mid-air. She quickly put it away when she saw Joey turn her way and they decided on the plastic fish. It was the goofiest thing they had seen and was so Jug that it made them laugh to look at it. Every time someone would walk in front of it or wave your hand it would wiggle and say…" Mm, that was a good worm… anymore?" Then, "I'm Captain Hook, take me to your leader." And worst of all, "Smells fishy in here."

They bought the crazy fish and were walking out toward the car in the parking lot when Joey, fishing around in his pockets, said, "Oops, I must have left my 5-dollar bill on the counter. You go ahead. I'll be right back." Joey took off running back to the glass doors of the hospital.

Just inside he turned to make sure Billie wasn't looking and snuck back to the gift shop. He brought the ring over to the volunteer lady. On closer inspection, he noticed that they weren't fish, but dolphins, however it was very nice just the same.

"Would this be for the young lady that was with you?" the volunteer, Marjorie, asked.

"Pretty obvious, right?" Joey admitted and she smiled.

"It's a beautiful ring… It's forty dollars."

"Ouch, forty? I only have a twenty left. I'll think of something else…thanks… Marjorie…right?" Joey answered looking at her name pinned to her volunteer smock.

"Yep, that's me. You are Josh Parker's friend, aren't you?" Joey nodded and turned around. "He's quite the talk of the town. Everyone is pulling for him. I see you and your mom all the time. Listen…that pretty little thing is Willie and Sarah's daughter, and you don't wanna lose that one! I'll make you a deal. Give my $20 now and give me the other $20 the next time you're in. I won't charge any tax and you can walk out with the ring right now."

"Really, wow! I appreciate that so much! She's going away, Monday to school and…"

"Smart son…Give her a little bit of you to look at every time she looks down at her hand…a bit of a romantic, aren't you? The world needs more of you!"

Back at the house Lilley and Don were sitting at the kitchen table drinking coffee and enjoying a spirited conversation about their adventure on the lake. Jessie had decided that the best way to be the center of attention would be to sit on Don's knee. Don did not object, in fact, he was getting quite attached to her and found her antics and unabridged comments quite hilarious.

Joey and Pam pulled up the drive and heard the laughter as they approached the door, raising their eyebrows at each other. As they entered the room, they greeted them appropriately, but both felt a twinge of apprehension as they walked to the back hallway.

As Joey turned to go to his room, Pam whispered, "Hey, Joe, come here for a minute." They went into Pam's room. Pam sat on the chair at the small desk opposite the bunk and Joey sat on the lower bunk's mattrass. "Do you think Don is getting a little aggressive? I mean, hasn't it been just over a week since they met?"

"Yeah, I know what you mean. When we came in, I almost felt like telling him that was Dad's seat. With Jessie bouncing on his knee like that, it was kind of tough for me. There's still a part of me that wants dad back but…"

Pam interrupted, "Well, yeah that's what I was thinking too. It's too soon, I think. I don't want to write off Dad yet, but…" She teared up thinking about the way it used to be.

"Pam, it's not the way it was, and it will never be. You had more time with Dad, and I guess you have a lot more of the good memories than I do. You knew him about three years longer than me, and those were his good days…Dad is not coming back. It's been hard to realize that but…he's really not sorry for anything, Pam. He has shown no interest in coming back and patching things up with Mom…or us. It's just over!" Joey teared up now too.

Pam moved over to the bunk and sat with Joey putting her arms around him. "I guess you're right, little bro. I guess we're like Daddy orphans, or something. Maybe we should be happy for Mom…even if it's just some temporary adult male company."

"Yeah, but…" Joey stood up quickly. "I get the bathroom first!" He darted for the door as Pam grabbed his t-shirt, almost ripping it off.

"Hey, you little creep!" she yelled and then laughed, falling back on the bed.

Joey and Pam joined the group in the kitchen and before long began sharing Ellen's idea about the plan against Paul Sinclair.

"That's exactly what I was thinking!" Said Don. "It's not like baiting Mark Sinclair into blackmail at all. We would just be providing him with a choice. For me the choice would be to accept our terms or go to court. He would see the court idea as very harmful to him and his business relations, especially when we go to the press claiming we have proof. I hope that doesn't mean I have a devious mind." Don chuckled.

Pam asked, "Why don't we do it tomorrow? I mean…go to Constable Roberts with the hypothetical scenario."

"I'm surprised you would want to see him again so soon," Lilley injected.

"Please, Mom. He is hot! But he is nice too." Laughs were all around and a groan from Jess made Pam stick her tongue out…then more laughs.

"I would rather have the proof in hand first," said Don. "If we come back empty from our little mission, all could be lost."

"I don't think so," Pam said quickly. "I think the Sinclair's, if they're as underhanded as you say, would jump at trying to smooth this over. By now, they likely know it was Paul, right? So, all you would have to do is tell them you have proof, and they would jump to have it just go away. So, if we have the proof or not, I think we should still take the same tact."

"Okay, I don't have the most devious mind here, tonight," Don laughed. "If you think they know it was Paul that could mean they looked for evidence or cleaned it up already. Let's hope they didn't think of looking under the boat."

Joey had left the conversation a couple minutes ago and was thinking of his friend, Jug, lying helpless in a hospital room. He stood up and announced that he was going to bed.

"Just a minute, Joey," Lilley said.

Joey sat back down.

"Something is bugging you. Do you not like the plan we are discussing?"

"The plan is fine. I don't care how we do it, if it works, and it sounds like it will. When we get so into the plan to crucify Paul Sinclair, it makes me think of why we are doing this. It's just kind of depressing when you think of a guy my age, lying in a hospital not able to wake up."

"Thanks for the wake-up call, Joe," Don said, nodding his head. "We all need to make Jug our motivation and not just vindictiveness like in my case. I've been so caught up in the revenge angle that sometimes I forget there is a young man fighting for his life that needs us."

Without saying anything more, Don stretched his hands out on the table beckoning with his fingers. Everyone joined their hands, while Jess grabbed Don's arm to be included. Then Don spoke up. "Let's not forget we are doing this for Jug."

"For Jug!" Joey shouted, and everyone repeated it enthusiastically.

"I think that Billie should be in on all our discussions," Joey said. "Her family is also affected by this…and so is she. I will text her about what we discussed here. Good night everybody."

"Well, good night, Joey," said Don. "I will take you fishing up the west side of the lake too some time."

"That would be nice," Joey answered wondering about the quick shift in conversation. Then he turned and began walking toward the hallway and gave a little kiss to a very sleepy Jessie slumped in Pam's arms.

"Of course, there is no guarantee we would catch another 75-pound lake trout…" continued Don.

Joey was already in the hallway and then quickly reemerged. "What? Another 75-pound lake trout? Another? Mom, what's he talking about?"

Lilley reached for the phone and flicked it a few times to find photos and stabbed the pic. She showed it to Pam first.

"Good God! I'm never going swimming in that lake again!"

"Let me see!" Joey pleaded. But before he could get a look, Don grabbed the phone away from Pam.

"Yup, that was some nice fish!" Don said in dramatic southern drawl, then laughed and held the phone up for Joey.

"Sorry, Mom, but Pam's right…Jeez! It looks like a giant speckled trout. I've only seen pictures of these in the paper once in a while. And you released it?"

"Yes, we did," responded Don, ready to defend his reasons.

"Thank you, for that," Joey said, completely surprising Don.

"What a beautiful fish. and she still lives! That's awesome!"

"Okay, Joe, there's two more things you have surprised me with. First I thought for sure you would be ticked that I didn't bring it home and second…you knew it was a female?"

"Sure, smaller mouth than a male," Joey uttered nonchalantly then turned and walked back to the hallway.

"I will call you tomorrow," Don called after Joey. We will go see Constable Roberts in the morning. That way Billie can go too, before she heads off to school on Tuesday.

The gathering broke up for the night. Don handed a very asleep Jessie to Pam and the kids all headed for their respective beds.

Don walked over and gave Lilley a little kiss on the cheek. "Thanks, Lill, I had a fantastic time out there with you and Jessie!"

"Thank you! I did too, but you made all this happen." She walked him to the door. "My kids are very thankful for your being here and for all you have done for us. And…did you just call me 'Lill'?"

"I guess I did. Sorry, if I was a little too…"

"No, it's fine. It's nice, actually. My dad used to call me that." Lilley's eyes were a little glassy.

Don saw that he had touched a nerve and stepped toward her and have her a warm hug. Then he turned for the door. "Sleep well. I'll see you in the morning."

Joey was quietly chatting away with Billie and filled her in on tonight's discussion. They decided that hearing each other's' voices was so much better than texting. They laughed as they decided that they were actually going to bed together.

"Joey, you sound really tired, so I'll say goodnight now. I love you!"

"I love you too. I'm not really that tired." Joey answered groggily. "I just start thinking about how everything is working out." He paused… "It would be so cool…if…we…prove…for Jug…I…" Then there was a long silence…

Billie giggled softly, kissed her phone and turned it off.

CHAPTER 13

The last "free" Monday before another long year of school and Joey was not looking forward to it in the least. School was tolerable when Billie was there but as of tomorrow, she was off to Elmvale, and the school week would be just a countdown to the weekend for Joey. Sarah had promised to bring Billie home every weekend so that Billie would agree willingly to attend the private school. In the end, the benefits would outweigh the negatives and the courses she was to take would likely set her up for a future in biology as either a health care provider or possibly a teacher. Today though, Billie was free to spend her time with Joey and there was some important business to do.

Joey was sitting having cereal at the kitchen table when he heard a car drive up the lane. Thinking it was Don arriving to pick Pam and him up for today's session with Constable Roberts, he quickly finished and put his bowl in the sink to wash out. Looking out the kitchen window he noticed that it wasn't the black pickup truck he expected. Instead, a small white car was parked in the lane. Then, the unmistakably rotund figure of Dr. Norman stepped out, shoving the car door shut with one hand and carrying a square box in the other. Joey went out to meet him a few steps from the side porch, invited him in and they sat at the table.

"I have something important for you and your family, Joe." Dr. Norman announced with a sober expression.

"I think I might know what it is," Joey answered. "I'll get the rest of the family out here…excuse me for a second."

Joey hustled back into the hallway and summoned his mom, Jessie and Pam. A couple of minutes later they were all sitting around the kitchen table in various states of awakeness with Dr. Norman at the head, his hand tapping the top of a cardboard box about one foot square.

"That was quick," said Lilley. "You didn't have to personally deliver it."

"It's the least I can do for you and your kids, Lilley."

Satisfied they were all present Dr. Norman presented the box to Lilley, who then passed it over to Joey. Joey slowly opened the box shoved the shredded newspaper aside and pulled out a beautiful oak box. On the side was a rectangular metal shield with an engraving that read, "Harriet – Our special Angel – loved and loving". Joey read the inscription out loud, set the wooden box containing Harriet's ashes on the table and stood up. He walked to the other end of the table and held his hand out to Dr. Norman. The old doctor took it in his massive right hand and shook it.

"Thank you, sir. This means a lot to me!"

"You are welcome, son. I'm sorry for your loss."

Without another word Joey walked out the door, stopping it from slamming shut, and walked toward the path leading to Little Beach. The burning in his throat and the stinging in his eyes, all too familiar in the past few months, started once more.

"I'm sorry, Dr. Norman, er…Grant. He's pretty emotional. They had a pretty strong bond those too."

"No need to apologize, Lilley. I hope that this brings some closure." He stood up. Have a great day."

Jessie was sitting on Lilley's lap as Grant exited the kitchen. All three girls sat there staring at the box with tear-filled eyes…the box… the pitiful surrogate of a beautiful spirit. They knew that was how Joey saw it and how much he wanted her back in his life.

Joey was not in the best of moods now. He had no bitterness for anyone in particular, just sadness again for his recent losses and the imminent absence of Billie on weekdays. He realized that Little Beach was the wrong place to go because of the flashbacks he got of a playful, happy Bernese Mountain Dog, splashing and chasing minnows there. He slowly turned and walked back toward the house thinking about the immediate future, looking for some positivity in the scenario before him. There was the new cell phone and the promise of "going to bed" with Billie each night. They had devised a plan. If one called the other, then the coast was clear to talk. If they texted there was someone within earshot or one of them was too tired and needed to sleep. He was also, no longer worried that Paul Sinclair was going to the same school as Billie. His confidence in Billie's feelings for him was as strong as ever. He heard Don's truck drive up the laneway and he quickened his pace. When he got there, Pam was already in the front seat talking to Don, so he slipped into the back seat of the crew cab.

They swung by Billie's place and headed for the Katunga County Sherriff's Office, William's Glen Division. Don had arranged to meet Constable Roberts at 10 am and they arrived a couple minutes early. The foursome led my Don and Pam with Joey and Billie trailing hand in hand. They walked up the sidewalk beside the parking lot toward a rather unassuming, one story brick building that sprawled for what looked like a few hundred feet like a strip mall. There was a green sign on the corner of the building labeled "Katunga County Public Safety Building", and then under that a smaller white sign with an arrow pointing to the right that read, "Sherriff's Office". This was the industrial part of town, and all the buildings were decidedly lacking in character and designed purely for function. Finding the Sherriff's Office door they entered and walked up to the counter, where a shorter, rather rotund female officer was placing a file into a file cabinet.

"Can I help you guys?" she asked cheerfully, sporting a name tag labeled, Officer Jenkins.

Don spoke up, "Yes, we have an appointment to see Constable Roberts at 10."

Officer Jenkins picked up a clipboard from the counter and after a quick perusal replied, "Yes, Don Archer?"

"Yes, that's me," Don answered.

She wrote down the names of the other three on the page on the clipboard.

"Okay, come on back here with me." She lifted a hinged portion of the counter and directed them into a glass encased office room. "I'll grab a couple more chairs. Just so you know Constable Roberts is now Detective Roberts as of a couple weeks ago." She pointed to the sign on the door and set the clipboard down on the desk. She left briefly and slid a couple more chairs into the room. "He won't be long, just make yourselves comfortable." Then she left closing the door on her way out.

"Wow, Detective Roberts!" Pam said in an admiring tone. "He's pretty young to be a detective."

Joey injected, "Hey, Pam, don't forget why we are here." They all laughed.

"I won't swoon…too much," Pam said raising her eyebrows and causing more laughing.

Detective Roberts entered closing the door behind him, shaking everyone's hand as he introduced himself. He paused ever so slightly as he shook Pam's hand and made a point of catching her eye. He was a tall, good-looking man, rather trim for a county cop, especially men with desk jobs. He had a black wave of hair in front, reminiscent of superman, Pam thought. His blue eyes sparkled when he smiled. Then he sat down behind his desk to listen to the reason why they had come.

"Wow, Pam, you have certainly cleaned yourself up! I knew there was a pretty girl underneath that costume I saw you in a few months back."

"Thanks, I guess people change when they see what could happen when they are on the wrong path." Pam suggested, maintaining eye contact with him and slightly blushing.

"Well, I wish that was true, but the sad fact is that most don't. You are a wonderful exception, and it is great to see. But…okay, what brings all you people here?"

Don decided to open the conversation on their behalf. "We are here to present a scenario, and we would like your opinion as a…" Don looked at the triangular name plate in front of him on the desk, "law enforcement, slash criminal investigations detective. We want to present you with a hypothetical situation involving a couple boats and an underaged perpetrator."

"Okay, wait right there. I think I know the case you are talking about. You're the other kid that was in the boat, aren't you?" Constable Roberts pointed a finger at Joey nodding suspiciously. "You know I cannot discuss details about an ongoing investigation, right? Wait a minute," now he looked over at Don. "You said your name is Don. Is that as in Don Archer? Now I am putting the pieces together and why you wanted to see me."

Don nodded with a grimace.

"I was about to call you today. You left your number with the officer that night, you rescued the two boys and claim to have witnessed the accident."

"Well, at least you have those facts straight," Don admitted.

"Well, do you have something to tell me about the accident? You might as well tell me your side of things while you're here. Are these other three privy to the information?"

"Yes, they are, and that was no accident. There is a history, a documented history of aggression on behalf of the suspect toward Joey, here. I can bring in another witness of a previous occurrence causing bodily harm…a broken arm to be exact."

Billie spoke up and Don winced, "My dad saw Paul, I mean the suspect chasing Joey," she put her hand on Joey's arm, "and causing him to break his arm."

"Is that true, son?" Roberts peered over at Joey.

Joey answered with a terse, "Yes sir."

"Okay, I'm getting a pretty good idea about why you guys are here. Billie, your last name is Magee?" He glanced over the clipboard filled out earlier. "You aren't related to Willie Magee are you?"

"That's my dad," Billie pressed her lips.

"Well, the plot thickens now doesn't it," Roberts emitted a stifled chuckle. "How are you sure that this was no accident other than the history between the two as witnessed by Willie Magee?

"I was tying my boat up at the town ramp, when I heard a power boat. I knew right away it was a Donzi because the sound is distinctive with the through-hull exhaust."

"I know what you mean," Roberts agreed.

Don continued, "Then I looked up and saw it heading east about 500 yards away at about half throttle. I also saw the rowboat the boys were in, to my left, closer to the western shore. Then the yellow-sided Donzi turned left sharply and headed back toward the smaller boat. The Donzi driver gunned the throttle and it looked like it was probably going 60 mph toward the boys. At the last second, it veered left, but it turned too late catching the boys' boat with its rear end. I could hear the sound and the large splash as the rowboat was flipped from the impact. Then the Donzi high-tailed it at top speed north up the lake. That's when I decided to go to the aid of the boys."

"Okay, the rescue part and head trauma to Josh Parker is well documented," said Roberts. "I hesitate to ask but who do you think the guilty part is…Paul who?

Billie and Joey leaned ahead in their seats, about to answer, when Pam held up her hand in a stop gesture and said, "No!" then there was a brief pause.

"So, Pam, I'm sure there is method behind your madness?" Roberts raised one eyebrow.

Pam stood up and paced the room, "If we tell you who we think it is and talk about this specific incident…one that you are currently investigating you can't give us any other information about it can you?"

"Not really," Roberts shook his head.

"So, can we talk about this in different terms? Let's say it was a car that was driven at someone to scare them, then swerved and inadvertently hit the person. If the driver of the car was a minor, what charges could be brought against him and if found guilty what penalties might he receive?"

"Have you ever thought of a future in law, Pam?" Roberts half joked. "You are right I can't give you information on this case but since Don and Billie here have given me information that will help me in my investigation, I might be able to help you with a hypothetical situation. I take it you just want to know, hypothetically, what a certain young man might be faced with if convicted."

"Let's say the young man was 15 years-old," Don winked at Pam.

"There are a number of possible outcomes. There are three degrees of assault in this state. The most serious cases are the ones where you can prove intent. In this ... hypothetical case. That may be fairly easy to prove but not guaranteed. The most egregious situation is one with intent that causes bodily injury by use of a deadly weapon. I'm sure that a boat, or should I say a vehicle, clearing his throat, used as a weapon in an assault charge would classify as deadly. At the very least a charge of careless operation of a vehicle could be made. As far as punishment, even a juvenile of 15 can be tried as an adult if it is serious enough. That of course, would bring about a more severe sentence. Family court is used to decide these cases.

In my humble opinion using the scenario you presented, on conviction, I think there could be jail time in a juvenile detention center, a fine of some kind or possibly community restitution. But of course, the worst thing for the accused family would be the shame. Although a minor's name cannot be publicized in the media, this is a small town, and the news will spread quicker by mouth than any newspaper. There is another thing that would trump the charges and the resulting conviction of course..."

Don interrupted, "It depends on how Josh makes out." Don didn't want Joey or Billie thinking about possible manslaughter charges just yet. "Thanks, Detective we appreciate the education very much."

"Are you married?" Pam blurted out causing a momentary freeze in the room.

"Jeez, Pam!" Joey, embarrassed.

"It's okay…No… 27 years old and still no blushing bride."

"Come on," Joey reached and grabbed Pam's hand and led her out of the office while Billie turned and grinned at Don and Detective Roberts who were both chuckling and Don gave Billie a knowing wink.

On the way back in the truck they discussed the results of the meeting.

"Okay," Pam started. "We didn't give him Paul's name, but he knows it's a Donzi and he knows Billie's dad can give background. You need to get to your dad, so that he doesn't give him Paul's name." she looked over the seat at Billie.

"She's right," Don agreed. "To really get the most out of the Sinclairs we need the blackmail factor to work."

Later at supper, Billie explained the situation to her parents, and they agreed to not divulge anything to Detective Roberts.

Lilley invited Don for supper and Don agreed. They had a lively dinner with laughter, silliness and Joey couldn't help thinking that this was like a real family. He wanted to invite Billie, but they agreed that it was better that she spent her last meal with her family before heading to Elmvale tomorrow afternoon. After everyone cleared the dishes and helped clean up Don asked everyone to sit down at the table again because he wanted to say something.

Lilley was still standing at the sink and Joey, Pam and Jessie took seats facing Don who was standing by Lilley facing the table. "Okay, I feel like I'm on one of those talent shows, because I need three 'yesses. I wanted to thank your mom for inviting me here…again! You all have been so good to me and made me your friend and I really like all you guys. That's why I need your opinion about something."

Pam spoke up, "Wait a minute. You are thanking us? What about the rescue, the cell phones, the dock and driving us around and playing detective with us? We are the ones that thank you…So unless your request is outrageous, I'm pretty sure you'll get 3 yesses."

"Alright, here goes…" Lilley turned around to face the kids too, leaning her back on the counter. "I would like to take your mom out to dinner, to a nice restaurant." He winced awaiting the verdict.

"A date? You wanna take mommy on a date?" Jessie shrieked. "I say yes!" She stood up waved her hand in the air bouncing on her toes, like she was in school and asking to teacher to go to the washroom.

"Absolutely yes from me," Pam said, also raising her hand.

Joey looked at his mom who was shrugging her shoulders as if to say that her fate was in his hands. Joey raised his hand and smiled, "Of course, Don!"

"Once again I get no say in the matter?" Lilley said, putting on a serious tone. The three kids quieted down, waiting for her response. She turned and faced Don, "Thank you, Don. I really do need some grown-up time. I accept!"

The kids cheered and Lilley and Don had a short hug.

Later Joey was "going to bed with Billie" on his phone. They were talking, not texting because tomorrow would be the start of a new chapter in their relationship. One of being apart and going to separate schools, no meeting, no walking home after school and for Joey not even having Jug, his friend, to walk home with.

"Hey Joey, Mom wants to know if you would like to come with us tomorrow and get me settled into the school dorm."

"Of course, I would, but how come you didn't ask me?"

"I was going to dummy, but Mom asked me, and I thought you would like to know that my parents like you being part of my life."

"Oh, believe me, I do! Your family is sure growing on me."

"I love your family too, Joey."

"Hey, Don asked Mom on a date tonight. Well, actually, he asked us if he could take her on a date."

"Aw, that's so sweet!" Billie answered. "I'll bet your mom was blushing!"

"Yeah, you might say that. What time do you want me at your place tomorrow. I got two lawns to do in the morning."

"We are leaving around 3pm. Do your lawns and we'll pick you up about 3:05 if that works?

"Yeah, great…good night…love you"

"Love you too…don't ever change, Joey!"

Joey could hear her emotion. "I won't. The same goes for you."

"You got it," she replied and ended the conversation.

CHAPTER 14

Joey finished his lawn maintenance duties and was showered and ready to go by 2 pm. He got his little ring box out and put it on the kitchen table. Lilley was at work at the Old General Store and Pam and Jessie were down at Little Beach trying to catch, or more likely, terrifying crayfish. Joey found some colorful wrapping paper in Lilley's sewing table/desk and wrapped up the little box and finished it off with a thin red ribbon made into curls like Lilley had shown him last Christmas.

Last Christmas…it seemed like a lifetime ago. So much had changed. They were not all bad changes but true to form, Joey seemed to dwell on the negative. His favorite person in the world, Gramps, was gone. His sweet companion, Harriett was gone. His lifetime friend, Jug was lying in a coma in hospital. Billie was going away to live in another town so he couldn't see her every day.

"Okay," Joey thought, "let's start thinking about all the good things. I can talk to Billie every day, and it isn't long distance to Montrose. Paul Sinclair won't be at school to push me around. Both Mom and I have a new friend and ally in Don Archer. Pam was back and was not only a sister but had somehow become a friend and confidante.

Pam and Jessie returned from their little outing and were thirsty, so they grabbed a couple juice boxes out of the fridge and sat with Joey at the table.

"Is that a present for Billie, Joey?" Jessie asked predictably.

"Yes, it is, nosey." Joey winked.

"What is it? It's a really small box. Is it a ring?" Jessie looked up, thinking she was teasing.

"As a matter of fact, it is a ring," Joey admitted.

Jessie sat back in her seat, disappointed. "You're no fun to tease any more, because you don't even care!" she crossed her arms, frowning. Joey chuckled.

"Hey, Joey," Pam perked up. "That wouldn't be a ring with two dolphins criss-crossing would it?"

"How would you know that?" Joey asked puzzled.

"The other day at the hospital, when you went back in to get the change you forgot, Billie told me she had seen a beautiful silver dolphin ring in there. She didn't ask me, but I was going to give you a heads up so you could get it for her some time as a gift. It looks like you didn't need any help from your older sister," Pam chuckled.

"Yeah, I saw her looking at it twice, but she didn't notice me. The lady in the store knew who Billie was and told me I should hang onto her. She gave me a great deal but I still owe her 20 bucks."

Just then a black SUV drove up the laneway and Joey stood up and waved at Willie through the kitchen window.

"I gotta go," Joey continued. "Billie's parents are letting me go with them to help Billie get settled in the dorm."

He snatched up the little gift, stuffed it in his pocket and darted out the door as Pam wished him luck.

Once in the back seat of the SUV beside Billie, Joey felt weirdly a part of something. It was like these people were his extended family. Willie and Sarah Magee were not people he was terribly shy around anymore but now familiar enough to talk to them freely or even hold their daughter's hand in their presence. Every day seemed like a new unexpected experience was unfurled to him.

"Thanks, Mr. Magee and Mrs. Magee, for taking me today. I really appreciate it." Joey offered.

"You're welcome son, and I know you might find it weird," said Willie, "but you can call me Willie. It's just less formal and I think we're friends now."

"Same goes for me, Joe. Just call me Sarah, please."

Joey and Billie exchanged smiles as Billie laid her hand open on the car seat and Joey accepted the invitation.

There, that was yet another new unexpected experience!

On the way to Montrose, they went over the plan to expose Paul Sinclair. Next Friday night's barbeque at the Sinclair's would set things up perfectly they hoped, especially in giving Billie some time to gather the proof she needed.

During the conversation, Joey asked meekly, "I hope I'm not being rude but, why do you guys do things with them? Are you old friends?"

He had heard Billie's explanation but wanted to hear it from her parents too.

Sarah answered, "It's awkward, Joe, if you want to know the truth. We were friends, we thought, but it got so that more and more business transactions were taking the place of friendly conversation. We haven't really broken things off with them because…well because…"

"Because we're wimps, that's why!'" Willie injected. "Neither of us want a confrontation but it might take that somewhere down the line. The business that goes on at these so-called friendly gatherings have been rather one-sided, with Sinclair Pulp and Paper the main beneficiaries." Willie looked over at Sara with a slight shake of the head. "Frankly, Sarah and I are nearing the end of our ropes with them. And, no, you're not being rude to ask. They have always had this idea that we might be like family someday by hooking Paul up with Billie. Well, you two have put a real snag in those plans, haven't you?" Everyone in the car smiled or snickered.

After a few minutes of silence there was a small shriek from the back seat. Sarah turned to see torn wrapping paper on the seat beside Billie as she was pulling a beautiful silver ring out of a small blue box. Joey couldn't wait any longer and the time seemed right. He was no longer hiding anything from Billie's parents.

"Oh, my God, Billie, a ring?" Sarah said excitedly but with some uneasiness that scared Joey, and Willie almost drove off the road.

"A ring!" Willie said, perplexed. "You got a ring at 14?"

"Relax, you guys," Billie said calmly. "It's just a friendship ring. Cool your jets!"

There was a definite sigh of relief from the elders, and a few more little squeals of joy from the back seat.

"How did you know I loved this ring? Did Pam tell you?"

"Actually, no she didn't. The other day at the hospital, it seemed like every time I turned to see what you were doing, you were admiring something on display there, so I went back to find out what it was and…"

"You didn't really leave a five-dollar bill back on the counter, did you?" Billie interrupted.

"Well, no, not really," Joey grinned.

"You are so amazing!" Billie checked out the rear view mirrow and snuck a kiss on Joey's cheek. Then she whispered in Joey's ear. "We can call this a friendship ring, but to me it means way more than that!" Then she leaned forward and showed off her little treasure to her parents. Joey beamed, and he felt more than rewarded. He meant it as far more than a friendship ring.

"Aw, is that ever nice sweetie!" Sarah remarked. Then she turned around a little more to see Joey's face. "Joey, that's so thoughtful!" Then she took Billie's hand and waved it in front of Willie's face so he could drive and have a look at the same time.

Willie smiled and winked at Billie in the rearview mirror. "That's awesome!" is all he said.

"Just a little going away present," Joey acknowledged, nonchalantly.

Billie didn't have to say anything. She just radiated her happiness by staring at her ring regarding it as a symbol of something so much greater. She laid her newly decorated left hand in her lap and squeezed Joey's hand with her right hand and mouthed the words, "I love you!"

Joey reciprocated by nodding and mouthing, "Me too!"

It took a couple hours to get everything in its rightful place in Billie's new home away from home. It was an "L" shaped room in the third story of a large, yellow-bricked Victorian house about two blocks from school. Elmvale School was located in a lovely, treed part of Montrose, a part of the city called, "Old West" because it was once the original hub. Now, other than a couple schools and churches, it was a lazy bedroom community, well treed and quiet.

About an hour after they arrived and in the midst of unloading the car, Billie's roommate, Rachel, arrived with her grandparents. Rachel was a very pretty red-headed Irish girl, looking for a career in marine biology. She was a couple years older than Billie and was set to graduate this year. Rachel's grandparents were slim and very fit for their age, each helping bring in some of her bags. Thomas had a wiry albeit slightly hunched body with an Arnold Palmer facial resemblance. Rachel's Grandma, whom Rachel called Gran, was a kindly, pleasant-faced woman more the Martha Stewart type but lithe and athletic. All involved in the gathering were congenial and the interchange of small talk was pleasant and affable. Joey thought the Irish brogue he had noticed in the exchange was quite a pleasing accent. Once things were settled, Billie and Rachel started getting to know each other, discussing their likes and dislikes and it appeared they had lots in common, including a boyfriend. Rachel's beau, Rick, lived in Athaca, about 30 miles east of Montrose. They had met during a track and field meet there. Rachel was quite a good sprinter and was competing in the 100. Rick, was watching the race and had approached her after the race to congratulate her and was struck by her sea-green eyes, wavy locks and fine, moderately freckled facial features. He was a sturdy muscular guy who competed in the shot-put event; a local farmer boy used to work and honest living. He arrived to greet everyone just as Billie, Joey and Billie's parents were heading out.

Willie had planned an Italian night out at Alberto's, a very popular restaurant in the area.

"Okay, who's for some good Italian food?" Willie asked as they headed down the front steps of the beautiful old house.

"You don't have to ask me twice!" said Billie.

"Ah, I didn't know we were going to eat out," Joey seemed a little embarrassed. "I didn't come really prepared for that." Meaning of course, that he didn't have money with him.

"Nonsense!" Sarah said, "When Willie and Sarah Magee say we're going out to dinner, you just tag along and enjoy. Let us have the pleasure of treating you!"

"That's very kind of you. Thank you." Joey said, humbled but comforted by Billie's grasp on his hand as they walked to the car.

Joey felt so good to be a part of this family. Still, there was something that just didn't sit right. It was the reality of his origin, his simple upbringing, his once quite complicated and dysfunctional family. He had not experienced this setting…ever. There was a feeling of awkwardness because he had not really participated in a formal meal out in such a fancy setting. Just the sight of the prices on the menu made him feel like he didn't belong here. About the only things he recognized on the pages were pizza and lasagna. When he noticeably, struggled with what to order, Billie gave up her desire for Fiorentina Steak, and ordered pizza for herself and Joey gratefully followed suit. He often struggled to make pertinent conversation or add any value to what was being discussed by Billie's parents, partially because of the extreme differences in what Willie and Sarah considered important in their lives compared to his meager history. Billie sensed this every so often and would step in and rescue him by either paraphrasing his attempts or touching his knee or hand to reassure him that he was among friends. Joey absorbed as much as he could and eventually by the end of the meal was feeling better about how to sit, how to handle the utensils, how to eat and speak properly. It was not that the Magee's were overly formal, it was more just the differences in the family's background to his and his intense desire to meet their approval.

After driving back to the dorm, they all got out and gave Billie hugs and wished her well for her first week. She reassured them that registration and buying the right textbooks and supplies were all that was likely in store this week.

"Why don't you walk her up to her room, Joey. We'll wait in the car," said Willie.

"Absolutely, thanks!" Joey took Billie's hand, then released it to open the door for her and they disappeared into the dark abyss of the foyer. They walked up the two flights of stairs and heard talking form Billie's room. Rachel's entourage was obviously still there. Joey let Billie take the last step up by herself, then he spun her around and they hugged each other tightly. Billie pulled back slightly bringing her hands up to chest height.

"I absolutely love this ring! The funny thing is, I don't even need to look at it to think about you because you are always on my mind. Thanks for being here to today! I love you! She gave Joey the juiciest kiss she could.

"I love you too and I will really miss you at school! Good luck, and I guess I'll see you Friday. Don't forget to go to bed with me." Joey chuckled. "I know you have a roommate, but even if it's text it's better than nothing."

There was one more kiss and Joey turned and began walking down the stairs.

"Make sure you tell me as soon as Jug comes around," said Billie.

"Will do."

The ride back to William's Glen was at first quiet and slightly tense for Joey, so he thought he would break the silence.

"Thanks so much you guys, for the dinner. It was great! I have never been in such a nice place, and the food was awesome."

"You're quite welcome, Joe. Can we call you Joey?" Sarah asked, turning to look at Joey.

"That would be great," Joey answered. "Only my closest friends and family call me that.

"Aw, that's nice Joey,"

"Besides, you guys said I could call you Willie and Sarah, so that's only fair." Joey joked and all three had a little laugh.

For the rest of the ride home the three talked about how they were going to set the hook and prove Paul Sinclair's involvement in the boating accident that resulted in Jug's horrific injury. It would begin with Friday's barbeque and getting a good photo of Paul with his boat, hopefully with the registration numbers on the bow revealed. Joey began to feel more and more at ease with Billie's parents. Just being with them made him feel more secure about his relationship with her. Willie divulged that he had already firmed up some business contracts with some of Sinclair's competition in the building supply business in preparation for the imminent dissolution of the Sinclair/Magee alliance.

"How is you mom doing, Joey?" Sarah asked out of the blue.

"She is so much happier since, well…" Joey stumbled, not finding the right words.

"That's great," injected Sarah, sensing Joey's discomfort. She knew about his dad's circumstance.

"Don's gonna take her on a date this week. They seem to be liking each other's company." Said Joey.

"He's had a rough go, after his wife's death," Willie added. "I'm sure they both could use a little camaraderie."

They pulled into Joey's lane as twilight was beginning to set in.

"I'll tell you if Billie has any news from school, Joey. Thanks for coming." Said Sara.

"No offense but, I might know before you," Joey risked saying.

"Oh, yeah…cell phones." They all had a good laugh. Willie backed the car out, waving to Joey on the way.

Lilley was sitting at her favorite spot on the couch reading and she looked up as Joey came in. He plopped down beside her.

"How did it go?" asked Lilley.

"Really good," answered Joey. "I thought Don might be here when I got back. Did you guys do anything today?"

"No, Don had to run up to his son's place in Tisdale, and I had laundry to do anyway…Listen, Joey, about that. Don and I are still trying to get a grip on being single. He's had more time than me but it's a bit of a struggle. We are just enjoying each other's company as friends. Newly found friends, at that. You never know what could happen in the future but for me…I'd like to be just friends for now."

"Do you still care about Dad, Mom?" Joey asked.

"He's your father and your sisters' father, so yeah, I do. He's lost his way and doesn't seem to care about us, but I don't wish him harm anymore. I did for quite a while, after everything came to a head, that night…well, as you know very well. But I can't hate him. He gave me you guys, and I have to believe he will find what he's looking for some day. I don't think I could ever love him again, though. He's just done too much damage. Maybe someday I will remarry but that feels like a long way off. Don has been through horrible tragedy and would love his wife in a second if she were to miraculously come back to life. It's hard for him and he may never get past that.

"He's such a good guy, though. I really like him," said Joey.

"Yes, he is, and I really like him too."

The week went by agonizingly slowly for Joey. There was never any good news from the hospital and school seemed barely tolerable, except for one class. Joey was able to take graphic art as an elective this year, and although Mr. Ward was a total computer geek, he was nice to Joey and encouraged him. Joey found the marriage of art and computers fascinating. He felt like he could unleash his creative talent in what seemed like, infinite ways using modern technology.

Just before falling to sleep at night was the best part of the day, because he was able to text and sometimes talk to Billie, share each other's day, and find the reassurance in a partnership that gave him strength.

He tried to play guitar a few times but found that his left arm was still too weak from the injury he suffered at the hands of Sinclair. His forearm had become a little smaller due to the atrophy of muscle tissue. It made it difficult to squeeze the guitar neck, especially when attempting bar chords. He admitted to himself that he was looking forward to a revenge of some kind, despite the guilt associated with those retaliatory thoughts. Guitar lessons were on hold until he got his strength back.

Joey had accumulated a good number of clients for lawn cutting and hedge trimming and was able to diversify his business and purchase more equipment. He was able to buy a used lawn tractor and trailer. After school he would hurry home and drive the tractor back to town and do a couple properties each night. The trailer was big enough to hold the smaller push mower, a weed whacker, a hedge trimmer, and a jerry can of gas. He paid cash for all his equipment and more jobs were coming in all the time as word of mouth spread around town.

Thursday night, Sarah called to Joey directly on his cell phone. This was a first, but inevitable since she was able to con Joey's number from Billie. It gave her a direct line to her daughter's confidant, and it felt good to both Joey and Sarah to be linked almost as family. Sarah and Joey were becoming good friends…almost an auntie-nephew-like relationship. Sarah had always wanted another child, especially a boy.

CHAPTER 15

Sarah and Joey arranged that Sarah would pick up Billie at 3 pm on Friday from Elmvale and drop her off at the Macpherson's in William's Glen, where Joey was finishing up some weed whacking and raking up grass clippings. When Joey saw the familiar car pull up to the sidewalk and the passenger door open, his heart raced. He wondered if it would always be that way. He dropped the rake and walked over to the car.

"Don't keep her too long, Joey. As you know we have an important night ahead." Sarah bellowed from inside the car.

"Okay, thanks for bringing her here." Joey yelled back.

Sarah drove off waving, and Billie and Joey stood there in a warm embrace on the sidewalk.

Joey stepped back, "I'm kinda sweaty from working. I hope you don't mind."

"I wouldn't care if you were climbing out of the sewer. It's so good to see you!" There was the requisite kiss and another hug. "What can I do to help you finish up here?"

"Well, you could hold these garbage bags up while I fill them with clippings. Then we will carry them over and leave them in front of Mr. Macpherson's garage, as he wanted."

They worked together for about a half an hour, and it felt so right to both of them. Billie actually enjoyed the exercise and just being reunited with Joey, and he was grateful for her being there and also sharing this part of his life. They filled 8 garbage bags and left them at the designated spot. Then they loaded up the trailer.

"So, you wanna go for a ride? I'll take you home, but you'll have to sit on my lap." Joey said in a devious tone.

"Jeez, what a girl has to do to get a ride," Billie joked, actually eagerly anticipating the physical contact.

Joey stopped the tractor in front of Dr. Norman's office and shut it off.

"What are we doing here?" Billie asked.

"Well, it's on the way to your house and I need to make my monthly donation," said Joey.

"Monthly donation?" Billie was still puzzled.

"I only decided today, really. I talked it over with Dr. Norman. His wife, Angela…I've never even met her, but she takes in dogs, rescues them. I think she calls it, "Happy's Place". If for some reason the owner can't look after their dog, she takes them and looks after them and then finds people who want them. It's kind of like an adoption agency for dogs, I guess. She has a good deal with the vet, obviously, so her vet bills aren't too bad but everything else like food, toys and her advertising and reaching out to the community is right out of her pocket. She relies on donations to keep her rescue going. Since Dr. Norman was kind enough to look after Harriet," a brief lump in his throat stopped him momentarily, "I thought I would help her out once a month."

"That is wonderful, Joey! I'm going to tell Mom and Dad about that. Maybe they can help too. You never stop showing me why I adore you!" She pulled him close and squeezed.

"Well, it's only a hundred bucks a month but that should buy food for a couple dogs."

"A hundred bucks! You must be doing well with your little business."

"Right now, I'm bringing in about thirteen hundred a month. I keep getting more requests and I might have to ask someone to help me out. I do 8 properties a week and if I get any more, I just won't have time."

"You told me you were doing well, but I didn't realize how well," Billie commented, still amazed.

"So, a hundred bucks to keep a couple dogs alive seems like the least I can do."

Joey swung his leg over the hood of the tractor and Billie stepped aside as he ran up the steps to the vet clinic, pulling a white envelope out of his pocket as he went.

The ride on the lawn tractor was probably longer than it would have taken to walk, but not nearly as enjoyable for these two. Billie sat crossways across Joey's lap with her arm around him as they putted the three blocks to the Magee home. They pulled up to the end of the laneway and had a quick kiss, not caring who might have seen, because to them, it just didn't matter anymore.

"Good luck, tonight," Joey said. "Make sure you text me about what happens."

"Oh, I will," assured Billie, with another smack on Joey's cheek, then she hopped off waving goodbye.

Willie and Sarah were getting ready to go over to the Sinclair's for the barbeque, but this was not just any barbeque. If there wasn't the ulterior motive behind the event, they probably would have turned down the invitation.

Sarah rhetorically asked, "You know, we are only going tonight because we have an agenda, right?"

"Absolutely, why?" asked Willie.

"Well," Sarah continued, "It just occurred to me that they have been doing what we're doing tonight, for years. It makes me angry to think of all the times we were together with them socially, and they were really only congenial to get our business. I was willing to look past Mark's arrogant loudness and Sally's displays of vanity, hoping there might be a little goodness in there somewhere. It's all been…for lack of a better word, phony. At times, I fell for their hospitality…like the night we all went out on the cruise in their cabin cruiser and had a few drinks as the sun set behind the hills. It was a beautiful night, and we really had a good time."

"Yeah, that was nice," agreed Willie.

"But do you remember what happened the moment we got back to their place?"

"Actually, I do," Willie recalled. "We all had a little buzz on from the drinks and Mark presented me with a lumber quote for the townhouse complex we were building. I did think it was strange that he had the paperwork so nearby the patio. Nothing had been mentioned previous to that about the construction. We were just sitting around making small talk and watching the last of the orange sky disappear into the hills across the lake…You're right, of course, but at the time I must have felt like he was doing us a favor by giving us a great deal."

"Exactly, so now we have purpose for our visit and so does Billie," Sarah affirmed.

The barbeques were informal affairs, but the upper class of the community would still be wary of their dress. For Sarha it meant designer jeans, a classy print top and fashionable sandals. For Willie it was the go-to navy dress shorts and white polo with a baby-blue cashmere sweater draped over his shoulders.

Billie had her dark brown front slitted skort outfit on. It was kind of flirty without actually revealing anything. Her top was a frilly white smocked blouse, flared at the waste and sleeves and just short enough to reveal a little tummy when she moved. She had dressed for intent tonight. She was going to show Sinclair what he couldn't have and rub it in his nose. She took a selfie in the full-length mirror on her closet door and sent it to Joey with the text, "How do I look?"

Joey replied with, "Too good for Paul Sinclair! You are sure making it difficult for me, but I know what you're up to. I want to squeeze your face off, you look so pretty!"

"That's sweet. Thank you! I have a job to do tonight, Joey. You will be in my thoughts every second. I will send you another pic when I'm home in bed. I love you!"

Joey was excited at the thought. "I can't wait! I love you too. Be careful!"

As they pulled into the Sinclair's concrete driveway, Sarah sighed. "Well, let the act begin."

They were greeted with the normal handshakes and the insincere clasps of fake hugs. Billie just stayed behind her parents.

Sally yelled back toward the kitchen, "Paul, Billie's here."

Billie was becoming tense and thought, "God, do you have to announce my presence!"

Paul came out and attempted a hug but Billie just allowed her shoulders to touch his and quickly patted his back to signal that it was over.

"Hey, Billie," Paul offered.

A terse, "Hey," was all she could muster.

"Food's ready and I'm hungry. I hope you guys are too," Mark said as he ushered them into the kitchen area. "How about a couple drinks first?"

"Yeah sure, thanks. Whiskey on the rocks for me and red wine for Sarah, if you have it."

Both Willie and Sarah welcomed a little liquid courage on this night.

They sat at bar stools at the kitchen island, while Paul sat in front of the multi-paned window overlooking the lake on a recliner. Billie stayed close to her parents to avoid any conversation with Paul. The sight of him was really starting to make her sick and knowing the secret he was hiding made him all that much more repulsive.

As the parents talked about the weather and how dry it has been and that it has impacted the building industry as well as the increased number of tourists this year, Billie was busy casing the large open area for photos of Paul and his boat. At the same time, she pretended to follow their conversation so that she could avoid Paul's eyes. Actually, she was being quite rude to Paul, but she was not much for phoniness. She thought she better make an effort to be somewhat affable so that Paul would not be suspicious of her actions, but her first words to him immediately put him on guard.

"So, have you been out in your boat lately?" It was just the only thing she could think of.

Paul squirmed in his seat slightly but had a clever answer. "No, not really. The boat's been broken for a few weeks now and I haven't got around to fix it. I think it needs a head gasket."

"A head gasket," Billie thought. "Nice try, you asshole." But instead, she said, "Oh, that's too bad."

Then she spotted the picture she knew she had seen before. It was propped on a miniature easel at about eye level between two rows of books on a full-length bookshelf beside the fireplace in the family room. The kitchen, sitting area and family room was all one big great room with beautiful big knotty pine beams. The family room was also vaulted with huge beams and the fireplace was enormous and built completely of granite rocks. The mantle was a gigantic beam, probably from one of the barns in the area.

Billie got up and walked over to the bookshelf pointing as she walked so that Paul would follow. The photo showed Paul posing with a costume Captain's hat, sitting on the back of the seat with one arm on the top of the windshield and the other on the back of the seat. As her eyes continued downward, she thought, "Bingo!" There were the registration numbers clearly marked on the bow, "NY 521394 SW.'"

"So, when was that taken?" Billie attempted reasonable conversation.

"Last summer, I think," answered Paul, still a little wary of her interest in the boat.

Billie sensed his cautionary demeanor and pretended to peruse other items and knick-knacks on the shelves.

"Cool rock," she said as she picked up a perfectly round stone about the size of a baseball. "I wonder how it got so round."

"That's one of Mom's river rocks. She's always bringing rocks back from her hikes along the shore. It gets that way from being washed down the river." Paul explained somewhat arrogantly.

"Okay, guys, time to eat," Mark announced. "I'll go grab the steaks and we can move into the dining room. I was thinking about eating outside but there are a lot of bugs around tonight."

Everyone made their way into the dining room, which was toward the front of the house just off the kitchen. Sally grabbed a salad bowl and a pot of potatoes off the kitchen counter and Sara helped bring a couple other bowls of vegetables to the table. As they arranged themselves at the table, Billie was feeling more and more uncomfortable by the minute. She could think of a thousand places she'd rather be and wanted to spend her weekend time with Joey. She reminded herself of her one task for the night and sat at the table beside Paul. Taking deep breaths, she tried to be as calm and natural as she could. Her mom and dad sat across from her with Sally and Mark at their customary positions at the two heads of the table.

Mark brought in a large silver platter of T-bone steaks that smelled tantalizing good to Billie, even though she didn't know how well she could eat sitting beside such a disgusting person. They passed around the food and continued to discuss nothing of any consequence. Then it became rather quiet as everyone dug into their food. Even though the aroma of the food was so mouthwatering, Billie found it difficult to eat. She felt a nervous edginess that made it hard to swallow her food. She looked up and noticed her mother was a little more serious than she usually was at these gatherings. Their eyes met and Sarah gave her a little wink and that seemed to ease the tenseness slightly. It reminded her that there were two allies in the room, and she wasn't on her own.

About halfway through the meal Billie asked to be excused to go the bathroom and thought that would afford her time to take a slight detour through the family room. It worked, and she got a couple quick photos of the captain and his ship without anyone noticing. When she got back and sat down Sarah gave her a little questioning nod and Billie nodded back in the affirmative. Willie also caught the exchange and smiled ever so slightly between mouthfuls.

Billie thought that with the job done and the fact that it had been so easy, she would now be able to relax. However, it was quite the opposite. The more she sat there, the more she felt agitated by being there. Willie and Sarah also felt that way and they began to exchange the odd communication that meant that they were done here. Yet, to make things work and not become too uncomfortable, they stayed the course, enduring Sally's nattering's about the new hair salon in town and Mark's recalling his football days, while Paul one-upped him, bragging about his completion percentage as the quarterback of the William's Glen Gryphons' team. It was excruciating for Billie, especially knowing that the person she wanted most to be with was standing by in the wings waiting for her.

Then the crescendo of the evening happened, partly by accident and partly coerced by Billie. Mark mentioned off the cuff that the neighbors "damn" dog was over sniffing around the barbeque when he was out taking them off the grill.

"The stupid thing," he explained. "I had to give it a boot in the ass to get him off our porch. People need to keep their stupid dogs tied up at home and not let them run around on other people's private property!"

Billie was seething inside and visibly becoming red in the face. Sarah seeing this, brought a napkin to her mouth and as she set it back down made a "calm down" motion with the palms of her hand. But she had to say something. She did agree that people needed to keep their dogs from trespassing but tying a dog up and leaving it outside all day was dog cruelty 101. It was something She and Joey had talked about many times and why he had trained Harriet to stay home or put her inside when he was away for an extended time. What Mark said was not such a big deal, really. It might have just passed by her had she not been so tightly wound up because of the stress and shear turbulence she felt in her chest. She wanted everyone to know that she disagreed and that somehow, they needed to know that she was with Joey and not their reprobate son.

"I don't think dogs should ever be tied up. I think it's cruel!" Billie managed. The silence in the room was deafening and Sarah almost gagged on her bun. "Joey trained his dog to stay on his property and she always did." There she had stood up for her beliefs and not sounded too angry.

"Who is Joey, dear?" asked Sally. "Did you mean Joe Burgess?"

"Hmm," said Mark.

"Yes," said Billie, and then she added, "Joey to me." She glanced quickly at Paul.

Sara and Willie just looked on, not even thinking of reprimanding her for being rude to Mark, but more hiding their pride in her guts to speak her mind.

Then came the statement of the night. It was like Billie was waiting for something like this to pounce on…and pounce she did.

Paul, trying to assert himself and his wealth of general knowledge made the worst comment possible. "Wasn't that a Bernese Mountain Dog?"

Billie replied coldly, "Yes, she was."

Willie and Sara were bracing themselves for what they knew would be the detonation of their daughter's temper.

Paul foolishly continued, "They're pretty stupid dogs. It died, didn't it? It probably left the yard and got hit by a car. Dumb dogs have dumb owners. I bet Joe-boy had a big funeral and invited guests. Did he serve food?" Paul laughed heartily and Mark worked to suppress a chuckle.

Sarah grabbed Willie's hand as if they were watching a thrilling movie and the climax was about to result in some catastrophe or death.

Billie stood up and threw her napkin down onto her plate, hard enough that it knocked her fork onto the floor.

"You couldn't possibly know about that dog! Her name was Harriet, and she had more love and heart than you ever will…and more between the ears too! You are the most ignorant jerk I have ever known. Somebody should tie you up, so you don't crap on other people. I never want to come back here again! I am done this make-believe relationship! Thank you, Mr. and Mrs. Sinclair for supper."

She raced to the door and slammed it behind her as the stunned audience at the dining room table watched her walk to the car and stand there leaning against it facing the road. What they couldn't see or hear was Billie crying and shaking with anger.

Sarah and Willie stood up too.

"I'm sorry things turned out like this," said Willie, and he meant it too. Things could have been so much better if they had just been genuine friends.

"Thanks for the meal… Sorry." Added Sarah. She took Willie's hand and they both headed for the door.

Mark stood up now, "Wait, aren't you going to finish your drinks. I have some business ideas for you too…"

It was too late they were already out talking to Billie.

"I'm sorry, Mom…Dad. I lost it! I've never been so angry and so hurt at the same time. I ruined things, didn't I?" She held her head in her hands weeping.

Both Willie and Sarah held her, and Willie cupped the top of her head in one hand, "I don't think I've ever been more proud of you!"

"That is exactly what I was going to say!" agreed Sarah.

They kept their clamp on Billie while Willie reached in his pocket and found the key fob, unlocking the car doors.

Still holding each other, Billie managed a tearful, "I love you guys!"

"What in the hell, Paul! Do you know how important our relationship is with the Magee's?"

"Yeah, I guess," Paul answered, head slightly bowed.

"Wasn't Joe Burgess the other kid in the rowboat you hit?"

"Yeah, but…"

"It's obvious, you idiot! It's not hard to tell how Billie feels about that Burgess kid." Mark continued. "We are not just facing a cover up to avoid bad press or a lawsuit, we are also now fighting the Magee's. We have to find a way of patching things up between the families or this is going to hurt our business big time!"

On the way home, which was only about a five minute drive, Sarah turned to face Billie who was still wiping tears away. "Did you get it?"

"Oh yeah, I got it. I'm going to print it out the size of a billboard when I get home!"

Billie showed Sarah her phone as Willie glanced over for a quick look.

"Billie, this has the boat's registration numbers clearly visible! That's amazing! I sure hope you guys can get the proof you need tomorrow."

"Great job there, detective Magee!" Willie said proudly.

"Can you believe the nerve of Mark? On our way to the car and he was trying to make a business deal!" Sarah remarked.

Later in bed Billie sent Joey the picture she had of Paul and the boat and wrote a long text detailing exactly what Paul said and how the night was cut short because she had blown up front of everyone.

Joey: "I am so proud of you! Are your parents cool with it?"

Billie: "They said they were proud of me too."

Joey: "Your parents stone me! They are the best! And you're the best too! Now, where's that other pic you promised me? LOL"

Billie sat more upright in bed propped up with a couple pillows. She unbuttoned the top two buttons on her night shirt and pulled it down over her shoulders. Then she took her hair and placed one auburn strand forward around her chin and onto her chest. She framed the photo so that no clothes could be seen but no indecent nudity either, and gave her best flirtatious look with lips slightly pursed. Then she clicked send and waited for a reaction.

Joey: "God you are beautiful! That's just too cruel!"

Billie:" LOL, thank you. Now, you're turn."

Joey sat up and tried to duplicate her pose and pursed lips but bared his upper body exposing everything from the waist up and sent it.

Billie: "Remember a few months ago when you thought it was weird that I called you beautiful. Well, you are…inside and out! I love you! Now we need to get to sleep because we have a top-secret mission tomorrow! Good night Joey!"

Joey: "Love you too…good night."

CHAPTER 16

Joey woke around midnight to someone rummaging around in the kitchen. Curious, he tip-toed into the room. It was Pam searching the kitchen cabinets.

"What are you doin'?" Joey said in a loud whisper.

Then he noticed tears on Pam's cheeks.

"What's the matter?"

Pam gave up her quest and plunked down on one of the kitchen chairs holding her head in her hands.

"It's still so hard, Joe! I've come so far but every once in a while, I get these urges. Sometimes, when I can't sleep, I remember how a good hit, or a strong drink would help me."

"So, you were looking for booze?" Joey wondered.

"Yeah, I guess I was. Sometimes I'm not even sure what I'm looking for. It's not as bad as it used to be, but it is still a craving, you know. It's not like a life or death situation anymore but it's still there. I can't believe I was so out of it a few months ago! They say that the cravings take a long time to go away and boy were they right! First, I start craving a cigarette and then I imagine what a joint felt like, then what a stiff drink, then the cocaine feeling hits me."

"Well, if it helps at all, I imagine Mom is pretty careful about having booze around. I think you're amazing for kicking it like you have. I will always respect you for that."

Pam stood up and walked over to Joey and squeezed him tight.

"You are the amazing one, l'il bro! That is exactly what I needed right now. Your support means so much, Joe! I love you for accepting me and welcoming me back."

"I love you too, sis. But don't tell Mom I told you that." They both suppressed their laughter and bid each other good night.

As planned, everyone met at Joey's at 8:00 pm that night. They would all wear as much black as they could. Don drove his boat over to the dock at Little Beach and tied it up. Sara gave Billie a ride to Joey's and was there about 7:45, completely dressed in black. Joey didn't have black jeans, but he did have a black hoodie. Don had a black track suit with a black hoodie as well. They looked like a swat team without the guns and black smudges under their eyes. It would have been slightly comical if not for their solemn intent. Pam was going to see them off and volunteered to stay home to keep Jessie company, however, she met with the group on the laneway. Don had docked his boat and emerged from the path to Little Beach, and they discussed their plan of attack and returned to the dock.

It was simple really, just troll northward up the shore in the dusk, reach a position just opposite Pike Point on the other side of the lake north of Sinclair's, then cross the mile width of the lake and wait until it was perfectly dark. When darkness set in, they would row around the point with oarlocks well lubricated for stealth and then position themselves outside the bay doors of Sinclair's boathouse. Nothing could go wrong, really, except for the fact that tonight, the Sinclair's bright yard lights were on. Those lights lit up the lake for

3 or 4 hundred feet off the shore. They were not turned on the night they had scouted the mission last week. All they could do was wait and hope they turned them off before they retired for the night. That meant waiting, possibly for hours in a small aluminum boat on the east shore just past Pike Point. The evenings were beginning to cool off much quicker as autumn approached. Perhaps they should have waited longer before heading out but here they were, in the dark waiting to complete their evidence hunting mission.

Sitting in the center seat, Billie and Joey sat with their arms around each other with Don in the stern. They whispered their conversations while the odd boat drove by some fairly close and others just a faint drone near the far shore. It was virtually impossible to see them anchored just off the shore in the blackness just on the north side of Pike Point, mostly hidden behind some exposed rocks with their lights off. Almost 90 minutes later the yard light went off and they got themselves in position, which meant only that Billie moved to the bow seat so that Joey had room to row. Don began to scratch around in his duffel bag for his camera equipment. The night supplied just enough light for him to assemble the telescopic pole and affix the camera and he set it back down on the floor of the boat to scour the shoreline with binoculars, as Joey methodically rowed on. Joey prayed they wouldn't turn the yard lights back on now because their little white hulled boat would literally glow in the dark this close to shore, but it remained dark.

"Hey, Joey," Billie whispered loudly, "What if they have motion lights on the boathouse?"

"I doubt if they will," Joey assured her. "They wouldn't be much good, at least on the lake side because every big wave would set them off."

"Good point," Billie affirmed.

They were about 200 feet away from the boathouse when Don motioned to Joey with his hand to stop. Joey stopped rowing and they drifted silently. It was a relatively calm night and the ripple of water splashing against the boat was largely indistinct. All three held their breaths using only hand signals. Once Don was satisfied that nobody was watching them from shore, he motioned Joey to row slowly on.

They reached the boathouse doors, drifting silently past the attached dock on the north side. The door on the south side housed Paul's Donzi. As discussed, Joey positioned the boat so that the bow was just past the south wall so that Billie could see from her perch in the bow if anyone was coming toward the boathouse or if a door from the house opened. The boat must not hit the side of the boathouse and the oars must not contact the boat or the boathouse. The slightest clunk could alert the pesky neighbor's dog or the Sinclair's. Don pushed out the telescopic 2-foot extensions until the camera was about 10 feet down into the water. There was a trigger, like a pistol grip at Don's end. When squeezed, a flash would signal the photo was taken, but there was no way of knowing if it was a revealing photo or whether it was even discernable. They would have to wait until they were significantly distant from the boathouse before they could examine the results.

Don was able to shove the camera into the boathouse about 7 feet and about 3 feet under the water. He squeezed the trigger and they all saw the water light up under the boat like an underwater fireworks display. He squeezed it 8 more times. Each time he brought the camera closer to the stern, hoping to catch all of the hull's secrets. He waited 10 or 15 seconds between each photo so that the water would not be lit up continuously. Then he pulled in the extensions and brought the camera on board.

"Hey, Don," Joey said with a breathy whisper, "Billie's photo shows the registration numbers on the bow. Is there any way we could get a pic of that?"

"I can't reach into the boathouse that far from here," Don replied.

Billie overheard and said, "Hey guys, there are 3 round windows here," she pointed to the south wall.

"That would be a little risky," Don suggested. "We would have to take pics of the two windows closest to the bow to be sure. I don't mind bringing the boat around to the side of the boathouse but the reflection of the flash off the boathouse windows would be seen for quite a distance. I am willing to give it a try if you guys are."

"I say, go for it," injected Joey.

"Me too," said Billie.

"All right then, ease us around to the side, Joey. There better be some green paint on one of those hull pics. We'll do the window closest to shore."

Joey expertly maneuvered the boat so that the stern was closest to the porthole style window on the eastern end of the boathouse. Don extended the camera pole up to the window, touching it with a very slight tap, then pulled the trigger activating the camera shutter. The reflection lit up the trees all around them and almost immediately the neighbor's dog on the south side started barking excitedly. In a knee-jerk reaction Joey went to get the boat away from the boathouse and inadvertently smacked the side of the boat with a loud metallic clang.

"Joey, row out and back up toward the point, quick!"

Joey pulled on the oars and got them about 100 feet out into the lake as the Sinclair's yard lights flashed on. The Sinclair's were alerted, and the worst-case scenario began to play in their minds. They had not trespassed and really done anything very illegal except maybe unauthorized photography. They were more afraid of what the Sinclair's were capable of doing to someone prowling around their property.

"Start the engine, Don. Let's get out of here!" Joey said, a little louder than a whisper now.

"No, get us around the point, Joey, as fast as you can! We will hide around on the north side of the point.

Two figures with flashlights were now approaching the boathouse from the Sinclair's back yard. The handheld flashlights were fixed on the boathouse and then flitted about on the dock and then around to the south side and as long as Joey rowed hard, they would be able to avoid them training the lights on them. They just rounded the tip of the point when lights lit up the rocks on the south side. They had made it to safety at least momentarily.

Just then they heard the twin motors of the Sinclair's 30-foot cruiser start up. Of course, they wouldn't use the Donzi, because it was supposed to be broken down. Joey peered over the rocks of the point and saw the garage doors on the boathouse roll up, the exhaust billowing out lit up by the interior boathouse lights. Then the boat appeared slowly backing out onto the lake. Sneaking away must have worked because they headed south just idling looking for whatever caused the commotion. They figured that the perpetrators were from the south since that had caused the dog belonging to the neighbor on the south side to be alerted.

"Should we make a run for it now?" Joey asked.

"No," Don said adamantly, "Keep rowing north and get as much distance as possible from them."

"They have a search light," Billie said from her lookout in the bow. "I can see a really bright light going back and forth along the shoreline."

"If we start up the engines, they won't hear us as long as they are running their engines," Joey suggested eager to get away from here.

"We are far enough away," Don said. "As long as we don't use any lights we should be able to fly under the radar."

Don started the outboard and almost immediately had the boat planed out and heading directly for the western shore. They all looked back to see if the Sinclair's boat reacted to them…nothing. They didn't see or hear them. 15 minutes later they found themselves at Little Beach and tied up to the dock.

"Wow, that was close!" Billie exclaimed loudly, grateful not to have to whisper.

"So, let's get into the house and see if we actually have anything worth the effort," Don said as he tossed the end of the bow line onto the dock and clicked the camera free of the telescopic pole.

They walked, feeling their way along with no lights, using their memory up the unlit path as stealthily as they could to the house making an effort to draw no attention to their position.

Lilley and Pam were waiting, playing a game of war on the kitchen table when the three mercenaries entered. Jessie had been asleep for an hour or so despite putting up a little fuss and insisting on staying up to greet the returning group. Pam was very crafty about getting her little sister to sleep, playing games until she basically just passed out.

"Ok, let's see what we got," said Don as he sat in the end chair closest to the door.

Everyone crowded around as he began to flip through all the photos. The first photo was the last one taken and immediately everyone cheered and saw the registration numbers on the bow as clear as can be. Billie got her phone out to make sure the Sinclair's hadn't tampered with the numbers.

She read them out as everyone observed Don's photo he had enlarged on the screen on the back of the camera. "NY 521394 SW"

"Perfect," said Pam. "Now, were there any signs of green paint on the bottom?"

They looked at frame after frame and all they could see was a few scrapes and some scum from sitting in the boathouse in stagnant water…nothing…not signs.

"There is one other thing I tried. I ran a video of as much of the hull I could reach and kept it running up and out of the water until the name on the boat could be clearly seen." Said Don.

He began to run the video, and everyone refocused on the 4-inch screen. Joey pulled up a chair behind Don and Billie sat on Joey's lap giving him her trademark wink. All watched intently and Lilley was the first to spot it.

"There!" she yelled. "Back up just a few frames."

Don clicked the back button a few times and paused it. There it was…a scratch line and green paint flaring from the line like the frayed plumes of a feather. This was real concrete evidence. Perhaps not irrefutable but how many Donzi's were seen hitting a green rowboat, and now have green paint on its otherwise white hull? Don took a photo of that frame. Then they continued to watch as the video came out of the water and revealed the name on the back of the Donzi, "Dreadknot" in block letters painted to resemble wood grain. Don raised his open right hand above his head and everyone took their turns high fiving.

"Our job here is done," Don announced proudly.

"Now, we have to work on getting some kind of compensation, right?" Joey suggested.

"Yes," replied Don.

"I think you guys should approach the Sinclair's as soon as possible," suggested Lilley.

"I will tell Detective Roberts what we've got and how decisive our evidence is. Then we will try to arrange a showdown for Monday afternoon or evening," said Don.

Pam went to bed and Joey and Billie took a walk down to Little Beach, this time with a flashlight. They walked hand in hand despite a light drizzle dampening the leaves and pine needles. They kicked off their sandals and Joey led Billie into the water until Billie was almost up to her waist and Joey mid-thigh in water not the least bit worried about getting their clothes wet. With the drizzle now becoming more of a downpour, they stood, their lips locked and excited by the dampness and each other's bodies.

Back at the house, Don was getting ready to leave. Lilley stood and walked over to Don as he leaned against the door frame.

"Don, thank you so much for what you've done for the kids… and me, "Lilley said softly.

"You're welcome, Lilley. Truth be known, it was almost fun, you know. The kids are unbelievable for their age. I think Joey and Billie really got something special there."

"I feel that too," Lilley admitted. "I just hope they can hold off until they're older before they start … you know, getting too intimate. I am beginning to love Billie like family, and I would hate to see anything happen that might split them up."

"Somehow, in the short time I've known them, I think you're safe. There is something bigger than just carnal attraction there. I see it every time I'm with them." Don paused, surprised by his own boldness and spilled out his thoughts. "What about us Lilley? Do you see any chance for a future?"

Lilley was calm and despite the abruptness, received the question without a hint of consternation. "I think, Mr. Archer, that time alone will tell. I'm still waiting for that first date you promised me," she said with a wink.

They both laughed and as Don began pushing the door open, Lilley grabbed his hand and she hugged him. He brought his hand down off the door and responded with a full embrace.

"Thanks, again," Lilley managed. "I think a lot of you, but I don't want to rush into anything yet. The ink on the divorce agreement is barely dry and there is still a lot of soul searching to do for me." She gave Don a quick tightening of her hug and stepped back. "You know it's raining out there, right?"

"Yeah, I know but it's still pretty light rain and it's only about 5 minutes to the boat launch. Take care Lilley. I'll probably see you tomorrow or Monday and …I think a lot of you too."

Don made his way down the path toward little beach just as Joey and Billie were heading back to the house.

"Good night you two," Don said as he passed them in the darkness.

"Good night Don," Joey answered. "Do you need any help with your boat?

Don decided to take Billie and Joey with him in the boat to the boat ramp. Billie could slip home easily from there as it was adjacent to her property. They could both help Don getting the boat onto the trailer and Don could take Joey back home after it was all loaded.

After Joey was finally settled into bed, his phone lit up and they exchanged their good nights, but Billie had something else on her mind.

"Joey, do you think we will make it?"

"What do you mean? You mean like, forever together? Funny, you ask that. I often wonder what will happen to us. I love you Billie, and that's all I know right now. I can't see how that could ever change. I want to be somebody though."

"I think I understand," answered Billie. "I will never stand in your way. You said exactly what I need to hear. I know we are young, and the odds are against us, but I don't see what could stop me from loving you. I wish I could just fall asleep in your arms right now! We will be somebody's … both of us…and I guess we have lots of time to decide stuff that comes after that. We could just fall asleep with our phones on, you know like we are in bed together."

"Yeah, that would be great…g'night."

"G'night."

CHAPTER 17

Joey and Billie spent Sunday together with a short visit with Jug and Ellen. Ellen was now going back home at night to sleep in her own bed but was often back to her son's bedside by 8 or 9 the next morning, hoping and praying that something good would happen, that today was going to be the day. But nothing changed and Jug showed no sign of coming out of his coma.

After their visit to the hospital, Joey and Billie took a walk around town. Joey showed her all the properties he looked after. She remarked on how ambitious he was and that he probably should hire someone to help him out. Joey was starting to think that way too and thought that maybe when he turned 16, he would get a used pickup and pull a trailer around with his hired help.

Right now, he had school to finish up and he had recently realized that perhaps some more serious effort needed to be put into his schoolwork, if he was going to make something of himself and keep pace with Billie. He knew he would never be into school as much as she was, but he could perhaps get into graphic design at Hancock College in Montrose. This thought had only been present recently and it was perhaps the idea that Willie Magee had planted in his head a few weeks ago. The idea that someday he might go to work for Magee Construction as a designer was exciting to say the least, but

Joey wanted Willie to hire him for his ability and not because he was in a relationship with his daughter.

Their walk ended at the diner just a block from the bridge over black creek.

"Can I buy you lunch?" Joey asked.

"I could eat," Billie replied coyly, but we could make it a Dutch treat.

"Okay… I have never heard of that. What does it mean?"

"It means we each pay for our own meals. Mom told me about that old custom. She encouraged me to offer that if you were to suggest going out to dinner."

"Well, I would sooner pay, just so this is like a real date, if you don't mind."

"Of course, I don't mind!" Billie released Joey's hand and they walked the last half a block with their arms around each other."

Just as they were about to reach the entrance to the diner, they were pelted with something that felt hard at first and then gooey and disgusting as a truck went whizzing by… Eggs! Slimy goo splattered all over them and the brick wall of the diner. Shell fragments littered the sidewalk around their feet. They both turned to see who had done this but all they could make out was the back end of an older green pickup truck. Now they were wiping the mucus-like egg guts from their hair, and it was running into their face.

"Joey! I can't see! Something hit me right in my eye!'

Joey turned his attention to Billie and began wiping the slop from her face and neck. "Jesus, who would do this! Are you ok? There must be two dozen eggs here. The sidewalk is totally splattered, and we are too."

"I think I'm okay, but my eye stings!"

Joey tried to clean Billie's face with his fingers. A few people were beginning to gather around them, and a woman offered him some tissue. Joey took it and tried to clear all the sticky mass away from Billie's eyes. Another older man who happened to be walking by across the road offered to help but there was really nothing anyone could do.

"Thank you, sir, but did you happen to see who did this?" Joey asked frantically.

"I didn't make out the people, but it was an older Ford F150. I would say mid 1970's, green with some brown primer paint."

Joey picked Billie up in his arms and carried her across the street and the short distance up the road to Billie's house. Billie hung on and buried her head into Joey's chest still not opening her eyes.

"Mrs. Magee!" Joey yelled. Then remembering what she told him, "Sarah!"

"Mom!" Billie joined in.

Footsteps came from downstairs and Sara entered the foyer.

"God, Billie, what happened?"

"Someone hit us with eggs," said Joey. "She got hit in the face and her eye is hurt. She needs it cleaned out. Can you bring a stool over to the kitchen sink?" Joey was surprised at his ability to deal with this so logically.

"Sure. Here set her down here." Sarah had a barstool in front of the sink and began to run water. "Let me see you honey," She grabbed a dish cloth and began cleaning her face.

"I think we need to get her to try to open her eyes so we can flush them out." Joey suggested.

"Okay," answered Sarah. "How do we do that?"

"Billie, I'm going to lift you up and put you on the counter so you can lie on your back and lean your head back into the sink."

Billie uttered a short, "Okay."

Once lying on the counter with her head back into the sink, Billie was able to open her eyes while Joey held her head to ease the strain on her neck. Sara managed to wring out some clothes and wipe around her eyelids. After a few flushes Billie was able to open her eyes without too much pain, but it looked like she was going to have a shiner. Obviously one egg had caught her directly in the eye, but it looked like she would be okay.

"I'm sorry, Sarah! I didn't see this coming!" Joey was near tears.

"Don't be silly Joey. This is not your fault in any way. Do you know who might have done this?"

"I have an idea," offered Joey. "Some guy who saw it happen said he saw two people in an old green Ford pickup driving away. I think I know whose truck it is. I'm pretty sure it was Wayne Litt's truck, but no one knows who was actually driving it."

"Is that Floyd Litt's son, the guy that owns the garage down at the corner?" asked Sarah.

"Yeah, I'm pretty sure."

Billie sat up with Joey's help holding a tea towel to her face. Joey put his head on her chest and hugged her.

"I'm so sorry Billie!" he managed.

"It's not your fault Joey!" She held his head with her left arm.

"No, it isn't." agreed Sarah. "What reason would Wayne Litt have for attacking you guys in such a foul manner?"

Joey lifted Billie off the counter and placed her on the stool. Both were coated in drying egg and their clothes were beginning to stink.

Satisfied that her daughter was going to be fine, Sarah said, "Billie, go and have a shower and change your clothes. Joey, follow me to the other bathroom. I will set out a pair of shorts and t-shirt of Willie's that should fit you. When you guys are out of your clothes set them outside the bathroom on the floor and I will put them in the wash."

While Billie and Joey were in their respective showers, Willie came through the front door, tossed his keys on the hall table and kicked off his shoes. He walked over to Sarah who was still showing signs of some distress. He bent down to give her a kiss and pulled back.

"What's the matter? And…what is that smell?"

"Let me pour you a drink," answered Sarah. "It's a long story."

She filled Willie in on what had happened and added, "Willie, you should have seen how Joey cared for Billie! He was so upset that she was hurt, and he wouldn't leave her side. He carried her here from the diner when she couldn't open her eyes."

"I have no doubt about that young man Sarah. You don't have to convince me. Billie's okay though, right?"

"Yes, she'll be fine. I think she's going to have a black eye from the impact of one of the eggs that seemed to hit her on or close to her right eye."

"Who did this?" Willie was becoming agitated.

"I think Joey might know. Listen, Joey was about to buy Billie lunch at the diner and that's where they were headed when they were attacked. I'm going to make up some hotdogs for them when they emerge from their shower."

Willie raised both brows and cocked his head to the side looking at Sara inquisitively.

"Willie, they are in separate bathrooms! Jeez!" Sarah laughed at his expression.

"I knew that," replied Willie sheepishly.

After a good fill of tube steaks, they sat around the coffee table in the family room and began to discuss who was responsible for the unprovoked assault. Billie looked much better, but her right eye was noticeably swollen. She sat close to Joey on the love seat facing Willie and Sarah on the couch.

"First, I want to say thank you, Joe, for looking after Billie and bringing her here so quickly."

"Of course, sir." Joey managed.

"Don't 'sir' me," Willie chuckled. "You know my name."

"Of course, Mr. Magee." Joey answered with a wry smile.

"Oh, a smart ass too," Willie laughed, and all joined in. The little bit of flippancy seemed to lighten the mood.

Billie snuggled into Joey, and he put his arm around her. Sara got up and brought back an ice pack, and Billie held it on her swollen eye.

"Sarah says you might have an idea who did this?" Willie asked.

"Well, I know the truck. It's Wayne Litt's. The older fella' that saw it happen said he thought there were two in the truck, and…"

"Go ahead, Joe. It sounds like you have some kind of theory," prodded Willie.

Joey continued, "Last semester, Paul Sinclair, Wayne Litt and John Mullen kind of pushed me around at school before I was rescued by one of the teachers who broke it up. Wayne Litt and John Mullen are both friends, or more like disciples of Paul Sinclair. Somehow, I know that Sinclair was behind this. He wouldn't dare be involved directly now after Jug's injury. I would bet anything that he paid those two to do this."

"Well, I guess there is not much we can do with no clear identification of the bloody idiots. I remember some kids throwing eggs out of a window on Hallowe'en a few years ago and the eggs actually cracked a car's windshield so they can make quite an impact."

"You think!" Billie snorted, looking past the icepack with her left eye.

Willie's eyes turned to Joey, "Well, you guys are lucky that nothing more serious didn't happen. How far along are you guys in collecting evidence against him? Do you have irrefutable proof?"

"Don is going to talk to Inspector Roberts today or tomorrow and we hope to confront Mr. Sinclair tomorrow sometime. I think we have enough proof, but as Don says, we may not have to use it. If we can convince him that we have proof, he might be willing to settle somehow."

"That's the language Mark Sinclair understands," added Sara. "Blackmail 1-0-1."

Don called Lilley shortly after lunch and asked her if she would like to go out for a dinner date tonight. He assured her that it was informal and that they would go by boat. Of course, she accepted freely, and they arranged to meet at Little Beach dock at 4 pm.

Pam had overheard the phone call as she entered the house from her walk downtown.

"You gotta hand it to him, Mom. He's a man of his word. I like him a lot. I'm glad too, that you can have some company your age to talk to and be friends."

"Thanks, honey. That means a lot. I like him too. In the short time we have known him…the things he has done for us…it's amazing, really!"

"I know, Mom. Just enjoy your dinner. I'll take Jessie up to the diner and have fries for supper if that's okay?"

"That's perfect. Here's a twenty. Doing something special will help her. I'm so glad you're back, Pam. I mean not just physically but…"

Pam took the money with a smile.

"Thanks, I know, Mom. It's hard though, sometimes. I almost blew it last night. If it weren't for Joey…"

Now it was Lilley's turn to interrupt. "I know about that too. I was awake and heading to the bathroom when I heard you guys whispering in the kitchen. It's all good, Pam. I love you, you know… and yes, I did hear Joey say that to you." They both laughed.

Lilley made her way to Little Beach as she heard the drone of Don's little boat approaching. The summer air was turning cooler but still comfortable and she relented to jeans and a crew neck sweatshirt for this outing. Don also in jeans and a Kamawog hoodie.

They headed north up the coast and reached the Duck Inn, a restaurant and outdoor patio right on the lake with boat slips. After settling into a nice table right along the railing next to the lake they ordered a couple beers and some finger food.

"This is awesome, Don! I'm glad you asked me."

"I'm glad too," Don replied, and they raised their pint glasses in an harmonious toast. It's hard to believe that in just a few short months that lake will be iced over and this patio probably full of white stuff. I can't bring myself to say it." Don laughed.

"I was here one time with Ellen," Lilley recalled, "one of our few lady's nights out…but that was a couple years ago. God, I wish that kid would wake up!" she set her glass down and stared out at the lake. Don squeezed her hand gently on the table in complete understanding, then sat back.

"Lilley, I was thinking. I don't think I'm going to go to the police with the evidence. If I tell Detective Roberts what we have, he would be obligated to investigate it further. It wouldn't be fair to have him withhold the evidence because we are looking for compensation from Sinclair. I think if we just tell Sinclair we have proof and threaten to go to the police that would be enough. What do you think?"

"I think you're right. It may even be illegal to put that on Roberts. I'm not sure. How do you plan to approach Sinclair?"

"I'm going to call him tomorrow and arrange to see him in his office. I know Joe's supposed to be in school, but do you think he could come with me?"

"Yeah, sure. I'll send a note with him to school. You can pick him up there. As long as the office knows, they will release him."

They both enjoyed a comfortable, relaxed evening on the patio, contented in one another's company. They sensed a bond developing but decided to just play it one day at a time. Later that evening at the Little Beach dock, they decided to part ways for the day. It was 7:30 and Jess had to be up for school the next day and Lilley wanted to make sure she was settled and ready for her big day.

"Thanks for such a nice relaxing evening, Don. I had forgotten what that was like."

"Well, I hope we can have many more, Lilley. I enjoy your company very much." He gestured for a hug extending his arms. Lilley accepted and kissed his cheek softly."

"I enjoy being with you too, Don."

"I will call you tomorrow after our confrontation with Sinclair."

Don hopped back into his boat and headed back to the lodge where he rented some dock space. He was going to stay one more week and figured it was dumb to keep launching it and dragging it around with his trailer.

"Hey Billie, why is your mom taking you to school tomorrow?" Joey asked as he reclined on his bed.

"I'm not sure exactly why, but she has a doctor's appointment in the morning. She hasn't really said what it's for. She says it's a checkup so, I'll roll with that, I guess.

"Hmm, okay. I really like your mom…just checking."

"That's sweet, Joey. I know she and Dad really like you too."

"I will text you as soon as I know what the meeting with Mark tells us. Personally, I hope it scares the shit out of him!"

"Yeah, me too," answered Billie.

They exchanged virtual kisses and bid each other good night.

CHAPTER 18

The school secretary entered Joey's geography class about at 1:00 pm and whispered something to Mr. Maclay's ear.

He pointed to Joey, "Joe Burgess, could you come here please?"

Joey got up and walked to his desk. "Yes, sir," Joey said, knowing full well why he had been summoned. Then he looked to Mrs. Kennedy.

"There's a Don Archer here to pick you up for your appointment," Mrs. Kennedy announced.

"Don't forget your cartography assignment, Joe,"

Joey loved cartography, "No worries, sir. I really like maps."

"I know you do, and I want a special effort from you." He winked and waved him off.

Walter Maclay was a kindly older teacher, a couple years past his retirement age. He loved his job and didn't know what he'd do if he wasn't teaching. He was a short, rotund man with a balding head a round face, speckled with many liver spots and framed by black horn-rimmed glasses. Joey liked him and found him interesting because he had been to almost every country in the world. In truth, Joey would often read an atlas rather than a novel or short story and the two had a good student /teacher relationship.

Don was waiting on one of the two chairs sitting in the hallway as Mrs. Kennedy and Joey appeared around the corner of the hallway.

"Must be important to miss school," said a rather austere Mrs. Kennedy. She was more like a strict teacher from yesteryear than a school secretary, but she ran a tight ship and kept the school firmly organized… a strictly by the book operator. "Come in here Mr. Archer and sign the book here for Joseph's release."

"Yes ma'am," said Don. Joey and Don exchanged grins but Don complied willingly.

"Thank you, Mrs. Kennedy," said Joey and the two made their way out and down the front steps of William's Glen High and jumped in Don's truck parked just across the road.

"Your release?" Don said muting his voice. "Is this a school or a penitentiary?

"Aw she's really a sweetheart but she does take her job seriously," Joey chuckled.

"Well, you ready for this, Joey," asked Don.

"You bet I am. I've been waiting for this for a while. Are we going right to Sinclair Pulp and Paper to meet with him?"

"Yep, it's about 10 minutes to the main plant on the way to Tinsdale."

"How are we going to approach him. Aren't you a little nervous?" Joey wondered out loud.

"Maybe a little," replied Don. "But just go in there knowing that we are in the right here. The Sinclair's are the ones hiding the truth. Before we go into his office, I want to pull over and chat with you about what terms we should ask for. We need to make sure he compensates Josh and Ellen and you as well."

They pulled over into a tractor dealership about 5 minutes away from the plant and discussed the terms they thought would be fair. When both were satisfied with the details they proceeded on to the plant.

They could see the large red and white stack and billowing white plumes of smoke or steam as they approached the site, then huge mounds of what looked like wood chips, belt conveyors and numerous buildings, big and small. The plant sprawled over several acres along Hawker River. The plant had been in the Sinclair family for 4 generations and consists of two separate plants. Although the name suggests that paper and pulp are the main products, the bulk of the business in the recent years has been the production of lumber for building. They invested heavily in the large saws and the drying and seasoning component of the business. As a result, the recent boon in construction has had a direct effect on the Sinclair's bottom line. Companies like Magee Construction were among the top clients and critical to the success of their business. In other words, Don and Joey knew where to hit them where it hurt the most.

They parked the truck in a large lot but close to the offices in a space marked for visitors and made their way through huge oak doors, an obvious placard for what lay within.

Don approached the receptionist's desk and announced, "Mr. Archer and Mr. Burgess to see Mr. Sinclair.

"Yes," she replied. "Mr. Sinclair is expecting you. Please take a seat through there." She motioned through to a hallway with beautiful wooden chairs upholstered in maroon leather lined each side of the hall. The walls were clad with frosted glass framed by oak casements and door entrances. They sat beside the door marked "Mark Sinclair – President" printed in gold on the frosted window portion of the door and waited for 'emperor' Sinclair to show himself. It seemed like 10 or 15 minutes before Mark Sinclair poked his head out of the office door – the mandatory wait was an obvious ploy to assert his importance and the premium required for a piece of his time. The two entered and sat in the chairs where Mark directed them in front of his massive desk. Everything in the room except for the windows were made of oak and framed wall panels of Georgia pine. It was a stately reminder of the years of prosperity for the company both resplendent and somewhat imposing to visitors.

"Okay, how can I help you gentlemen?" Mark asserted in a formal tone. "I assume that this is not a business call Don, bringing the boy, here along with you."

"Oh?" Don answered, not the least bit impressed with the person or his office. "Why would you say that?" This was an obvious suggestion that Joey's presence would imply a connection to the boating incident, but Mark was not willing to bite on this or concede quite yet. "And this is Joe Burgess, not just any boy, Mark," Don pressed on.

"I am aware," replied Mark. "Perhaps you could get to the point, Don. Time is money you know."

Don could not have written a better introduction for his presentation. "Well, that is certainly a convenient segue for our motive here today. I will get to the point…and here it is. We have proof that your son Paul caused the boating incident resulting in Joe's friend, Josh Parker suffering a coma and fighting for his life in Four Counties Hospital."

Mark was visibly squirming in his seat. "You're crazy! Maybe we should just stop this absurdity and put an end to this meeting. What proof of any kind could you possibly have? Our Donzi has been out of commission for a month now."

"Who said anything about a Donzi?" Don pounced on Mark's glaring slip of the tongue.

"I think he means the Donzi belonging to Paul. The one with the registration numbers, 'NY 521394 SW' and named 'Dreadknot'?" Joey read confidently from a folded paper he had retrieved from his jeans pocket.

Mark sat up now searching for the right words now, afraid of another verbal blunder. "You are just bluffing. I could charge you for attempted blackmail!" His voice was now rising to levels not necessary for an enclosed office and his posture was stiff and agitated. "You're just like all the rest…out for money! You need to leave!"

"Okay, but do you really want us to go to the police with our evidence?"

"What evidence? You know the registration numbers of our boat…so what? Anyone can look that up with the right connections."

"What about the photo evidence and eyewitness accounts?" Don said calmly.

Mark, beginning to stand, slumped back down into his high-backed leather office chair and realized he was beaten. He could not have this going public. He sat a few moments more wiping his mouth with the forefinger of his right hand and looking down scanning his desk as if the answer to his problem lay somewhere in the stacks of lumber orders. His reaction, he realized was an absolute admission of his liability. Don and Joey knew that he didn't really have to see the proof they held because his reaction said it all.

"What do you want?"

"We thought we would leave that up to you. Surely you could think of a fair compensation. Of course, there are two scenarios here, right?"

"You are really enjoying this aren't you, Don? You just have a personal vendetta because of our past business dealings, right? The business dealings where I came out on top!"

"You mean the dishonest, unethical dealings that temporarily left me bankrupt? You bet I am! But when there is a young man facing death because of your son, this is a whole other level of corruption! His mother has experienced untold grief and suffering. Maybe he lives. Maybe he doesn't. Do you want your son facing manslaughter charges? That could really color your business image couldn't it."

"Like I said, what do you want? You want a new boat?" He threw his hands up in a question looking at Joey. "You want money?

Mark stopped and fidgeted, looking around the room again for answers. Don and Joey both knew that they had him where they wanted and would not break their silence or suggest anything unless required.

"Look, I will buy you a boat! For Christ's sake, it was a lousy little rowboat! I will get you an aluminum boat with a motor." He paused and he knew that was not going to be sufficient. Don and Joey remained silent, knowing that the more he spun his tires, the deeper he would be stuck and looking for a way out. "I'll get the Parker's a new boat too…and build them a dock."

Still no reaction from the two opposite his desk. "Where's this proof? You haven't shown me anything that proves my son had anything to do with this."

He realized that he had basically admitted his son's guilt by offering these minor compensatory offerings.

Don broke his silence. "What would you expect someone to do for you if it was your son lying in a hospital bed with his very life on the line? I can show you the photos. I can also show you the video."

More silence. Joey felt like his lottery numbers were about to be announced. Don's plan was working flawlessly to this point. Of course, Mark was mulling over the idea that there was an actual video of the incident, when it was really a video of the underside of the Donzi.

"Let's go Joe, he obviously doesn't think we are serious." Don put his hands up on the arms of his chair as if he was about to stand.

"No, wait! Okay, we didn't realize he was involved at first, but we were able to put it together eventually. We know Paul was harboring a grudge on Joe, here. It was all about that little Magee bitch!"

Joey rose out of his seat and Don pulled him back down.

"You bastard! You better come through or I'll go to Detective Roberts myself with our evidence!" Joey yelled, sure that the receptionist was wondering about the proceedings.

"Okay, okay…Let me think about this. I still don't know for sure that you have any proof though. I mean, I haven't seen it myself."

Don nodded at Joey and joey pulled the mini digital recorder out of his pocket. "We were only going to use this if we absolutely had to."

Joey pushed the play button… "No, wait! Okay, we didn't realize he was involved…"

There it was…basically a confession on top of the evidence collected. Now it was show time. Mark Sinclair had better come through with something acceptable or they would put their demands on the table.

Sinclair got up and walked to the door. "Jean, cancel my 2:00 o'clock appointment and if anyone shows up, I'm not here." Then he walked back to his desk, clasped his hands and began to talk more resolutely. "Okay, you win. Boats for Mr. Burgess here, and Josh Parker as well as a dock. $100 000 to his family if he survives and $500 000 if he dies."

Don and Joey swallowed but didn't flinch. They could not have even suggested this size of settlement! Instead of accepting excitedly, Don simply took a deep breath while Joey was struggling to breath at all.

"So, you think that young man's life is only worth $500 000?" Don postured nonchalantly. He found Mark's eyes and studied him dauntlessly." He was like a UFA fighter about to break his opponent's arm and daring him to tap out. Meanwhile Joey had placed the recorder in front of him on the desk but had pressed the record button once more."

"Look, you win, okay? $500 000 for the family and 1 million if he dies!" Mark dropped his head into his hands and was looking like he was about to break down. "There has to be a time frame here. I mean he could die tomorrow or wake up tomorrow. I mean who knows? Can we date this October 15th? That's a month from now?"

"Okay, agreed, and don't forget the boats and the dock," said Don. "And if you think you might renege…we want it in writing before we leave. He nodded to Joey who reached for the recorder and pressed play and played back the entire conversation.

Mark reached into his desk drawer and pulled out a pad of paper, wrote out the entire agreement and signed it. Then he showed Don his signature on his license to verify it.

"Right, well we will see our way out," added Don. "You know, to save you having to smile congenially in front of your secretary and playing your honorable businessman game."

As they left the building and were walking toward the truck both were saying quite audibly, "Yes, yes, yes yes!"

When they were a few miles away from the mill, they stopped once again, pulled over the truck and got out walking along the side of the road to relieve their tension then turned to one another and hugged jumping up and down, screaming like they had just won the championship game of the NBA or NHL or the World Cup!

Joey shared the success of the meeting with Billie by sending her a thumbs up text and, "Will talk to you tonight."

Joey and Don were literally bubbling over when they arrived back at Joey's house. They tried to calm themselves before entering the screen door but Lilley wasn't buying their fake solemnity.

"Okay, tell me what you got!" she said.

They couldn't hold back and both began talking at once creating a totally undiscernible clatter. They both directed the other to say their side of the story with a palms up gesture towards the other.

"Okay," volunteered Don. "We will each say one phrase each until it is all out on the table."

"Sound intriguing," answered Lilley. "But, just a minute. I'll get Pam. I'm sure she would be quite interested. She went back into the hallway and returned with Pam and all sat calmly at the table.

"Okay, Joe. You get the first two words," offered Don.

Joey cleared his throat. "Jug lives. Family gets $500 000." Both Lilley and Pam covered their mouths and sat down staring in amazement.

"Oh sure, give me the bad one," Don said, but continued. "Jug dies. Family gets a million.

"Oh, my God!" Pam burst out.

"I get a new boat with an outboard motor," Joey said unenthusiastically thinking about Don's last statement.

"Parkers get a new boat and motor as well as a dock," Don said putting his hand on Joey's shoulder and recognizing his distress over the thought of Jug dying.

Don held up the officially written agreement signed by Mark Sinclair.

CHAPTER 19

It was now October, and the air was definitely changing. The trees were sporting the lastest in fall colors and the wind whipped the lake into swirling dark blue furrows. Little Beach looked so much different, darker and colder, at least by color. Orange and yellow splotches decorated the small bay's surface with a flotilla of maple and poplar leaves surrendered to the autumn breeze, gradually stripping the trees and transforming them into majestic skeletons. The wind brought the pine scent indoors and the entire lake district smelled of the forest.

Joey was busy collecting and splitting logs for the wood stove. The lawns and once burgeoning shrubs were now becoming dormant. Grass was not needing trimming and now he could focus more on preparing for the winter season. After school time was spent hacking away at logs and stacking manageable-sized firewood into the shelter behind the house. Today, however, was Saturday and Billie had pedaled her bike over to Joey's and the afternoon was for only them… together… alone.

It was midafternoon, and they were both shrouded by a large shawl Joey had absconded from the living room couch. They sat on the end of the dock, Billie surrounded by Joey's arms, legs and the mohair shawl, staring out onto the grey/blue water that just a few weeks earlier was more a reflection of a baby blue sky and warm sultry air. They just held on to each other as if they were meant to be and as if they always were. There was no doubt about the other, no feelings of jealousy, no backbiting. If they disagreed on something they worked it out or just left it alone. Neither wanted anything to come between them.

From the first moment Joey had seen Billie today, he noticed a difference in her, something about her face and the way she carried herself. The twinkle in her eyes that he loved so much was not as effervescent. She seemed content to just snuggle into his arms and did not volunteer what exactly she was thinking.

Joey looked over at the clear cool water and the sand, stones, and submerged weeds and immediately thought about the things he missed about this place.

"Jeez, I miss Harriet! She used to follow me all around the bush and would splash away in the water like a little pup. She was such a good, sweet spirit!" Joey fought the emotion but the swelling in his throat made him swallow.

"She sure was," Billie said. "And beautiful too!"

"Billie, I know something is eating at you a bit. Have I done something to put you off?" Joey shifted his butt on the dock to his right so he was more beside her now and could see her eyes.

"You are something else," Billie acknowledged. "I doubt if there is a guy in the world that could read a girl like you can."

"You're not any girl, Billie. I imagine you know me well enough to know if something was not quite right."

"Yeah, you're right. Okay, maybe I need time to get a handle on this, or maybe I need to think about what it really means…but…"

"You're scaring me now!" Joey interrupted.

"It's Mom. She thinks she may have breast cancer!" Billie began to sob slightly just hearing herself say the words.

Joey felt her tremble and then take a deep breath while he held her tighter and stared off out at the lake trying to take in her words. "But…how? What…" He couldn't really fathom the thought and knew so little about it that forming a sensible question was difficult.

Billie saved him from the struggle. "She had a mammogram last week, you know, that morning she drove me to school. It's like an x-ray and it showed some lumps that aren't supposed to be there. Tomorrow she is having a biopsy done."

"You mean like they are going to cut her and take a lump out? Joey asked.

"I don't think so. I think she said it's called a core-needle biopsy, so they do it with a needle. I know she is scared, and I am too. You are the only person who knows so we have to keep it quiet until we find out for sure." Billie buried her head back into Joey's chest and let out another deep breath.

"I'm sorry," he whispered softly, stroking her cheek with his fingers. "Hopefully it's nothing," Joey said, attempting to be positive.

"Yeah, hopefully."

That evening, after supper as Mark Sinclair sat out on his deck overlooking the lake he contemplated what he had agreed to. It occurred to him that he needed some kind of assurance that Don and Joey wouldn't go public but realized it was virtually impossible to prevent them from doing so if they decided to. He had never been a man to believe firmly in a man's word which is partly why people resisted trusting him. No one was hurt more personally or financially by Mark's business dealings than Don Archer, so how could he trust him to keep his word?

Not really knowing where he was going with this, he reached into the pocket of his hoodie pulled out his cell and dialed Don's number.

"Hello, Mark?" Don answered, expecting him to be the last person he'd see on his phone screen. He had intended to call Mark, though, to refine some of the details of the agreement.

"Don, I'm a little worried about the deal we made."

"Why is that?"

"How do I know you won't go public anyway, even after I hand over the boats and money?"

"Funny you should have trust issues, Mark," Don answered, sarcastically. "What if I put in writing that you called me to take a look at the Donzi that day because it had mechanical issues. I could testify that it wasn't running and therefore it couldn't have been Paul."

"That might work. Why would I call you though? You aren't a mechanic."

"Let's just say you knew an old associate that once owned a Donzi, which, in fact, I have. I even have some old paperwork to prove it."

"Okay, can you do that right away?

"I'll stick it in your mailbox tonight but there are a couple other things. Willie Magee knows all about our agreement. He has agreed to continue to do business with you provided you give him an extremely generous discount on your lumber products."

"Oh, the joy just continues, doesn't it!" Mark sneered.

"Well, I guess you have your son to thank, don't you…And by the way those boats and motors better be new, good quality aluminum, and with a minimum 15 horse power. I will need you to deliver the first one this Saturday to the town boat ramp. I will be there at 1:00 to see that it gets delivered to the Burgess dock."

"Yeah, yeah, okay. When is this ever going to stop?"

"When you're paid up in full. I will get that signed note over to you shortly."

Mark threw his phone unceremoniously onto the glass table on the deck just as Sally arrived and handed him a glass of wine. She sat on the other side of the table in an identical chair.

"Bad news, or just more from our friend, Don Archer?"

"Both," growled Mark. "This is a hell of a mess! I just want it to go away! That kid has to be held accountable somehow. Any ideas?"

"As a matter of fact, I do have an idea," answered Sally smugly. Remember how you said that after he graduates from high school you would take him around on your sales trips to our big clients and pay him as he learned the ropes?"

"Yeah, but that was before all the shit hit the fan!"

"Exactly. I think what would teach our dear son the most would be to learn the pulp, paper and lumber business from the inside out." She raised an eyebrow and Mark could see where she was going with this.

"That's a great idea! We will start him doing grunt work and operating machinery under Gordon Jenkins the crew chief in the pulp mill. Maybe a few months of 12-hour shifts will knock him down a peg or two. We will make him earn his way up instead of handing it to him. He's been avoiding me like the plague lately, and frankly I didn't want to talk to him much either until I had a plan."

He raised his wine glass and Sally reached over with hers for a mutual clink, somewhat mitigated by the decision.

Joey's phone rang with its locomotive voice making them both jump. He fumbled around under the blanket, and retrieved his phone from his jeans pocket.

"Hello?"

"Joey, it's Mom. He's awake Joey! Jug's awake!" Lilley could barely contain her emotion.

"Holy crap! Really? We'll be there as soon as we can!"

Joey grabbed hold of Billie, turning her to face him with his hands on her shoulders. He could not keep it in, and he broke down as he stared into her eyes and then looked down tears flowing uncontrollably. Billie gently raised his head with her hand. She knew those weren't sad tears when she saw his face. Joey seized her and held her tightly as he trembled.

"Is it Jug?" She felt his head nod. "Oh my God, Joey! Oh my God! Let's go now!"

Joey helped her up and he scrunched the blanket up and pinned it under his still sore arm and grabbed Billie's hand. They jumped from the dock and ran up the path to the house.

Once inside Lilley and Pam were there standing like they had been pacing.

"How did you get here so fast?" exclaimed Lilley as she ran over and embraced them both.

"Group hug!" Pam said as she ran over and joined in on the scrum.

When they pulled back, Joey asked, "Is he okay, Mom?'

"We need to talk about this…let's sit down."

They sat around the kitchen table as Jessie emerged from the back of the house holding onto a barbie doll in one hand and a brush in the other.

"What's going on? She asked in a worried voice.

"It's okay, Jess," said Joey. "Come over here." He patted his knee and she squeezed in between the table and his lap.

"Jug woke up, honey. That's really good news."

"Does that mean he's not going to die?" Jessie asked as she plunked her doll and brush down on the table.

Everyone kind of looked at each other at the table and Lilley spoke up. "Yes… yes, that's exactly what it means! This is a happy day!"

"I sense a 'but' coming," reasoned Joey.

"Hence the reason for not rushing over there," said Pam.

"Yes," said Lilley, "It's not like we can just go over there and see Jug and expect everything to be just like it was before the accident."

"We talked to the doctor about that a week or so ago," Joey said nodding with understanding. "He is not likely to remember much. In fact, he might not even know who he is."

"That's right, Joey," Lilley stepped in. "We can all go over there but I think we should go one at a time and not overwhelm him. I think, Joey, you and Billie should go first. You are the closest to him…but don't expect any miracles."

Joey hugged Jessie with his right arm and reached over and squeezed Billie by the shoulders with his other, each with excited smiles.

"What happened to your eye, Billie?" Jessie wondered, tilting her head.

"I will tell you all about it later. Ok?" answered Billie.

"I can run you guys over if you want," Pam said, as she looked over at Lilley who nodded with approval.

"Sounds good, honey. I'll stay here with Jess and give Ellen a call back to see how things are going and tell her you are on the way. I'll also call Don as he will be anxious to know this news as well."

The three of them piled into the old Chevy and rattled off down the road at a brisk pace while hope and anticipation filled their hearts. When they got to the hospital, Pam suggested that she stay in the parking lot until Joey texted her to either come in or that they were on their way back out.

When Joey and Billie reached the room, the door was closed. Some moving shadows could be seen against the light of the window through the glazed strip of glass in the door. Joey knocked lightly and after a couple seconds, Ellen and a nurse came to the door and stepped out into the hospital corridor. Joey noticed a doctor sitting on a stool beside Jug's bed but was unable to see his friend as the Dr's back and shoulders blocked the view. The nurse closed the door behind her and motioned over to the chairs in the small waiting room across the hall. Once they were all seated, Ellen on one side with Nurse Gillespie and Billie and Joey huddled together on a small love seat styled bench facing them, Nurse Gillespie began addressing them. She was a short, rather rounded figure with a kind, wholesome face. She looked like she would be just as comfortable carrying pails of milk at a dairy farm as the clipboard she held. Her dirty blonde hair was held in a donut like bun encircling her head. Her smile indicated that she had found her true calling, and the crow's feet in the corners of her eyes swept past her thin wire glasses frames giving away her penchant for smiling and revealed how she approached others with love and compassion.

"Ellen tells me you two are good friends of Josh. I am new to this wing, but I have some experience with coma patients. Do you understand that Josh will not be exactly as you knew him…at least not for now?"

Billie and Josh both nodded their heads simultaneously, Joey with a muffled, "Yeah."

The doctor has determined that he has a GCS of 10. That stands for Glasgow Coma Score. We measure things like if his eyes open to various stimuli, if he speaks or is able to respond verbally and to what extent he can feel and respond to physical stimulus. Each of those three things are graded out of 5, so 15 is completely awake like we are right now. 3 or under is … well let's say the prospects are grim. Josh has been in and out for a few hours since early this morning but now seems to be responsive but confused with some memory loss. His score is about 12, meaning he as a moderate to minor brain injury. To make an already long story shorter, we think his chances of a full recovery are probably 95%. There may be some lasting effects but it's impossible to tell at this point.

"That's great news then, isn't it? I mean he's going to live and come out of his, right?" asked Joey, as Billie squeezed his hand.

"That's right, Joe!" Ellen stood up, wiped the tears from her tired anguished eyes that had felt so much pain in the last several weeks. She extended her arms and Joey stood and embraced her.

"This is the best news!" ever he exclaimed. He patted her softly on the back and sat back down.

"Come here dear," Ellen extended her arms to Billie and she accepted her warmly as well.

"I'm so happy for you Mrs. Parker…for all of us!" Billie stepped back and the three sat back down facing one another again.

"You two are dear friends to my Josh, and I am very happy that he has such wonderful people as you in his life. His recovery will surely be accelerated because of your care and friendship…and you two, if you call me Mrs. Parker one more time, I'm going to call you Joseph, Joey and you Catherine, Billie!" They all laughed briefly.

Joey thought he had not seen Ellen smile since the boat incident over a month ago. It was as if a huge weight was being lifted from all of their hearts.

Ellen's phone rang and she pulled it out and had a tertiary glance. "It's your mom, Joey. Jane here will tell you what to do." She gestured at Nurse Gillespie and got up and walked down the hallway with the phone to her ear.

"Okay, guys, as Ellen said, my name is Jane and I was assigned to Josh just last night when he was showing signs of stirring."

"Pardon me, Jane," Billie spoke up, "How do you know so much when you're…" she hesitated.

"Just a nurse?" Jane completed Billie's sentence.

"No, not JUST a nurse. Nurses are the most amazing people I know."

"It's okay, dear. I am actually working toward getting my doctorate, and I specialize in head trauma."

"Sorry, I didn't mean to pry. I'm just interested in medical things and…anyway go ahead. I'm listening."

"Well, you seem like a bright kid, and you can get hold of me any time if you pursue a career in this field and need any advice."

"Thanks," Billie answered.

"So, yeah…" She leaned forward in her seat and spoke noticeably quieter as if she was divulging private or personal information.

"Ellen tells me that you're pretty well informed, but I want to impress on you that Josh may or may not remember you right now. He did finally call Ellen 'Mom' about an hour ago, so things are improving. He is in what we call a minimally conscious state. You can go see him but speak calmly and don't stay too long. I will come for you in about 10 minutes."

As they entered the room, they both noticed nothing much different from the last visit when Jug was totally out of it. He was slightly propped up with tubes and wires coming out of both arms and from under the covers. The only possible distinction on this day was that Jug's eyes were twitching and opening and closing. They walked over to the window side hand in hand looking down on their friend. It was never easy coming here but at least now there was some hope and even though the lumps in their throats were causing involuntary swallowing they were able to hold it together. As they studied his face and the opening and closing of his eyes it looked as though he caught each of their eyes once in a while, like he was trying to focus on his new guests.

"Jug?" Joey uttered, softly.

"Hi Jug," Billie added, also delicately as Jane had instructed.

Nothing came from Jug but just the struggling of his eyes to fix on their faces. Then his left arm, the one nearest to them rose from his side and his index finger pointed shakily at Joey and fell back onto the bed. Joey placed his hand on the back of Jug's hand avoiding the protruding IV hose. He felt Jugs fingers slightly squeeze together as if in acknowledgement.

"Jug?" Joey tried again still quietly and calmly but still no verbal response from Jug.

Billie tried the same tactic with a little touch and gently issuing his name. It was clear that he was not quite ready to communicate but something told them that he recognized them.

"Do you think he knows who we are?" Joey asked.

"For some reason, I think he does," answered Billie. "There's something about the way he is trying to look at us and why would he raise his arm up like that?"

They continued to say his name and received very little response for the next few minutes. Then Jane came back into the room and stood beside them.

"Anything?" she asked.

"He raised his arm and it looked like he was pointing his finger, but he didn't say anything," Joey answered.

"And it looked like he was trying to focus on us, but it seemed like it tired him," added Billie.

"Well, I think we better leave him now and let him rest. I think you can agree that he is quite a bit better though, can't you?" Jane said cheerfully.

"Sure can. Hopefully he makes a little improvement every day," said Joey.

Jane motioned with her nod and pointed with her hand to the door, and they all headed for the hallway.

"Aww…aaaa," desperate attempts to speak came from the hospital bed behind them and they turned and retraced their steps.

Joey and Billie both looked back at Jane as if to ask permission to stay a minute longer. Jane nodded her approval and the two resumed their position beside the bed, but nothing more seemed imminent.

Then… "Jaao…Joee…"

It was all he could muster and it seemed like he fell back into a sleep or passed out like a drunk might after a bender.

"He said my name!" Joey said excitedly, looking back and forth at Billie and Jane.

Billie held onto Joey's arm and shuddered excitedly. "He's going to make it, Joey. I know he is!"

"Let's go now guys," advised Jane. Then smiling brightly, "I am really impressed with that!"

As they gathered again in the little waiting room across the hall, Ellen once again joined in the group.

"Ellen, Jug said Joey's name!" Billie burst out.

"Really! Wow, you guys need to come by here every day. That is really good news! Right, Jane?"

"That is awesome news, Ellen! It tells us that there is lots going on in his brain and to be able to recognize people is a very positive signal."

Billie put her arm around Joey and hugged him tightly with an excited expression.

"Okay, you guys, another group hug is called for here!" Ellen stood up and opened her arms once again and all four joined in.

Joey and Billie said their goodbyes to Jane and Ellen and headed down the hallway toward the elevators with their arms around each other, smiles on their faces and smiles in their hearts. Where they walked with tentative steps of uncertainty a half hour ago, they now strode quickly and confidently as if at any minute they would both jump up and click their heels.

"I'm so happy, Joey!" Billie said as Joey pushed the large glass doors of the entranceway open for her.

"Me too!" said Joey. Then he stopped and pulled her into him kissing her sweetly on the lips. She looked up at him with that twinkle in her eyes that he adored. "Thank you for being with me through all this."

"Where else will I ever be?" replied Billie.

CHAPTER 20

On the way home from the hospital Joey asked Pam to stop around at Dr. Norman's so he could make his monthly donation to Angela Norman's dog rescue service. After he had left the car and was making his way up the steps to the office Pam turned to Billie.

"Do you have any idea the difference you have made in my brother's life?"

Billie looked a little embarrassed and didn't know really what to say to that except what her inner voice told her, "He has made a huge difference in my life too, you know."

Pam looked a little confused, "How could you need him? You have everything you could ask for…money, great parents, popularity. You could have anybody you wanted for a friend. And look at you. You're absolutely gorgeous!" Pam laughed sincerely.

"Well, thanks for that, but everybody sees things differently, I guess. I have never been in need of anything material. You're right about that. My life is not all that you see on the surface, Pam."

"Wait a minute," Pam interrupted. "You don't seem 14 years old to me. It's like you are twenty something. Does anyone ever tell you that?"

"Actually, a lot of people," admitted Billie. "Maybe it's because I used to read all the time. It's like I have the answer because I've read it somewhere, you know?"

"But seriously, Billie. "I used to see Joey as a moody little brat that just wanted to be alone and didn't care about anybody but himself. Since he's been around you, he's become…I don't know…nice, warm, loving. How did you do it?"

"I didn't do anything. He's always been that way. I think he needed someone to really see him and feel him. Yeah, he had Jug…a buddy to hang with and he and his gramps had a great close relationship, but he needed someone to share everything with."

"So, have you shared everything?" Pam said with a smile and a wink.

"Wow, you get right to it don't you? No, we haven't, and that is part of the mystique of Joey. If I told you that a teenaged boy didn't care if he had sex until he was old enough to make a full commitment you would laugh and say, 'where are his hormones?', right? He loves me, Pam, and I feel it deeply. He would do anything for me, and I would for him."

"I know he does, and I know you do. It just seems so…I don't know. Do you think you guys can make it all the way? You know, all the way to the little house and into marriage and all that? I mean, the odds are certainly against it."

"We have talked about that," Billie answered quickly.

"Of course, you have" said Pam, sarcastically. "Did you guys just jump into your twenties and decide to skip your teens? I mean aren't the teen years all about experimenting and yes, screwing up and learning from your mistakes?"

"For most, I think you're right," said Billie. "Joey learned a lot by watching others and if you don't mind me saying, from your father's abuse."

Pam looked out the car window sadly contemplating their home life over the last few years.

"I'm sorry. I am out of bounds. I didn't mean to…"

"No, you're not. You are just stating the obvious and you're right. We all had to grow up too fast. We both lost our teenagerhood, especially Joey because he is still in his mid-teens." Pam paused…" But I'm still curious about you. I know it's none of my business, really, but what drew you to him?"

"Remember I told you that I read a lot?" Pam nodded. "Well, there's a reason, and I've really never even been through this with Joey but, I'll try to explain. I have things…just things. I have a couple people I can really call friends but most of the people who call me friends aren't real. You say I'm popular. What makes a person popular? In William's Glen you are popular because you have things, just things, money, in other words. People would hang around me so they could be seen as being liked by me, so they could appear popular too. It took me a couple years to realize this and when I did, I kind of withdrew into myself. I didn't want to be with people who just used me to be popular. I became a reader just because I was lonely. I didn't have anyone who wanted to know the real me, a genuine, what's the word? I guess it's soulmate or kindred spirit. Even after I met Joey, I was cautious, but I gradually came to realize that with him, what you see is what you get. There is literally nothing I couldn't tell him or share with him."

"No way, you're 14!"

They both laughed as Joey returned to the car.

"Well, I see you guys are hitting it off pretty well," said Joey, looking for a reaction.

"Instead of looking over at Pam and saying nothing or maybe giggling or something, so that you might be a little embarrassed, I'll tell you why we were laughing. We were laughing because she is convinced that we are not 14. The reason for that is because I love you so much!"

She turned and put her arm around his neck and kissed him softly.

"Yep, no way you guys are 14!" Pam repeated.

Now, all three laughed.

"Hey, Billie, you wanna come back over and I'll do some tube steaks on the barby?" Joey suggested his spirits obviously uplifted after their visit to the hospital.

"Sounds like a plan," answered Billie. "I'll just text mom and tell her what I'm doing."

While Billie was texting Pam pulled up on the road in front of their house. Don's Truck and a boat trailer were in the laneway.

"Hmm, I wonder if we should walk in on them?" Pam asked.

"Pam, it's not like that. At least it's not like that yet but I'm pretty sure there is a little spark there." Joey answered as they exited the car and strode up the laneway.

"Uh, looks like Don got a new trailer. This one looks brand new," observed Joey.

"They all look the same to me," replied Billie.

Lilley and Don were at the table and Jessie was over playing on the rug in front of the TV as they entered the hallway.

"Hey guys," Don said. "How's Josh doin'?"

"Hey…He's, well, let's just say it's going to be a long recovery but he is actually awake!"

"He said Joey's name!" Billie added excitedly.

"That's wonderful!" said Lilley.

Jessie ran over and took her position on Joey's lap.

"Hey joey, you should see…"

"Shh, Jessie, you promised," Lilley interrupted.

"But…"

"What's going on here?"

Jessie moved over to Pam's lap as if she was looking for a more comfortable seat and slightly annoyed that she had been silenced.

"Yeah, what's the secret you guys?" Pam added a little puzzled by the secrecy.

"Don, I think you should deal with this," said Lilley. "You did all the work on this."

All the kids sat there with their mouths a little open. Billie reached over and put her hand on Joey's shoulder as if she was beginning to understand the scenario about to be unfolded.

"Well, you probably noticed a boat trailer in the laneway." Don paused. "Let's put it this way. Why don't you go and take Billie for a ride in your boat, Joe?"

Billie patted his shoulder with two quick taps, "I knew it! Joey, your boat…get it?"

"Really?" Joey's eyes were wide as saucers. "Seriously? Already? And a trailer?"

"Well, you don't exactly have a boat launch over at little beach, do you?" said Don.

"Holy, crap!"

Pam reached over from her seat around the corner of the table and offered a high five. Joey gladly accepted the invitation with a good smack. Then Jessie, not to be left out, did the same.

"Congratulations, little bro. You're a boat owner" Pam announced.

"God, I don't know what to say! How did you manage the trailer?"

"It's amazing the power of leverage, or blackmail…whatever you want to call it," answered Don.

Billie pushed on Joey's shoulder so he would turn toward her. "I think you should say, 'Do you wanna go for a ride Billie?' don't you?"

With nothing else to say, Joey grabbed Billie's hand and they were out of there in a flash and down the path to Little Beach. They slowed up as they approached the dock to take in the sight of a beautiful 16-foot aluminum boat with a carpeted floor and new 15 horse 4-stroke Johnson outboard. Joey pulled her up on the dock and got in the boat reaching back to help her in. It had vinyl, removeable seats, three in total; one to operate the tiller where he sat, one on the opposite side on the middle seat, where Billie positioned herself and one in the middle of the seat in the bow. It was like a dream come true for Joey! It was something he envisioned for himself down the road after he had established himself in a permanent occupation and settled, maybe 5 or 6 years from now. He sat there staring up and down the boat and took hold of the throttle arm and touched the top of the motor as if he was caressing a new pet. Billie was fixed on Joey's face and covered her mouth about to cry for the joy she knew he was feeling.

"This is not just a fishing boat. This is a great little boat!" Joey burst out.

Billie got up and sat on Joey's lap, "I'm so happy for you, Joey! You deserve it for all the shit you've been through…pardon my French! Let's take her out for a spin.

Billie walked up to the bow line and unhooked it from the cleats on the dock and Joey looked after the stern line. He examined the set up and began pumping the bulb on the fuel line. Then he pulled out the choke…

"Hey, this thing has a battery and electric start…sweet!"

He pressed the orange button on the control arm and the motor sprung to life immediately. He revved the throttle by cranking the handle a few times. The motor purred and quieter than he had ever heard an outboard motor. He thought it was likely because it was new and they were becoming more and more muffled due to the improved technology. He slowed the idle and pushed the gear lever into reverse and backed away from the dock. Then he pointed the boat out into the lake and headed out full speed into the calm evening water of the lake. Both were smiling ear to ear and hooting whenever they jumped a small boat wave. After a couple minutes Joey slowed the engine down and turned it off facing the setting sun to the west directly over Little Beach. It was 7:30 and the sun was already painting the clouds in amber and orange hues. They both took positions on the floor of the boat with their backs against the middle seat arms around each other. It was a cool night, but the excitement and the comfort of each other's company warmed their bodies and their hearts.

"Billie, I hope we can be together forever, and do this forever."

"Me too, Joey! It's beautiful, isn't it, so quiet and peaceful!"

She turned and gently brought Joey's face to hers with her right hand and they kissed so passionately that they both had watery eyes and then enveloped one another tenderly as Billie slunk down into Joey's chest completely fulfilled and happy.

"Billie, I forgot to tell you the reason I was so long at Dr. Norman's today. He usually doesn't see me put the envelope in their mailbox, but Angela saw me and asked me in for a minute. Do you remember the Telfers up on the Tilson Line?"

"Yes, that was horrific! The poor woman! Mom was so upset about that. Didn't he hit a transport truck head on? I know Mrs. Telfer was part of Mom's charity drive last summer."

"Yeah, it's pretty sad. Well, I guess Mrs. Telfer couldn't deal with their dog after her husband was killed so she turned it over to Angela's rescue. She usually takes senior dogs but this dog is a 4 month old Bernedoodle. I swear, she is the cutest little dog I've ever seen! She ran right over to me when I bent down. It baffles me how she could just give it up like that."

Billie looked up, "Maybe the dog was too much of a reminder of her husband. It's hard to say but I know Mom was so traumatized by the death of our dog that she will never have another one. People react to trauma in different ways I guess."

"I would love to be able to rescue that beautiful little dog. She has the same markings as Harriet but because she has poodle in her she would have a longer life. The trouble is, it costs about 400 bucks to sign her over to someone."

"Look!" Billie pointed up into the darkening sky. "A shooting star!"

"Oh, yeah…that's cool!"

They lay their heads back for a few more minutes taking in the wonders of the infinitesimal expanse and the wonder of the jewels in the sky above them. Drifting silently with just the lilting lap of the small ripples against the boat's hull and the gentle rocking of the little boat they began to feel like they could easily just fall asleep in each other's arms. After a few more minutes of pointing to each new star slowly establishing its position in the sky as the darkening background of space revealed it, they resumed their riding positions and thought that they should head back before they were caught in the blackness without lights.

When they got back to Little Beach and tied up the boat securely, they headed for the house, arm and arm, barely able to see where they were walking and giggling with every misstep and root they stumbled on. It was one of those nights you don't forget, a milestone, a special event shared with the person you loved. They both felt that intensely.

Before they got to the house, and within earshot of the conversation and sporadic laughter heard from the kitchen, Joey stopped Billie and looked at her seriously.

"Billie, I know you don't really like talking about it but if you can't talk to me, who can you talk to? I want to know how your mom is. She means a lot to me too, you know. She accepted me, no question. I know it's because of how she feels for you, but she has been so…"

"We don't know yet, Joey. She goes in again on Monday and they are going to go over the pictures they took and see what she has to do from here."

"I know this is weird but tell her that I send my love. I do love you and your family, Billie!"

"I know you do, because I feel the same way about yours. When we can go to bed each night on our phones, it's like I wouldn't be able to sleep if we missed a night."

Joey chuckled, "You too, eh?"

"Well, when we go to bed Monday night, I will let you know if there is any news about that."

She hugged Joey tightly and Joey could feel as she squeezed him that she needed this embrace a little more than most.

Monday came and after school Joey checked in with Ellen, calling her on his cell as he walked home. Nothing much had changed other than Jug was apparently able to say "Doctor" after Ellen had repeated it a few times. It was like he was an infant learning to talk all over again.

Joey managed to partially put that aside by directing his attention to his new boat. He took it for short rides rationing the gas as best he could. He would have to take on some more jobs in town to be able to drive and maintain his new toy.

He was strumming some chords on his guitar about 9 pm when his phone barked. He decided that a dog bark was a better ring tone than a locomotive, irritating enough to get your attention but not blaring to the point of scaring him into heart failure.

"Hey, Billie," he said softly, propping the guitar against the wall beside the bed.

"Hi," Billie replied, and then there was an uncharacteristic and noticeable pause.

"What's wrong? I feel like you are hesitating or something." More silence.

"Mom does have cancer, Joey!" another pause.

"God… I'm so sorry, Billie!"

There was something about hearing Joey's voice that caused Billie to lose her voice and her composure. She was like a young child who scraped her knee but didn't cry until she saw her mother. Joey was her shoulder to cry on but right now all she had was a cell phone pressed between her ear and her pillow. Her throat ached and she didn't have the words to really tell him how awful she felt.

"I wish I could be with you now!" Joey whispered. Then he too, sensed her pain and although he did not make a sound the tears streamed down his cheek. "They have lots of treatments now," Joey offered desperately trying to console her.

"I know, but it's already stage 3. The cancer clinic says that they think it's in her lymph symptom and it's spreading. She needs surgery…radiation and…" She could not finish, and she wept openly, uncontrollably.

"I'm coming to you. Meet me at the front door of your place in 30 minutes," Joey said emphatically.

"But, how…"

"Just trust me." He turned off his phone.

Joey knocked lightly on Pam's door and after no response he opened it and tiptoed over to her as she slept on her side facing away from him. He gently shook her shoulder and whispered.

"Pam…I need you. Can you help me?"

She opened her eyes and was startled as she turned and faced Joey.

"What the hell, Joey! What's going on? …Okay, okay, I'll meet you out in the kitchen." Joey left and she got up throwing on her bath robe and wiping the sleep from her eyes.

She sat across from Joey, immediately noticing his distress and when he looked at her, he began to sob again. Pam got up and came around the table and sat in the chair next to him cupping his head with her hand.

"God, Joey, what's wrong?"

"It's Billie's mom, Sarah. She has cancer and Billie is lying in bed crying and I want to be with her so much it hurts!" His tears flowed once more.

"Get your clothes on. I'm taking you to her! Now, let's go!"

Joey threw his arms around his sister and cried shuddering against her shoulder.

"I knew you would," Joey managed to say.

They left a note for Lilley and promised to be home in time for Lilley to have the car for work.

They pulled up in front of the residence and they could see Billie inside the big glass door in a house coat and slippers.

"Go to her and comfort her. She needs you to just hold her bro. I'll go to work with Mom in the morning and pick you up so you don't miss too much school. I love you, little bro!"

Joey approached the front door and Billie turned the dead bolt and let him in and then locked it once he was inside. They stood there embracing, both in spasms of grief but comforted by each other's company.

"Joey, you didn't have to come…"

"Would you have stayed home if I was in pain?" he answered. "Show me where you sleep. I want to just hold you all night."

That's exactly what happened that night. They held each other and found themselves drifting in and out of sleep mixed with periods of shudders and pain induced spasms and lots and lots of tears. As the darkness became shades of grey and the birds began to chirp, they faced each other bundled in arms and the legs intwined. Joey knew he had to leave soon as he didn't want her to get in trouble for having a boy over all night. He brought his hand up and gently wiped her still moist cheek. She opened her eyes and seemed somehow less stressed than she had just a few hours ago. She buried her face into his chest and held on tightly.

"I should go. I don't want you to get in trouble. Phone me tonight and we'll go to bed on our phones again. I don't want to ever leave you Billie!"

"Thank you for being there for me, Joey. I love you so much!" She held on even tighter and sobbed into his chest.

Joey gently extricated himself from under the covers, still in his jeans and t-shirt. He sat on the edge of the bed and slipped on his runners as Billie rolled over and put her hand on his back.

"Talk to you tonight," Joey whispered. "I will always love you, Billie. We have to be strong…for your mom. We will get through this!"

He bent over and kissed her sweetly. Then he covered her up, put his hand on her head, got up and tiptoed stealthily to the door, pulling his hoodie over his head, and left without a sound. Once outside he texted Pam and they arranged to meet at the coffee shop a couple blocks from Billie's residence. Pam delivered Lilley to her work and picked up Joey as planned circled around through the drive-thru and bought coffees.

On the way back to William's Glen sipping on coffee, Pam asked, "How bad is it? What stage of cancer is it? Do you know?"

"Billie says it's stage 3… metasag…metesatig…meta…"

"Metastatic…That means it has reached other parts of her body and it's spreading," Pam interjected. "I'm sorry Joey, but that's not good."

"Will she die from it?" Joey asked, reluctantly.

"A friend of mine from the residence had a mother with breast cancer. I'm not sure what stage it was but she told me that there was a good chance of her making it another 5 years or so."

"So, she will die from it," Joey whispered to himself, trying to get a grip on what it really meant. He had dealt with death before with Gramps and even with Harriet, but this was Billie's mom, a young woman in the prime of her life.

Sarah Magee spent a good portion of her adult life raising money for others less fortunate than her. The tragic irony that she should be struck with cancer was obvious to all those who knew her.

Willie and Sarah struggled mightily with this while alone with each other but would not let it influence their interaction with friends or business associates.

She began treatments as soon as she could starting with chemotherapy. It would likely mean that a double mastectomy would be in the near future and even the removal of her lymph nodes since her cancer was aggressively spreading. That would be followed by radiation, hormone therapy and immunotherapy.

One warm fall day, Joey took his boat out on the lake after school and caught 5 pan fry sized perch. He took them home filleted them and bagged them with salt and flour. Later that afternoon, just before the supper hour, he arrived at the Magee's house, laid down his bike on the sidewalk and rang the doorbell. He didn't know what else to do. He just wanted Sarah to know that he cared and that he knew that she was going through a difficult time.

The door opened and Sarah stood on the threshold looking surprisingly ordinary. Ordinary was a good thing in Joey's eyes, not exactly sure what he expected her to look like. Perhaps he thought she might look sickly or off color and feeble.

"Joey, Hi! Come on in."

"Aw, that's alright, Sarah," Joey had trouble meeting her eyes and didn't really know where to look. "I can't stay. I just thought you might like these." He held up the freezer bag. "They're perch, caught fresh today and ready to cook or store in your freezer," he said proudly.

"That's so sweet! Thank you!" She was aware of his uneasiness and noticed his inability to look at her in the eye. Her shoulders slumped and she tilted her head, touched by his sensitivity. "Joey?" He looked up now into her eyes and felt his lip tremble. "It's okay, sweetie. We are going to get through this!" She set the bag of fish on the hall table inside the door stepped out and embraced him warmly.

"I'm sorry!" Joey said almost unknowingly. He couldn't hold back the tears and they stood there momentarily. Sarah's eyes also filled as she looked out toward the street over Joey's shoulder.

Then he released his hold on her and turned wiping his eyes and walked toward his bike.

"Billie told me what you did for her the other night… thank you!"

There was a pause as he wondered how many mothers would have approved of him spending the night with their daughter, even though Billie would have told her the full context of the visit.

"And thanks for the fish. How about we have a little fish fry on Saturday? We will do them up on the barbeque."

"Sounds good," answered Joey, looking up at her and nodding, forcing a half-smile.

"We all love you, Joey. You mean a lot to our family, and I really appreciate you making the effort to come over today."

Picking up his bike and looking back Joey managed, "I love you guys, too." Then he struggled desperately to catch his breath.

He mounted his bike and road away with tears streaming down his face and trembling. He had to pull over into the park and sit on the bench where Billie and he had sat many times. After gathering himself and drying off his face on the sleeve of his sweatshirt, he continued home.

CHAPTER 21

In the following days and after the fish fry which was, by all means, a normal get together between friends…friends who were more like family, Sarah's appearance was changing. She seemed puffy or slightly bloated and Joey just assumed it was the treatments that were causing the change. Yet Sarah, herself, did not change. She maintained her warm, loving nature and upbeat personality as well as her sense of humor. Willie tried his best to be as strong as she was, but Joey could notice a faraway look in his eyes every so often. He noticed this because Billie and her dad were two peas in a pod that way. He knew when Billie was down instantly, and Willie had all the same markers.

This all seemed like a cloud, like something out of a fantasy, too weird to be true. But somehow Joey knew this was reality. That night when he and Billie said goodbye to each other it was not the same. It was colder and Joey couldn't maintain any eye contact with Billie. His entire world revolved around her and in a time like this he couldn't reach her. She closed the door on him before he could ask what was wrong. But of course, he knew and thought it best to not press her.

The days and the weeks flew by and every night while they still communicated on the phone, Joey asked Billie the same question.

"How's your mom doing?"

What was Billie to say? Nothing really changed. Little by little Sarah's hair fell out. Little by little her body paled, and her skin turned gelatinous. Little by little Billie didn't want to answer Joey's questions. Nothing had ever driven them apart before, but this was too much for her. She wanted to share everything with Joey, but she was too impaired by her communion with her mother and her condition. She couldn't see any further past the immediacy of her basic anatomical connection with her. Finally, she didn't answer Joey. She couldn't bear to talk and turned her phone off before she went to bed. She couldn't find the strength. She lost her connection with everything that was outside her bond with her mother.

A month went by, and Joey had not even seen Billie. He couldn't reach her. He called and he called. He texted and there was no response. Just weeks ago, they had gone to bed together via their phones, but nothing seemed to get through to her now. Joey was starting to fail at school, starting to revert to his sullen self and it took its toll both in his school life and at home.

Pam caught him down at the dock one chilly fall night. She had known that things weren't right with him, as everyone else around him did, and she had her theories as to why that was. He was sitting at the very end of the dock, cross-legged and head down. Pam was leaning on a sapling where the path gave way to the opening at Little Beach.

"I know you are hurting, Joe. Is there anything I can do to help?"

"No," he answered abruptly.

"Please, little bro…let me help."

"How can you help. I don't need anything!"

"Yes, you do...She loves you, Joe. I know she does. Just give her space."

"Space? Space? She always told me that we should share everything and not hold any secrets." Joey swiveled around on the dock and faced Pam, wiping the remnants of his previous thoughts from his eyes.

There was a long pause and Pam gathered her thoughts. She knew what she wanted to say but it was such a sensitive subject that she needed to calculate her words.

"You know her mom has cancer. You know Billie is an overly sensitive person, right? Joey...if our mom had cancer, how focused would you be on anyone else?"

"I would still...I would still love her!' Joey lowered his head a cried into his knees.

The next thing he felt was Pam enveloping him in her arms and cradling him in his sorrow.

Joey sputtered, "I care about Sarah too. Why won't she let me into her family's circle. We've always been so close and now I feel like I'm just...some guy she knows and not..."

"She will come around Joe. Please have faith in her. She needs you to be faithful and hang on. It's something she really counts on you for right now."

"Why? I just don't get it! If I was really down and sad, the only person in the world I would need would be her!"

"You are not in her shoes right now, Joey. It's a complicated thing for her."

Pam held on to Joey for a good 20 minutes out at the end of the dock at Little Beach. Then they stood up with her arms still around him and walked him back to the house.

Still distraught, Joey could not go to bed. No one meant more to him than Billie and he felt estranged, abandoned, and could not console himself.

It was 1:30 in the morning when Joey's phone went off. He was still cradling his head in his arms at the kitchen table and his eyes were like sandpaper, sore and itchy.

"Hello?" Joey answered.

"Hi Joey… I'm so sorry!"

"Billie…Joey couldn't combat his emotions. "I love you. I want you to feel better! I'm so sorry…do you not love me anymore?" He couldn't hold it in and completely broke down.

"I've treated you so wrong. Please forgive me!" Billie pleaded. "My world just came crashing in on me and then I realized that my world is nothing without you! Of course I love you. Please forgive me!"

"But you shut me out, Billie. All I wanted was to make you feel better and you shut me out! I haven't even seen you for weeks. I wouldn't do that to you!"

"I know!" Then Billie broke into a full-on sobbing and could not contain herself any longer either.

Their phones were silent, neither knowing what to say next, and both found themselves trying to sleep with heavy hearts and unfinished messages. There was nothing that could be said that would stop the hollow hurt in Joey's heart or the intense sorrow in Billie's.

Joey had no idea what to do next. He felt a little better to hear her say that she still cared about him, but where was she? Should he make the move to go and see her? He couldn't. It was she who shut down on him. Was that too selfish? Her mother has cancer. How could he really know what that was even like?

It was cold and grey outside and Joey's heart felt the same. He had pulled the boat and trailer with his lawn tractor all the way from the town ramp to a clearing behind the house. He covered the boat up and put some gas treatment in the tank and drained all the water out of the motor. The November winds were cutting as Joey found himself walking into town along in front of Jug's house. Jug was showing slight signs of improvement every day, but it was a slow process. He thought it weird that Billie had called him and said how sorry she was and that she loved him, but it was now two days later and there was still no more communication between them. Joey didn't know what he should do but didn't want to intrude on her family's personal life. He didn't know where he was walking but he ended up standing on the road in front of Billie's house just staring at the front door. He desperately wanted to walk up to the door and knock on it and have Billie throw her arms around him and give him the magical twinkle. He couldn't find the courage. If Pam could see him now, he thought, she would not question that he was only 14 years old.

    He decided to turn and walk away and just hope she would make a move to him soon. By the end of the day, he was beside himself and needed to talk to someone. He opened the door to the girls' bedroom where the kitchen chairs were supporting a network of sheets and blankets draped around the room forming a huge tent. One end of the blanket was tied to the top bunk and it was tied with clothes pins to the chairs and over the desk on the other side of the room.

    "Pam?" Joey half whispered, not hearing any sounds.

He saw the blanket pop up in the middle with, obviously Pam's head touching the roof of the tent structure. She emerged holding her index finger to her mouth indicating to be quiet.

She took Joey by the elbow and whispered as she pulled him out of the room, "We were playing barbies and she fell asleep, so I just started reading my book."

They found themselves in the living room and Joey explained how he was not sure what he should be doing, and Pam continued to advise him to let Billie have her head.

"She called you to reassure you that she still felt the same about you right?"

"Yeah, but that was yesterday, and I haven't heard a thing from her. I just don't know what I should do. I know she's at home and not at school, so something is not right but…"

"Joe, that's an understatement. Her mother has cancer! She needs time. Billie is probably trying to help her mom with everything around the house. Cancer treatments can take a lot out of a person. I bet she calls you tonight again."

"I guess you're right," Joey admitted head bowed. "I am being too selfish, just thinking about how I feel. What do you think I should do?"

"Talk to your older and much wiser sister," Pam quickly asserted, and both found some much needed laughter.

"I can't seem to concentrate at all in school," Joey added. "It's like I'm not really there at all. Maybe I just gave too much of myself to her. When she's not there it almost feels like a part of me is not there, you know?"

"I have not had any relationship with a guy like that, but I know what you are saying, and my advice remains the same."

They heard a car drive up the laneway and assumed it was just Lilley coming home from work. Then a knock came to the door. Since the weather was getting colder they could not see who it was because the inner wooden door had no windows.

"Hmm, wonder who that could be?" Pam wondered and as she walked toward the door, she noticed a black truck parked in the laneway. "There's a black truck in the lane."

"Probably Don," said Joey. "Maybe Mom and him are doing something tonight."

Pam opened the door and a black and white ball of fur barreled into the house and ran directly to Joey and in walked Don and Billie!

Joey was mauled immediately by the bernedoodle from Angela's rescue. He fell to his knees on the floor and they frolicked wildly as he looked up and saw his visitors. Billie ran in and she too fell to her knees and threw herself onto Joey, wrapping her arms around her. They laughed loudly as the pup tried to nuzzle her way between them. After a few minutes the pup walked away wagging her tail frantically sniffing around the room and scouting out what was likely remnants of Harriet's scent.

"I'm so sorry, Joey! I love you so much!"

They sat on the couch holding one another tightly.

Joey looked up to see Pam nodding her head in an, I told you so, way.

"What's all this? Joey burst out still exuberant from the puppy's wild entrance. "And how come you came with Don? This is weird! Don, what's going on?"

"You better ask Billie there. She's the architect of this episode." Don said smiling and pointing to Billie.

"It's me, saying sorry Joey! I can't imagine how you must have felt, not hearing from me for a couple weeks!"

"Three weeks, four and a half days to be exact," said Joey. "But you don't have to explain anything. I understand why…I think."

Jessie had now arrived on the seen as the puppy emerged with her from the hallway. She had been unceremoniously awakened by a frantic deluge of puppy slurps.

"Hey, whose dog is this?" she bellowed.

Pam and Don positioned themselves on the three remaining kitchen chairs and Jessie scrambled into Pam's lap. It was as if they were watching a TV show and were eagerly awaiting the explanation that Billie was about to give.

Billie looked over toward Jessie, "That is Louise. She is a rescue that Dr. Norman's wife, Angela had at her house. And she now belongs to Joey!"

Joey looked confused and looked to Billie completely baffled. "What in the world are you talking about?"

As if on cue Louise jumped up onto the couch and lay beside Joey, resting her head on his thigh. Joey pet her softly on her head. "I know this pooch. I would have taken her, but the cost was just too much for me to handle and…wait…you paid for this?" He looked at Billie, head tilted still perplexed by this sudden turn of events.

"Well, if you would let me explain without interrupting, I will tell you!" Billie feigned frustration. "Last night after I called you, I went to my mom and told her that I had not spoken to you for a few weeks. She was completely shocked by that and wondered why. She had no way of knowing that I had wrapped myself up so much in her sickness that we hadn't been communicating. I should say…I wasn't communicating. We cried together last night, and we both felt so bad for you. She knows what you mean to me, Joey. We both thought about ways we could make it up to you and that puppy there on your lap was the only thing I could think of. You mentioned her to me that time we stopped by Dr. Norman's and you gave your donation to Angela. Since Dad was on a trip out of state and Mom wasn't feeling the best, she called Don and we arranged to pick up Louise and bring her to you."

Louise looked up and pawed Joey in the chest. Her feet were huge, and her legs looked more like a spider monkey's than a dog's, but she had the cutest face he had ever seen and she stole his heart immediately.

"I'm so sorry, Joey!" Billie buried her head into Joey's chest as she trembled and cried.

"Hey, I told you, Joey, didn't I? I told you she would come around!" said Pam proudly.

All had a little laugh and Louise perked up to see Lilley coming through the door with some groceries in her arms. She set the bags down on the counter and Louise scampered over to see her.

"Look at you!" Lilley squealed playfully. "Aren't you a beautiful little girl."

"So, you were in on this too, Mom?" Joey asked nodding.

"I called your mom first," said Don. "When Sarah called, I wanted to make sure it was all right with your mom to bring another dog into the house.

"You guys...I don't know what to say. She is absolutely awesome, and I love her but to be honest." Joey searched his heart and felt emotions once again rising to the surface. "Although this couldn't have been a nicer surprise for me, I feel kind of guilty."

"What do you mean, honey?" asked Lilley.

"I was thinking about how much I missed Billie and afraid to show up because, well, I didn't know what to do. I didn't know what was appropriate and I got all caught up in being just sad and feeling lonely. I should have been thinking about your mom more, Billie, and not just how bad I felt!"

"That's because I didn't keep you in the loop like I should have. I shut you out. I didn't mean to I just couldn't leave Mom. That is until she gave me heck and straightened me out. She wants to see you by the way. She loves you too, Joey. She really does!"

Now there were no dry eyes in the house. Well except for Louise's but she was busy trying to get Joey's sock of his foot.

"But the fees to adopt her and the trouble you went through…" Joey was trying to put together the events leading to this wonderful moment.

"Mom offered to pay for everything," said Billie, pushing back a little so she could face Joey better. "When she told Mrs. Norman who it was for, she refused to take anything. She said that you deserved to have that dog more than anyone she knew. Remember how we used to talk about Karma, Joey? Well, this is Karma and Louise belongs to you and … maybe me someday?

PART TWO

THE SINCLAIRS

Karma brings about inevitable results either in this life or the next depending on what we do with our existence. For the purpose of tying up the loose ends here, we will dwell on this life. Even though we don't always see the results of our actions immediately, eventually we will. We will pay or we will be rewarded, if that's the way you like to think of it.

People like the Sinclair's are around us everywhere. They are users, manipulators and sociopaths. You could stop reading right now and surely make a list of the people who fit that description. There are sociopaths like Mark Sinclair and people like Sally who are attracted to sociopaths. It's like the ultimate bad boy character because they are usually smart enough to get away with whatever self-serving endgame they are focused on. Why people would be attracted to that is difficult to imagine but when the two come together and produce an offspring you get a Paul Sinclair. You can't really fault someone like Paul for being who he is. It's all he has known from his earliest memories. Nevertheless, the world is full of these types, and we must navigate through our lives understanding that.

Mark Sinclair's purpose was to come out better than his competition, his clients and basically anyone he associates with. That's his mantra, his raison d'etre. Coming in last is just not acceptable and coming in second is the same as coming in last. It doesn't seem to matter to these people, who they hurt along the way. The most accurate definition of these kind of humans would be humans without a conscience. If a building collapses because of their shoddy workmanship or materials, they just want to be excluded from blame. They would sooner hire lawyers to fight the inevitable lawsuits than lead rescue operations for the victims.

Even people who are involved in large transactions like the Magee's can become duped by the Sinclair's of the world. It's not so much that the McGee's are gullible or stupid. It's because they trust and have put their faith in people who they have dealt with honestly throughout their life.

Mark and Sally Sinclair suffered major losses in business once they had estranged the Magees. But seven years later they are still doing well enough to maintain their pulp and paper and lumber business as well as diversifying into outdoor furniture like garden swings and patio accessories. Karma has not really caught up with them, at least that's what they think. They wouldn't recognize bad karma because one of the necessities of sociopathic people is that in order to survive, they must also be extremely narcissistic. Paul was in and out of trouble many times since his parents forced him into manual labor in the mill. Making him work was more a punishment for the shame he caused them rather than a life lesson to make him a better person. He still gets pretty much everything handed to him because it's part of the Sinclair image. Unfortunately, this backfired on Mark and Sally because Paul is now serving time in the county jail for mischief and disorderly conduct as a fall out from one of his frequent binges. He is struggling mightily with the maturation process, still harboring his diehard disciples from high school, and choosing conflict with those perceived to be weaker. Paul is probably categorized as a vulnerable narcissist and a victim of his parents' psychological neglect and abuse. He still must be treated by those around him like he is special. If he isn't treated that way, he becomes anxious and lashes out. Mark and Sally are unable to recognize their failure as parents. It's just not in their makeup to admit such failure. Paul's lack of direction was in their minds, purely Paul's choice and nothing they could have done about it.

Mark and Sally give to charities and appear regularly in social news columns as benefactors and pillars of society because they need to, not because they are trying to make a difference. They would never donate to a charity unless their names were somehow up in lights. They need to surround themselves with worshippers to feed their ego's appetite. There is no real benevolence there at all. They have this distorted image of themselves, and their importance needs to be constantly stroked by others even if they must orchestrate it themselves.

Even at 14, Billie and Joey saw these qualities in Paul Sinclair and knew they wanted nothing to do with him. The irony in all of this is that most of the town of Wiliam's Glen and the entire county knew how self-involved the Sinclair's were. Many were able to use it against them and even gain monetarily. All you have to do is praise a narcissist and they will give you things. Feed them like a puppy and the puppy will do his/her tricks. If you tell them how great they are, they will not only believe it but reward you for saying it. The funny thing is the narcissist often can't tell when they are being used. It's a balance that seems to work for all involved as long as you're on to them. This is how the Sinclair's coexist with the world around them. They screw people who are new to their underhanded ways and help those who satisfy their egotism. They would give money to see their name on a new wing of the hospital but walk around a struggling senior trying to get his wheelchair over the threshold of the doorway into that hospital.

In a simple small town setting people like the Sinclair's have very few friends because their way of doing things clashes with this type of society. They need to dress up, go the city and hobnob with other socialites with equally shallow personalities. Small town people base their happiness on being part of an honest life, a day's work for a day's pay. The Sinclair's and people like them continue to thrive financially and live in their trifling, superficial existence of self-indulgence without guilt or empathy for others.

THE PARKERS

Josh Parker, (Jug) recovered from the boating mishap that left him comatose for several weeks. Except for a few minor speech problems like a hesitation and a slight stammer as well as a complete loss of any memory of the episode on the lake, Jug was pretty much his normal, goofy self.

With the money the family received begrudgingly from the Sinclairs, they built a small dock behind their property similar to Joey's and made some improvements to their house. Ellen is now back working in Montrose in the law office and Jug used some of the money to pay for his university education. It's autumn now and Jug is in his final year of university, attending North Eastern in Montrose. He graduates this coming spring from a four-year accounting program. He has accepted a position with Magee construction where he will be part of their office staff involved in managerial accounting, internal auditing, and taxes. Jug has also found a local niche in preparing taxes for people in William's Glenn…a kind of under-the-table enterprise.

For about 6 years now, he has been involved with Billie's cousin, Olivia from England. This relationship started when he was 15. That summer, it was Olivia's turn to visit Billie for the holidays as Billie had done the year before in England, much to Joey's chagrin. The relationship started in the early days of Jug's recovery from his head injury. He was by no means back to normal when Olivia first met him. Jug was not yet able to pilot his boat around due to his lack of motor coordination. At this time, he used crutches to get around and was attending therapy once a week in Montrose. Joey would pick Jug up at his new dock and ride across the lake to the Magee's and the girls would join them. They had some great times that summer, fishing, swimming and just hanging out, between Joey's duties at his still burgeoning landscape business. By the end of the summer, Olivia was beginning to see through Jug's damaged body and mind and found a warm, funny character lurking inside.

They wrote for two years and when Jug was 17, he had saved enough money to make the trip over to England. Billie and Olivia had put an end to the every-other-summer trips because they were becoming more involved in the development of their own careers, and they needed to work part time during the summer holidays to further those ambitions. Ellen and Olivia's mother discussed the idea of Jug's visit and decided to accommodate the two by allowing Jug to "board" with them in England for a week. The two hit it off so well that they didn't want to separate when it came Jug's time to return home. They decided that maybe they wanted to be more than just friends and after a tearful goodbye they vowed to see each other again soon. The next summer Olivia came over to William's Glen for 2 weeks and that's when things became a little more serious. Jug's personality and most of his physical abilities were back to normal, they were now 18 and in love. Moonlight cruises and romantic walks replaced the video games and adventurous escapades with Joey. Of course, Joey had his own sweetheart to spend time with.

At 19 Olivia was accepted into Teacher's College about an hour way from William's Glen. Although not her parents' first choice, they agreed to let her come and live in residence at Johnstown college and become a teacher. True to his character, Jug had purchased a Volkswagen beetle and painted it lime green, with a brush, no less. He had become sort of a town character, not the town fool but a funny, unique and likeable character. Every Friday you would hear the distinctive ringing sound of the Volkswagen engine as it headed east through town to pick up Olivia in Johnstown and a couple hours later the same sound as it returned for the weekend.

The foursome became even closer throughout the years, sharing many outings, parties, celebrations, good times and bad times. Olivia and Billie were always family but now the four of them were very much kindred in their relationship.

Now at 21, Jug and Olivia live over near the high school in a rented house. Olivia landed a kindergarten job in William's Glen Public School and loves it, while Jug is well entrenched at Magee Construction and doing tax returns on the side. They're not married but very much together and in love and everyone in town is expecting wedding bells any day now.

Rumor has it that a certain acquaintance of Don Archer's has been seen calling on Ellen from time to time. Speculations abound, but when you see a late-model black Escalade in the Parkers laneway some nights, how can a small town's tightly knit grapevine resist the scuttlebutt?

THE ARCHERS

Yes, the Archers… as if that's a surprise. Only two years of dating with Lilley and being more of a father to Jessie, Pam and Joey than Hank had been, especially in the last few years, Don had more than proven himself to the family. All involved heartily approved of the union but it's funny how it all played out.

Don was always a romanticist, which is why he was so eager to help Billie by staging the presentation of Louise to Joey. He loved the drama and the happy ending that day brought everyone.

Don's weekly trips to William's Glen became 2 or three times a week as he and Lilley found a variety of reasons to do things together. Since it was not a long drive from Montrose to Lilley's, she didn't hesitate in asking Don to watch Jessie, if Joey and Pam were not available. This was more than just a convenience though. She knew when she got home he would be there and she liked that feeling. Obviously, the baby-sitting gig was just a ploy to have dinner together later that night or possibly an outing which at times involved everyone, even Joey and Billie when she was around.

One night when they returned from a boat ride, Lilley hustled Jessie up to the house quickly before she peed herself and Louise bounded along jumping on their heels like it was part of a game. Joey found himself alone with Don as they secured the lines of the boat.

Don reached out and touched Joey's shoulder as he was turning to walk up the path.

"Joey, I need your opinion about something. There really is no one I need more to approve of what I'm going to ask you. You've come to mean a lot to me…like my own son, and…"

"Don, if you're about to say what I think you are, of course I approve. You mean a lot me too! My whole life got better when you came into it! My mom has never been happier and it's because of you. In fact, I was wondering why you were taking so long!"

"Thank you, Joey! I intend to propose to your mother this weekend, but I want it to be special. For now, you're blessing was what I really needed. Do you think your sisters would agree?"

"Absolutely, Don. Do you see how Jessie reacts when you are in the room and sits with you all the time? She completely thinks of you as her dad…and you know how fond Pam is of you. She could not deal with life at all when Dad was around. Now that he's out of the picture, well, you've been like a close friend and yes… family, to all of us. I know we all want to see you become family, officially!"

Don extended his hand to Joey and Joey ignored it and opened his arms wide for a huge man hug accompanied by firm slaps on each other's backs. "Thank you, so much Joey!" They stood there in bear hug for a few seconds, then Don stepped back scratching his chin. "I have a plan…"

That Saturday in mid-June, the Magees and the still Burgess family, planned a huge fish fry disguised as a sweet sixteen birthday party for Billie. Don Archer was also invited as he was truly one of the group, as well as Jug, Ellen and friend. Billie had decorated the back yard with Joey's help, stringing Christmas lights between poles and setting tables with balloons taped to them as center pieces. Willie had begun construction of a bigger boathouse and although the top living quarters were not completed there was an additional boat slip added earlier in the spring. Balloons also adorned this structure as well. The day was perfect with only a slight breeze, a few wispy clouds and temperatures in the mid 70's.

Joey, Lilley, Jessie, Pam and Louise arrived by boat and tied up to the new dock. Shortly after that Jug, Ellen and Al, Ellen's "friend" arrived securing their boat across the end of the dock. Don, walked over from the lodge, only a couple hundred yards away, where he was renting a cabin for the weekend. Everyone, except Jessie was seated at the tables and enjoying conversation and a few drinks while Willie filled his new propane deep fryer. Jessie and Louise were frolicking around chasing an old chewed up soccer ball, Jessie giggling and Louise playfully growling as she ran off with the ball. She had never learned the art of returning the ball to the person who threw it. She just figured that if the human threw the ball, the human didn't really want it. So, she ran around the yard with her tooth caught on a seam and the ball hanging from her face while Jessie chased trying to get the ball back.

At the end of the row of picnic tables, sat Sarah, now confined to a wheelchair to assist with her mobility. She had not responded much to treatment and although now in stage 4 of metastatic breast cancer the disease had quickly spread to many other organs. She was weak and short of breath, her body only a thin reflection of what it once was. Nevertheless, her presence was as elegant and upbeat as ever. Perhaps the hardiness of her laugh was not quite as robust, but the effervescence of her animated conversation was still there. She gestured wildly with her hands and never looked down once, her face always beaming with her trademark smile. Everyone knew that her days were numbered as did she, but there was no room for pity and especially not today.

This was Billie's day, for the most part. Unlike other well-to-do families, Mark and Sarah did not believe in spoiling their only offspring with lavish gifts. When it came to giving her an actual present, it would be done in private and likely it would be something sentimental. Today, however, they wanted to present Billie with something very special.

When it came time, the food was gone and the happy birthdays were sung, Sarah pushed back her wheelchair and stood up, slightly wobbly, leaning on the end of the table. As she stood, everyone recognized that she was about to speak, and their boisterous exchanges turned to muffles and then silence.

"I want to thank all you wonderful people for coming today. It was truly amazing how Billie has surrounded herself with such honest and good people. Willie and I feel so blessed to call you our friends… possibly even family some day?" She winked at Joey and that brought some chuckles and blushes from Billie and Joey. "We don't usually allow gifts to be given at our own family's birthday get togethers, but I decided that today I would break the habit. I don't really know how to say this and please forgive me if I stumble. Billie, my goodness, I guess we messed up giving you the name Catherine!" Another round of laughter… "You are now sixteen, well, officially not until tomorrow, but it has been so quick! It's just a tick in time since you were in Willie's arms, no longer than the distance between his elbow and his hand." Both Ellen and Lilley brought their hands to their faces, Ellen wiping her face with a napkin and Lilley a flick of her finger. "I want you to have something that you will always cherish and maybe pass on to your own little girl someday."

Billie's tears came suddenly, and she sniffed and wiped her eyes. Joey put his arm around her as if to say that he understood, feeling her tremble. She sensed that her mother was saying goodbye and she was not quite ready to hear that. Despite the scream that lived in her throat she hardened herself bravely, swallowed and forced a warm smile toward her mom.

"Willie, could you give me a hand here," she asked nodding toward her husband.

He stood and walked around behind Sara, unfastened her necklace which had been hidden by her blouse and placed it in her hand. Willie gave her a kiss on the cheek and sat back down.

"Oh, Mom!" Billie could not hold back her tears as Joey squeezed her on one side and Willie on the other both with arms around her, one high, one low.

Sarah held up the magnificent gold and diamond necklace featuring a large tear-drop shaped emerald dangling from the bottom. "This necklace has been in our family since the early 1800's and was originally given to your great, great grandmother by your great, great grandfather. My mother passed it on to me and now I want to pass it on to you. I am so very proud of the young woman you have become and the choices you have made in your life!" Then a tear, she swore would not make its appearance today, unmistakably traced down her cheek.

Billie raced to her mother and held her tight, both trembling and both understanding the significance of the timing of this gift. To say there was not a dry eye there that day would be a gross understatement. Everyone took their turn to get up, congratulate Billie and exchange hugs with them both. It was a truly beautiful, albeit heartrending moment which turned into more like a half hour of hugs and hand shaking. Then Willie Magee tapped his beer glass with a fork until all had quieted and took their seat. No one had even noticed, Pam sneaking around the side of the house with Louise on a leash.

Willie began, "I too want to thank all of you for coming her today. I think, for me, it's a day I will always remember, and I hope you will remember this day too, Billie." He reached out his hand and Billie took it, kissed the back of it and pressed it to her cheek smiling up at her adoring father. "And now, with Billie's approval and in fact her insistence there is something else special happening today. There is someone else here that will, no doubt, remember this day forever as well. So, I'm going to ask Lilley to do something you might find odd." He put both hands down on the table and fixed his eyes on Lilley sitting across and over a few seats from him. "I want you to call Louise."

"You want me to call Louise?" Lilley was completely perplexed and even a little nervous. "What on earth for?"

"Mom," Joey cocked his head and caught Don's eye as well, "Just do it, okay?"

"Okay, I'll play along but sure wish I knew what you were up to …Louise? Louise? …Weezie!" Everyone burst into laughter. Exactly what this crowd needed right now.

Around the corner of the house bounded Louise. Lilley swivelled her chair around and Louise sat in front of her with her head cocked to the side as if to say, "Well? You want something?" Louise brought her paw up trying to get at something on her neck. There was a red felt bag hanging from her collar by its golden draw string. "I suppose you want me to see what's in here, don't you?" Louise tilted her head back and forth, her tongue hanging out, panting. Lilley untied the string and reached into the bag feeling the unmistakable shape of a ring.

While she was doing this Don had positioned himself around behind her and was down on one knee. She drew out the beautiful diamond engagement ring and everyone oohed and awed knowing full well what was transpiring. Lilley's head bowed and she sobbed into her hands.

"Mom, look behind you," Pam announced.

Lilley turned and saw Don down on one knee.

"Lilley, will you marry…"

"Yes, yes, yes! I love you!" It was their turn to stand and hug each other as glasses clicked and cheers and laughter resumed.

That was a fantastic day! It was a day Joey would never forget either. Billie's sweet sixteen birthday party had turned into an engagement party for his mom and for him the most poignant moment was when Sarah referred to him as family while presenting Billie with the family heirloom. He knew in his heart that Sarah would not see Billie's 17th. The day was monumental and so damned bittersweet!

THE BURGESS – MAGEE'S

That Summer, following Billie's sweet sixteen party and Lillie's official engagement to Don, things moved along quite nicely for Joey. He was very busy at his landscaping business and had found out from the guidance department at the high school that he would be able to attend the Montrose school of fine art in a year's time after his graduation from William's Glen High. He was able to purchase a 2009 chevy Silverado from his landscaping efforts and got his licence about a week after his 16th birthday. He used it to haul around a small utility trailer carrying his mowers and other equipment. It was only a plain Jane, with wind up windows and a regular cab with a bench seat, but Joey was proud of it because he had earned it himself.

Two smaller construction projects were now underway. Don had secured a double lot on Skogie Lake, about a mile north of the Sinclair's old house. The Sinclair's had moved away from William's Glen and now lived in a very nice log house in the country closer to their plant. Don was going to build a home for Lilley and himself, complete with all the amenities to accommodate kids and a mother-in-law suite, not really intended for mothers-in-law but more for older kids that may want to visit.

The other project was Willie's boathouse. Joey volunteered to help him with it, his motives obviously not entirely unselfish. He could learn about building from Willie, as well as get to know him better and at the same time be closer to Billie.

In February, with the landscape frozen and the lake a sheet of ice and snow, Sarah's prognosis changed from bad to worse. Willie spent almost all his time at home trying to get Sarah to eat something as her appetite and her body became weaker and weaker. She slept most of the time and the doctor began to suggest that her time was running out.

Dr. Jane Wilson, a leading oncologist from Montrose General, who happened to be a friend of the Magee family would make weekly visits to the Magee home but was now encouraging Willie to move her where she could be watched and monitored 24-7. Both Willie and Sarah were set against moving her and opted for home hospice services. Dr. Wilson made the arrangements, and she was now visited daily by a palliative care specialist, Nurse Josey Michielson. She was an extremely empathetic nurse who understood not only the physical needs of a terminally ill patient but the psychological, emotional and spiritual side of it. Knowing you are going to die soon is a complicated thing. Sarah had eventually accepted her fate and was no longer scared of the inevitable, a concept that neither Billie nor Joey could grasp at their tender ages.

Joey and Billie sat on the thick rug on the floor in the family room of the Magee's with their arms around each other and Louise curled up in front of the fireplace. They were watching a horror movie on a popular streaming service but neither seemed all that interested in it.

"Are you really watching the movie, Billie?" Joey asked as he had noticed Billie frequently glancing out through the huge windows to the winter scene beyond them. The moon was reflecting off the crystalline speckled snow drifts accumulating against the back patio door.

"No, not really. I'm just enjoying sitting here with you. I guess the comfort of being with you is something I need so much right now. I know Mom's going to die and I'm trying to wrap my head around it. When you hold me, it helps me sort of hide from the reality of it all."

Joey reached up and grabbed the remote from the coffee table and clicked off the TV.

"It was a crappy movie anyway," he said trying to get her to smile. She was cradled in his arms and between his legs both facing toward the TV and the fireplace. He moved his head to the side to catch a glimpse of her face, maybe her mouth slightly upturned, but there was no reaction. She just turned, caught his eye briefly and looked beyond him and back to the wintery landscape beyond the glass.

"It's beautiful, Joey. Isn't it? I mean the snow…how it sparkles in the moonlight. I know it's beautiful, but it doesn't seem to affect me the same. It's like, just a cold bitter winter's night. Mom would run and get her phone and take pictures of it, like she did every night when the setting sun was putting on a display over the hills on the other side of the lake."

"Doctor Wilson said that Mom won't really die from breast cancer. It's when it spreads or metastasizes to the other organs like her lungs and her brain.

"I can't believe how much I'm going to miss her, Joey!" Billie fell into a deep, silent cry with no sound just deep shuddering breaths, while her body quaked with spasms of trembling. Joey held her tighter, and she turned sideways grabbing his t-shirt in a tight fist and buried her head into his chest agonizing into a seizure of uncontrolled sobs.

Willie came out of the back hall and saw his daughter wrapped in the arms of the boy she loved and the tear trickling down Joey's face. He continued into the kitchen and began to make a cup of coffee, his heart heavy. After pouring it in a mug he entered the room where Billie was still convulsing in pain against Joey's chest. Joey looked up at Willie through his watery eyes, his lip quivering, his head shaking in bewilderment side to side. Then he rested his head back down on the top of Billie's still holding her tight. Willie set the mug on the table and sat down on the couch next to the two kids on the floor, his hand gently cupped the top of Joey's head. His eyes were also wet not just from his pain but also from seeing his daughter so distressed.

"I love you both, very much!" he managed in a quiet barely audible voice.

"Oh, Daddy!" Billie got up and sat in Willie's lap like a toddler might and wrapped her arms around him and they both held on to what was left of their family.

"Thank you for being here for her, Joe!" Willie said, firmly, looking out past Billie's head. He held his daughter kissing the top of her head and stroked her auburn hair as Joey stood up. Louise stood also and tried to jump on top of them, poking her snout into Billie's cheek licking frantically. That was just comical enough that all found the ability to laugh and cry at the same time.

"Weezie, you are one little clown, aren't you!" Billie said through sniffles.

"Well, I should go. It looks like I'm going to be shoveling out some walks tomorrow if this snow keeps up."

"You're a good man, Joe. I can't wait until you come and work for me in a few years. It's, as they say, hard to find good help these days."

"Thank you, sir…I mean Willie," Joey let out a slight giggle. "I can't wait either and … I love you all too!" Then he bowed his head and just cried.

Billie stood up and embraced him as he was about to make his way to the door. "Don't you ever leave us!" Billie blurted still unable to control her emotion.

"I'm not going anywhere." Answered Joey as he wiped away a tear on Billie's cheek with his thumb.

Louise was already standing at the front door like a pointer indicating the direction of a kill, as if the door would magically open because she willed it. Billie walked Joey to the door holding his hand and arm with both of hers. They kissed sweetly and said their good nights.

Joey walked out, opened the door of the old chevy pickup and Louise bounded up into the passenger seat and off they went into the snowy night.

The call came at 3:45 in the morning. Before Joey could find the phone on the side table, he knew what the call meant.

"She's gone, Joey!" There were no other words from Billie. All had been said earlier that night.

"Should I come over, Billie?"

"No, the ambulance is taking her away, now. Just come in the morning. We talked to her, Joey. She said she loved you and hoped that we would have a beautiful life together! I love you! I just can't talk!" She clicked off her phone and Joey sat up in bed, his heart pounding dumbfounded and numb.

Joey loved Sarah too. She wasn't just his girlfriend's mother, a future mother-in-law. He felt her warmth and caring nature from the first day he met her. She had always trusted him. It was not anything she ever said. She treated him as an adult, even when he was just 14 and Billie and he had just begun to discover their feelings for each other.

The way she talked to Billie and him was with an understood respect. She knew her daughter well and if Billie loved this rather rough young man, then he must be okay. The early days weren't all milk and honey. There were a lot of bad days Joey was forced to deal with, especially when his abusive father was still at home. Things began to change for Joey after Gramps passed away and Billie had grown to love him as more than just a friend. Sarah was there through all of it and always added a kind word, some encouragement or humor. Other than Joey, she was really Billie's best friend. It was not a typical mother-daughter relationship. She let Billie have her head and Billie always seemed to remember who she was, upholding the honor of the Magee name by acting appropriately. Billie did this because of her admiration for her mother and her father, not because she was told to or because she was afraid of being scolded or losing privileges.

Joey knew he would never get back to sleep so he got up and went into the kitchen and through habit put 4 slices of bread in the toaster. That aroused Louise and she sat staring at the machine where crunchy bread came from. When they popped up, he buttered them and smeared cherry jam thickly over each piece. It was something he did when he wanted a little pleasure, something to make him feel better. He took a bite, tore off a corner of the toast and tossed it to Louise. After another bite, he pushed the plate ahead buried his face in his hands and wept.

The funeral was massive. Joey had not seen so many people in one small funeral home. True to form, the Magees had organized a small unpretentious affair right in the small town of William's Glen and not some posh wake in the city. Of course, they could have afforded just about any kind of celebration of life, but they were from humble beginnings and vowed to go out the same way, a trait respected by many of their family, friends and business acquaintances. Billie's cousin Olivia, and the Wilmot's were there all the way from England. There were people young and old from near and far, some on crutches, some in wheelchairs some who were obviously cancer patients. Most wanted to say thanks to Sarah for what she had done with her life and how she had affected others. Sarah had headed up so many charities throughout her life and given so much that now the hearts she had touched wanted desperately to at least say goodbye. The love and good will overflowed the building as beautiful music played and pictures of her life were everywhere.

Billie wanted Joey to stand with her in the reception line and Joey felt honored to be an accepted member of the Magee family. Every once in a while Billie would grab his hand and squeeze it, especially when she saw an old friend of her mom's.

"Remember the song you wrote for your Gramps?" Billie said looking up at Joey. "I know exactly now what you meant when you said, 'he made us proud of him even the day that he died'"

"I'm so proud to have known and loved your mom!" Joey answered. That brought tears to both of them.

All day they fought back the tears, persistent heart wrenching sorrow, and shook hands and gave hugs. It was difficult to speak as words were strangled in their throats. It was an exhausting day and Willie, once a tower of strength and confidence looked so completely defeated. Joey remembered so vividly the day he lost Gramps, but Sarah and Willie had been together far longer than Joey had even been alive. There now was a lost, empty look in Willie's eyes. Their marriage had been an example of devotion and true friendship that in today's world was becoming more and more uncommon. When a person like Sarah dies you question many things about why we are even here and especially why a person of her character and benevolence should be taken away. Some things are beyond reason and the question, "why".

It was Lilley and Pam's turn to console Billie and her dad in the same room where Lilley's dad and Pam's grandfather were paid tribute. Later following the ceremony, Lilley, Pam and several women that were associated with Sarah's various charitable organizations put out sandwiches and finger foods back at the Magee home. People stood around with drinks in their hands and most talked about irrelevant things as if this was just a social gathering. The whole day was beginning to wear on Willie.

"I know everyone means well, but I wish everyone would just go now," Billie whispered to Joey as they sat on the love seat in the family room.

They found themselves sitting and standing, sitting and standing over and over. Every time someone approached to express themselves, they stood and pasted on a simulated smile and thanked them for coming. Really, all the two of them wanted now was to be alone and they suspected that Willie felt the same. When Jug came in the room the three of them just had a group hug with very little said. Jug pulled up one of the dining room chairs that had been placed around the perimeter of the room.

"I don't understand these things," he said. "Why do people stand around and talk about the weather and everything else under the sun except about your mom?

"We were just kind of talking about that," answered Billie. "I wouldn't mind if they were laughing about some funny thing that Mom did, you know? But it seems that they can't deal with it. It's like they are afraid to talk about Mom, because it will make us feel worse.

If they only knew how impossible that was!" Joey gently squeezed Billie's hand resting on the seat between them.

Willie never took a seat all day, and Olivia and her mom and dad were busy serving people and bringing out drinks for all the visitors. Now that many had left, they were now cleaning up in the living room and the dining room where all the food had been set out. Sarah's sister, Mary was suddenly overcome and began to cry out loud and Billie's Uncle James had to usher her back into one of the bedrooms to console her.

"You know, if Mom can see what's going on here, I don't think she would like it one bit! She accepted that she was going to die, over the last two months and she would want people to celebrate her life and not mourn so much. But I know how they feel, especially Aunt Mary, Mom's only sister. It's like funerals aren't for the person who died, it's to comfort those who will experience the loss. I guess I'm dreaming but I wish there could be happy funerals. I mean, Mom is not suffering anymore. She hated being dependent on Dad and me and doctors and nurses and she hated the way she looked and felt. She didn't want people feeling sorry for her and that was the hardest part…to see her like that. She was such a strong person, such a good person and such a funny person!"

Billie now broke down and deposited herself into the shroud of Joey's arms, hiding her face with her hands, pulsing in sobs. There was no place to run or hide that would feel better than right here with the person she felt closest to.

When all the guests had gone and everything had been cleaned up and put away, the adults; Willie, Mary, now calmed from her earlier breakdown, and James sat around the kitchen table drinking whiskey and wine, nibbling on left over cheese and crackers and were trying to each put in their version of their loss. In the family room Billie and Joey sat with Jug and Olivia continuing their conversation. It was during this melancholy day that Jug and Olivia could see in each other the tender loving side. From this day on they felt the attraction that would inevitably bring them together.

Finally, everyone had left. Olivia, Mary and James had gone to bed. Jug had gone home and all that remained were Willie still sitting at the kitchen island reading over some of the cards left to him and sipping on a scotch on the rocks and Billie and Joey. They were both still cuddled on the love seat, neither one wanting to give in to sleep which periodically forced their eyelids closed. Willie saw his daughter curled up in Joey's arms and felt a tear dribble down his cheek confused by it. Did he feel sadness, or did he feel a happiness in knowing that his little girl was loved and would always be in the arms of that young man? He put down the card he was reading and grabbed his drink and took a place on other love seat facing them. Hearing him enter and sit down they both sat up more but still embraced.

"No, don't change your positions, guys. I just came over to tell you both, how proud I was of you today. I couldn't have asked for anything more out of either of you. Your mother whispered in my ear and told me how much she loves you both!" More tears began to flow, and Billie got up and snuggled into one side of her father. His large arm engulfed her, and his hand came up and tousled her hair like he always did. Then he patted what was left of the seat beside him gesturing to Joey. Joey nestled in on the other side, Willie's arms around both.

"This was a hell of a day," Willie continued, "Now it's up to us to be strong and carry on. We have a lot to accomplish, the three of us. I have a business to run, a boathouse to build with you, Joe and you both have schooling to finish up and careers to begin. It's going to be different without her, but she will be in our thoughts, and she will be whispering in all our ears as we do what we need to do. We have to mourn because we can't really help ourselves, but she would want us to get on with things and pick ourselves up and carry on." Willie looked left and right at the two. "I'll leave you to say your goodbye's but I just want you to know again, that I love you both!"

"Me too Daddy!"

"Me too, future Daddy!" An actual chuckle came from each of the three as Willie got up and left them.

Each year that went by since the passing of Sarah, new challenges were presented and met. Pam was seeing Detective Robert's brother, Cliff, an employee of the William's Glen Public Utilities Commission and a very well-liked town character. He was really good for Pam in a number of ways. His old-fashioned philosophy and good-ole-boy nature was comforting and Pam found a home with him, literally. Much to Lilley's chagrin, originally, Pam moved into his apartment over a vacated store downtown. Later, Lilley would come to realize how good he was for Pam, and she began to love him like a son. Pam was also finishing up her diploma in cosmetology and was also learning about nail, facial and skin care. Joey found this so ironic as he thought about his creepy sister's gothic appearance of a few years ago. Nevertheless, Cliff had negotiated with the owner of the store and had purchased the entire building so that Pam could set up her salon and esthetic services and they could live right above her work. It was for Lilley, a dream come true that her daughter had found the straight and narrow and was about to make something of herself and become a respected member of the community.

Jessie was blossoming into a ridiculously cute and freckled red head. She reminded Billie of Anne of Green Gables, from a book that

Aunt Mary had given her when she was about 10. Jessie was funny and playful and actually, quite a character as her grade 7 teacher diplomatically described her on her mid-term report card. She was happy and well-adjusted albeit slightly mischievous. Don had been a savior for their entire family. He needed Lilley and her entourage as much as they, especially the impressionable Jessie, needed him.

After three years of part-time construction on Willie's boathouse, it was nearing completion. One day, shortly after Joeys 18th birthday, on a warm Saturday afternoon, Willie, Joey and Billie were sitting on the dock which ran around the perimeter of the structure. They were eating sandwiches that Billie had made for them. She had become the goffer as in go for this and go for that. If they ran out of deck screws she would run down to the hardware store, if they needed food or occasionally a cold beer she would run and get that, while occasionally helping the two with the finishing touches and the actual construction.

"I got a few things I want to run by you kids to see what you think," Willie said, trying not to spit out food as he ate his tuna sandwich. "Billie, since you use your mom's Honda all the time to run errands and go to school and all, how would you like to actually own it?"

"Really, Dad? My own car! Wow, I was wondering how I was going to earn enough to by one and I don't want to have to rely on you and Joey to take me places. That's amazing!" She scooched over on the planking, leaned in and hugged Willie giving him a kiss on the cheek. "Thank you so much!"

"Well, it's almost your 18th birthday, and I hate shopping, so… this works out great for both of us/" All three laughed and Joey jostled Billie's shoulder, and each threw a smile to the other.

"There's something else too…I've been thinking about this for a long time, and I want to know your thoughts…from both of you. As you know we are just about finished the boat house and we have been talking about getting renters. I will put an ad out next week and you two can sniff around and see if you know of any respectable person that wouldn't mind living in a boat house. It should fetch a pretty decent rent. It has two bedrooms, a nice bathroom a sort of sitting area and a kitchen with all the appliances…"

"And the view from the porch off the kitchen has to be worth something too. You can see down the whole length of the lake," Joey chimed in.

"Exactly, but that's really not what I wanted your opinions on. I was thinking that once you guys are finished school and you both have jobs, you might want to live here?" There was a pause while Billie and Joey looked back and forth at each other in disbelief.

"Wow!" Are you kidding?" joey exploded.

"Holy Cow, Daddy, you are full of surprises today, aren't you." Billie gushed as she moved over to put her arms around Joey.

"Of course, if living near your dad is a little uncomfortable, I would understand. You would also have to cover the expenses like heat and hydro and any utilities and so on."

"Willie, do you know how much I've dreamt about living at the lake? To be living right on the lake would be better than a dream come true, for me!" Joey said, shaking his head still having difficulty believing what he was hearing.

"I know, or at least you two have convinced me that you are lifers. In a way you remind me of Sarah and me. Of course, my motives are not entirely selfless. Billie, your mom and I married fairly late in life. She had you when she was almost 37."

Billie felt a twinge of unfounded guilt knowing that Sarah was unable to have children after she was born. It was a natural infertility due to Sarah's age and Willie's too. He was 9 years older than Sarah and although still youthful and healthy not as fertile as he once was either. Nevertheless, somehow Billie felt to blame and thought that they might have wanted another child.

Willie continued, "We were older for having kids and now I find myself close to retiring. I could retire now but there are a couple of reasons I won't…not yet anyway. One is that I'm not ready to. I'm not sure what I would do, to be truthful. My company is basically my life other than you two. I know everybody says I don't look it but I'm going to be 62 in a few months. I won't be keeping such a hectic pace forever. When I do retire, I would like to live here."

"Of course, Daddy, I would hope that I can be there for you when you are older, like you cared for me when I was young."

"Thank you, sweetie, I wasn't sure how I was going to word that and now I don't have to. The other thing is…I want to keep my business going strong so that Joe…Can I call you Joey?"

"Of course, sir…I mean Willie," Joey joked.

"Okay so that you, Joey can become entrenched in the business and one day take it over. How does that sound, son?"

"Well, I'll answer that once I get by the fact that you just called me, 'son'" They each laughed. "But seriously, you are going to do all that for me?" Joey asked with incredulity.

"No, not just for you, Joey. For our family. Once I do finally retire, I would want you two to take over the house and let me have the boathouse for my later years… So, what do you guys think?"

"Dad, that's a lot to take in. I think we would be the luckiest people alive, that's what I think!" Billie put her arm around Joey and squeezed.

Joey was still shaking his head. "It's like I can see our whole future starting to materialize. We still have some school left and careers to start but I am absolutely pumped about this! How could a young couple be so fortunate!"

"You may be fortunate that way but it's not entirely without earning it. You have shown me that you care for my daughter… well, more than I could ever have imagined a boyfriend could. And because you fit my ideology of what a son-in-law should be as well as a future employee and possibly business partner, the decision was pretty easy for me. Now, don't you two split up on me now!"

"Yeah, that's not going to happen," Joey said holding on to Billie and giving her gentle shake.

"You can bet on that Dad!" Billie confirmed.

"I have a little announcement myself," Joey said, rubbing his chin and winking at Billie. "I know beyond a shadow of a doubt who I'm going to spend my life with, and I want to be supportive not just emotionally but financially too. So, because of that I have decided to sell my landscaping business. It is now fully operational 12 months of the year and I have accumulated a lot of machinery over the last 4 years. My customers have been contacted and although they are disappointed to see me go, they were happy with who I chose to take it over. Charlie Mathers has been asking me for a couple months now if he could buy it. His family is backing him, and they are willing to pay me what I'm asking so…I guess that's my news for the day."

"A smart decision, Joey," injected Willie immediately. "I notice that Billie didn't seem surprised and that tells me that you two talked it over. That's something that when you become legally married you will need to continue. Communication is everything, the way I see it. To be honest, my only doubt lately was how you were going to manage that business, finish your education and take on the graphic art job at the firm. I guess you just answered that question and I hope you got enough money to cover your equipment and that you factored in the turnkey business he will be inheriting."

"I sure did," said Joey proudly. "I am putting some away for a very special purchase though." Billie smiled and blushed as Willie put two and two together.

"We talked about getting engaged, Dad, but we thought we didn't want the community to start rumors about how young we are and all that, so we are going to wait a year or so."

"Why?" said Willie, seemingly puzzled. "Just make it a long engagement. It's not like everybody doesn't know you guys are a couple. You would bring no shame to me. In fact, you would be solidifying everything we have been talking about today."

That took the couple by surprise, and both reached for their answers.

Joey turned his palms up as if in wonder, "You don't think we're too young to be engaged? We just thought…"

"What is too young? In a blink of an eye, my wife has gone." He stopped struggling for the words and to keep himself together. "What I would give for a few more years with her! Do you know how precious time is? Our life is only one tick in time. The older you get the shorter life is. When you are your age, you think that it will never end, but it will. Go after what you want for yourself now. If you want to wait a couple of years to get on your feet financially before you get married that's great, but I sure have no problem with you two getting engaged. None whatsoever! In fact, I will throw in some money to help you buy the damn ring. What do you think of that!"

A group hug was undeniably appropriate as they all stood and locked up together.

"Excuse me for a minute. I'll be right back." Willie left them on the dock and trudged up the tiered stone walkway to the back porch and entered the house.

Billie and Joey sat back down on the dock, their legs dangling inches from the clear lake water. They both studied their reflections as they looked down into the calmness.

"I can't believe what a day this has been!" Billie said still watching her mouth move in the reflection and seeing Joey's face beside hers.

"I know. I'm having trouble just taking it all in. I just don't want to disappoint your dad. I mean I need to get top marks in my final year. I want him hiring a fully qualified and highly skilled designer."

"You won't. Joey, he loves you! Do you think he would be disappointed in me if I faltered in any way?"

"No, but you're his…okay, I see what you mean. Maybe it's just my own pride. I cannot fail."

"And you won't."

Hearing footsteps behind them they stood up and turned to face Willie.

"It's Saturday. This place only needs a few finishing touches which I am fully capable of. Now, I told you how I felt today so there doesn't need to be any doubt with me, okay? I suggest that you take this," he handed Joey a cheque, "and go talk to your mother, Joey. If she feels like I do, than get your butts over to Montrose and go engagement ring shopping. Let me know if it's going to happen after you talk to

Lilley, and I will make plans to host an engagement party right here on the deck next weekend… Now, go!"

"My God, Willie… a thousand bucks? This is too much!"

"Don't you tell me what's too much for my daughter!" He slapped Joey playfully on the shoulder and Billie ran into her father's arms.

"Now, git!"

They ran and jumped into Joey's old truck and drove north up the coast to Lilley and Don's new house.

"Mom!" Lilley was trying to start some begonias in a circular garden surrounded by rocks near the front steps.

"Whoa! What's your excitement, you two?"

"Where is everybody else?" asked Joey, still anxious, Billie clinging to his hand.

"Well, you know Pam. She's out to lunch with Cliff and Don promised Jessie a soft ice cream cone so they're down at the dairy. Would you please tell me what's going on?"

"Mrs. Burgess…er I mean Lilley; do you think we should get married in a couple years? Joey understood why Billie had stepped in and took this tact. He was just going to blurt out their engagement, but Billie knew his mom all too well.

"Well, sure, I guess, but that's two years from now. Why are you so… You guys are getting engaged aren't you!" Billie and Joey just stood there holding hands and smiling. "Does Willie know what you are planning? My God…this is exciting!"

"Mom, Willie sent us here and told us to get your blessing before we actually go buy the engagement ring."

"Jeez, Joey!" Lilley began to tear up, throwing her arms open and wiggling her fingers on both hands for the two of them to come to her. "I sure love you both and I only want to see you happy. You definitely have my blessing! God! I can't wait to tell Don! How are you going to pay for an engagement ring? You said you were going to save the money you got from your business."

"Mom, what do you think I was saving it for? Anyway, I will have lot's left over. We are going over this afternoon to Montrose to shop for one." Neither wanted to say that Willie had given them all that money so that Lilley wouldn't feel compelled.

"Two!" Billie spoke up. "Do you think the girl is the only one who gets a ring. You are going to need one too. I want me to be on your finger at all time!" She gave Joey a little squeeze.

"Well, I guess you two better get going then. I want to see that ring or rings as soon as you get them!"

What an amazing day that had been for them! Billie called her dad on her cell and he of course, was not surprised. They found two rings at Noshes Jewelers and agreed to be conservative with the money. They found two rings for just over $1000 and vowed that they were not going to be influenced by commercials and the idea that they had to be expensive to be meaningful. They would have worn bamboo hoops if they had to. Billie's was a classic solitare with a thin gold band shaped with a notch in the setting where the addition of the band would fit in on the wedding day. While Billie was talking to a highly perfumed sales lady about how to clean the diamond, Joey whispered to the salesmen at the counter where the diamond was once housed and purchased the wedding band slipping it in his pocket. He would keep it under lock and key until the big day arrived. Joey's was a black tungsten band with gold edging and a heart engraved through the brushed finish. It was very different, and he asked the jeweler to engrave "Billie" on bottom opposite the heart.

Billie could not take her eyes off the diamond as they drove home, and Joey drove with his ring hand on the steering wheel so he too could admire his. Joey pulled the old truck into the rest area about half the way back home where they sat looking at their rings until what they had just done completely sunk in.

"I love you Billie, and I will love you forever!"

"I love you too, with all my heart!"

"Billie, I need to do something."

He started the truck back up and before long he was parked in the guest parking lot of Gramps' old residence.

"Come with me." Joey and Billie got out of the truck and Joey led her out past the picnic bench where he and Gramps had so many heartfelt talks. They disappeared into the forest on the path behind the tool shed and within two minutes they were at the base of the huge beech tree hand in hand staring at the carving of "Billie and Joey".

"Oh, Joey, of course! This place it's just so, I don't know… meaningful. It's where we first shared our personal secrets. It's where we lay with each other laughing, crying, contemplating life and the heavens. It's where I first learned the meaning of 'Remember Who You Are'… it has to be here!"

While Billie looked up into the streams of sunlight filtering through the young leaflets, Joey was down on one knee. Billie felt her hand being tugged and she looked down at him, her eyes tearing up.

"I knew you would make this a memory I wouldn't forget! But before you say anything I want this to be done in a special way…just ours. I know what you're going to say, and I don't want you kneeling to me."

Billie got down on both her knees and Joey put his other knee to the ground and they held each other, knees padded by the wild grass and soft moss, staring into each other's eyes.

"Billie, I love you! I always have and I always will! Will you marry me?" Joey could barely get it out, but he forced himself to look into her eyes while the tears streamed from his.

"Yes, yes yes! You are my true love, and nothing will ever change that!" She held on so tight, Joey hadn't realized she was that strong. They pushed back slightly and kissed more deeply, more passionately then either had ever done before. Neither could see the other clearly and their tears mixed on their cheeks as their faces pressed together in the passionate joy of the moment.

The following Saturday, true to his word, Willie had a catered party in the back yard. He could not contain his happiness. He was able to muster some of the women from Sarah's charities to decorate the yard and he even hired a disc jockey. Joey couldn't help thinking about how much he loved the community and how much everyone invested in their happiness. He remembered how Gramps used to say how much people care about each other in small communities. Everyone was there. Really, they only ones absent were Billie's Aunt Mary and Uncle James and Cousin Olivia. They did send a video call to Billie and Joey during the party, but it was too much to expect them to make travel plans like that in less than a week. Billie held a microphone up to her phone at the DJ's table and everyone applauded the congratulatory message all the way from England.

It was a great night with one heart-rending moment and a feeling in those closest to the family that one important person was missing.

Billie walked Joey out to the end of the dock and looked out over the lake as the sun painted the sky orange and purple over the hills on the other side. They stood there both thinking the same thing as Billie tried desperately not to cry. Joey held her as she laid her head on Joey's shoulder and she wept deeply.

"I know, Billie. I miss her too! But I know she is so happy to see us together!"

In another tick, the next two years had gone by. As it turned out, Willie didn't have to look far for a tenant for the boathouse. Joey was more than willing to pay a fair rent to be close to his girl. He had money from selling his landscape business, was playing his guitar and singing in small venues to keep up his skill and add a few bucks to his wallet. He even wrote a novelty song called, "Willie, Billie and Lilley" which was popular with the families concerned and the local community who knew them. He also found a niche with his artwork, painting, sketching and even doing digital renderings of people's pets. Some people would pay good money to have their beloved animal immortalized in that way.

Staying in the boathouse had its drawbacks though. It was tough on weekends for Billie and Joey to stay apart. They managed for most of the time to respect their reputations and those of their parents, but on days Willie was in the city with no chance of being caught, their carnal attraction couldn't be resisted. Although they satisfied their hunger for each other, and their lovemaking was very intimate, they didn't cross the line. Billie would always remind Joey that her mom was watching them and when their wedding night came around, what was left to consummate would be special, exquisite and memorable.

Billie landed a great job at Four Counties Hospital in William's Glen. She would be a medical sonographer or an ultrasound tech, in layman's terms. This would be the perfect situation for her as she could use her nurturing persona and be involved in the medical field without being too close to the blood and guts world of surgical medicine. She would get her actual certification after a couple years of on-the-job training or apprenticeship. The only thing she was leery of was her exposure to prospective cancer patients, in particular breast images. She knew in time that she would view her role as a person who helped catch the cancer early, but her mom's passing was still too real and not yet just a bad memory. Joey was wondering how the continual exposure to pregnant women would affect Billie's maternal aspirations. They both loved kids but some planning would be needed before they would be delving into parenthood.

Pam and Cliff were now living the life of a married couple above Pam's beauty salon, both doing quite well and in love. Lilley could not be happier for her once confused and wayward daughter. Although they still hadn't tied the knot, they thought it best to wait another 6 months to a year since this was Joey's and Billie's year and they didn't want to compete or otherwise dilute the salience of that special occasion.

Joey's family house was bought by a local trucker with a love of fishing and Lilley was able to negotiate some extra money for the docking space he would inherit. Joey docked his boat at Willie's boat house, and they built a lean-to on the south side to shelter it from bad weather. Now that he was occupying the boathouse, he and Louise would often be seen trolling along the shoreline of Skogie lake in the evenings. Louise would eagerly anticipate Joey's landing of a fish. As soon as it was obvious that a fish was on Louise would start pacing around in the boat. After unhooking the fish, Joey would let it flap around on the floor of the boat briefly and Louise would hunker down on her haunches as if she was to engage the fish in play. After a good laugh at Louise's antics, he would return the fish to the water as soon as he could wondering what the fish thought of its scary encounter with the hairy monster from above.

The wedding took place in the Magee's back yard the last Saturday in June. As luck would have it a thunderstorm rolled through in the morning, soaking much of the equipment set out for the gathering. Fortunately, no damage was done except for a couple tent pegs holding the door flaps pulled out from the strong winds. The tent was a huge 60-foot-long white rental with three 20 foot poles holding it high and windows, and it reminded Joey of the old days when the circus came to William's Glen.

Neither Billie nor Joey wanted a big wedding. A big show was not what they were about. They wanted it as casual as possible and even encouraged their guests to wear casual clothes. Typically, though, anyone above the age of 40 seemed to be rather formally dressed, some with party dresses and suits, while the younger generation wore summer casual dress; fashionable but not formal. Billie wore a beautiful crepe midi dress with spaghetti straps, and an orange and white floral pattern. Her hair was braided by Pam that morning. She had large looping braids encircling her head with wispy strands of auburn cascading in ringlets from the braided crown. A strategically placed sprig of white baby's breath accented the updo. She accessorized her outfit with a pair of white Converse running shoes to affirm her desire for a casual affair. Joey wore his best jeans leather moccasins and a plain pastel orange t-shirt. Together they could have posed for a magazine typifying casual cottage country fashion. Willie, under strict instructions from his daughter, was dressed in casual attire. He looked very distinguished with his white slacks, black alligator belt, plain blue t-shirt and a light blue blazer. Both Billie and Joey remarked on how debonaire he looked, like a millionaire about to board his yacht.

Willie didn't exactly have a yacht, but he did have a nice 26 foot Doral, which was pulled around and tied to the dock on the north side of the boathouse. The podium was on the lake side so that all the wedding guests would face out toward the water and the boat would be front and center. It was there that most of the wedding pictures were taken posing on the boat, the dock and along the shoreline.

The lines of tables and white folding chairs were festooned with white streamers and bunches of white balloons. There were clusters of white balloons spaced on the white tablecloths and weighted down by small bean bags. Between the balloons were vases with single white roses and springs of baby's breath. The podium was flanked by speakers on stands and a microphone on a boom stand. On each side of that were large white decorative baskets with gorgeous bouquets of white carnations and roses set in a back drop of green foliage. The large bouquets were provided by Lilley and Don at their insistence and both Billie and Joey had to admit that they were a magnificent addition. Despite the air of informality and simplicity the scene was in vogue and elegant.

The wedding party was somewhat smaller than most, again deferring to simplicity and bucking the formal and traditional way of doing things. Billie's entourage consisted of Willie, Olivia as maid of honor, and Pam as a bridesmaid, while Joey had Jug stand as best man with Lilley and Jessie as the ring bearer. Don had agreed to act as sort of a master of ceremonies and kept the affair in order making announcements and introductions. Louise was given free reign and Joey knew she would never go too far from him or Billie for that matter, with so much food around.

Both had agreed to write their own vows and the entire ceremonial portion was to be short and officiated by Willie's friend Judge

Casey of Montrose. The two were friends from their teen years and more recently golfing partners.

The ceremony was difficult without Sarah's physical attendance and many times her name came up in the speeches, but the references were largely humorous and light. Don began by welcoming everyone to the affair and acknowledged that Sarah would have been overjoyed to have been there but that he was confident that her presence was being felt by everyone who knew and loved her. He had Willie come up and he too welcomed everyone and presented Judge Casey and the prospective bride and groom. There were tears of happiness and of sorrow, but everyone was able to hold it together for the sake of the intended couple. Louise greeted everyone with wags and slurps and was a great source of levity throughout the day. When Judge Casey took to the podium, he had Billie and Joey come and stand on each side of him along with the small wedding party. He was a rather portly man and in spite of his being just in his fifties, he had lost most of his hair and was deprived of perfect vision. He had a brown cardigan loosely buttoned over a white polo and grey slacks with shiny patented brown shoes. Billie and Joey suspected that this was about as informal as he could get. He looked out over his half glasses and read from a script he had placed on the podium. His words were kind and meaningful and reflected his admiration of the Magee family. He then introduced Billie and Joey and they came to the podium together standing side by side and facing their guests.

THE VOWS

Billie unfolded a wad of paper onto the podium. "Thank you all for coming here today and for making this such a special time for Joey and Me." Already the importance of the day and the absence of her mother made her hesitate, but she continued unable to clearly see her audience. "I have known Joey since early on in high school. Even before we spoke to each other I noticed him. I can't explain why. There was just something about him that seemed special." She turned now and faced Joey and a lump in her throat made talking difficult. She gently swiped away a tear. "When I say to you Joey, that you are my one and only true love that is not just something I made up to sound good. It couldn't be truer. I tried to think of everything I would promise to you today and it is really endless. I can't imagine someone loving another person more than I love you!" Joey reached both hands out and gently took hers, his eyes pooling like hers.

"I vow to continue loving you for the rest of my life and to never forget how special our love is. We bucked the odds and when people called us too young or that it was just a puppy love, I knew in my heart it was much more than that. I vow to honor, respect, support and encourage you and to be at your side through whatever life brings. I vow to be the best mother…" she paused, and Joey looked up quickly "… to Louise!" Everyone roared in laughter, especially at the look on Joey's face! "I vow to show my love to you always and fight for you fiercely through good times and bad, forever. I vow more than anything to be your best friend and that one person that you can laugh with, cry with, and hide nothing from. Of course, that doesn't apply to birthday's and Christmas." More laughs from the crowd.

Jug yelled out, "Don't forget Father's Day!" Again, the guests all laughed, still remembering Billie's reference to being a good mother.

"I also vow to uphold my mom's values by cherishing you like she cherished my dad by loving you and never taking life too seriously because we are only here for a short time, and I vow to make your life the best I can make it. I love you so much!"

Willie brought a tissue out of his pocket and discretely wiped his eyes, knowing that any mention of Sarah would be tough.

Billie completely broke tradition and grabbed hold of Joey and the two hugged and cried together in front of everyone. There was literally no one there without a tear in their eyes…Except maybe Louise who was lying in front of the podium chewing on her bone.

Joey realized that it was now his turn because of the silence and because Billie stepped back and smiled at him with nothing more to say. He fiddled in his pocket and brought out some papers and scrunched them all up and threw them into the shelf under the top of the podium.

"Okay so…what she said…" He stopped and looked out over the crowd, and they erupted with laughter.

"Great speech, bud! "Jug yelled out again.

Then Joey looked into Billie's eyes and held her hands caressing her knuckles with his thumbs. The guests all quieted down, and Joey heard a faint, "awe" from someone. He thought it may have been Jug's mom, Ellen or maybe it was Lilley.

"I did have my vows all written down, but you stole all of mine so now I have to wing it." More laughter from the crowd.

"Billie, all those vows you made, all those life experiences; good, bad…way before we came to stand here and promise to endure all that life throws at us, we had already experienced most of them. We have loved each other since we were 14 years old and as you pointed out we weren't given much of a chance. Heck, we both talked about it then and wondered what our chances were. It turns out there was no chance… (pausing as people looked a little puzzled) of me ever loving anyone else other than you!" Joey looked into Billie's eyes smiling with a wink. A few gasps of relief and muffled chuckles from the audience. "Since we were 14 years old, I have felt that you were part of me. You rescued me from myself, and you have always felt like family to me." Joey looked back out over the crowd. "We have already endured so many things together. We supported each other and encouraged each other, cried, laughed, and experienced most of the things we now vow to continue doing. It's like we don't really have to prove anything to each other because we have both dealt with criticism, and even abusive people and bullies. We have experienced tragedy, and the passing of loved ones and even as young teens we were by each other's side. And now we experience what only seems to be the natural growth of our relationship. We exchange vows that we have made to each other for a long time, but now in front of our family and friends." Now, firmly holding Billie's hands he continued looking sincerely into her eyes. "I vow to uphold everything you said you would in your vows and to love you as I have since the first day I met you. If it weren't for you coming into my life…well, it scares me to think of what might have happened!"

Joey turned to face all the guests who were mesmerized by the devotion being displayed in front of them. He faced them holding Billie's left hand in his right hand as Billie turned too. Then they both, in unison, recited the words that they had practiced while attempting to look into every eye in the crowd at least briefly.

"On this day, we both promise to love each other fully, through life's mountains and valleys. We promise to make a home of love, kindness and respect, a home where each of you gathered here today is always welcome!"

They released their hands and stood back facing each other. Joey nodded at Judge Casey and he stepped between the two. Joey lifted the podium out of the way and set it to the side which kind of spooked Louise, but she found another place to lie down just outside the tent.

Judge Casey began, "In all my years of officiating weddings, I don't think I have ever felt as involved emotionally. You two have really captured us here today." He looked from one to the other and then faced the audience. "It gives me great pleasure to officiate the uniting of these two fine young people, although I get the feeling that I might be about 6 years too late!" Everyone laughed..." It seems you two have shared your hearts for a very long time. Now Joey and Billie will exchange rings as a symbol of the promises they have made to each other here today. I would like to call on Jessica Burgess to bring forth the rings?"

Jessie stood up from the seat in the front row and it became apparent why Joey had moved the podium. Jessie was dressed in a white sun dress, her red braids also weaved together streaming down her back, another of Pam's masterpieces. She was barely 5 feet tall and as cute as a button as she moved slowly toward Judge Casey, holding a white satin pillow with two rings pinned neatly to the top. She smiled through her new braces and looked back and forth at Joey and Billie both mouthing, "I love you" to her as she approached the judge. He took one ring and Jessie backed up to the side a little nervous. He handed the ring to Joey and as they planned, he began without any instructions.

"Billie, I give you this ring as a symbol of my love and dedication. Please wear this as a daily sign of my love and commitment to you."

Billie held out her hand and swallowed hard, quivering with emotion, allowing Joey to slip it onto her finger. Then she stepped back and Jessie came forward again. The judge picked off the other ring and handed it to Billie.

"Joey, I give you this ring as a symbol of my love and dedication. Please wear this as a daily sign of my love and commitment to you."

Now it was Joey's turn to hold out his hand as Billie was forced to turn the tight-fitting ring several times to get it on a rather sweaty finger. Then they stood back and stared glassy eyed at each other again but still holding on to both hands.

Off to the side, Judge Casey swiveled the microphone over and announced, "By the powers vested in me, I now pronounce you man and wife!"

Cheers rang out and confetti flew everywhere. He didn't have to tell them to kiss. He had barely finished the pronouncement and they were locked and whispering, I love you's in each other's ear. The sudden commotion scared Louise as she ran around looking up at everyone, tail between her legs. Then she found Joey and Billie and scampered up to them recognizing her favorite humans. Billie bent down and patted her on the head.

"I can see you every day now!" Billie chortled still wiping tears and laughing at the same time.

It was a wonderful day with bittersweet moments and heartfelt expressions of love. It was the kind of wedding that they both dreamed of despite the absence of people that were so close to them. They were and always would be there in their hearts and minds. It was not the beginning of a wonderfully close relationship, but a continuation, a waypoint in their journey together. The day was not fancied by decorum or pomp and circumstance and that made the focus be on the relationship itself and the deep venerated love that had been maturing through the past 6 years. It represented freedom to both, a day that marked a point where they could just be together as one without wondering if they should be. Even the scene was so much a part of their being, the lake and the lapping waves against the shore and the boathouse cribs, the setting sun over the rolling hills in the west and the sweet smell of the pines with the background sounds of laughing seagulls. No building or sterile structure could possibly duplicate the atmosphere that enveloped them that day.

They stood arms around each other at the end of the boathouse dock staring wistfully into the orange and coral colored sky pointing out the purple and pink pastel wisps of clouds. Louise had followed them, and she too became part of the trio, silhouetted against the majestically colored background. A gentle, warm breeze that stirred the sparkling water at their feet caressed their faces and the strands free from the braids of Billie's auburn hair waved and fluttered around her face and neck. Joey turned and held Billie's face gently with both hands exploring her entrancing blue eyes and kissed her lips softly as she quickly and passionately responded, both once again holding each other tightly, trembling and completely enchanted. A small head leaned softly against the back of Joey's right knee.

THE END

A TICK IN TIME

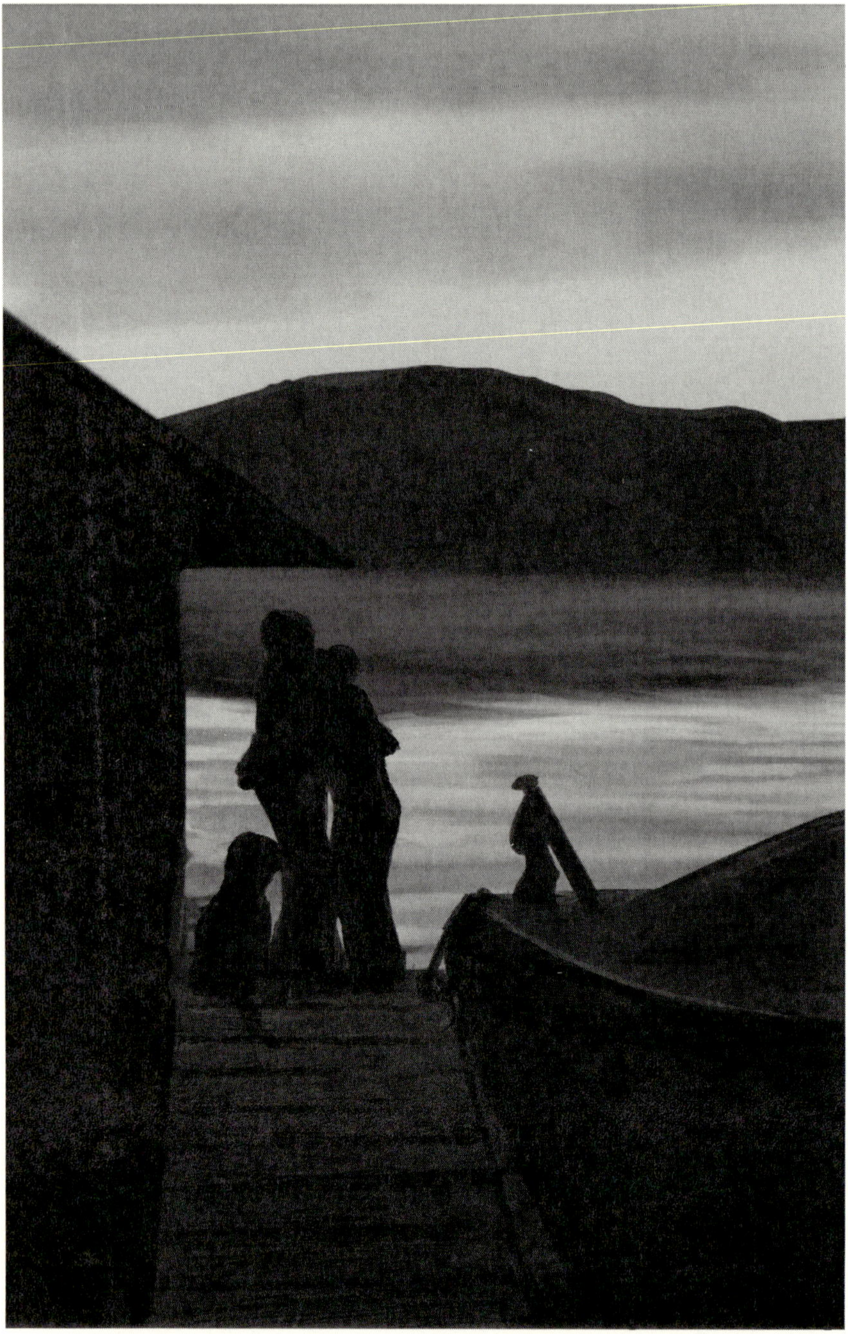

ACKNOWLEDGEMENTS

There are so many people I need to thank. My parents gave me encouragement in all the right places and there's that thing called unconditional love that can never be overemphasized. My sisters Peggy and Mary Jo and my kids and grandkids have always encouraged my music, my art and my writing. My friends were always there to support me even when I didn't deserve it. My students will always be my main source of motivation because it's through my interactions with them that I learned the most about life. Believe me, teachers learn far more than they teach! Without my wife Cathy, this book may have never been published. Since she reads almost a book every two days, I figured that she might know what she is talking about. Her love and encouragement are the reasons you are reading this right now. Her words were, "This has to be published," and I always do what I'm told.

 I also want to thank all the wonderful dogs that have been in my life. You will learn from them as much as you let yourself. It's science, and the love drug oxytocin has been fairly recently discovered present in dogs (and presumably other animals) and is considered the reason that they crave human affection and bond to us so faithfully. Their love is genuine, unselfish, and unmistakable.

 All you need is love.